Struggle Me This

—for Ann Smith, in memoriam

Struggle Me This

SJ

ISBN: 978-1-943661-55-8

Sij Books
booksbysij@gmail.com

Printed in the USA

The bullet from the Hyena's Makarov, traveling 2,300 feet per second, traversed and exited his skull just above his left eyebrow, a little toward his ear. A gush of blood and cerebrospinal fluid splashed from the entrance wound as he slid to the cement floor.

Emma screamed. She could see the holes in the wall where the bullets had entered her tiny house of poles and mud. The propane fridge hissed. Reece gasped for breath, and Emma was beside him, clearing his airway, lifting his head, applying pressure to his wounds with her bare hands. She glanced for a phone, muttered "Shit" and yelled for help. He was bleeding badly and needed fluids right away.

Irigit banged on the door, shouting wildly in the cool night air, losing his hat made of scrap cloth. Dogs snarled and yelped in the distance. Barra, Mariam, and Isaac ran from their rooms. Just a few compounds away, Afewerki had heard the shots and imagined the worst.

Emma saw Reece's pupils weirdly getting larger, getting smaller, getting larger. His respirations grew ragged.

"Reece! Breathe, you bastard! Goddammit." Blood soaked her pajamas. With each beat of Reece's heart growing ever faster, blood spurted. A massive hematoma was already forming on the side of entry.

Irigit stood back to let Isaac kick in the door. It shuddered, then groaned open. In they came, shouting. Emma yelled for IV fluid and an IV kit. "Oh God," she said, watching Reece's pupils blow wide open in the candlelight. Afewerki burst into the room, taking it in. He had passed the Hyena along the path, the administrator drinking from a wine bottle, huddled between his bodyguards.

"Afewerki! IV, get an IV! Normal saline! Afewerki!" Reece seemed to snore, the shadows of the candles pooling with the blood.

Afewerki spun and raced out to the clinic. The night lit by crowded stars, he tripped on a rock, fell sprawling, and rolled to his feet. His hands stung. A rock had dug into his kidney. Down the hill he flew, alone. At the clinic gate, he double-fisted the door and yelled for the guard.

"Abet!" yelled the guard.

Afewerki pounded. The door seemed a portal into another world, one that would never open. The guard inside asked who was there.

"Afewerki!" He began to think in Italian. "Apri la porta!"

The gate opened a crack, and Afewerki pushed past the guard, who held his rifle like a snake. He ran to the dark clinic door. The lock. The door was locked, and only Isaac had the key. "Merda!" He turned and ran and suddenly had to stop to catch his breath. Down the hill, Isaac sped. He was trying to remove the key from around his neck. He ran into Afewerki, grabbing his shoulders, and both fell to the ground.

"Quickly!" said Afewerki.

The lock tumbled to the dirt. Afewerki barged into the clinic past the staring guard. A small group of men had begun to gather just up the hill. They held rifles and doolahs. One held a hand grenade with a spoon detonator, a relic from World War II.

Inside, Afewerki grabbed a bottle of Icelandic IV fluid

and looked at the label. D_5W. He needed normal saline. D_5NS. *No.* There. *Yes.* He pushed a bottle of normal saline at Isaac and told him to run. Afewerki grabbed an IV kit, 18-gauge, and a drip kit. He paused. Did he need iodine or alcohol? No time. He ran, hitting his shoulder against the rough door frame. Another bottle of fluid! He ran back and grabbed another liter.

Reece's respirations continued ragged in a high-pitched whine. The blood pulsed with each stroke of his heart. Emma stared at his face, holding a pair of underwear to the entry wound and a folded bra to the exit wound. She noticed his jaw trembling as if trying to speak. His nose was prominent, looking down from above. Blood slicked her pajamas. Around her stood Barra and Irigit. Mariam sat in the lone chair, praying with eyes open.

Isaac entered with the bottle of fluid. "He is coming!"

The wide-open gate allowed a few bystanders to enter the compound. They stood, whispering. Afewerki split them down the middle and dropped a bottle of IV fluid into the grass.

"Afewerki!" shouted Emma.

Barra and Irigit moved back. Afewerki rushed in and handed the IV kit to Emma.

"Hook the tubing to the bottle! Flush the line!" Emma tore open the kit and marveled briefly at the opaque, white, plastic IV catheter. She turned his head sideways, looking for the jugular. She would need to lower his head so the vein would bulge, but that was impossible. She yelled at Barra to lift Reece's feet. Blood ran from the wounds. She spotted the vein and in one movement slid in the catheter. A gush of blood spurted, and she removed the needle. She held up her hand for the IV tubing, felt it, and jammed the tube dripping saline into the IV. "Tape! We need tape." There was no tape.

Afewerki leapt to his feet and ran out the door, pushing his way through a small crowd hesitant to venture close. *Tape!*

A country of sixty million people, Ethiopia would not have its first neurosurgeon until 1991 with the arrival of Tadios Damtie, fresh from training in the United Kingdom. At the very moment the bullet entered Reece Meyer's skull, the chief of surgery at Black Lion, Dr. Girma Tadesse, who would look after Reece, was enjoying a bottle of Austrian Riesling brought into the country by his fellow faculty member at the University of Addis Ababa, Dr. Wayne Macomber of Flynt, Michigan.

It had taken the better part of the following day to evacuate Reece Myers from the tiny village of Godo, first by jeep to Alem Ketema and then by helicopter to Addis Ababa. Emma did not think he would survive the jolting overland ride to AK.

Twice he seized in the jeep and once on the flight to Addis. The bullet had entered just above his right eye and exited just a bit higher on the opposite side above his left eye. No one believed he would live, and the Mission delayed a transfer out of the country to Nairobi, reasoning, according to Dr. Guthrie, the Baptist Mission's veterinarian, that further travel would certainly kill him, that he needed to stabilize, and that Reece's family should be consulted in the United States. Emma was a wreck. Dr. Tadesse took over Reece's care, his primary concern being the possible death of this young American.

Within an hour of his arrival, Dr. Tadesse examined the X-ray of Reece's head. There was no CT scanner, which would have proved much more useful in assessing tissue damage. From all appearances, Reece was in a coma, responsive only to deep pain, which, Dr. Tadesse emphasized, was better than no response at all. The Makarov round had entered Reece's head rather cleanly, not in a tumbling motion. The entry hole was roughly the size of the bullet, and the exit wound resembled an ugly slit. An intracranial pressure monitor, tied directly into Reece's spinal canal, fluctuated around 30 mm/hg, indicating excessive pressure from the brain trauma.

Emma removed the pads from Reece's eyes and dripped in saline. She wiped the excess, pulled his lids closed, and replaced the pads, covering each with a strip of silk tape. The adult intensive care unit had to share an ECG monitor with the recovery room, but his cardiac function was the least of anyone's worries. At the edges of his bullet wounds, Dr. Tadesse had discovered nearly microscopic threads, metallic in nature. The fibers were difficult to distinguish from the flesh and showed up on X-ray as a shadow. He passed it off as another mystery of life and mentioned it to no one.

Reece existed in a fugue state. He could hear everything around him, but could not move or respond. Light came and went. He was trapped inside his head, which felt bloated. He wasn't quite sure who he was or what had happened. The voice of the woman with a Southern accent he could understand, and from her, he began to fathom that he had been shot. Where was he? He longed for her to touch him and speak. The other voices were strange, a strange English, and then another language he could not understand. The tube in his airway drove him mad. The ventilator breathed for him when he didn't want it to. He couldn't relax. Occasionally, deep sleeps came over him, against his will.

"Reece? It's Emma." She took a warm washcloth and ran it across his cheeks and forehead. "It's about noon. I just ate lunch, a club sandwich at the Hilton. Dr. Guthrie made me get a room there for a few days. I have to go there at night to sleep. Swam in the pool for half an hour this morning. The water's too hot, though."

Who are you? Where am I? It seemed to Reece that he was speaking, but the woman whose name was Emma did not respond. Another voice, a man. He felt his hand being squeezed.

"Hey there, good buddy. It's Dr. Guthrie. I came by to see you and let you know what's going on. The doctor says you're stable."

Emma spoke. "Reece, they're here to draw some blood. They want to check your blood oxygen level. Hold on."

Reece felt something cool on his wrist, a dull, deep pain streaked into his left hand. Someone was inserting a needle into his radial artery. He understood, and it hurt like hell.

"All done." Emma held pressure over the puncture site with a wad of gauze.

"Like I was saying," resumed the man's voice, "you're still considered to be in critical condition, but you're fairly stable, which is good news. I hope you can hear me, so I'll just keep talking."

Dr. Guthrie told Reece he had spoken with his grandparents and his fiancée, Kristin. He had remembered that Reece's parents were dead. Everyone at the Mission was praying for him. Everyone at Mission headquarters back in Virginia was praying for him. Dr. Tadesse would be by to see him soon.

"Has he responded at all?" asked Dr. Guthrie.

He must be talking to the woman.

"No, but I feel like he can hear us." Emma wore fitted jeans, a sleeveless lavender top, and tennis shoes.

"God willing," said Dr. Guthrie.

"Has that fucking Hyena been arrested yet? He damn well did it, even though he won't admit to it."

The Hyena.

"Emma, watch your language. We do have to keep the faith, you know, even though I get you." Dr. Guthrie wore his signature tight, short-sleeve shirt, white.

Emma frowned, wanting to say worse. Why was she getting so attached to this guy, Reece? *He understands what I've been through.* She didn't want to lose him, for the sake of his grandparents, even for the sake of Kristin. Would Kristin come to visit?

"The Hyena is under investigation by the wereda administrator in AK. From what I gather, there's bad blood there. He's made himself unpopular with lots of folks in the zone," said Guthrie.

Reece coalesced images of the Hyena in his mind. He had been working as a nurse in a small village in Ethiopia. It seemed so strange. The Hyena was a bad man. Apparently, the Hyena had shot him, but why? The last thing he could remember with certainty was eating peanut butter fudge on an airplane.

When the Abba Paulos heard of the shooting of the ferenj, he stopped his work. A monk, healed of his skin infection at the Baptist Mission clinic, he had been hand-hewing the rock church near Godo for eleven years. He had one day kept the Hyena's henchmen from raping Emma and had sent curses down upon them for their actions. When he had first met Reece in the clinic, he knew he was one of them. How he knew it, he did not know, but he was certain, nonetheless.

Abba Paulos prayed to God for the healing of the ferenj and prepared to make the journey to Addis Ababa. He gathered his fly whisk, a candle, three matches, his leather-bound Old Testament written in Ge'ez, two palm-shaped magnets, and placed several handfuls of kollo, dry sorghum nuggets good for snacking, into a leather pouch that he attached to his waist. He would walk and take rides as they came. Perhaps the Addis Ababa bus driver would offer him a ride from Alem Ketema into the city. He could not afford to pay the fare of fifty birr. The sun was rising, and he closed the door to his simple house with a piece of wire.

Dr. Tadesse ground his knuckle into Reece's breastbone. Reece responded weakly, clenching his fists. His pupils were mismatched. The left pupil reacted to light, but the right did not. He had taken Reece off the ventilator that morning, and thus far, Reece had done well, breathing on his own.

"He is strong inside his heart," said Dr. Tadesse. "I am hoping for the best. We must watch and see." He had witnessed no one survive a gunshot to the head. That the bullet was of sufficient caliber to pass through his head and exit instead of bouncing around inside his skull had probably saved his life. He wondered if Reece would be blind.

Emma, standing on the other side of the ancient hospital bed, held the rail and glanced from Dr. Tadesse to Reece. She had been in Addis for three days and needed to return to the clinic, but she wanted to be near Reece. That afternoon, Reece's fiancée Kristin was supposed to arrive in Addis. She wasn't sure she wanted to meet her.

Reece listened to the conversation between Dr. Tadesse and Emma. He felt pain in his lower back. There was always a pressure in his bladder. He had a catheter. His legs ached. He felt much too warm, blankets being piled on top of him despite the hot weather outside. His thoughts ran to the Ark of the Covenant. He must have been reading about it in his Bible. He imagined Moses communing with God through the Ark. Sparks and fire...

It took the Abba Paulos twelve hours to walk the forty kilometers from Godo to Alem Ketema. He'd had water twice, once at the Jara River and then again at the Wenchit. Ascending the escarpment into AK, he'd taken a ride in the back of a Toyota pickup, a Mission vehicle, along with a farmer and his long, wooden plow. The Abba had been to many strange places while dreaming, but he knew it was more than just dreaming. The places he visited were very real. He had seen things he was unable to describe without appearing to be crazy. He just kept digging his church, his life's work. This ferenj, who had been shot in the head, was the only other of his kind that he had met. The Abba knew that it was up to him to do something, although precisely what that was, he was not sure.

Reece coughed, throwing out great wads of phlegm that clung to his lips. It was his fourth day in the intensive care unit. The windows to the street stood open, and a stale breeze of manure and onions wafted through the gauzy curtains. The nurse wiped away the mess from Reece's mouth. He was stable, but with petit mal seizures on occasion, his fingers and toes twitching for minutes at a time.

Reece tried to turn his eyes toward the nurse but could not tell if he was successful or not. She was golden-skinned and had a sharp jaw. Her long hair was tied into a ponytail. She was careful when she turned him from side to side. Of a sudden, he felt like he was floating. He felt himself contract. His vision went black. His heart rate increased to 120 beats per minute. His fingers and toes trembled. He...

Just outside of Alem Ketema, the Abba Paulos dropped by the Mere Amanuel Church to pay his respects to the priest, Matthias. The priest was not in, attending the funeral of a woman and infant who had died in childbirth. The debtara, Fanuel, a church deacon, welcomed the Abba with a glass of curdled milk from a clay pot.

"Tell me of your journey," said Fanuel.

Since he did not quite know why he was traveling to see the injured ferenj, the Abba only said that he was traveling to Addis Ababa to take care of some business, that he would be there less than one week.

"How is the digging?" asked Fanuel.

"God provides the enjera, and I provide the pick," he said.

Fanuel laughed. "Yes, and the Church of St. Gabriel, how is it?" He knew that a new tabot, the replica of the Ten Commandments consecrated by the Patriarch, had been installed at the church in Godo. The rumor was that the Icelanders, who had arrived in Godo before the Baptists, had stolen the church's original tabot and hidden it in a cave.

"All is well," said the Abba. "Our people will be blessed. The crocodile can no longer reach the monkey."

"Ah, yes," said Fanuel. "The eyes of God are much too strong for the eyes of hyenas."

The Abba nodded. He had rather liked Dr. Thorsson and the Icelandic nurses Svana and Eydis. They had visited his church in the rock on three occasions and left valuable gifts of money, teff, and birzz, the honey drink, which he especially liked.

The Abba and Fanuel talked into the dark. Tired, the Abba spread a woolen blanket on the church floor. He lit his candle with a single match and settled in for the night. Dogs mauled one another in the distance.

Reece had drifted down in the bed, the head being raised ten degrees to keep him from aspirating the liquids being forced down a feeding tube. Try as he might, he could not blink his eyes. Each time Dr. Tadesse came by, he would ask Reece to blink his eyes and squeeze his hand.

With the nurse's help, Emma pulled Reece up in the bed, then turned him on his left side and stuffed a hard pillow behind his back to keep him there. Heat stifled the unit. A trickle of sweat ran down her back, and felt cold.

"Reece, you've been here five days. When are you gonna wake up? Dr. Guthrie says I have to leave tomorrow. There's a plane going up to AK." She took a comb she had brought and combed his greasy hair.

Dr. Guthrie arrived with a guest. It was Kristin, Reece's fiancée, fresh from the USA. Emma turned and watched Kristin watch her run the comb through Reece's hair. She felt a little empty pocket of air develop beneath her heart.

The Abba Paulos arrived in Addis Ababa. A taxi driver, high on qat, had given him a ride from Mookaturi into the city, saving him a day or two's walk. He had never been to Black Lion Hospital and imagined it as a tall, white building, icy in appearance. He imagined that inside it was very complicated and that the smell of death would be heavy. The taxi dropped him across from a building eight stories in height. The ground was denuded, patches of brown and pink dirt.

Kristin, in tears, walked toward Reece's bed. She wore a white dress with a narrow red belt. Curls of brown hair surrounded her thin face. Emma came around and embraced her. Dr. Guthrie stood back, clearing his throat. Reece's eyes were black, and a swath of gauze encircled his head. An IV dripped into a line anchored in the crook of his arm. The pale orange feeding tube was taped to his nose and forehead. His face glistened with sweat, his eyes staring straight ahead. A smell of wet tennis shoes and alcohol permeated the open room.

Kristin leaned in and spoke into his ear. "Reece...It's Kristin. It took me four days to get here. I'm...so sorry. Oh, my God..." His hand felt cool and did not respond to her grasp. What was she to do? *What happens next?* She felt sick to her stomach. Was this woman named Emma his nurse?

"He's been unresponsive, except to pain." Emma knew that Kristin was a nurse as well.

"Are you his nurse?" Kristin looked around the vacuous ICU, dimly lit, two large rooms connected by an archway.

"Sort of. I'm Emma. Reece worked with me in Godo." Emma put the comb on a small bedside table.

A charge of electricity. "Yes. Emma. I'm sorry. Reece *was* shot?" She felt like she was speaking for the first time using words that made no sense.

"Um, yes. The village administrator, we're pretty sure, fired through the wall twice. Afewerki saw him just afterward with his pistol." Emma saw that Kristin's shoe was untied.

"Reece was inside his house? And the guy could see him in the house?" A deep welling of sorrow came over

Kristin. Her mother had complained when she left the dog, the Cocker Spaniel, Walter...that they would have to feed and walk him. Her mother did not like dogs or Reece.

"I'll step out for a few minutes." Guthrie turned and walked away with his hands in his pockets.

"He was inside my house. It was after Bible Study." Emma searched for words.

"Your house?"

Emma felt trapped. "Reece gave his bed to a man who needed a leg amputated. The man had lice. Anyway, I told Reece he could sleep on my floor."

Kristin touched Reece's neatly combed hair. The IV dripped by gravity. A metal urinal sat on the floor.

"It just happened, out of nowhere. The Hyena is an evil man. He shot Reece through the wall."

"The Hyena?" Reece had mentioned him in a letter. "He sounds horrible. Is he in jail?"

"No," said Emma. "There's no proof so far that he did it. He denies it. It was just for one night, Reece in my house, I mean, until the man could be evacuated to Addis, here, in fact, to Black Lion." Thinking of the man's rotted leg made her want to puke.

Reece went stiff, his breathing dropped an octave, and his toes and fingers began to twitch. His hands curled inward ever so slightly. The bed shook, but just barely...

Reece seized for nearly an hour. Drenched in sweat, the quivering in his hands and feet subsided. His breathing relaxed, his eyes staring at the ceiling. The nurse had let Kristin dribble some saline into his bloodshot eyes.

"How long can you stay?" Emma was exhausted, and

before going to Godo was going back to the Mission guesthouse instead of to the Hilton. Staying there just made her feel guilty. But Kristin was staying at the guesthouse, too.

"I don't know how long I can stay," said Kristin. "Dr. Guthrie talked about taking Reece to Kenya, to a larger hospital there, or maybe to Rome, but I don't understand why he can't just come home. He said the Mission would pay for it."

"It's just risky, with Reece being so critical. If his intracranial pressure doesn't stabilize, they may have to do a craniotomy to relieve some of the pressure of the hematoma on his right side. He's still seizing even though he's on Dilantin, which is in short supply around here."

"I guess so," said Kristin. Reece looked so dead. She was frustrated that the hospital did not have the means to do an EEG on Reece. What if he were brain dead? But his heart was so strong, and he was breathing on his own. He could be comatose for years.

The nurse, Edit, came in to hang the Dilantin and push 60 ccs of water into Reece's feeding tube. She was tall and beautiful. Her father had been a general in Haile Selassie's army. She injected 50 milligrams of generic Dilantin into the bolus feeder and let 100 ccs of normal saline fill the tube. It would take an hour to drip in. She checked his vital signs. She held the thermometer up for Emma to read. It was in Celsius, and Emma could not tell that Reece had a fever.

The Abba Paulos navigated his way through the complex hallways of Black Lion Hospital. He was getting close, feeling Reece's presence. He and Reece both knew the others from the other places. The Abba had embraced his heritage, but Reece had not. To himself, Reece had explained away the strange night visits as merely childhood nightmares, night terrors, and then as the very real entry of Satan into his thoughts. God had created the heavens and earth, not the infinite earths.

The Abba wore his golden-yellow skullcap and dirty shamma of matching color. His tire sandals made little sound on the maroon-tiled hallway floor. The brass cross around his neck was heavy. With him, in the folds of his robe, and the bag at his side, he carried most everything precious to him, including the magnets.

"Hallo," he said to a man wearing a white coat. "Excuse me. Where may I find the ferenj called Reece? He is nearby?"

The resident in training from nearby Addis Ababa University took in the sight of the Abba Paulos. Everyone knew of the ferenj Reece in the ICU. "Yes, Father," he said. "Follow me," and he took him to the adult intensive care unit on the second floor.

To assuage the fever, Edit crushed then pushed 500 milligrams of paracetamol down Reece's feeding tube. "He is fever," said Edit, practicing her English as if Emma and Kristin were still there. She looked across the room, panning the fifteen other patients. She would like someday to visit the United States, but laughed at the absurdity of the suggestion. Occasionally, the power went out at the hospital, and the generators almost always failed, sometimes because the hospital could not afford the diesel to run them.

It was 7:25 p.m., and Edit's shift should have ended an

hour ago, but no one had relieved her. She snacked on a little box of frosted cakes from a local pasticceria, sharing them with another nurse. As she ate at the nurse's station, Reece's fingers and toes twitched, then trembled. His jaw clenched. His black field of vision sparkled with bright lights, white, red, and orange. Kristin had been there. She had touched him...

Edit rounded her patients, eight in all, all critical and in dire need of baths, dressing changes, and medications. She was already two hours over her scheduled twelve-hour shift. She could only do so much. A man in yellow garb pushed through the heavy wooden door onto the unit. She watched him walk past the nurse's station and stop. He seemed very confident of his mission, as if he knew exactly what he was doing. The other nurse spoke with him first and then pointed toward Edit. The lights flickered. Occasionally, when the power went out, patients died.

The Abba Paulos walked forward, glancing at a thin woman on her back from whose direction emanated a terrible smell, a smell of feces and death. "Tenesteling," he said to Edit.

"Hallo. Dehina newot?" asked Edit, showing respect to this middle-aged man of the church.

"Dehna negn," said the Abba. He could see the ferenj in a bed against the outer wall, just a few beds over. He pointed and said that he had come to see the ferenj who had been shot.

"Yes, Mr. Myers," she said. "He is here. You know him?"

"He has visited my church, which I have been building for many years into the rock. God would have me here to pray for him. He gave money to the church. A terrible thing has happened to this young man."

"He was shot by the village administrator?" asked Edit. She stood at the foot of Reece's clean but messy bed. She noticed the Abba's muscled forearms and gnarly hands.

"No one is knowing but perhaps the birds that fly by night. One man is evil, yes. Perhaps he did it." The Abba approached Reece, gazing at the IV, the feeding tube, the bag hanging on the bed filled with urine. Gauze covered Reece's eyes, making him look dead. "He is called the Hyena."

Edit winced at the thought. Hyenas were awful creatures that lived near the city dump.

The Abba approached Reece. "He can hear? Ato Reece?" he said, calling Reece mister.

"Perhaps he can hear, only God knows. He has many visitors during the day, and they speak with him. His fiancée is coming here from the United States."

"Ah, very good," said the Abba. He was tired and wondering where he would spend the night. It seemed he would have to go to the Mercato and find a room. It was Thursday, the first day of the Assumption of the Virgin Mary, which meant he would be fasting. He could feel the weight of the magnets he carried.

A man who had been moaning across the room began to curse. Edit excused herself and ran over to the young man who'd had his leg amputated. He was the man who Reece had let sleep in his bed the night he was shot at Emma's. The leg had come off neatly above the knee.

"Mendeno?" asked Edit of the man. He sat up in bed, a look of panic on his face. He panted and clutched at his chest. She knew that look and suspected that he had thrown a clot to his lungs. The man's neck veins pulsed rapidly. She called for her co-worker to summon the doctor on call.

The Abba turned his attention to Reece. His mother had explained to him how he was a son of God, that his father was from far away, from beyond the sky. The young man lying before him was a son of God as well. Reece would have the layer of mesh embedded into his scalp as he did. The Abba prayed daily and meditated on the wonders of the universe. Living alone, he never spoke of his knowledge to others. He would be accused, no doubt, of being possessed by evil spirits, of having buda, the evil eye.

He muttered a prayer for Reece, looked back at the group of three gathered around the man who had been shouting, and brought forth the magnets. They fit his hands. He placed a magnet on either side of Reece's head, engaging the mesh. A faint glow...

The Abba returned the magnets to the pouch and looked back at the nurses and a doctor surrounding the bed across the room. The man seemed to be having trouble breathing and was shouting for his father. The Abba made the sign of the cross in the air and kissed the cross around his neck. He could not be sure that the ferenj would be able to find his way among the many worlds that he understood to exist, but his instincts and his dreams had assured him that he had to help. He said a brief prayer.

He exited the intensive care unit and asked a man lying in the hall with one arm how to get outside. The man pointed and said to follow the stairs down. The Abba thanked him and, within a few minutes, walked into a deserted green room filled with yellow chairs. A door led into the just-cooling evening air. The city was loud, cars and trucks, and he wished for the silence of his simple home.

Walking, he spotted a young man on a motorcycle, lounging on the sidewalk with a chewing stick in his mouth. The Abba's neck itched, and he touched where the staph infection had been and worried that his trouble would return. He would have to visit the clinic in Godo when he returned and receive more medicine.

With a furrowed brow and mustache, the young man, dressed in a bright red, yellow, and green soccer jersey, sat sidesaddle on his Platina motorcycle. Fingers interlocked with his thumbs pressed together, he surveyed the Abba in his golden-yellow garb.

"Mendeno?" he said. "What's the problem?"

The Abba thought about the twenty birr in his pouch and how he needed to conserve his money. He asked the young man if he could take him to the Mercato, where he could find a cheap room. The young man said he needed five birr for the gasoline. The Abba laughed and said that God would provide him seven times that if he only would do this favor. The young man also laughed and motioned for the Abba to get on and hold tight to the bar behind him. It was the Abba's first motorcycle ride.

The young man navigated back alleys to Uganda Street and snaked his way into the seething Mercato, bustling with vendors, restaurants, music shops, shoe shops, a coffin factory, and cheap hotels. The street was muddy and wet. The young man stopped in front of a store that sold bright red and blue brooms. Its steel doors yawned open, easily shut in seconds, should there be trouble. "You can find many hotels here," he told the Abba, revving his engine.

The Abba Paulos dismounted and bumped into a man pushing a wheelbarrow full of limes. The man scowled and kept moving. He saw a man with black teeth wearing a broken Scuba mask and a red leather coat. The man leaned against a yellow barrel and held out his hand. The Abba blessed him under his breath and began his search for a hotel.

Blessing and praying for many people, the Abba wandered into the recycling area of the Mercato, where worked the poorest of the poor, turning garbage into useful products. There was a small five-room hotel there, the Abyssinia, that charged only three birr per night, but for the Abba, they reduced the price to two birr. The patron, a woman with the strange name of Patricia, stored used plastic jugs, yellow and blue, on top of the hotel's corrugated steel roof. In his room was a homemade bed of wood, a blanket, a three-legged stool, and the stub of a blackened candle. He smelled wood smoke, urine, and sweat. He was hungry and fasting, but would have a bowl of the famous minestrone he had heard about for his dinner, but only after darkness fell completely.

At Black Lion Hospital, Dr. Tadesse listened to Reece's chest. His heart was strong and regular. Lung sounds were fairly clear. He listened to Reece's abdomen. He could hear tinkling sounds and growls indicating that the stomach and bowels were working. Reece was having diarrhea, but that was to be expected from the liquid food being pushed into the feeding tube. The bandages were off his head, and the bullet's entry and exit wounds, now just purple clotted marks, were healing with stitches. His eyes were still black, and his intracranial pressure elevated, but the seizures had abated.

Kristin held Reece's sweaty hand.

"Reece. Reece." She was exhausted. He would be flown back to the States in a few days. He would be placed on a medical jet for a flight back to Birmingham, Alabama.

Reece stared straight ahead, his eyes wide and wet from the saline Kristin dripped in every hour or so. He drifted in and out. He couldn't tell what year it was. He dreamed of working at a clinic in the countryside with two nurses and a doctor from Iceland. The dream interludes were peaceful. Afewerki was there. The Icelandic nurse Eydis was attractive. Was he engaged to this Kristin? He sensed that was the case, but couldn't remember. He'd been shot in the head by the Hyena, but that was all that was clear. Kristin holding his hand felt nice. Where was Emma? She had left to go back to work. But where?

With Reece stabilized, his pupils equal and reacting to light, the Baptist Mission placed him aboard a Med-Jet headed to Birmingham, Alabama, and the University of Alabama Hospitals. Emma rode with the entourage to Bole Airport and stayed to watch as the jet ascended and disappeared into the clouds. He had barely started massaging her neck when he was shot.

Dr. Guthrie put his hand on Emma's shoulder, and they walked to the Toyota van. "He's a tough nut for sure," he said.

"Yeah," said Emma.

"He was the last hire for relief work for us. It'll just be you until we shut down the operation in Godo. You, okay with that?" The buttons on his shirt strained.

"Yeah, I guess. I was getting used to him in the clinic. We were a pretty good pair."

"You still have the team to work with, Afewerki to interpret for you. Do you need another few days in Addis before you head back up?"

"No, the next flight up will be good for me." She felt lighter than air and watched Dr. Guthrie open the van door with a key.

Dr. Guthrie navigated out of the airport parking area and onto Bole Road toward Meskel Square. He hit a tremendous pothole, and the front left tire went flat. "Shit," he said and then apologized to Emma.

Delivered by ambulance to UAB Hospitals, Reece, on a stretcher, rode through the endless hallways and across the enclosed walkway to the Spain Wallace building to the sixth floor, where he stayed in one of the large rooms at the end of the hall. Inside was cold and bright with fluorescent lights, while outside, the hot summer of August pounded the town with sunshine and heat.

Kristin had returned home to her parents' house to regroup, shower, and prepare to stay with Reece for two days before she returned to work at Carraway Hospital across town. Walter, formerly Stones, the Cocker Spaniel she and Reece had named, was proving to be a handful. Her mom threatened to sack him if he kept peeing in the house. Secretly, Kristin wondered if her parents were hoping that Reece would die.

"Hello, Mr. Myers, this is Debbie. I'm your nurse today. I'll be taking care of you for the next twelve hours. You're back in Alabama now. You were shot in Africa, I believe. You're doing well."

Debbie checked the ECG monitor, normal sinus rhythm. She took his vital signs, noting that his heart rate was elevated at 110, but his blood pressure, respirations, and temperature were normal. He would need a new feeding tube, which she would place soon, to receive his meds, which included Dilantin, and his meals, which would consist of cans of Ensure. She put a diaper on him and a blue pad beneath his hips. She raised the head of the bed to 30 degrees and cut off the overhead light. She threw back the sheet to check on the catheter, re-covered him, and then turned him on his side, putting a foam wedge behind his back. She washed her hands and hurried out of the room to check on her other seven patients.

Reece knew that he was in the hands of a good nurse. He pondered the long flight. His ears had nearly ruptured on the descent into Birmingham. He desperately wanted to hear the voices of his grandparents and his dead parents. Kristin was very good to him, but he could detect the strain in her voice. She could not miss working any more shifts, she said. He still could not remember being shot, in the head no less, but did remember being in Emma's tiny house. He sensed another seizure coming on. His fingers curled inward, and his body trembled.

Emma lit the white candle beside her bed and leaned against the crooked wall, a pillow behind her back. She turned at random to a devotional in her copy of *My Utmost for His Highest*. She had not continued the Bible study that Reece had started. "He must increase, but I must decrease." John 3:30. The piece ended with "You may often have to watch Jesus Christ wreck a life before He saves it." But what about wrecking a life that was already saved? That was Reece, a missionary no less, shot in the head by the fucking Hyena. She closed the book and entered into prayer for Reece and to ask forgiveness for her foul language. But sometimes, enough was enough. How much could one person bear? She was certain that Reece didn't love Kristin. She could feel it. He had explained he felt guilty about leaving her and had proposed on a whim. She was a fabulous person in her own right, but he had begun to love her, Emma! Shot in the goddamn head! Emma shook. Tears came to her eyes. She was so lonely! *He freaking understood!*

He had been leading the team in a Bible study about the Ark of the Covenant. He had some strange ideas, but the Scripture seemed to back them up. She remembered him speaking of the sons of God, the children of angels who had relations with humans. It was in the Bible. Maybe that was no stranger than Moses parting the Red Sea. Reece was smart, kind, and had great legs!

"I am so angry!" she shouted into the darkness. Right away, she heard Irigit bounding across the compound. He knocked on her door, speaking rapidly.

"Chicorilla. No problem," she said from her bed.

"Ishi," said Irigit, whistling and returning to his post.

Less angry after her outburst, she recalled Reece's hands on her shoulders that night. His hands had felt so nice. They had slipped into her scrub top, a thrill running through her body. Gunshots.

Emma reached for her prayer notebook and began to pray for each name, that God would bless, guide, and protect.

Reece laid on his back, slumped in the Clinitron bed. Below the mattress skin swirled silicon-coated beads that made him float to keep his skin from breaking down. He seemed mired in his magical mattress. It was like being in soft mud.

The TV was on, always on, tuned now to MTV. Guns 'n Roses' "Welcome to the Jungle" played. Reece listened, but could not focus his eyes on the TV. When would Kristin come again? She massaged his feet, which felt so good.

The nursing assistant came in. Her name was Debbie Dee. "Today is Fri-day, Mr. Reece. Fri-day." She said this each time she came into the room.

There were two narrow, floor-to-ceiling windows in the room. He thought it must be daylight by the brightness. Reece wished that Debbie Dee would tell him what month and year it was. He wasn't even sure what planet he was on.

The feeding tube itched his nose. The attending physician was considering placing a permanent tube through his side, directly into his stomach. EEG studies showed that he was inside somewhere, but it would likely be a lengthy hospital stay.

Debbie Dee sat down for a minute. She needed to give Mr. Reece a bath, but first, she wanted to finish her word search puzzle.

Emma was weary of Ethiopia. The famine was winding down, and Dr. Guthrie had mentioned that the clinic in Godo could be closed soon. There were plenty of other opportunities for her if she wanted to remain a missionary. She decided, though, that she would rather leave and return to Alabama to see about getting a job at UAB Hospitals in Birmingham. That's where Reece was. She wondered about Kristin and their plans to be married. A rooster crowed. A dove slid along the tin roof.

There was a knock on her door. It was Afewerki, ready for clinic. It was Tuesday, market day, and limes filled his pockets. He sucked one and put a piece of the peel in his nose for the pleasant smell.

"Coming out soon!" she said. A pot of water warmed on the stove. She dipped in a bandanna and washed her face. She washed her hands and arms. That was enough. She imagined her hair looked a mess, but didn't care.

She scraped open the door and looked into the compound. The sun shone bright, the grass green. She could hear the team talking in the dining hut. "Hey," she said.

"Shall we eat?" asked Afewerki.

"I don't feel hungry?"

"Are you sick this day?

"No."

Barra came out of his room singing. He had a bright smile, as usual, a little too bright for Emma. "Good morning, doctor!" Since the shooting, he still maintained what seemed to be a working relationship with the Hyena.

"Good morning, Barra. Afewerki, you eat. I'll just have some tea."

"Are you to be sick?" asked Barra.

"No," said Emma.

"Ah, come to join to us. We will read from the Bible, no?"

"I'll get some tea and come in for a while."

Barra called for Irigit to bring the teakettle from the cookhouse. "You see, I am bringing tea to you."

She said, "Thanks." They would read and talk in Amharic and laugh in Amharic. She would just listen. She had been able to speak with Reece. A sickness drained through her body.

Reece lay naked in the reclining chair. Debbie Dee had cranked him out of bed with a lift and placed him on a blue absorbent pad. The rectal tube had proven to be a mess, and Reece was again wearing diapers. Debbie Dee dipped a washcloth in hot water treated with liquid soap and scrubbed his body from top to bottom.

The door was wide open, and his grandparents walked in. "Oops!" said Horace. "Oh my," said Dora. They backed up, bumping into one another.

"It'll just be a few minutes," said Debbie Dee. She was petite, had large hips, powerful arms, and cold sores in the corners of her mouth.

Reece shivered, exposed. Debbie Dee turned him on his side. His right arm flopped over the chair arm. She washed his back, which felt so good. She dug into his crack as the last bit of washing. Reece flinched. "Hey, you moved," said Debbie Dee. She would tell the nurse.

Wearing gloves, she slathered on hospital lotion and rubbed his back, especially his sacral area, where bed-sores were likely to occur. She turned him back over, shot baby powder onto his privates, reapplied the diaper, and put him in a clean gown. He was good to go for twenty-four hours. She gathered the rags, towels, and dirty linens and shoved them down the laundry chute in the hall.

Reece felt fresh but relieved that the bath ordeal was over. He stared straight ahead. They had removed the nee-dle from his spine that measured intracranial pressure. People entered the room. Don Henley sang on the TV.

"Hey, Reece, it's Granny," said Dora. She had been crying on the way to the hospital, and her eyes were puffy. She wore a turquoise pantsuit. It was Saturday, and she'd had her silvery-black hair done for church the next day.

"Grandpa's here, too," said Horace. He had his hands in his pockets, fiddling with change.

They stood there looking at him, a kind of miracle they thought. All of the doctors seemed to think he should have died.

Reece stared straight ahead. He could see half of both of them as they hovered near him. He wanted badly to speak and tried, but nothing would come. He struggled to move a finger.

"You look good," said Dora. There was one chair in the room. "These lights are too bright." She found the switch that turned off the overhead panel light.

Yes, thank you.

"Everyone's praying for you, son," said Horace. He always called Reece son or boy.

Reece wondered if it mattered. He knew he would emerge from his current state as a completely different person. God was dead.

"We had fried okra last night," said Dora. "I thought about you while we ate. I know you love fried okra."

Jesus, fried okra. Since his arrival, he hadn't tasted anything but hospital toothpaste and the lemon mouth swabs. He tried to move his eyes. *Did they move, just a bit?*

"When you come back around, I've got some potatoes I need you to plant," said Horace. "I could use your help. I'm eighty, you know, although all the ladies think I'm sixty." He laughed.

"Shut up," said Dora.

Ha, Granny doesn't pull punches.

Debbie Dee walked in. "Y'all doing okay? He's a handful that one." She took a comb and arranged Reece's drying hair.

At 2946 Zephyr Road, Reece Myers sat in the tiny living room, staring at the rug. He was going to Luby's with his parents. Two days prior, he had run away from home, had ridden nearly three hundred miles on his Suzuki TS 90 before the piston head had melted. He'd tried to sell his bike at a pawnshop to buy money for a bus ticket to Alabama, where his grandparents lived. The owner of the pawnshop was an off-duty police officer.

A junior in high school, Reece hated school with a passion. It was his thirteenth school in twelve years. His parents never went out to eat. He remembered one outing in Fort Knox, a restaurant beside the Grant's department store in Radcliff. He had ordered the fried clams. He'd had no clue what clams were. He had liked them but had not eaten them since. That was four years ago. It was just after noon.

An hour earlier, George Hennard washed his hands inside the fancy brick house that his father owned. He had not seen his parents in over a year. They let him have the house after he was dumped as a Merchant Mariner for marijuana use. George was more or less a loser, but what could they do? He gathered his two pistols, a Glock 17 and a Ruger P89. Two weeks earlier, he had tried to sell them in Austin. Boxes of ammo filled the dining room table.

George looked out the window. His 1987 Ford Ranger sat in the driveway. He had a big fancy house but no money. He couldn't afford gas for the Ranger and had quit his job at the cement plant two weeks earlier. He felt sick about having to ask his asshole dad for money. Maybe that wouldn't be necessary any longer. He saw an attractive woman pushing a baby carriage in the Texas sunshine pass by the house. He thought about blowing her away, but let her go. He would have to chase her down, and that would create a scene.

Reece's dad, a sergeant at Fort Hood, and his mother entered the living room. Was he ready to go?

"Yeah." He wore his bell-bottom jeans, and a blue knit shirt. The song "You Can Ring My Bell" ran through his head.

Outside, the Texas heat hit him. It was Wednesday, and Reece was supposed to be in school. The wind blew at a crisp clip. The school counselor had recommended that he take off the week, which was fine with him. His mom opened the door of the Bobcat hatchback and let the front seat tilt forward so that he could squeeze in. Cramped, he looked out the window at the pink-brick house. There was a fence around the front and back yard. It was flat without trees. Across the street was an apartment complex.

George Hennard took US 190 West from Belton to Killeen. It took him twenty-two minutes. He drove the speed limit and maybe a little slower. He turned on the radio. It was disco, and he turned it off. Disco made him think of women. Past Nolanville and Harker Heights, he continued on the expressway toward downtown. It was four-lane all the way with a wide grassy median. There was a music shop. His Steely Dan tape had broken. He needed a new one. He pulled off the expressway and parked. The guns lay on the passenger seat. *So what?* Once parked, he had to remind himself why he had parked. *Oh yeah, the tape.* He went inside. It wasn't much cooler than outside, hot for October.

The cashier noticed this guy come in, pick out the tape, and arrive at the register all in less than a minute. *The Royal Scam* by Steely Dan. He paid with cash. Hennard looked thin, with a red face, and a thin nose capped his face. His black hair grew long, and his bangs curled under.

Reece's dad took Zephyr Road to W.S. Young and then took a left after half a mile in lunchtime traffic. He passed the mall and turned left onto the expressway toward Luby's. Reece had never been before. He wondered what he would order. Maybe hamburger steak with gravy. Perhaps they would have lasagna. Who knew? He thought about his insufferable classmates at the high school. He hated them down to just a handful.

The bronze Bobcat made better time on the expressway and then crossed the median into the Luby's parking lot. Luby's loomed freaking huge and stood alone like a sentinel on the Texas flatland. He waited for the seat to go forward and stepped onto the pavement with his Converse tennis shoes, green. He'd once ridden in the back cargo area of the Bobcat all the way from Alabama. That had been hell.

George sat in his truck, thinking about *The Fisher King*. He cranked it and turned the AC on low. He had about a quarter tank of gas. He struggled to take the cellophane off the cassette tape, finally using his teeth. He thought briefly about how he'd had to change schools because of his father's job. His dad was a fucking surgeon and had moved them willy nilly from place to place. He reached for the nearest gun. He was about to put it in his mouth. It wasn't his fucking fault, though. He'd tried to make friends but that was fucking impossible when the kids had been together since kindergarten. They were all paired up, boys and girls. He turned the key in the ignition, and the starter whirred and ground. The truck was already running. He looked at the clock, flashing a random time.

The cute receptionist inside welcomed them to Luby's after a short wait in line. The place was hopping with very few empty tables. It smelled like his school cafeteria on a good day. She led them to an empty table in an open area with ten other tables. Booths lined the walls. Ceiling fans spun lazily, stirring the cool air.

It took about three minutes for the waitress to reach them. "Hey, y'all. Welcome to Luby's. I'm Amanda. Y'all know what you want to drink?"

Reece recognized her from high school. She was in the same grade. She had no clue who he was. His mom ordered water. His dad ordered black coffee, and Reece ordered sweet tea. One special that day was fried cod with two vegetables and a dessert for $5.99. Reece wondered if that included the drink. Fried fish and ketchup were royal. He looked at his parents sitting there. They seemed invisible. He thought about the coming Monday when he would have to return to school. He shook his head and muttered to himself.

"What's that?" asked his mom.

"Nothing."

Amanda returned with their drinks.

George pulled out of the parking lot. He had to wait for

nearly forty-five seconds before scooting into traffic. Up ahead was Luby's. Why not just stop in and have a nice lunch? He had about twenty bucks left to his name. Might as well make the most of it. He slowed and tried to imagine the menu. He couldn't remember if they had a salad bar. He thought about how the waitresses would say, "Table for one?" He thought about how those two girls in his neighborhood were afraid of him. He hadn't had a date since the fucking Merchant Marine threw him out. He swung into the Luby's parking lot and stopped. He didn't know that the brake fluid cable was rubbing against the right front tire. He saw the plate-glass window beneath the Luby's sign. He put the Glock on his lap and floored it.

Reece concentrated on moving his index finger for hours on end. He thought it had moved, but no one was there to see it. Debbie was his nurse, and Debbie Dee was the nursing assistant. God, he longed for something cold in his mouth. He now had a feeding tube that entered his stomach through his abdomen. He could feel the warm Ensure and taste it when they pushed it in.

"Let's clean your mouth," said Debbie Dee. She seemed frozen in the 1970s. Big hair. She tore open a foil pouch that held glycerin swab sticks. Reece hated them. She stuck the lemony, gooey swab into his mouth, coating his gums and tongue. She imagined it felt good.

Reece focused on moving his eyes. He could tell she noticed.

"Oh, Jesus, Mr. Reece, you done moved your eyes." She walked to the foot of the bed. His eyes followed her. She walked to the opposite side of the bed. *Barney* was playing on the TV. She thought maybe Barney had something to do with it. "Babydoll, that's super fantastic! Wait'll I tell Debbie. Boy, your family is sure gonna be proud." She high-fived him by raising his arm from the bed. She hit the call button.

Thank you, thank you. He felt exhausted. His eyes hurt as if he'd read the *Iliad,* the *Odyssey,* and *Ulysses.* Immediately, his mind wandered. He tried to focus. What had he just done? Had he moved his finger? He couldn't remember. He stared at Debbie Dee.

"What'cha need?" asked the unit clerk, answering the

call button.

"Tell Debbie to get down here. I got something to show her."

Debbie Dee took his blood pressure. 122 over 78. Debbie walked in. She'd had a weird conversation with a resident who was Reece's primary caregiver.

"What's up?"

"He done moved his eyes. Watch." She moved from his left side to the foot of the bed. Nothing happened. "Well, I swear he moved his eyes. He did. Didn't you, good buddy?"

Reece thought, trying to listen. He could hear Debbie to the right. There was too much going on. He needed to rest his eyes. He blinked.

"He blinked," said Debbie. "I saw that. His family will be glad to hear this."

"Yeah, but he moved his eyes, too. Come on, Mr. Reece, don't be stubborn."

Reece felt like he had been staring at the ocean from a porch in North Dakota. He closed his eyes.

"I'll be damned. He closed his eyes," said Debbie. "Yeah, just keep watch on him. That's great, though. Wow."

Debbie Dee puffed out her chest. She felt that she alone had brought Reece one step closer, and maybe it was true. She noticed the curtains were closed and opened them. She changed the channel from PBS to MTV. Reece struck her as a music-loving kind of guy, and she was right. It was "Run to You" by Bryan Adams.

Reece knew the song. It made him feel good. He imagined that his finger was tapping to the beat beneath the sheet, and it was.

Afewerki told Emma it was a terrible idea to walk to Alem Ketema. The shifta would rob them. There were hyenas. The walk was long with many climbs. No other ferenj had ever done such a thing, and the people would murmur. And what would the Mission think?

But Afewerki determined that Emma was serious about walking to Alem Ketema. He conscripted two daily laborers and one of the warehouse guards, who owned an AK-47, to accompany them. He filled Emma's backpack with cold enjera soaked in wot, crunchy sorghum nuggets, matches, two Icelandic IV bottles filled with water, and a light blanket. He could walk the twenty-six miles in a day, but thought that Emma could not. They would have to spend the night along the way. It would be perilous. He wanted to leave when the moon was still up, but Emma insisted on having a big breakfast and leaving a couple hours after sunrise. She wanted to enjoy the trip, to enjoy the scenery, to soak in the adventure.

After a breakfast of eggs with fresh peppers, Emma was ready. She wasn't sure how long she would be gone, so had left word at the clinic that it might be closed for two or three days. She thought about the Abba Paulos and how he was concerned for Reece. He had returned to the clinic, the staph infection on his neck reoccurring. He had traveled to Addis and visited Reece at Black Lion Hospital. He was praying for Ato Reece.

"Let's do it!" said Emma. She felt alive.

Afewerki tried to smile. He could only think of the long,

long walk and the dangers. His leather shoes were old, and he worried they would not make the entire journey. He led the way, a shamma over his head and shoulders to protect him from the sun. Emma followed, followed by the workers, Abdu and Lema, and the guard Mekdem with his rifle.

They took the road out of town at first, but, to Emma's surprise, soon left the road and followed an ever-changing network of footpaths that led over boulder fields and through rock outcroppings. The shifta tended to ambush foot travelers on the main roads.

After three or four miles, Emma's feet complained. The bright sun made it very warm, and her feet were hot. She imagined blisters forming at the ends of her toes. Mostly it was downhill, with rolling sections as they descended to the Jara River. She had imagined that she would see wildlife, but there were only a few birds and small lizards.

"Where are the lions and giraffes?" asked Emma.

Afewerki walked twenty feet in front of her, trying to encourage a faster pace. "You must go to Awash," he said, referring to the river valley. He stopped and pointed to a pair of bearded vultures circling very high above. "These are our lions."

"Maybe they will eat you," said Emma.

"No, they will only eat the ferenj."

"Ha!" Emma looked around her at the vast spaces. In the far distance stood the escarpment leading up to Alem Ketema. But first, they had to descend to the low places, the kolla, and cross two rivers.

It took four hours, but soon they descended to the Jara. A simple Bailey bridge crossed at a narrow point. The river pooled in long sections of standing water, connected by narrow rivulets. They surprised a group of naked women bathing there.

"Are there crocodiles?" Emma waved at the women, who had submerged in the still water.

"Yes, the azo, but into the canyons," said Afewerki. He'd seen them firsthand on a helicopter ride with Terry. They made his skin crawl. He led the way across the wooden bridge reinforced with short steel trusses. The planks were four inches thick. "A helicopter is coming." He shielded his eyes, scanning the distance.

"Oh, great," Emma watched as the helicopter passed overhead, most likely on its way to Godo.

"It is Terry," said Afewerki. "Perhaps we should wait?"

Emma was frustrated. This was unexpected. "No, let's keep walking. Maybe I have a point to prove."

Abdu, Lebna, and Mekdem looked to Afewerki. He indicated they should walk across the river and see about drinking water. They were thirsty.

They crossed and stepped back onto the rocky, dusty road. "We must stop here and drink," said Afewerki. "For a short rest."

"But not for long," said Emma. "Is the water safe?"

"You should drink the bottle water." Afewerki took off the pack and retrieved a bottle for her.

They rested for twenty minutes with little conversation. Emma was the first to hear the helicopter this time. They all listened as the helicopter drew nearer. It circled above them and slowly descended to find a landing area. Emma could see Terry's bearded face encased in headphones.

The others were on their feet, greeting the helicopter.

Afewerki waved. Terry landed the craft within fifty feet of a large black boulder. Immediately, everyone but Emma made for the helicopter. Abdu, Lebna, and Mekdem crouched, almost walking on hands and knees, following Afewerki. This would be their first helicopter ride, and they were not about to lose the opportunity.

Emma scowled and made her way to the helicopter. The downwash felt good. She grabbed Afewerki's hand and stepped up inside. Abdu, Lema, and Mekdem crouched and grinned in the space behind Terry. They should have all taken seats and buckled in, but Terry gunned it, lifting and circling above the river.

It was only then that Emma realized that Dr. Guthrie was in the front seat to the right of Terry. "Damn."

Reece had been back in Birmingham for three weeks. Kristin imagined that she would quit her job and spend nights on the small couch in his room at the end of the hall. God, she worked in a hospital, too. Was her whole life destined to be spent in hospitals? Did she love this guy, Reece Myers? She was his fiancée. That mattered. *Right? But what about Emma?* Emma and Reece shared something that Kristin and Reece did not, a life event. Reece had been shot inside her little house. *Was that the first time he'd spent the night with Emma?* Kristin gripped the stick shift of her Toyota, choking it, sitting inside the dim hospital parking deck. What would Jesus do?

She wore fitted jeans and a red gingham shirt. She hadn't had a haircut in three months, and her head of curls nearly covered her face. She walked across the walkway into Jefferson Tower, turned right, and headed for the walkway to Spain Wallace Tower. She knew some of the nurses who worked there. One of the building's namesakes, George Wallace, had been a patient there, a urinary tract infection.

In the elevator up to six, a woman asked her for change for a dollar. Kristin had ninety-five cents, and the woman said no. She stepped off onto six and turned left for the southwest unit. A wheelchair sat in the hallway. The smell was predictable, like a new shoe with a tinge of wintergreen. Bright fluorescent lights. She glanced at the unit clerk inside the nursing station. Did she wave? At the end of the hall was Reece's room. It seemed to come to her versus her going to it. She glanced into a room to her left, a woman with gray hair on a bedside commode.

Reece lay slumped on the electric bed, his feet jammed against the bottom. Debbie Dee was off duty, and everything was a crapshoot. There was no dedicated nursing assistant on the evening shift. The sheet was wrinkled beneath his back. He could feel it. *Damn. Goddamn. Fuck.* Someone had come into the room.

Kristin walked in. It was eight p.m., but the blinding light made it seem like midday. Reece was askew in the bed, his eyes open, searching. The room smelled like soured Ensure and feces. "Oh, Reece," she said.

Reece knew the voice. He imagined that he turned his head, but only his eyes moved. She was there, Kristin. He would give anything to say anything. He focused on moving his mouth. Nothing.

Should she tell him about the resident, Brad, who was hitting on her back in CCU at Carraway? He was cute, muscled, and destined for greatness. He reeked of success. Kristin bit her lip. She was engaged to Reece. *What to do?* She glanced at the ECG. She examined the IV pump, dosing him with normal saline. His face glistened with oil. "Hey, baby," she said.

Reece focused. *Kristin.* She'd come to Ethiopia. He'd been in the hospital there. He moved one eye toward her and then the other. One of their last dates had been at the zoo. He'd taken photos with her camera. How long ago was that? *Years? Months? Days?*

Kristin took a clean washcloth into the bathroom and ran the hot water. She soaped the cloth and went back to Reece.

The warm rag felt so good on his face. He closed his eyes. She scrubbed his face, especially his nose, and then rinsed the rag and washed his face again, removing the shiny film of oil.

The evening nurse, Constance, walked in. She wore thick glasses, a 1950s look. "Thank you," she said. She didn't bother to introduce herself and checked the catheter bag, half full, which was good. Everything seemed in order. "You have a visitor, Reece," she said on the loud side. She nodded her appreciation to Kristin and left for the next patient. Kristin rolled her eyes, a flunky getting by when no one was paying attention.

Reece blinked. He lifted the fingers of his right hand. He was desperate to communicate. *Emma.* She was in Ethiopia. He'd been in Ethiopia. A cartoon character, the Hyena had shot him in the head. He could only imagine him as drawn in black-and-white with red lips.

"We're supposed to get married. Remember?" asked Kristin. That seemed like a dead deal.

Married. Reece processed that word. Had he been married before? He thought about his parents. They'd been married for how long, eighteen years? *Shit.* He went back to Emma, her healthy chest, her crooked smile. His last memory was of the top of her head, his hands on her breasts. Who had shot him in the head? *The Hyena. But how? From where?* Did he have a hole in his head, a scar? Was the bullet still inside his head?

"Reece," said Kristin. "Look at me."

Reece closed his eyes. He opened them. He smelled baby powder. Kristin was there. She was real.

Inside the helicopter, Emma removed the long, sheathed knife from her waist. Inside, it was so loud that no one could talk. Abdu, Lebna, and Mekdem glowed with looks of wonder on their faces. It was their first time to leave the ground. They stared through the Plexiglas windows, absorbing the experience. Their children would be amazed. Dr. Guthrie talked to the pilot, Terry, through the headset as the Bell 412 spun toward Godo. Strapped in, Afewerki and Emma faced Abdu and Lebna. Mekdem sat on the floor with his AK-47. Terry had made him unchamber his round.

"She says she needs a radio," said Dr. Guthrie. "Doesn't feel safe."

"Can't blame her, though, since Reece was shot," said Terry.

"That was tough," said Dr. Guthrie. He'd just had this image of Emma as being made of steel, indestructible. Her need for safety surprised him.

They were climbing, staying above the escarpment as it towered. Below, the road to Godo snaked.

Emma was embarrassed at being intercepted before she reached Alem Ketema. She felt compromised. If Reece had been there, she wouldn't have worried so much. The last she had heard, he was still alive, but who knew? He could die at any time, or perhaps even worse, live as a vegetable for years and years. Where was God in all of this? She surveyed the browns, reds, and greens passing beneath them. She looked at the door release. It would be so easy to step out, fly for a moment, and end it all. Hell, Reece didn't love his fiancée. He loved her, Emma. She wanted to scream.

Terry and Dr. Guthrie continued their conversation. Terry was surprised at Dr. Guthrie's attitude. He'd been around, though, seen a lot. But still, Emma deserved to feel safe. The other feeding stations had radios. He was surprised that she had stayed in Godo after the shooting.

Emma unbuckled her chest and lap strap. Everyone was looking out the windows. She leaned forward. The breath seemed to leave her lungs. She saw the spurt of blood from Reece's head. He was falling to the floor, crumpling.

"Holy shit!" Terry saw the door-open light. He looked back and saw Emma standing, pushing on the door. He turned the copter sharply to the left. Emma fell backward onto Mekdem. He had no idea what to do, a look of shock on his face. Emma managed to stand and head back to the door. The copter dropped, quickly circling. Emma fell forward. She was on her knees, crawling toward the door, which was partially open. She wanted to die.

Terry dropped the copter fast and had to veer right to keep from slamming into the ground. The ground was steep. Emma was in the door. He turned the nose uphill and dropped.

Emma jumped.

George Hennard, thirty-five years young, crashed through the plate glass of Luby's in his Ford F-150. It was twelve-forty, lunch. He was wearing a seat belt. He gunned it, running over three tables. The first thought was that he needed some mint chewing gum. He looked through the windshield at the chaos. People ran toward his truck, thinking he was hurt. A man, Michael Griffith, was at his window, a veterinarian. He thought it was an accident. He wanted to help. Hennard shot him in the chest through the window at point-blank range, killing him. The truck still ran. He turned off the ignition. The cassette played "Don't Take Me Alive."

He opened the door. He felt strong. The cries and silence made him feel like iron. He fucking hated women and spotted his first target. "The women of Belton are to blame!" he yelled.

Suzanna Hupp reached for her purse where she carried a .38. *Fuck,* she'd left it in her car. Hennard came at them. Her father, Al, jumped up and rushed Hennard. Hennard shot him in the chest, killing him. Very few were running, though. Most were hiding beneath their tables. He thought about how lonely he was. He thought about how he should adopt a cat. Maybe that would help.

"All women of Killeen and Belton are vipers!" he yelled.

Hennard strolled through the restaurant looking for women to kill. He felt compelled to shoot everyone he locked eyes with, including men. His gun made loud noises. He loaded. He wanted to punch the bitches, but his hands held two guns, a Ruger and a Glock. "Another One Bites the Dust" ran through his head, and he laughed. He thought about his father, the doctor, always working and berating him for being lazy. They'd fucking moved ninety dozen times when he was growing up.

He fired. He fired. He looked for heads with long hair. He fired. He fired. People knew it was no accident. They hunkered down. Jimmie Eugene Carruthers jumped and ran toward the steam table. He was trying to reach the kitchen. He tripped over a leg. As he sprawled, a bullet crashed into his skull.

Hennard then focused on those on the ground, hiding from him. He ambled, aiming and firing. When someone leapt and began to run, he fired multiple shots. The Ruger and Glock were empty, and he reloaded the Ruger. He fired three times and worked his way to a wall to cover his back. It was strangely silent. He looked at his truck, twenty feet away. Had he driven through the window?

He reloaded the Glock. It was louder. He liked the sound. He fired at long hair. A man rushed him. Lt. Col. Steven Charles Dody. Hennard held up both guns and fired each, hitting him in the chest. It was amazing how the bullets stopped forward progress. He thought about his job at the cement plant, how the supervisors got free coffee but not the worker bees. He had to pay seventy-five cents at a machine. He'd gotten used to it, but still...

He came across a woman and her four-year-old daughter. He pointed at the woman's head. She was on top of her daughter. He wondered what it would have been like if he'd been a girl. He imagined that his father would have been more attentive. Maybe he would have recommended that he go to college and become a doctor like he was. Instead, he'd wasted three years in the Merchant Marine. *What a fucking mess.* Hell, he was ready to shoot his mother in the head. He kicked the woman in the ribs with his steel-toed shoe. Time stood still. She looked up at him. "Get up. You can go," said Hennard. "Go!" The woman, gasping, dragged her daughter to her feet and ran toward the smashed front window.

Reece could see the inevitable. They were trapped. The gunman was ten feet away. "Lie still," he said.

In an adjacent dining room, there was a crash of glass. Customers were breaking out. Hennard refocused. He shot and killed the next three, two being men. He needed a drink. He liked cheap vodka. He turned back and saw an elderly woman cradling a man he'd shot. No need for her to be sad. He shot her in the head from fifteen feet away. He moved toward the steam table. He liked chicken-fried steak with brown gravy. There were no servers. He fired two shots through the ceiling. He entered the adjacent room. Tables sprawled upside down. People ran toward the broken glass. He emptied both guns, and four people fell.

He reloaded and walked toward the broken window. He felt a breeze. He saw an unmarked police car slam on its brakes in the parking lot. He saw flashing lights from the road. He said a short prayer and moved back into the restaurant.

Reece lay still. His parents were about to die. Hennard walked over. First, he shot the woman and then the man in the backs of their heads. A woman jumped up. She was running for the broken window. He turned and fired, bringing her down. He moved on. Reece cowered like a dead dog.

Hennard mused. The servers wore yellow shirts. Where were they? The kitchen staff wore white. The servers at the steam table wore green. He'd make sure and take a tour of the kitchen before his bullets were gone. He didn't know it was Boss's Day. In a single sweep at two tables, he'd killed three school board members.

Next door at the Sheraton, the Department of Public Safety was training Killeen police officers on how to prevent auto theft. They were on break. A woman ran toward them screaming. They had heard shots and ran to their vehicles for weapons. Sergeants Jody Fore and Bill Cooper entered through the crashed window. At the other end of the room, Fore saw his target, shooting at people on the floor. Fore fired four rounds from his 9 mm service revolver. Sergeant Cooper crouched and moved forward from table to table. A coffee mug exploded near his head.

Two other officers entered through the shattered glass. Hennard went to his belly, firing at Fore and Cooper. They returned fire, the room erupting into mass chaos. Fore and Cooper moved forward, now within twenty feet of Hennard. They fired. He was hit. Hennard rolled onto his back. He put the Ruger to his temple and pulled the trigger.

Emma face-planted into the rocky dirt like bones covered with skin. She felt it, tasted it. The pain to her forehead and shoulder. The fall had been over a dozen feet. Her first thought was of her goddamned father. He'd fucking wrecked her. She should be working hard as an RN back in Birmingham. Maybe she would have been a doctor. *Motherfucker.*

Terry landed the Bell 412. Dr. Guthrie unbuckled and jumped down. He forgot to duck and ran toward the rear rotor, which was poised to slice his head in half. At the last second, he veered left and ran around the back of the copter. Inside, Terry went through the motions of cutting the engine. He pushed his door open. He was still buckled. *Fuck.*

Emma rolled onto her back. Her forehead throbbed. Her eyes blackening, blood flowed from her nose. She saw the sky, blue with sheep clouds. Was she broken?

"Emma!" said Guthrie. "Hey, Emma!"

Emma heard him but did not have the wits to reply. He was blocking her view of the sky.

Terry dropped to his knees with Guthrie. "Emma!"

Emma had six older sisters and one younger brother. She liked to eat at Duck's Barbecue, take out, pulled pork with Carolina slaw, and vinegar sauce. Her mom worked there. Shadows hovered over her. She looked between them, savoring the blue. Reece was dead. He was in heaven, singing hymns. *Fuck.*

"Emma!" Guthrie wiped at the blood from her nose.

Her breathing was slow and irregular. Her pupils were equal, which was good. There was a huge red knot on her forehead. "Emma!"

Afewerki was out of the copter, standing there, in shock. She had jumped. He'd thought they were very high. He wasn't sure. She was still alive. *Jesus Christ.* This was worse than Reece being shot in the head. He thought about the scar on his back, a stab wound from when he was seven. He'd dropped a pencil, his precious pencil, and another boy had grabbed it. He had grabbed it back. He was lucky to be alive.

Emma tried to focus. She was lying on top of rocks. It hurt like shit. *Reece?* She struggled. He was dead.

"Dammit to hell," said Dr. Guthrie. "Should we stabilize her?" He was afraid that her spine was compromised.

"She turned over, though, right?" asked Terry.

"Yeah, right," said Guthrie. "Let's see if she can sit up. "Emma!" He explained what they needed to do, that they would help her stand.

Emma wanted to die. She felt them trying to help her stand. Her head felt limp at the end of her neck. She'd helped her brother buy a car, co-signed with him, but he'd stopped making the payments. She tried to raise her neck.

"Again," said Guthrie. He lifted her head. Terry bent her legs.

Emma gradually understood. She tensed her body. What was the difference between shampoo and conditioner? Not much. She felt herself rising from the ground. She saw the helicopter and remembered.

"Damn," said Guthrie. He and Terry kept Emma from collapsing. "Up! Up! Stand! Do it!"

Emma heard him. She stood, locking her knees. She thought about her latest daily devotional: "Let those who suffer according to the will of God commit their souls to Him in doing good...—1 Peter 4:19." *What does it mean? Was she not suffering? And what was the good?*

Terry landed and watched everyone disembark. He thought Emma should come to Alem Ketema for a while, but Guthrie was in charge. Dr. Guthrie decided to stay with Emma for a couple of days to ensure she would be okay. It was the devil's work, her jumping from the helicopter. Terry had nearly plowed the copter into the ground, trying to get down once he realized that Emma was going out the door.

"I need to lie down," said Emma, walking up the steep hill between Guthrie and Afewerki. Already, whispers of what she had done were breezing through the small village. Perhaps she had buda, the evil eye?

Dr. Guthrie put his hand on her shoulder. "You'll be fine. No work for a couple of days. We'll play cards tomorrow, take a walk, eat some enjera, and get fat." He forced a laugh. The station would be closing in a couple of months, but he hadn't told her. He needed her to stay until then.

"We must treat the cut on her head," said Afewerki. "I will go to the clinic. I will get the key from Isaac."

Emma's forehead throbbed. She imagined a line of a hundred patients, half of whom had worms. She would cure them, and they would be back within two weeks. She thought about her father grabbing her breasts. She thought about the Hyena and his men attacking her while trying to visit the monk carving a church into the rock. She thought about Reece, falling sideways, buckling, blood squirting from the bullet holes.

Irigit loitered at the open gate with a worried look.

"Your eyes are purple," said Guthrie. "I'm concerned." He walked her to her tiny house and pushed open the door. Inside was warm. The tin roof creaked in the sun.

Emma stepped inside and went for a chair. She put her face in her hands, hearing the hiss of the propane fridge. She smelled plain wax and pressed on her plastic eyes, making black spots appear from the sides.

"Look up," said Guthrie. "I want to check your pupils again."

Emma looked up. Dr. Guthrie's shirt was tight, too small. Why were all of his shirts too small? He seemed a million miles away. Flies buzzed her face, but she didn't care.

Guthrie peered into her eyes and swiped at the flies. The pupils were equal. "You gonna be okay? You have to be. God is your rock. Don't forget that."

Emma processed his words. What if she had died? Who would replace her? Would it matter? It didn't take a rocket scientist to treat tapeworms.

"It's 4:20. Dinner'll be soon."

Emma laughed. "I'm not hungry. Is Reece alive?"

"Yeah. He's alive, as far as I know."

There was a knock at the door. Afewerki had antibiotic ointment, 2x2 gauze pads, and some silk tape. "I have," he said.

"Need to wipe off the dry blood on her nose," said Guthrie.

Afewerki put the supplies on the table. There was clean water in the fridge. He poured some cold water from an IV bottle onto a 2x2. Her blood stained the gauze as he wiped.

Emma winced. She looked at Afewerki. He was a good

man. She knew he was attracted to her. She was flattered, but could only think of Reece.

"Looks better," said Guthrie.

Afewerki put the finishing touches on the bandage. He'd brushed his hand against her hair. He looked at his handiwork and smiled. "You are okay now."

Emma tried to smile, pressing her lips together. Her knees and shoulder hurt. "Let me rest for a while."

Guthrie thought. "No, let's go for a walk."

Emma shuddered. "No, let me sleep."

"The devil wants you to sleep," said Guthrie.

Afewerki stood, dumbfounded. "Perhaps she is tired."

Guthrie frowned. "Want to visit the donkey cave?"

Emma processed his language and laughed. She put her elbows on her thighs. She couldn't stop laughing.

"What?" asked Guthrie.

Emma put her face on her thighs, hiccupped, and sat up. She felt drained, hopeless. She needed a plane ticket to Alabama and would visit Reece in the hospital. He would respond to her presence by sitting up. Maybe he would tell a knock-knock joke. "Life is killing me."

Afewerki nodded. She was speaking in riddles, the gold covered in wax. "What a hell."

Emma stood and walked to her cot. She rolled onto it shoes and all, turning her back to them.

Emma dreamed about the night Reece was shot. The bullet went through his testicle and lodged in her uterus, impregnating her with a child that turned out to be a runt yellow hyena with black spots. She shook herself awake, surrounded by pitch black. She could hear a light snoring. *What the hell?* She sat up in bed, the springs squeaking. What day was it? What was the dread in her chest? It flooded through her. *The helicopter. Reece.* Her face flushed in the dark. She felt impotent. How would she ever face the world again? She wanted only her mother. God, her mother needed to quit smoking.

She reached over her bedside and felt for the flashlight or box of matches. Her hand found the box. She struck a match, and the light at first blinded her. She held the match above her head and looked toward the front door. A blob figure sat in the chair near the table, the source of the snoring. A flood of information. Dr. Guthrie was sleeping in the chair. She had tried to kill herself. She was in Godo. A village in Ethiopia. It was 1986. Back in Alabama, people watched TV and ate popcorn cooked in microwave ovens. In Ethiopia, babies died from diarrhea. Nothing made sense, or did it? She'd order a pizza from Domino's if she could. They would deliver it to her door. She could request extra sauce. *Hell.* She fell back on her pillow.

A rooster crowed, and doves scratched claws on the tin roof. Emma opened her eyes. She half expected a monkey to walk on her face, Marvin, but he was dead. She pinched herself. What time was it? She looked at the Timex on her wrist. Nine-twenty. The light seeping through the cracks indicated a sunny day. The chair by her table was empty. A lone fly drilled her left eye, and she hit herself in the face and winced. She hoped it was Sunday, no clinic. It was Monday, the longest clinic lines, and she was almost two hours late. She screamed inside her head and pulled her hair. She just wanted to crawl back inside her mother and start over. She said a brief prayer, asking for strength.

There was a knock on her crooked door. She lay there, staring at the ceiling. Maybe they would go away. *Maybe not.* She threw back the Mennonite blanket and pushed her legs over the cot's edge. She stood in her pants and shirt and nearly blacked out.

The knock came again. "Emma!" It was Dr. Guthrie.

"Hey!" said Emma. "Hold on." She checked her zipper. She felt her face. It was sore and oily. She craved a hot washcloth, or a *washrag,* as her mother said. Her hair somehow hurt at the roots. She saw her tiny refrigerator and stove. The shelf with Italian tomato sauce and Australian cheese. She was wearing socks. Where were her shoes?

"Abet?" she said to herself.

"Take your time!" said Guthrie. He'd had Afewerki open the clinic to treat what he could without Emma. The line had been pretty long, the day promising to be hot. But now it looked like rain, or did it? He missed his wife back in Addis Ababa. She would understand. She would be shocked. Reece had been nothing but a signature of bad luck. But God knew best. God's will was often puzzling. Within thirty days, the Mission's business manager would be killed in a plane crash, and he would have the same thought seconds from impact.

Emma slowed. She deserved a break. She'd traveled over eight thousand miles to help others. The people liked her. She was doing well. One day, God would separate the sheep from the goats. She thought about how tasty goat meat was, on a level with that of sheep. She splashed her face with water and dried it with a bandanna. "Come in!"

Dr. Guthrie waited for the door to open. Inside, Emma

waited for the door to open. She grabbed the latch and pulled after a moment. The light was blinding. "Hey."

"Hey," said Guthrie. "Just checking. Want to have breakfast?" Abebe had made scrambled eggs with goat bits, green peppers, and crumbled enjera. His mouth watered, thinking about it.

"Yeah, need to eat." Emma felt like a rock at the bottom of a well. She appreciated his energy, but was it artificial? If she'd tried jumping back in the States, she'd be locked up, tied to a hospital bed. She remembered her mother again. She'd worked forty-two years at the same barbecue shack, longer than Emma had lived.

"Great. Can I come in?" He came in.

"Yeah." Emma sagged onto her bed, the springs complaining.

"No clinic today. Got it? Afewerki is taking care of that. All is well in God's eyes."

"I appreciate it," said Emma, and she did. She felt she was falling down a ragged cliff, bouncing, breaking bones as the wind whistled through her hair.

"You are one heck of a survivor, Emma. God is watching over you. What happened in that helicopter was the devil's work. What's important is that you persevere. There's good work left to do here, God's work. God has called you here, remember that. You are one of the toughest ladies I've ever met." He also thought she was pretty. The way her breasts swelled her scrub top. She was incredible. But God, she'd jumped from the freaking helicopter.

"I'm sorry," said Emma. Tears rolled down her hot cheeks. She needed a woman to talk to. Guthrie was just a bit clueless. She wondered if Zenebek was in the cookhouse. But she couldn't speak English. Maybe they could just hold each other.

Guthrie leaned forward, elbows on knees. The only thing he could do was pray. He bowed his head. "Dear God, Heavenly Father, visit us during this trying time. Please bless Emma. She is your child, dear Father, and needs you now in this difficult time." He fought for more words. "Amen." He looked at Emma slumped on the edge of the bed.

"Thanks." She brushed back her dingy blonde hair, half expecting it to come off like a wig. "You've been helpful. Maybe...maybe I need to go home."

Irigit rapped on the door. Breakfast was ready. He'd removed his tattered hat before speaking and held it over his heart.

"Hungry?" asked Guthrie, glad for the distraction. "Come on." He forced a smile and stood.

Married? April? Kristin. Alabama. Reece felt an urgency in his bladder, as if his bladder was the size of a dime. He strained, eyes closed to relieve the pressure, but nothing. *Urinary tract infection?* It was Saturday, according to Debbie Dee. *She must live in the hospital.* She secretly gave him liquid Nyquil during the day to help him relax. It only cost six bucks, but was worth the price. Made her shift easier.

Reece moved his right hand against the sheet, over and over. He focused on raising his head from his pillow, which seemed impossible. But he could feel the tension in his neck cords. He imagined sitting up in bed, standing, and walking to the nearest McDonald's for a Big Mac, the combo. His stomach rumbled. He still had the damn feeding tube. Ensure, mostly vanilla. The vanilla sensation made him want to vomit, but he couldn't. Debbie Dee pushed it in with a 60-cc syringe as fast as she could. Couldn't she just drip it slowly so he couldn't taste it? Hell, what control did he have over anything? *None.* Debbie, the nurse, was the best, though, asking him questions. Did he want an ice chip in his mouth? She didn't wait for an answer, but at least she asked.

What if his heart stopped? Was his life in the hands of Debbie Dee with the permanent cold sores? Was he on a heart monitor? He didn't know. Did he need a bath? Where the hell were the doctors? He felt like a misfit toy.

The TV blared, a shopping channel. Hummel figurines. Reece thought he would explode. God, if he could just raise a cup of water to his lips. That fucking Hyena had shot him in the head. He vowed to hunt him down, castrate him. He remembered a pet hamster. He'd built it a special cage. One day, he'd let it play in the space between the window and the screen. He'd pushed down the window in a hurry and squashed the hamster's head. It lived, though. *Fuck*. His mother had driven them to a vet, but the office was closed. The hamster, Abdullah, lived, but was slow after that, off balance, much like he felt. *Fuck*.

"Hey, buddy!" It was Debbie Dee.

Reece imagined what was next. He lifted his right hand an inch, but she didn't notice.

"Babydoll, we're gonna do airplane aerobics." She'd seen a video on how to exercise while you were stuck in a plane seat.

She bent his legs at the knees. "Push down! Push! Like you're tryin' to raise your behind."

In the spirit, Reece tried, but nothing happened.

Debbie Dee, always practical, moved on to the next exercise. "Okay, you're gonna raise your arms over your head. Easy as pie." She imagined the staccato music of the video.

Reece couldn't even imagine his head in relation to his arms. He sent a signal to his arms. Nothing. *Shit*. Debbie Dee raised them for him. Debbie Dee thought about her new boyfriend, Gene. He was a character. He could tie a cherry stem with his tongue and knew at least three card tricks. He wasn't bad looking to boot.

"Let's do it!" Debbie Dee used language from an inspirational video she'd seen at the YWCA. "Tried by the fire!" Her own words.

Reece searched. Was he human? He was on his back,

floating, staring at the overhead light. What lay beyond? *Captain D's?* He wanted some fried fish and sweet tea. *Hush puppies. Crunchies.* What the hell would it take? Was Debbie Dee the measure of his progress? *Hell and shit on toast!*

Emma nibbled her food. Her face hurt, as did her shoulder. How far had she fallen from the helicopter? She felt shame, anger. Why hadn't the Hyena shot her in the head instead of Reece? She had to get out of Godo.

Guthrie sat across from her in the dining hut. The rest of the team, Isaac, Barra, and Mariam, had already eaten.

"Life is killing me." This was her new mantra.

"God is good," said Guthrie. He wished he had better.

"What about the investigation? Will the Hyena ever have to answer charges? He did it. He shot Reece. He's bragged about it, according to Isaac."

Dr. Guthrie wanted to say there was no law in Godo other than the kebele courts, which mainly dealt with land disputes, and that nothing could be done. The Hyena was the law in his realm, although the kebele ran the village behind his back. The Hyena was a public eyesore, who was necessary to the structure. If it weren't him, it would be some other tool flexing his muscles. What did it matter?

"Do you think I'm a virgin?" Emma looked at Guthrie's eyes, a light blue.

Guthrie wondered if he had heard her correctly. He returned the look. *Best not to speak.* She was trying to convey a larger message, surely. And there was that confounded stirring in his pants. God, it had been years since he'd had sex. He had three sons in boarding school in Kenya. One was about to graduate. The devil was a clever son-of-a-bitch.

"Do you think I'm pure as the driven snow?"

"Emma," said Guthrie. "You are righteous in God's eyes. You have answered the call. Few can say that. Less than one percent."

She'd smoked marijuana. She'd had sex with a stranger. Her father had fingered her and sucked on her breasts. She looked at her tennis shoes. She tried to keep them clean, but it was hard during the rainy season. "I'm a sinner," said Emma.

"And so am I," said Guthrie. "God's grace…" He tried to decide if he was still hungry. He took a swig of water from the IV bottle. He heard the gate open.

Afewerki appeared in the doorway, lifting the flap. He hadn't had breakfast. Speaking rapidly in Amharic, he directed his words at Dr. Guthrie. He sat in a plastic chair and helped himself to enjera soaked in wot juices.

"What?" asked Emma. The sunshine outside called her. She needed to take a long walk by herself, perhaps to visit with the monk carving the church into the rock. *Abba Paulos.* She would leave him some money. She knew he had traveled to Addis Ababa to visit Reece at Black Lion Hospital.

"Emma, Afewerki needs help in the clinic, but I'll do it. You finish eating and rest."

"I don't think so. I need to work."

"No, really. Rest, Emma. You need it."

"Yes, you must to rest," said Afewerki.

"I'm here to work," said Emma. If she'd had a cloth napkin, she would've thrown it onto the table as a challenge.

There was a shriek from outside.

Guthrie stood and stepped out with Emma right behind him. Zenebek stood outside the cookhouse, clutching herself. Irigit was laughing and peeking inside.

"What is it?" asked Emma.

"Mendeno?" asked Guthrie, walking that way. "A snake?"

Zenebek was beside herself, shaking and trying not to laugh for crying.

"Let's take a look." Guthrie peered into the dark room. A low fire of coals. He looked at the poles on the underside of the slanted roof.

Barra came through the gate with a wide smile. "What it is?"

"Snake," said Emma. She wasn't afraid of snakes. She followed Guthrie into the cookhouse. The enjera basket lid was askew. A snake in the enjera. She lifted the lid.

"Careful," said Guthrie. "Could be a mamba or an asp."

"Who cares?" asked Emma, and there it was, a brilliant green snake coiled on top of the gray flats of enjera. Didn't look poisonous to her. She squatted.

"Emma, no."

Emma felt a power course through her body as she reached and grabbed the snake behind the head. It made a tiny gasp and coiled its body around her hand. It looked like a green fist of snake. Her eyes were blackened and her forehead bruised with scabs from the fall. She looked crazy.

"The Jesus Christ!" said Barra as Emma emerged from the cookhouse. Zenebek's mouth flew open.

"Emma, please be careful," said Guthrie. "Could be poisonous. What are you going to do now?"

Emma walked to the back of the fenced compound, the

snake gripping her hand. Its white mouth wide open. She passed Afewerki along the way. He said nothing. This was very bad. No one touched snakes. They were cursed. Only Dr. Guthrie followed her to the far corner.

Emma grabbed the snake's tail and pulled it away from her hand. She was afraid she was choking it. Why not just let it bite her? She let go of the head, and the snake swung from her left hand. She dropped it in the grass, and it shot away.

"Was pretty," said Emma.

Guthrie shook his head. Now the people would talk.

The previous day saw some storms to the east and north, but the silence and dead heat promised something spectacular, memorable. It was a day off for Kristin. She'd gone to the zoo alone, trying to recreate days there with Reece. The monkey house depressed her with its deflated gorillas and lackluster orangutan. It was as if they had died, but their hearts kept beating.

She walked to the snake house. She hated snakes, but something was calling her. She passed two young mothers pushing strollers, walking as if the world was okay, as if they owned it. Inside her, a white-hot point of envy glowed. She was ready to have children with Reece. He'd begun to move his eyes and fingers, but what would that lead to, or not? Sweat gathered in her eyebrows. The heat was something else. A yellow cast absorbed the sky, which worried her. Little did she know that a bank of black clouds in Cottondale, Alabama, was assembling and beginning to circle, sending threads of spinning cloud to the ground as if testing the waters. Within thirty minutes, no less than ten tornadoes would be spotted, most just throwing up dirt and debris, but one persisted and withdrew to the sky to incubate and fester.

Inside the cool snake house, a little boy with Down syndrome pressed his face to the glass of a timber rattler, smearing it with saliva. His mother urged him along, wanting him to see everything. Kristin paused in front of the green anaconda, coiled in its lit glass enclosure. It was green and had black spots and black stripes emanating from its eyes. Something held her there. The snake was immobile like Reece, trapped. The life seemed to drain from her. Maybe he would be better. She was going to see him after the zoo. Her mother wanted her to cut ties with him and move on with her life. Had he not spent the night in that other nurse's house? Perhaps God had punished him for betraying her. The snakes were creeping her out. She turned for the door but had to wait for a woman in a wheelchair to be pushed through the door by a younger man. She was combing her thin gray hair with a black comb.

"This here be the snakes," said the man.

"Well, hello snakes!" said the woman. She was missing her front teeth.

Kristin slipped out. A few fat raindrops fell, just one every few feet, but then stopped. She wanted to see the flamingos, pink with black beaks, standing on one leg. Why didn't they fly away to Florida? She walked downhill, past the turtle well and toward the square pond. There were ducks.

Out in the open, she got a good look at the sky. A thrill passed through her shoulders. Her church had given her a new brown leather Bible after hearing about Reece being shot. The pages were so thin but sturdy. She liked to leaf through them, lighting upon random scriptures. She'd never been one to underline or write in the margins, though.

Initially, the tornado was white and ragged, perhaps an F-3, coasting at first south and then back east following the I-20 corridor as if led on a leash toward Birmingham from Tuscaloosa. As it gathered strength, the swirling cloud gained a girth of half-a-mile wide and began to tint black. Those who saw it failed to believe that such a thing was possible. The massive tornado stalled, hovering hundreds of feet above the tender earth and then moved forward as if put into gear with a purpose to rip, implode, and terrify.

Kristin felt vaguely hungry but knew it was a mistake to eat the overpriced food at the zoo. Some ice cream would be nice, though, and she bought a lemonade Popsicle. She wished she'd left the window cracked in her Toyota. Reece had wanted her to sell it so they wouldn't have any debt when they married. He drove the old Chevy Citation that his grandparents had given him. The plastic interior was a bloody maroon. She liked his grandparents, but she felt that maybe they blamed her for what had happened to Reece. Perhaps she was bad luck. Or was Reece bad luck? She would marry once, that was it, and God had determined that Reece was the one. Who was she to question or doubt despite the misgivings of others?

She considered buying Reece something from the zoo gift shop, but that was pointless. In the parking lot, the weather became clearer. In one direction, in the distance, hovered a dark gray infused with purple, and in the other, bright sunshine and clear skies. The two didn't mix very well. Tornado weather ran across her lips, but she didn't care. Her parents had a basement, but she hated going into it. Cloth scraps for making quilts and paper bags full of books and encyclopedias filled the room

She drove to UAB Hospitals, marveling at the angry sky. She decided not to turn on the radio. What was the point? Within ten minutes, she was inside the parking deck across from the ER. The air hummed, thick, electric.

Saliva filled her mouth, and she swallowed. Inside, the halls were strangely empty. She took the walkway across the street to Spain Wallace Tower. In the distance, the sky seemed to have tripled in height, a deep-sea blue.

Anyone with the TV or radio on knew that a mile-wide tornado was ripping through Adger, leveling five churches along the way. The tornado lifted as if atoning for the carnage and moved toward Birmingham, passing over Bessemer, gaining strength, orbiting entire houses, cars, and trucks in its grip. In a Toyota Tercel, Teresa Ledbetter had crawled into the back of her car when it lifted from the ground and began the spin cycle up the wall of circling cloud. She buried her face into the bosom of her precious three-year-old Cassie and screamed, dizzy, crazy, and the cloud released her a thousand feet from the ground, tumbling.

What the heck? Patient beds were in the hallways. Nurses and doctors were busy pulling beds from rooms, although some had so many tubes and attachments that they were left for last. Kristin understood and ran to the end of the hall. Reece was there, in bed. Where was Debbie Dee? Should she push him into the hall? There was a narrow window on two sides of the room. She rushed to the window and looked. Her heart dropped. She yanked the plug on the Clinitron bed. Reece sank into the mass of polyester beads inside the mattress casing. She pushed, but the bed was locked in place. She kicked the lock. The bed moved. Outside, debris circled, crashing into the windows.

"Hey!" It was Debbie Dee. She grabbed the foot of the bed and pulled. Kristin pushed. Metal pounded the brick façade and smashed the south-facing window. A sucking of air from the building sounded like a dog dying in a hot fire.

Reece thought the world was ending, but strangely, that was better than his current state. He could feel the building shaking, tearing apart. Kristin looked beautiful in her purple, short-sleeve shirt. He thought that perhaps it was a tornado, but wasn't sure. It seemed more like an earthquake. He lifted his hand, but no one noticed. He thought that maybe he sat up in bed. His bed slammed against the door frame. Paper flew through the air. A roar. There was screaming, but no one could hear. Kristin went to her knees, gripping the bed. The top floor of the building left with its massive AC units.

The godfather of all tornadoes stalled over downtown Birmingham, grinding buildings together like corncobs, bricks spilling like corn kernels. Winds in excess of 250 mph destroyed everything, sucked the shit from sewers and sprayed it over Red Mountain into surrounding suburbs. On channel six, meteorologist James Spin ranted in an ecstatic orgasm of live devastating information until the TV tower spun away into cotton candy. For the first time, he was afraid and heeded his own advice to seek shelter, but there was none in the studio. The building exploded into a million pieces.

Reece saw black daylight. He focused on the debris flying through the air. His bed rolled toward the aperture. He looked at the sky, listening to the roar of God. He felt a pain in his leg and then in his chest like darts. As if hanging from a cliff, Reece endured the tumult. It did not occur to him to pray. The storm was moving north, eager to devour Fultondale, Gardendale, Morris. Where was Kristin? The storm would not abate until it reached Cullman County. Two hundred and thirty dead, the hospital in a shambles, another ninety to go, not counting dogs, cats, and livestock.

The dulling roar, as if someone had taken the vacuum cleaner downstairs. Reece enjoyed the view through the ragged tear in the building's new roof. Water dripped. The sky looked a pinkish yellow. He smelled an electric fire. He tasted blood in his mouth. *Kristin?*

Kristin helped a nurse, Sandra, to stand. She was bleeding from somewhere. The back of her scrub top was soaked red. "You need help," said Kristin.

"Yeah," said Sandra. "Debbie Dee!"

She was crumpled in the corner of the hallway, her face crushed, a bloody fountain.

"Oh, God," said Kristin. It seemed that someone was playing a xylophone in slow motion. *Reece,* his bed jammed halfway back into his room. There was no ceiling, the top ripped off like paper. She looked back down the long hallway, expecting a giant bowling ball to come crashing through. A bed sprawled on its side, the patient on the floor. The freaking lights were still blazing.

"Reece?" She looked into his eyes, twinkling, it seemed. No bleeding. "Jesus."

"Hey," he said. He grinned.

"What?" asked Kristin. "You said, 'Hey.'"

"Hey," said Reece. It was all he could say. He kept grinning. He could smell the death, feel the carnage. It was just more of the same. God was crazy, and he felt better for it.

Guthrie considered having Lenore Thurmond come and spend a week or two with Emma. Lenore was a career missionary, jumping from place to place in East Africa, trying not to get old, trying not to die from boredom. Her husband was a retired bigwig with the Mission Board. Lenore's huge head of silver hair defied gravity. Guthrie needed to get back to Addis to do his clinics and plan other trips upcountry. Plus, the sheet-fed press that printed Amharic Bibles had broken, and he needed to order parts from Germany.

Zenebek and Irigit murmured with one another, commenting on Emma picking up the snake. She must be charmed or some tool of Satan. Emma was heading to the clinic to work, against the advice of everyone, including Dr. Guthrie. She felt powerful, alive, and walked down the hill to the feeding compound and the clinic.

As she passed those squatting in the lane, waiting for their turn with the ferenj, her vision focused. They needed her, and she would do her best. Afewerki was her trusted partner. She pushed through the wooden door covered with tin roofing and headed straight toward the misshapen clinic. Emma slapped her hands together and imagined a puff of white smoke. She dared anyone or anything to take her away from her mission. *Reece.*

Occasionally, Emma paused and looked outside the clinic door for just a splash of sunshine on her face. Activity filled the compound, and she felt needed, as if she were moving the feet of a giant, its face unseen in the clouds above.

"What's next?" she said. Forty or so were waiting. She wanted something other than worms or diarrhea, maybe a nasty accident. Trauma was challenging.

Afewerki missed going back and forth between Reece and Emma. In walked the Abba Paulos, his neck red with oozing, itchy red bumps. Emma greeted him and bowed slightly. He was in his golden yellow garb with the skull-cap.

"Is he shaving his neck?" asked Emma. He must be.

"My goodness. He is using a razor from the Icelanders."

"Huh," said Emma. "How many times has he used the razor?"

"For many months," said Afewerki.

"No wonder," said Emma. "Tell him to throw it away and quit shaving."

Afewerki did, and the Abba looked hurt. It was his prize possession. He lifted his jaw as Emma stroked his neck with a gauze 4x4 soaked in peroxide. His neck foamed. She could see each follicle, red and swollen. She measured out another ten-day supply of tetracycline. The Abba rose, sad but feeling better.

Emma slapped her hands together. She felt bright, in charge. The sun glowered in silence directly over-head, noon. She would skip lunch. She hoped Afewerki wouldn't mind. "What's next? Spina bifida? Kidney trans-plant? Lazy eye?" She laughed, and Afewerki frowned.

In walked an ancient woman, bald except for a thin down of hair.

"Mendeno?" asked Afewerki as he helped her sit on the plank bench balanced on two biscuit tins. The old woman turned his stomach with her rank smell.

The woman began to talk as if delivering a defense to a PhD dissertation. She used her hands and stomped her right foot for effect. She looked up and looked down, something like a smile on her face, but not quite.

"She is one hundred years old," said Afewerki. He didn't believe it. "She has heard that you fell from the helicopter."

"Oh," said Emma. "Uh, she looks it. What's the problem?"

The woman had not stopped talking, patting her leg often, and pulling up her dress.

"Many years ago, a bullet entered her leg," said Afewerki. He rolled his eyes. "The bullet is ready to come from her leg."

"How does she know?" asked Emma.

"She can feel it is time."

The woman laughed. Emma laughed.

"Show me."

Afewerki instructed the woman to show Emma the bullet.

The old woman grinned and pulled up her dress, revealing her thighs. There was a bulge just above her right knee. The skin there was paper-thin. Emma felt the knot. It was there, a bullet as the old woman claimed.

"I need a scalpel and some alcohol wipes."

Afewerki sighed and retrieved the supplies.

"I can almost just pull it through the skin," said Emma. Her heart raced. *Who shot her?* "Afewerki, who shot her? Why?"

Afewerki asked the old woman. The old woman laughed and told her story, which took a few minutes.

"The Italians were invading Eritrea. She was shot. The Italians were beheading soldiers and placing the heads on their vehicles. She is one hundred years old."

"Damn. She must've been a teenager." Emma opened two alcohol wipes and scrubbed the area over the bullet. The woman smelled like syrup. "Open the scalpel." She moved in closer but avoided breathing on the site.

Afewerki peeled back the wrapper. He plucked off the plastic sheath and held the scalpel out for Emma.

"Gonna be a little sting." With a firm and steady hand, she cut below, up, and over the object. Dark red blood welled and began to run. "Four-by-four." Emma took the gauze and gripped the bloody area. She tugged, and the bullet came out, looking like a bloody suppository. She laughed.

The old woman laughed and clapped her hands.

Afewerki felt like he might vomit.

With Spain Wallace Tower destroyed, it was necessary to move Reece out, and Kristin volunteered to take him to her parents' house without asking them. Was there any other choice?

The ambulance delivered Reece to 3425 Forrest Lane. A cool $800 was charged to the system. Reece had no insurance. Kristin was at work. She had wanted him in her room, but her mother had the paramedics tote him into the basement where she made quilts. Reece felt inches away from the three-foot fluorescent tubes in the drop ceiling. Would he wind up at the garbage dump? Where was Kristin? Where were his grandparents? Did he have a dog? He lay there, moving his eyes and lifting his right hand.

Kristin hurried home from her extra evening shift. She'd been imagining wedding dresses. She pulled into the driveway. The house seemed dead. It was Tuesday, and her mother would have made chili without beans, just hamburger meat. Her father worked at City Hall. He liked to watch the news. The chili was good with sweet rolls or crackers. Sometimes her mother made cabbage to go with it.

Reece could touch his face. He touched his face again. A skinny orange cat jumped onto the bed and onto his chest. It was a twin bed, his head lying flat. The solid contact with a mattress weirded him out. He was used to floating in the Clinitron bed. But he somehow felt more grounded. He thought about saying motherfucker. In the fluorescent brightness he mouthed "Motherfucker." The cat, Wallace, swished his tail in Reece's face and lay on his chest, purring.

He's here! Kristin ran into the split-level house, first going upstairs. "Mom!" She ran to her bedroom. No Reece. The tornado had spared their neighborhood, but houses within a mile had been ripped and strewn. "Mom!" It was eleven-thirty p.m.

"Hey, baby, settle down. He's here, in the basement. Your room wasn't big enough." She was not so old, but her shoulders had begun to slope, the corners of her mouth with distinct lines.

"What?" Even the animals weren't relegated to the basement. Her pet squirrel, Harvey, lived outside, but that was to be expected. She hurried into the basement, turning the corner. *Which room? Not the sewing room.* Reece lay flat on his back in the sewing room with a deep brown comforter over his legs. He wore a t-shirt, a 10K race he'd run before Ethiopia on a Thanksgiving Day.

Reece's hand was mid-air, stalled. He turned his eyes toward the shadow. *Kristin.* "Hey," he whispered.

"Reece?" Kristin was amazed that he was alive. He was speaking! Nearly every patient on the floor above him had been killed, sucked into oblivion. Everyone thought that Debbie Dee had been killed, but she was alive in the neuro at Carraway. She was an angel.

Kristin took his hand and brought it down. "You're in my basement. You're in Alabama. There was a tornado." She thought about making the sound of a tornado.

"Hey," said Reece. It was all he had. He could see her, not a direct sighting but close enough. She was beautiful.

How would he make a living for Kristin? Was the engagement still on? *Probably not.* Where were his grandparents? He remembered the sucking sounds of the tornado. Were they alive? His chest and leg hurt. Was the catheter still in? He couldn't tell. He needed to pee.

"Pee," he said. He rolled his eyes, ashamed. It felt as if he had cold ice cream on his nose.

"Pee," said Kristin. There was a plastic urinal on the bed. She'd never seen his penis before. It was now or never. She pulled the sheet back a bit and found it, limp. She put it inside the urinal and covered him with the sheet.

Was he urinating? He couldn't tell. He willed his body to pee, and it did. It felt good, but when did it stop? He couldn't tell.

"I'll leave it there for a few minutes," said Kristin. Beneath the stress, she could see Reece. He was definitely there. It would just take time. She had faith in God. She thought back to her party days in nursing school. She could sure use a drink, but those days were gone. At least while she lived at home. Vodka and cranberry juice. She could taste it. *Damn.*

It had been a long day. Emma was exhausted, as was Afewerki. They had skipped lunch at Emma's request. The floor was a mess of 4x4 wrappers and peroxide puddles. Emma imagined working at a convenience store in Japan. She'd have to make sure the inventory was not expired. She imagined a can of expired pineapple chunks. What would she do? Would anyone notice? Did it matter?

"Emma?" asked Afewerki.

"Yeah?"

"We are leaving now?"

"Any more patients?" She looked outside the clinic door. She saw the guard and waved. "Bucka."

Afewerki was relieved but famished. He was sick of the clinic and the nasty smells. There had been one woman with gonorrhea. Her husband had visited a whore in Alem Ketema.

There was a timid knock at the gate. The guard opened the door. "Abet?" He saw a man with an older woman coughing and holding her dress as if it held gold.

The woman was the man's mother. He said that God was punishing her. That she would die soon. He pushed her through the open door, and she almost fell.

The guard looked over to the clinic door. Shouldering his rifle, he held out his hands. What could he do?

"Oh no," said Afewerki. "One more."

Emma washed her hands with soap, the water dripping into a biscuit tin filled with pus and blood. "Really?" She came to the door. An old woman was bent over, her hands at her crotch. "Bring her in."

Afewerki asked God for patience. He extended his hand to help the old woman, but she wouldn't take it. Nearly doubled over, she stepped up one step, then the next, and into the clinic. The familiar smell of smoke and milk.

"Mendeno?" Emma led the woman to the bench seat, but the woman would not sit. She moaned and spoke in a high voice.

Emma and Afewerki turned to the man, the woman's son. He seemed stymied and began the story. His mother had been gathering firewood near Sokoro Stream, perhaps half a kilometer beyond. Maybe it was a demon from there. He stopped, unable to continue.

"What?" asked Emma. "What happened next?"

Afewerki prompted the son, who was wringing his hands. He appealed to his mother to continue the story and went to the doorway, looking out.

The woman mumbled, bent over. She was in tremendous pain.

"What?" asked Emma. She went to her knees, her hand on the woman's shoulder. "What?" She wanted to say, "What the fuck?"

Afewerki listened. He was stymied. "She says that the devil has pulled her from the inside."

Emma had a hunch. "How many children has she had?"

"Eleven," said Afewerki. "What does it mean?"

"Can I look beneath her dress?" asked Emma.

The woman straightened. Her eyes said, "Yes, please help me."

Emma pushed the woman's knees apart, and there it was.

"Jesus the Christ," said Afewerki. He looked away.

"Oh, mama," said Emma. "Her uterus has everted." A bag of pink, shiny flesh hung between the woman's thighs.

The son walked outside, trying not to vomit.

"She needs to lie down," said Emma.

"In the floor?" asked Afewerki. His appetite was gone.

Emma could see no other way. "Yeah, in the next room." The laborers had added a small room to the side of the clinic.

The woman stumbled there, and Afewerki instructed her to lie on the floor. Holding her flesh, she nearly fell. Emma caught her. Afewerki took her other arm. The woman squatted with a groan. She feared she would die.

"Tell her to sit and then lie back," said Emma.

Afewerki followed her instructions. The woman fell back, lying on the cement floor. The woman let loose her burden with a low moan, looking at the slanted ceiling of the room.

Emma parted her legs and pulled up her dress. It looked like a bloody red pancake. It had to go back inside, but how? She thought about the babies with everted anus's from diarrhea and had an idea. "We need cold water," she said.

"Cold water?" asked Afewerki.

"Yeah, tell the guard to go to my house and bring back two bottles of cold water from the refrigerator."

The woman moaned, reaching down to affirm what she already knew.

Emma put her hand on the woman's forehead. "Tell her that we're going to help."

Afewerki mumbled and stood to run back to the compound for the cold water.

Kristin held Reece's hand for as long as she could without falling asleep. "Hey, I'm going to lie down on the floor," she said. Her mother had called her for dinner. Kristin was exhausted.

Reece nodded. Did he love Kristin? His mind turned to Emma. Was she still in Ethiopia? He'd been shot in the head, *right?* He remembered the sound of the roosters and then the dogs fighting in Godo. The overhead fluorescent light was off. *Thank God.* He wanted to turn his head, but couldn't. There was a small light somewhere in the room. He examined the acoustic panel of the drop ceiling. Looked like worm trails. Kristin was already snoring. Was she really on the floor?

Would he ever work again as a nurse? A chill slipped across his body. He imagined an older man with white hair. *Red birthday cake.* Was he dreaming? Kristin's mother didn't like him, and now he was in her basement. *Shit,* the tornado at the hospital. That had been wild. He'd always wanted to see a tornado. Now and then, he'd dream about tornadoes. At the last second, he'd find something to grab onto as the wind sucked at his body.

The room smelled of litter box and samples of cloth. A small window, just above the ground outside, sloped to a steep street. A faint light in the dark room. "Hey," he said. He thought Kristin was close. *On the floor?* Did she still have the Cocker Spaniel puppy? Walter, or was it Stones?

Kristin opened her eyes. *What the heck?* Where was she? She sat upright and looked around. The basement.

She was in the basement. "Hey!" She stood and felt dizzy. She grabbed for a bed rail, but there was none. She lumbered against the wall. "Dang."

"Hey," said Reece.

Kristin righted herself and went to her knees beside Reece's bed. "Hey. It's me." She could only think of "Sweet Home Alabama," one of Reece's favorite songs. She didn't get the part about Neil Young.

"Touch me," said Reece. "I don't feel real."

"Baby," said Kristin. She put her hand on the mattress and ran her hand across his forehead. "You're real. So real."

"What about the Hyena? Is he real?" Reece felt he might rise from the bed and shoot through the roof.

"The Hyena." She'd not met him, but Emma had mentioned him. He'd shot Reece in the head. Reece had talked about him in letters. "You're safe. No hyenas here."

Reece imagined the Hyena, drunk off his rocker, flashing his pistol. He yearned, somehow, to be there again.

Just that morning, a friend of Kristin's had told her that Reece was a tool of Satan. God was punishing him, but for what she couldn't say. God took care of His own. This friend suffered from scleroderma and looked like a burn victim. *Is she bitter?* Reece had just completed two sentences. The tornado had loosed his tongue. Was that a sign from God or Satan? Everyone at church was praying for her. But were they praying for Reece, too? Wasn't God on the job regardless? She didn't know.

Emma placed a few folded grain bags behind the old mother's head. The woman's eyes pleaded for help. Emma talked to her in a soothing tone and squeezed her hand. "Ishi. It's going to be okay."

Afewerki returned with two bottles of cold water and Isaac.

"Okay, good, we may need you, Isaac," said Emma. She spoke to the woman and released her hand. "I need a pair of sterile gloves and the tub of ointment."

Afewerki brought her the supplies. His stomach churned. He held the ointment while she put on the gloves.

"Okay, Isaac, you will hold one leg. Afewerki, you will hold one leg. Put the bottled water on the floor here and take out the stoppers."

The woman lay on her back, breathing deeply. She was worried that the ferenj would solve the problem with a knife.

"Okay, take her legs and lift just a bit." Afewerki clarified her orders for Isaac. He looked like a lost child about to discover that his parents were dead. Emma pulled back the woman's dress, exposing the everted organ, glistening in its juices. Isaac looked away. Afewerki could only stare.

Emma dipped a gloved hand into the ointment and lubricated the red, veiny uterus, one that had given life to so many babies. With her other hand, she took a bottle of cold water and poured it over the organ, gently pushing it back inside. The flesh seemed to respond, shrinking just enough as Emma worked it into the woman's vagina. She finished the first bottle and reached for the second. The woman moaned as the cold water crept up her back on the cement floor. She was so embarrassed, but what could she do?

Like shrinking a penis, Emma emptied the second bottle of cold water. Still, half of the placenta remained everted. "Lift a bit higher."

Afewerki and Isaac lifted higher, avoiding eye contact.

Emma now used both hands, dipped in ointment. She focused and reminded herself that there was no hurry. It was like a puzzle, one piece at a time. Gradually the organ disappeared, until there was only the vagina framed in graying pubic hair. She imagined the uterus wadded inside the woman's pelvic cavity. Being careful and slow, she inserted her hand into the woman's birth canal, seeking to find the uterus's proper place within.

Afewerki thought his neck would break with the strain. He was holding a bare, dirty leg, the skin calloused and cracked. He looked at Isaac, who seemed to be in a trance. He looked down, just a glimpse, and saw the back of Emma's head. He looked again at Isaac and saw that his eyes were open. They gazed at one another, and the old woman's moans were the only sound. Isaac was the first to smile. Afewerki immediately shut his eyes, but could not help a deep grin. Isaac stifled a laugh. Emma looked up. Afewerki broke into a low laugh. Isaac's eyes watered, and he openly laughed, seeking a deep breath, but it wouldn't come.

"Hey," said Emma. "Almost done, mama." She looked into the eyes of the mother and grandmother. She could feel the soreness and blackness around her own eyes. "You guys need to shut it."

Isaac felt his grip loosening on the old woman's knee. He was laughing now, full force. Afewerki burst into hysterics. "What a hell!" he said, letting the woman's leg dip down. He felt weak and useless, but could not stop.

"Hey!" said Emma, her right arm deep into the woman's vagina. She felt a twinge of despair and comedy and feared the worst. "Dear God." She felt the organ was back in its rightful place and withdrew her hand, a laugh on her face. She told herself, *Shut it!* but broke into her own fit of laughter. On her knees, she bent over to catch her breath. It was like a dam released.

Isaac lowered the woman's left leg and then Afewerki the right. The woman had closed her eyes, fearing the worst. Perhaps she had given birth to a monster in the process. Why were they laughing? Emma could not catch her breath and tried to stand. The poor old woman lay on her back with nothing but laughter in her ears.

Emma bent over, gloved hands on her knees. They were a mess. She coughed and then, with great urgency, yelled, "Bucka!"

Startled, Isaac and Afewerki stumbled erect, and serious looks creased their faces. Afewerki thought of his mother and sobered. Isaac was beyond hope, and he stepped into the clinic and then into the yard, still laughing, his eyes watering, his diaphragm hurting.

"Jesus Christ," said Emma. She withdrew her gloves, one into the other, and tossed the ball of gooey latex into the biscuit tin. She kneeled again beside the old woman and smoothed back her graying hair. "You're okay. Ishi, mama." She worried that the minute the woman stood, her uterus would flop back out. "Afewerki!"

Afewerki had sobered. "Yes, Emma."

"This woman must rest for three days and, if possible, she should lie down. No lifting of anything, especially children, for two weeks. The uterus could come back out."

Afewerki spoke to the old woman in a low and serious tone. She nodded, her eyes wet with tears.

"Okay, here's where the rubber meets the road. Help me help her stand. Tell her not to bear down at all."

"Ishi," and he told the woman.

Together, they helped her to stand. Dizzy, she turned, walked into the clinic, and sat on the bench.

"God, I hope she can make it home okay. Is her son still here? He needs to know what we told her."

"He is outside," said Afewerki. He called to the son and murmured instructions to him. He saw Isaac near the gate with his head down, leaning against the fence.

"Ishi," said the son. "Xavier meskin." He took off his hat when he said that.

Emma sat beside the old woman, patting her leg, hoping all would be well. The woman seemed so healthy otherwise. Emma said a brief prayer with her eyes open, challenging God to do the right thing.

"What a hell," said Afewerki.

A major portion of downtown Birmingham between the Civic Center and Five Points South lay in waste. Usually, the tornadoes turned north, staying west of I-20/59. The Bell Telephone Tower had lost its top and three floors beneath it. UAB Hospitals was in a shambles, especially Spain Wallace Tower, where Reece had been. The entire building was closed except for the labs and outpatient center on the ground floors. Patients had been transferred to Cullman, Huntsville, Montgomery, Anniston, Tuscaloosa, and a few to Emory in Atlanta. The story was major news in every venue, even internationally.

Kristin set up a small black-and-white TV in the basement for Reece to watch. There were at least six UAB patients in the intensive care units at her hospital, Carraway. She adjusted the UHF aerial for Channel 42, which featured morning news, more talk about the tornado, and in-depth coverage, including survivor stories.

"Reece, I have to go to work. Okay? Mom's here all day. I'll be back by four. I'll call and check on you. Okay?" She had requested a transfer to day shift and was surprised that it had been granted.

"Okay." His vision was still blurry, and he focused on her face framed in brown curls. "My grandparents? The tornado."

"They're fine and can come any time," said Kristin.

"The light in here seems...pallid," said Reece.

"Pallid?"

"Insipid."

"Maybe it's because you're in the basement. It's dim without the overhead light, but that makes it too bright."

"Oh," said Reece. "I'm in the basement. I need a drink."

"Hey, I have to go. A drink of what? There's Gatorade here."

"Katikala," said Reece. "I want to get drunk with the Hyena."

"What? Drunk? With the Hyena? Reece, be serious. Are you joking? He shot you." She pinned her name badge to her scrub top.

Reece raised his left hand and then his right. "No. I'm not afraid of him."

Kristin leaned over and kissed him. She wondered if they were still engaged. Did his being shot change that? She'd had to argue that point with her mother. "I hate that I have to go..." She squeezed his hand and bounded up the hollow carpeted stairs, meeting her mother, who stood there with crossed arms.

"Is he wearing a diaper or what? You know I can't do anything with that. He needs to be back in the hospital. We're not equipped to take care of him," she said.

"He has a urinal, and yes, he is wearing a diaper. It would be super if you could put a bedpan under him if he needs it."

"Honey, I can't do that. I'm not a nurse. Maybe they have a bed at Carraway. I'm going to call and check on it. His grandparents think it's a good idea, too."

"Does Dad get off at noon today?" asked Kristin.

"No, five, but he's not a nurse either," said Gert.

"Ahh! I have to go." Kristin pecked her mother on the cheek, grabbed her keys and a white sweater, and left through the front door. Outside, the sun shone friendly, seventy degrees, a perfect day. "Jesus, help Reece," she said.

Reece watched the news and then extended coverage of the tornado. He recognized a lady who was being interviewed. He'd kissed her in a Christian bookstore several years back. He'd bought an album by Stryper. *The Yellow and Black Attack.* Her house had been destroyed, and she'd lost four German shepherds. He guessed she was still single. She looked forlorn, standing in front of the rubble of her home, arms crossed, just pieces of things, complete destruction. He practiced moving his arms and legs, nodding his head back and forth. Every few minutes, he reached up and touched the scars on his temples where the bullet had passed through.

Next up was *The Price is Right.* Reece turned his head from side to side, trying not to drool on his pillow. A woman from Arkansas won with a bid of one dollar for a can of oven cleaner. His neck hurt, and he relaxed.

On his back, he thought of Ethiopia, Godo, Emma, Afewerki, and the team. The clinic was always busy, always something surprising, like the little boy with flies in his ears. His family had thought he had gone deaf, but it was just an amalgam of wax and dead flies. Once that was out, flushed with hydrogen peroxide, he could hear just fine. He grinned. *Fuck. Sorry, Jesus.*

"Hello?" Gert came down the stairs. Around the bed, there was junk piled against the walls. It looked like a fire hazard. She'd promised to check on him every couple of hours.

Reece looked down to see if he was covered. He wasn't sure if he was wearing underwear or not. He waited for Gert to come into view. She came just to his right side, and he turned his head. "Hey."

"Hey. Need anything?" She fidgeted. She hated that this had happened to Kristin. Was she going to marry a vegetable? "Uh, do you need anything?"

He saw the Gatorade on the little table beside his bed. "Can you help me with the Gatorade?"

Gert was shaking. "Yeah." She held the quart bottle somewhere in front of his face. Reece lifted his head just a bit, waiting. She managed to get the drink to his lips and tilt it without spilling. She watched his throat move as he swallowed.

"Thanks."

Gert had to get upstairs and finish her Bible study. "You're welcome." She backed away, disgusted, taking the Gatorade with her.

Terry brought more grain, milk powder, and soybean oil with the helicopter and took Guthrie back to AK. He'd also brought letters for Emma and the team. Emma held her stack, placing one in front of the other. The letter from Kristin caught her eye. She had to read it first. Clinic, though, was in full swing. It would have to wait.

Afewerki looked bored. Too many patients with headaches and stomachaches, worms. And so many young girls wanting lotion for sex. When would it end? He yawned. He dreamed of traveling to the United States and escaping his dull existence.

"Aiyee!"

There was a woman at the clinic door. She looked frantic. Before her was a younger woman, perhaps seventeen. There were two patients already inside, both with tapeworms.

"Mendeno?" asked Emma.

"What a hell." Afewerki listened to the woman's pleas, her abnegation of all that was reasonable. Did such things happen in the U.S.? He listened to this woman who had broken the queue.

"What does she say?" asked Emma.

"It is hard to understand." He questioned the woman, and she raised her voice to a new fever pitch.

Emma pulled down the lower eyelid of the woman in front of her. Nearly white. *Damn.* She had two young ones with her, both breastfeeding from a mother with anemia and tapeworms, slowly taking her to the grave.

"The woman has tried to kill herself. She has swallowed many pills," said Afewerki. "How do you say it?"

"Suicide," said Emma. "How many pills? What kind of pills?"

The mother wept, stumbling over her words, asking her daughter for confirmation.

"Six pills for malaria," said Afewerki. He rolled his eyes.

"Oh." Emma watched the distraught mother, who believed that her child would die. "Eggs. We need four eggs. Send for them, okay?"

Afewerki looked surprised. *Eggs?* "Eggs?"

"Yes, four eggs." Emma motioned for the young woman to come inside. She extended her hand and led her to the end of the bench on the door side of the clinic. "Chicorilla," said Emma. The mother came in as well, and Emma nodded.

Afewerki relayed the message to Barra, who was in the warehouse next door, and he went in search of four eggs.

"It will be soon," said Afewerki.

"Ishi," said Emma. "Until then, this woman needs niclosamide."

Afewerki opened the five-hundred-count bottle of niclosamide and handed the woman two brown tablets. He explained she must chew and swallow, and that dead and dying worms would appear in her feces. She should always wash her hands after defecating, if possible. She chewed and swallowed, a solemn ceremony to be shared with family and friends later that day.

It didn't take long for Barra to locate four chicken eggs. He paid fifty cents for the brown eggs and brought them to the clinic, curled in his shirt-tail.

"Amenseganalo," said Emma. Facing her was the young woman. "Afewerki, break the eggs into a cup." She then told the woman in English to drink the eggs, and all would be well. She reached over and patted the hands of the worried mother.

Afewerki translated. The mother broke into a cheerful smile. When Afewerki presented the girl with the raw eggs, the mother encouraged her daughter mightily.

"In the name of God," said Afewerki.

She took the cup and gulped down the eggs. The girl gagged and stood, bent over. She looked afraid, panicked.

Emma held her. "The bucket, the biscuit tin," said Emma.

The woman heaved. Afewerki was just in time.

Emma held her, rubbing her back, feeling that all was well. "Ishi."

Afewerki gagged, trying not to puke. Maybe he should have moved to Addis Ababa and looked for a job there. There was the coffin factory in the Mercato. What about the Wabe Shebelle Hotel? They served club sandwiches. *Merda.*

The young woman heaved a slick of mucus and eggs, with a trace of white, powdery chloroquine, into the biscuit tin.

Emma held her until she was through. "Enough," she said. She looked at Afewerki. "Tell her and her mother that all is well. She is cured."

Afewerki placed the tin on the cement floor. He relayed Emma's message.

The mother dropped to her knees. "Xavier meskin," she whispered.

Reece was alone. He felt alone. He was alone. It seemed that he was in Ethiopia and then back in the States. Back and forth. The TV droned. Noon news. The tornado coverage, interrupted by ads for dog food and allergy medicine, transfixed him. Kristin suffered from seasonal allergies. The women in allergy commercials were always thin and pretty, wearing glasses.

What the hell was he supposed to eat? He was starving. It was noon, and Kristin's mom descended the stairs. She was supposed to push in a can of Ensure, followed by 100 ccs of water.

Gert stood as far away from the bed as she could. She fingered a pile of yarn on a folding table. The tube was in his side, secured with a stitch and tape. His shaved head now growing half-inch spikes creeped her out. Wasn't it enough that she had to look after Kristin's paralyzed pet squirrel who lived in a plastic swimming pool covered with chain-link fencing? This was above and beyond.

"Hey," she said. "I have to give you this can of Ensure, vanilla."

A TV chef was giving details on how to cook chicken tetrazzini—thyme, mushrooms, breadcrumbs.

Reece felt wild. He lived in a basement, below ground. The house sat on a long hill in Birmingham. The driveway was steep. He felt out of kilter. He was an invalid in freaking Birmingham, Alabama. How many times had he ridden his bike up that hill?

"Shit on toast," said Reece.

"What?" asked Gert. "Do you not want it?"

"Want what?"

"The Ensure."

"Is that what's keeping me alive?"

"I guess," said Gert. "Kristin told me."

"Sorry. Yeah, no problem. Except I can drink it. Why do I still have a tube in my stomach?"

"The doctor—"

Reece reached and pulled out the tube, tearing the stitch. "Jesus, that's done." He held the wet tube like an eagle on his wrist.

Gert couldn't decide if she should run and hide or praise God. She took a deep breath. "Can you just do that? Here's a garbage can."

Reece studied Gert's face. "You, okay?"

"No. I'm a wreck."

"I'm a wreck, too."

Suddenly, Gert felt better. "We're both wrecks. Ha."

"I want to see some crazy shit going on!"

"What?"

"My apologies," said Reece. "I keep seeing the future, or the past."

"Can you drink this without a straw?"

"And why am I not eating food, for God's sake? I mean, really. I can't walk yet, but my teeth are fine."

"Oh," said Gert. She didn't know if she should let him eat. "Let me call Kristin to make sure. I can make you a turkey sandwich."

"Jesus, that sounds good," said Reece. He had an urge to say, "Lick my balls, tooty fruity." He tried to sit up and fell back.

Gert put down the Ensure and put out her hand. "Here."

Reece took her hand and pulled until he was sitting up. "Dang, my stomach is so weak. It's hard to stay up." He reached for the Ensure.

"Here."

Reece took a big sip and fell backward. "Damn."

Gert looked baffled. What was she supposed to do?

Reece turned to his side and hefted himself up onto his elbow. "Yeah, I need a straw. Do you have one?"

"I think we have some from McDonald's. Let me check." She trotted up the stairs. She usually did her needlepoint and watched the morning game shows. There was the prayer chain as well. Was she going to be Reece's caretaker? That wasn't in the cards.

Reece rolled off his elbow. Would he and Emma have connected had he not been shot? He hoped she was safe. Had the Hyena been punished in any way? His vision blurred. He burped. "Ugh."

Gert stepped back into the room with a straw. "You, okay?" He looked dead for a second.

"I'm sorry. I can't drink any more of that. I need the turkey sandwich. Sorry. Am I wearing a diaper? Jesus H. Christ. How far is the bathroom?"

"You have a urinal." She felt like a lost balloon.

"Well damn. That needs addressing, don't you think?"

"You can't get up just yet." She wrung her hands. She was afraid he wanted to get up, that he would fall and break something.

He went back up on his elbow, a look of satisfaction on his face. "Nice tits."

"What?" asked Gert. "You need to watch your mouth. I

can't believe you said that." She backed away as if she had spotted a giant cockroach.

Reece laughed. *Why did I say that?* "I'm sorry. It just came out. Not sure why." He was thinking of her mound of Venus. That made him laugh.

Gert backed away to the stairs. She went to the den, took the phone from the wall, and dialed Kristen at work. She looked down and noticed that her blouse was unbuttoned one button too many. Her hands trembled.

Reece coughed, and the pressure in his head rocketed. "Fuck-damn!" He had to get out of bed and sit up. There was a small couch, covered with boxes and junk. The orange tabby jumped onto the bed, tail raised. "Hey, Wallace." Reece reached, but was too jerky, and the cat jumped off the bed. "Damn." He couldn't believe he was in Kristin's basement. He felt like a fungus growing in a stale pot of coffee. The thought consumed him.

He rolled to the edge of the single bed. It was maybe three feet to the carpeted floor. *Here goes.* He let his legs slide off and went to his stomach, clutching the fitted sheet. He'd make his turkey sandwich if he had to. He was on his knees. He looked like he was praying. He breathed a bit heavy. "Shit." *Watch your language.* "Well, hell." He wasn't one to curse so much.

Gert finally got another nurse to get Kristin to the phone.

"Mom? Is Reece okay?"

"He pulled out his feeding tube and said he's going to walk to the bathroom. He said I had nice breasts, no, tits!"

"What?" Kristin needed to start a new IV in room three. She was planning on skipping lunch since she was so busy. "Mom? I guess he's fine without the tube. He'll need to start drinking and eating."

"Yeah, I figured that," said Gert. "I wish your dad were here. Reece is scaring me."

"Mom! He's lucky to be alive. Just give him liquids. See if he will drink the Ensure."

Reece crawled like an inchworm. He was halfway up the steps. The air in the basement was killing him. He wanted to be with his grandparents, not in Kristin's basement. He breathed like there was bread in his lungs.

Kristin could hear an IV pump beeping. "Mom, I've got to go. Just check on him every hour or so. He'll be fine. Okay?"

"Okay, but this has to change. I can't take it."

"Bye, Mom."

"Bye." Gert turned. She heard something. "Reece!" He scuttled along on his hands and knees in the hall. His gown draped around his arms, his butt exposed.

Reece collapsed into a ball. He was out of the basement. *Thank God.* He felt he could sleep and did just that.

At patient eighty, Emma felt her spirit breaking. She could so use Reece. He had been a part of the clinic. He had carried half of her burden, but so briefly. Afewerki was a godsend, but she needed a partner, perhaps a life partner. He had been so close, just inches away, to being hers. When the clinic closed and the Mission withdrew, she would return to Birmingham and visit Reece in the hospital.

"I need a quick break," said Emma. "I'm going to just walk around the compound for a minute."

"Ishi," said Afewerki.

"Be right back." She stepped down from the clinic and turned toward the warehouse. Barra seemed always to be inside doing something, rearranging the grain bags, but she wasn't sure. She walked downhill, looking into the distance toward AK. All was brown there, but with the green of shrub close by. She looked at the ground, black dirt with infinite rocks. Beyond the fence were the graves of epidemics past. She circled the helipad and turned back uphill. She paused and looked at the little clinic with the warehouse beside it. That's where she worked. Outside the fence, a line of villagers snaked up the hill. She couldn't see how many were left. It was maybe four o'clock. Her stomach rumbled.

Emma took a deep breath and stepped back into the tiny clinic. The next two patients were there, each on a plank spanning two biscuit tins. This was her life. This is what she did. Afewerki nodded to an old woman to his left. "She is the first." He knew what she would say.

"Mendeno, mama?" asked Emma.

The woman spoke slowly as if with emphysema, taking deep, noisy breaths. She spoke at length, her saggy eyelids rolling as she blinked.

Afewerki was blank.

"What is it?" asked Emma.

Afewerki controlled his voice. "She wonders why your face is bruised and there is a snake…"

"Snake bite?" asked Emma. She could feel the knot on her forehead.

"No, the snake has crawled into her vagina. She needs you to remove it. It will grow into a hyena." He turned and stared out the open door.

Emma squatted, looking up at the woman. *What to do? Move on to the next patient?* She knew that Afewerki was on the verge of laughing. Maybe that was the best reaction. "Afewerki?"

"Yes?" He did not turn to face her.

"What do we do?"

"Perhaps she must see…the priest."

"Huh." She thought. The woman was so sincere. She would try something.

"Take her into the new room." The new room afforded some privacy.

Emma gathered a bottle of the Icelandic IV fluid, normal saline, a drip kit, and a red rubber catheter.

"What will you do?" asked Afewerki.

"I'm going to drown the snake. Tell her."

Afewerki looked surprised. He took the woman into the room and told her that Emma would drown the snake in her vagina. He spoke in a serious tone. Perhaps Emma was right.

Emma entered. "Let's have her lie down and bend her knees. You sit at her head, maybe hold her head."

"Ishi," said Afewerki. He explained what was needed to the woman. Wide-eyed, she followed his instructions.

Emma punctured the IV bottle with the kit and plugged the IV line into the catheter with the flow cut off. She handed the bottle to Afewerki, who held it above his head. "Tell her I'm going to put this catheter into her vagina and drown the snake."

Afewerki mumbled Emma's words. The woman nodded and parted her legs. Emma drew up her dirty dress. Slowly, she inserted the catheter. Should she say some magic words? She reached for the clamp on the IV line and released it. The fluid bubbled and began to flow. Emma decided to pray out loud. "Dear God, please help this woman. Deliver her of the snake that is in her vagina. Help her to know that she is cured and that you are her protector in all things. In Jesus' name. Amen."

The fluid flowed rapidly in then back out, creating a small puddle between the woman's legs. It took five minutes or so for the entire liter to empty. The woman held her eyes closed, believing. What else could she do? The snake would most likely kill her otherwise.

"Let's let her rest for ten minutes, and then she can go," said Emma.

"Okay." Afewerki spoke to the woman, and she nodded, feeling like a great chasm had been crossed.

The next patient was a boy of ten, without his mother or father. Emma looked at him, all alone. This was unusual: a child at the clinic without a parent. "Mendeno?"

Afewerki was curious. What would be the problem? He

stood there and put his hand on the boy's shoulder. "Tell us," he said.

The boy seemed very anxious, distressed. His face was in his hands. He spoke. "I am not well," he said.

"What is the problem?" asked Afewerki.

The boy was embarrassed. "I am swollen."

"He is swollen," said Afewerki.

Emma looked at the boy. He had a full head of curly hair. His legs looked normal. She looked into his face. "Where?"

Afewerki hesitated. "In his genitals."

"Oh," said Emma. "Does he know why?"

"Let us look," said Afewerki.

The boy dropped his pants, standing with his uncircumcised penis slightly erect. There were dozens of bug bites on his groin. His penis was swollen, three times the size it should be. The head looked like a water balloon.

"My my," said Emma. Maybe fleas, maybe chiggers. Did they have chiggers in Ethiopia? She wasn't sure. She tried to think. "What's his name?"

"He is called Gatto, the Cat." Afewerki rolled his eyes. Cats were scarce in Godo. Dogs and hyenas in abundance."

"Nice," said Emma. She liked cats. His penis didn't look infected, just swollen. Chiggers were a bitch back in Alabama, especially in summer. "Let's dose him with Benadryl, diphenhydramine, fifty milligrams now and twenty-five tomorrow. Tell him that it will make him sleepy. Then, let's swab those bumps with permethrin."

"Ishi," said Afewerki. He found the plastic bottle containing diphenhydramine and shook out three pink capsules. He explained to the boy what he needed to do. He prepared a half-cup of water from the water can. Next came the milky permethrin.

The boy, with wide eyes, nodded. He felt that his life was over otherwise. "Amenseganolo. Xavier meskin," he said.

"Chicorilla." Afewerki escorted the boy from the clinic and motioned for two more to enter. The woman with the snake in her vagina was still in the new room, absorbing her fate.

"The woman can go." Emma knew that she would see a hundred patients that day. She felt like a clown at a carnival, Snow White at Disney World.

Afewerki, with a stern voice, caused the woman with the snake in her vagina to stand and leave the clinic, confident in her cure. In came a young girl, thirteen, with a baby, followed by a farmer with his hat in his hands. Only eight more in line.

Emma thought about dinner. She hoped it wasn't too spicy, maybe a potato wot, denich, maybe some greens, goman. God, she hoped it wasn't the volcanic dorowot.

"What?" asked Emma.

Afewerki translated. The young girl spoke in hushed tones. She had recently married a shimogele, an old man, perhaps fifty. He was rich, owning thirteen oxen. He had twenty children. His old wife was dead. She couldn't get excited about sex. He was ugly. His penis was small. He smelled like pee and talla. What could she do?

Emma rolled her eyes. Get a gun and blow out his brains is what she wanted to say. *Damn, what to do?* "Afewerki, what to do?"

Afewerki didn't hesitate. "She must pretend to have the

evil eye, and he will divorce her."

"Hell," said Emma. Seemed like good advice. She spoke with great urgency to the young bride, and Afewerki interpreted.

"Seven more, Emma."

Reece slept on the floor, curled in a ball for an hour. He awoke with yellow shag carpet in his mouth and looked around. He was at the top of the stairs. He saw the piano. Kristin was pretty good at the piano. He turned and looked down the hallway toward the bedrooms. Straight ahead was the den with the TV. Bright sunshine filled the room. Could he walk? Why not try? Where was everybody?

He pushed himself up to his knees. His arms were so weak. He felt his heart rate jump as he tried to push against his toes. He fell back on his knees. "Damn."

From the kitchen, Gert heard something and went to the den, speaking to him through the doorway. "What can I help you with?" She didn't want to touch him. She hated the sight of him. Why did Kristin have to get tangled up with a psycho?

"No, yeah," said Reece. He managed to sit on his knees, his hand pressed to the wall. "I'd like to stand."

"Are you sure?" asked Gert. "Maybe we should wait for Kristin to get home." Reece's backside was shining. She tried not to look.

"When is that?"

"In an hour."

"Tell you what. Bring me a chair to grab onto, a dining room chair."

Gert went to get the chair. She just wanted to read her Bible, crochet, maybe call her mother. She pushed the chair into the hall.

"Yeah, thanks." Reece sat up again and put his hands

on the seat. He pushed down and pushed up with his legs. "I'm weak." He went back to his knees. "I can freaking do this." He pushed down with his hands. Up came his legs, and he locked his knees. He teetered at the top of the stairs that led down to the front door. Sweating, he gasped for breath.

"Dear God." Gert couldn't figure out how she could help. It was like watching a baby try to swim, going under, going under. She put her hand across her mouth.

Reece's foot slipped, and his knee hit the carpet hard, burning the skin. "No." He pushed up again and locked his knees. "Yes."

"Please be careful."

Bemt over, Reece's head hit the seat cushion, his hands gripping the back of the chair. With a mighty heave, he stood and reached for the top of the chair. For a moment, all was well. He stood, bent over the chair, but standing.

Gert shut her eyes. He swayed back and forth.

Reece pushed and went erect. He was standing, his heels hanging over the top stair. "Oh!" He swirled his arms and fell back into space, down six steps, hitting hard against the front door.

"No!" said Gert. Her first thought was that he might be dead, and how that would solve several problems. He lay there, moaning with his eyes open, flat on his back. What could she do? Call an ambulance? Put a pillow under his head? She knew that the hospitals were flooded with tornado victims, but surely there was a bed somewhere. She went down the stairs. "Are you okay?"

"I don't know. This floor is hard."

Gert fetched a couch pillow from the den and placed it

under his head. "I'm calling an ambulance."

Reece vaguely understood. "No, wait, don't. I'll be a good boy."

Gert dialed 911 and breathed a sigh of relief.

"Damnation," said Reece.

At 3:45, Kristin drove up the hill to her parents' house and saw an ambulance in the driveway. "Oh my God!" She pulled in front of the ambulance on the street. She searched for her emergency flashers but couldn't find the button. Without turning off the engine, she ran up the driveway. A stretcher stood at the bottom of the steps. Was he dead?

She tried to open the door, but it was blocked. She could see inside the side glass. Reece was on the floor. "No!" She turned sideways and slipped through the narrow opening.

"Ma'am!" said a paramedic. He'd entered through the back door with his partner.

"Reece." Kristin knelt beside him. "What happened?"

"She pushed me down the stairs."

"What?"

"I fell. Just kidding."

"You're bleeding." She lifted his head, seeing a gash in the back.

"Maybe," said Reece.

"Ma'am, we need to position him to open the door. Are you his sister?" asked the paramedic.

Kristin looked at him and noticed her mother standing there, terrified. "I'm his wife, I mean fiancée. He was shot in Africa. The tornado demolished his room at UAB. He needs to stay here. Reece?"

"Yeah, baby?"

"You want to stay here, right? You came up the stairs, so you must be getting better."

Reece thought. Her mother didn't like him, and neither did her dad. "I busted my head open. The hospital might be a better deal."

Kristin was confused. *What to do?*

"We're here," said the paramedic. His name was Ken. "They have some rooms at Carraway, or at least room in the hall." He noticed Kristin's scrubs stamped with the Carraway logo. "You work there?"

"Yeah."

"Let me go back until I can walk," said Reece. "It should only be a week or so. I'm feeling like firecracker ice cream."

"He's right," said Gert. "He needs better care than he can get here. I'm not a nurse."

Kristin hated having him so close and then taken away. "Okay, Reece, if you think it's best."

"Yeah, thanks. I'll be up and about in no time." He tried to smile and managed a half grin, but then realized he was peeing himself.

Emma kept looking at the pile of white letters on the shelf. *What does Kristin have to say? How is Reece?* There was also a letter from her pastor. Had he heard about her suicide attempt? Would her mother find out through the grapevine? Had she really jumped? She didn't feel depressed, just sad and angry. Weren't you supposed to be depressed when you tried something like that? Her forehead was sweating, the wound healing, stinging.

"There are two more." Afewerki leaned out of the clinic door and nodded for them to enter. He knew what they wanted.

The first young lady of fifteen years stepped up and extended her hand to her friend. Both had golden skin and fleeting smiles. They wore colorful headscarves and long green dresses with bare feet. Standing close to one another, they stumbled into the wall, laughing.

Emma's back was killing her from bending over all day. Her breasts hurt, and she was thirsty. "Mendeno."

"Ah, they have both the name of Mariam," said Afewerki.

The more robust Mariam spoke in a whisper, giggling. The other seemed wan, her eyes a bit vacant.

"What is it?" asked Emma. She pressed her hands to her back.

"They are sleeping with the jeep driver. They want lotion to have sex."

The pale Mariam sat on the bench, leaning on her elbows.

"Huh," said Emma. This was not the first request for lotion for sex. "Lotion is for the hands and not safe for sex. It will cause irritation and possibly infection."

"Yes, I will tell to them."

Mariam stood listening intently, blushing. She giggled, and then a worried look crossed her face.

"Ai yi yi," muttered the one sitting on the bench.

Emma squatted and lifted the girl's head. Something was not right. "Mendeno?" She looked at Afewerki. "Her name is Mariam, too?"

"Ow, yes."

The girl put her hand to her stomach. She had diarrhea, and she had lost weight.

Emma checked the color of her lower eyelid, which seemed a little pale but not equating to severe anemia. "Her neck seems swollen." She palpated the girl's neck, feeling large, swollen lymph nodes. "Does she have a sore throat?"

Afewerki translated.

"No," said Mariam. She explained she was having terrible sweats at night, that it caused her to be very hot and then very cold. She only had one old blanket, and what was she to do?

"How much weight has she lost?"

"She is saying five kilos. That is a lot."

"More than ten pounds. Is she eating?"

"Her appetite has gone. She only eats some bread."

"She's been sleeping with the jeep driver? Is he sick as well?"

The girl looked at her friend, but she did not know if the driver was sick. He had told them to get the lotion from the clinic.

"Probably buggering them," said Emma.

"What?" He motioned for the other Mariam to sit on the bench. She blushed and sat.

"Anal sex," said Emma.

"No, no, that is very bad." He made a sour face. He hadn't thought of that.

"You need to ask her."

Afewerki asked and coughed.

Both Mariams looked at one another in surprise and were silent. The Mariam, who was ill, cried. Emma put her hand on her forehead.

"She's burning up with fever. Geez." She walked to the shelf and took a thermometer, cleaned it with an alcohol wipe, shook it down, and had Afewerki put it in her mouth. Emma rolled her tongue, imagining the thermometer in her mouth.

Outside, a brisk breeze blew. The guard stood in the center of the compound, his shamma flapping. He held his hand to eyes, watching large crows circle overhead. He would shoot them, but bullets were expensive. When would the ferenj leave? It was getting late.

After three minutes, Emma retrieved the thermometer. "Wow, 102.4."

"That is very high." He told Mariam that she was very sick, and her tears returned, doubling in force. Her friend sat with her hands in her lap. "Shall we give paracetamol?"

"Yeah, five hundred milligrams. What is her diarrhea like?"

Afewerki popped the lid from the paracetamol tin. Emma drew a cup of water from the container into an orange cup. Mariam examined the white pills in her hand and then swallowed them one at a time. She mumbled.

"Her diarrhea is painful. She wants the injection," said Afewerki.

Emma brushed her hair back with one hand. "If I knew what the problem was, perhaps I could. She doesn't seem to have an obvious infection, unless it's the diarrhea. Is she having lots of gas? Burping eggs?"

"No, just to be very hot and burns," said Afewerki. "She is having this for many days."

"We could try a sulfa drug, I suppose," said Emma. "But not an injection, tell her." Her stomach roared, and the other Mariam laughed.

"She will take," said Afewerki. "She is misery otherwise."

Emma counted out a ten-day supply in a paper envelope and handed it to her. The packet disappeared into the folds of her dress.

"I wonder," said Emma. She shook her head as if in disbelief.

Reece relaxed on the stretcher, half inside the house and half on the front porch. His gown was wet in the front. The paramedic talked on the two-way radio. Reece didn't have insurance.

"Mom, he can just stay here." Kristin felt exhausted. She stood at the head of the stairs with Gert.

Gert fiddled with the curl of hair behind her ear. "But he said he wanted to go to the hospital." She ground her teeth. "Your dad will be here soon, and I need to get the casserole in the oven."

"Do you have the eight hundred they need to take him? For God's sake, he was a missionary. He was shot in the head," said Kristin.

"He can ask his grandparents. How about that?"

"They're on social security. Plus, he would never ask them to do that."

Reece faced the road. The occasional car passed, slowing down to rubberneck at the flashing lights. He could hear the conversation between Gert and Kristin. He waved at a car.

The paramedic, Bill, with a handlebar mustache, returned from the ambulance. "I'm sorry, sir, but we're going to have cash or put you back in the house." The other guy was already pulling Reece back inside. Bill held the storm door open.

"I'm back," said Reece to no one. The tiny landing barely fit the stretcher. The walls were a light marigold, the carpet cream, the popcorn ceiling without moldings. Who would clean the urine off the floor?

Kristin put her finger to her lips and made a face at Gert. "He's going into my room. Reece, you're coming into my room." She took two steps down, turned, and glared at Gert.

Gert put her hands on her hips. "No, he is not. No sir, no ma'am."

"Did you even think to call his grandparents when he fell?" asked Kristin. "You have their number."

"He crawled up the stairs, and maybe he should call."

Bill and his buddy needed to go to a nursing home. A woman had fallen and broken her hip. "Ma'am? Ladies? Where shall we put him? We have another call."

Kristin took two more steps down. "In my room. Up here, down the hall on the left past the bathroom."

Bill squeezed inside. "Let's walk, Mr. Myers. You can do it. One on each side." He undid the belt across Reece's lap.

Gert stormed into the den and turned on the TV. What else could she do? "She is not sleeping in that bed with him. No sir, no ma'am," she said to the TV. She buttoned the top button of her blouse and folded her arms across her chest. She had almost gotten rid of him.

Reece leaned heavy on the paramedics and tried to walk between them. His legs felt like tingly springs, and he was dizzy. Flashes of light. He just went with them. He looked at Kristin and tried to smile, her face framed in brown curls. She made delicious peanut butter fudge. Her small breasts looked perky.

"Well, hello again," he said, laughing. He grunted as he crested the top of the stairs. Along the wall hung photos of Kristin and her sister.

Kristin opened her door. She threw back the comforter. She needed a pad to go under him. She stripped a pillowcase and laid it on the sheet. She could hear Walter barking outside, probably at a squirrel. "Here," she said. She'd dreamed of Reece coming home early from Ethiopia, had prayed for it, and here he was.

Bill eased Reece onto the bed, and he flopped backward, legs dangling.

"I'll take it from here," said Kristin. "Thank you."

"Not a prob," said Bill, and they were on their way.

"Thank you," said Reece, a bit too late. He felt Kristin sweep his legs onto the bed. He went to his side. She pulled his hips, moving him to his back, somewhat in the center of the double bed. The room was a light purple with dark curtains, girly.

Kristin stood back with her hands on her hips. "There." What else could she say? She leaned down and kissed him on the lips and ruffled his oily, thinning hair. His breath smelled bad. "Bad breath, you bad boy."

"Sorry," said Reece. His teeth felt furry. They hadn't been brushed in days. "I need some gum." He shifted onto his side and raised on one elbow, taking deep breaths. He could feel pressure on the back of his head where he had fallen. "Is my head bleeding?"

Kristin had forgotten about his new injury. She parted his hair, and there was a blue knot with a short gash. "No bleeding, but I need to put a pad on the pillow." She wanted to laugh.

His stomach muscles weak, he fell back from his elbow. "Your mom is pissed. She was talking to the TV." It felt so good to hear words coming from his mouth. "I have a headache now that I think of it."

"I'm pissed that she had them put you in the dingdang basement, in the sewing room no less." She looked into the hall, past the wall thermometer. The five o'clock news played. Her dad would arrive in exactly ten minutes. He worked as a clerk at City Hall. She hoped he would be in a good mood. "I wonder if she called him at work."

Gert went from the den to the kitchen, getting her foot tangled with the long phone cord. "Fiddle faddle!" She'd forgotten to put the casserole in the oven. She turned on preheat, 350 degrees. The green patterned linoleum, cracked, was too expensive to fix, and Edwin wasn't handy like that. If she'd married the electrician like her mom had wanted, she'd be rich by now, and none of this mess would have happened. She grumbled. The oven wouldn't beep when it was time to put in the casserole, so she set the egg timer for fifteen minutes.

Reece imagined a little tunnel in his head where the bullet had passed. His little finger tingled, and he wondered if there was a connection. "Maybe I liked the basement with the little TV. I'll be underfoot here."

Kristin sat on the bed. "No, you're not. They'll just have to get used to it."

"And me, too." He thought of Emma and her little house, how the rain poured off into a steel drum. He could almost reach out and touch the place.

"What are you thinking about?"

"Huh?"

"You're thinking about something."

"Just about how miffed your dad is going to be when he gets home. He owns this place. Your mom runs it, though."

Reece tried to remember what he had been thinking about.

There was the sound of tires in the driveway and then a door closing.

"Oh brother," said Reece.

Emma fretted over this thin Mariam. Fever of unknown origin could very well be the best diagnosis, but the detail of the night sweats had caused her to remember. Back in the States, HIV and AIDS were sweeping the country. They had just developed a new and better test for the virus. She'd never seen someone with it, but this young woman could be her first.

"Afewerki, does she have anal sex with this jeep driver?"

"Oh my? Must I ask?"

"Yes, you must."

Afewerki murmured the question.

Without looking up, Mariam said, "Ow."

"Yes, this thing is true," said Afewerki. He shivered at the thought.

"She could have HIV or perhaps even AIDS. I'm worried about her." She wasn't even sure if there was a treatment. She would die a horrible death, perhaps become covered with the purple lesions of a rare sarcoma.

Afewerki knew of AIDS, but not HIV. "We must wash our hands," he said.

"Yeah," said Emma. "No more sex for her, please tell her. She could give other people the fever, tell her."

Afewerki told this to both of them. The Mariams looked at each other and then at their hands.

"She could be highly contagious, and the jeep driver, too. We need to track him down, the pest." Emma sensed the unfurling of an epidemic before her eyes, but she had little power to intervene. She watched Afewerki soap and rinse his hands in the green biscuit tin. She heard singing.

Barra knock-knocked on the door. "My friends, hello! The day is very long, no? Shall you come soon to eat with us?" He smiled his white smile.

"We're still working," said Emma. She was no longer hungry. Barra made her think of a shiny bug with a hard shell.

"Ah, yes, these young girls have come to you." He stepped into the clinic, examining the shelves. "Yes, God to bless them, no?" He laughed a short laugh.

The Mariams frowned and gazed at the floor.

Afewerki spoke in a soft tone to Barra, and his eyes grew wide. He folded his hands and nodded, then stepped out of the clinic in a hurry.

"He is speaking with the Hyena, I've heard," said Emma. "Why is that?"

Afewerki looked out the door to make sure Barra had left. "We must pay him some money to keep this clinic. Barra gives to him each week."

"What? You're kidding." She should not have been surprised at such a thing. "Damn...But these girls. What to do?"

"The driver is paying them for sex. They will still need the money." Afewerki yawned. He was hungry.

Emma wanted to pull her hair out. "We must find that driver. When is he coming again, ask them."

The Mariams spoke at once. They did not know, perhaps soon, perhaps market day on Saturday.

"Do they need a place to stay? They can stay at the shelter. We can feed them."

"They are working for their fathers, carrying the water.

They cannot leave."

"No more jeep driver," said Emma in a stern voice. "And no more sex. You must listen."

The girls nodded, and the well Mariam helped the unwell Mariam to stand, who then spoke to Afewerki.

"Yellum!" he said and told them to leave.

"What?" asked Emma.

"The lotion she is asking again," said Afewerki.

The more Emma thought about Barra giving money to the Hyena, the madder she got. She would confront him at dinner. She heated water in a pan and dipped a cloth to wash her face. She could smell her feet. She glanced at the two small holes in the plastic that lined her walls, the bullet holes. She remembered the letter from Kristin and hurried to read it. Where was it? It was beneath the pan of water. *Damn.*

At the door, a knock.

"Abet?" Emma turned and saw Zenebek peeping in. She made the motion of putting food to her mouth and pointed toward the dining hut. She smiled and hurried away.

The letter. She opened it. It was three pages long. "Dear Emma..." She sat in the lone chair. *Holy cow.* She was so cut off from the world. Her mother could die, and it would be two weeks before she knew. She learned that Reece was still at UAB Hospitals in Spain Wallace Tower. He had begun to move his eyes, but that was all. She felt sick. Kristin wanted to bring him to her house, but she couldn't quit her job to take care of him there. Emma longed for him to be back with her, working in the clinic. He would track down the jeep driver and give him hell.

The second page detailed how grateful she was to Emma for keeping Reece alive after he was shot. The ink had run out, and she'd used a different pen to finish the letter. She wanted to know if Emma had a crush on Reece. *What the hell?* She wanted to know when Emma would be returning to the States. Would she try to visit him? *Hell yeah.* Emma scanned the last paragraph and let the letter fall to the floor. God, what could she do? Perhaps she should consider striking up a romance with Afewerki. Is that what Kristin wanted? Kristin had looked so helpless standing beside Reece's bed in Black Lion Hospital, like a baby hedgehog. Reece deserved better. She stood and paced, realizing how hungry she was. *Barra.* She would go and confront him now. Maybe she would confront the Hyena, too. The bribe money was Reece's blood, which still stained her cement floor.

Edwin walked up the steep driveway, mounted the steps, and opened the door. He'd tried to talk with Reece about the Second Coming before he left for Ethiopia, but he'd shown little interest in the topic. It wasn't surprising that God had punished Reece, but for precisely what, he wasn't sure, unless it was infidelity with that other nurse.

Edwin opened the storm door and jiggled the doorknob. Locked. That was strange. He was missing the news. He should have stayed longer at City Hall, addressing the multitude of tornado-related snafus, but he didn't feel it was his job to put in extra hours. Only two years to go until retirement anyway. He hesitated. What should he do? Knock on his own door? He pushed the doorbell.

Gert hurried to the door, realizing her mistake. "Hey."

Edwin entered. He couldn't smell casserole or stuffed bell peppers, to be more exact. "It's Tuesday, right?" He handed his brown blazer to Gert and walked up the stairs. Something wasn't right. He looked back at the door. Did he smell pee? He eased into the den, backed up to his recliner, and fell into it with an *oof*. There was more coverage about do-gooders flooding the city, trying to help with the clean-up after the tornado. More than likely, some of them were in town to steal. *No doubt.*

Gert could hear Kristin talking to Reece in her bedroom and winced. The egg timer went off in the kitchen. Gert skirted the long way around through the formal living room into the kitchen.

"Bell peppers ready?" Edwin's feet were up, his shoes pushed off.

"Just getting it in!"

Edwin suddenly remembered that Reece was in the basement. Where was Kristin? "Honey?"

"Yes?"

"Is Kristin in the basement with Mr. Myers?" The TV flickered in the dim den. A man had traveled from Little Rock, Arkansas, with his chainsaw to help out. He was sleeping in the back of his Ford Ranger. He didn't have the money to buy gas for the chainsaw. "Stupid."

Gert stood beside his recliner. He reached up and touched the small of her back. "Where's Kristin?"

"Well, she's in her room." She fidgeted. "With Reece."

The recliner went straight, and Edwin's feet hit the carpet. "What?"

"Pray about it before you do anything, okay? He crawled up the stairs—"

Edwin muted the news. "Did what?"

"Then he fell and hit his head on the door. The ambulance came. The paramedics put him in there. Kristin told them to. I was going to call you..."

"Baloney biscuit." He couldn't believe it. "You get on that phone right now and tell his grandpa to come get him. He will not sleep in my daughter's bedroom. Who does he think he is? Coming in here like that." He stood, his fists clenched.

"Let's pray, sweetheart." Gert took his hands and bowed her head. She had an urge to go to her knees and beg, but for what she did not know.

Edwin recoiled, but then saw the wisdom in her words. He began. "Dear sweet Jesus, you have visited us and laid upon us this burden, which we gladly bear in your name. We only ask dear Lord for patience and guidance regarding Mr. Myers. We understand that this is temporary, that the devil has had his day, but that you, Sir, are in charge."

"Amen," said Gert. The water purifier attached to the kitchen sink spigot was clogged.

"That b-a-s-t-a-r-d has to go and soon," said Edwin. He took the phone from the cradle and handed it to Gert. "Call his grandparents. I'm going to talk with Kristin."

"Hey, Dad," said Kristin. She'd changed from her scrubs into loose jeans and a blouse in front of Reece. She tried to fill the doorway. "You're missing the news."

Briefly, Edwin realized that was true. *What to do?* "Young lady, is Mr. Myers in your room? That is unacceptable." He folded his arms across his chest. "Mommy's on the phone right now with those grandparents of his." He looked back to see Gert holding the phone in both hands like a baby bird. "Gert..." She hung up.

"Dad, no. He needs to be with me. This is his home for now."

"Flibber flabber," said Edwin. "I'm going to have a word with him. We agreed that he would stay in the basement."

The dog barked outside. Wallace walked through the den with his tail erect.

"Hey, Boo Boo," said Kristin. She picked up Wallace, who purred. "And no one agreed to anything. You put him down there. It's damp and dark, maybe like the rest of this whole dingdang house." She paused. "I'll sleep on the floor." She walked into the den.

Gert thought it best to check on the casserole and did

so, taking a long look at the foil-covered pan. Warm air filled the kitchen.

Edwin set his jaw. He was five-seven with short, graying sandy hair, kind of chunky. He'd thought about joining a gym, but he didn't like all the grunting. Why couldn't people just work out without drawing attention to themselves? He walked past Kristin into the hall toward her room.

"Dad, no."

"Don't 'Dad no' me." He cleared his throat. He knocked twice and entered with Kristin close behind.

Reece lounged in bed with a contented look on his face. He had a headache. How much more could his head take? He looked at Edwin. Maybe if he got close enough, he could drag him into bed and kiss his face. "Hello...sir."

"Uh, hello," said Edwin. "You've been misplaced."

"Like the island of misfit toys," said Reece.

"No. Like this is my daughter's room. Kristin's room. It's not godly." What would the pastor think?

"Her room isn't godly?" Reece coughed.

Edwin stuttered. "God is punishing you. You have to get your vertical," and he made a vertical motion, "with your horizontal." He made a horizontal motion.

"Dad," said Kristin from the hallway.

"I'll need a protractor," said Reece.

"I'll bet you've never been inside a Christian bookstore," said Edwin. His cheeks flushed with rage.

"I'll bet you've been inside a Christian," said Reece. The smile went away. What was this, leapfrog?

"Gert!" Edwin tried to spin on his heel but stumbled into the wall. He turned left and went into his bedroom and closed the door.

Reece felt for the urinal between his legs. It needed to be emptied, but he decided to wait.

Emma forgot her bottled water and slipped into the dining hut. It was just about time for the kerosene lantern. Everyone was there: Mariam, Afewerki, Isaac, and Barra. But no Reece.

Emma took a chair, silent. Two bottles of birzz, the honey water, sat on the table, both empty. The cold enjera in front of her on a platter was soaked with juices, but with no meat on top. She took a fold of dry enjera and pinched a wad of the juicy part. The spicy juice flamed her mouth, and her stomach growled.

"We are praising to God," said Barra. "He is good, no?" He was full and felt a little sleepy. He watched Emma bring her hand to her mouth. She was using her left hand. Everyone watched. She switched hands.

Emma chewed and put her left hand beneath the table. She felt their stares and sudden silence. *Of course, I have a crush on Reece.* She wanted to get drunk and read the letter again. She could slip some generic Valium from the clinic and sleep for two days. *What would it matter?*

"This is dirty," said Barra. He stared at the large platter. He glanced at Emma.

"Ai yi," said Afewerki. He shook his head no at Barra.

"What is dirty?" asked Emma. Barra looked small in the dim light. His shirt matched exactly the color of his pants. He seemed to be wearing a body suit. She expected him to burst into song at any minute. She looked at the faces, all downcast. "What?"

"The hand," said Barra. "It is unclean. You must not. We

can no longer eat this enjera." He chuckled, and his white teeth flashed.

"But I am full," said Afewerki.

Emma processed Barra's words. It hit her. "Oh! I'm sorry. I forgot."

"It is yours, this enjera," said Barra. "Zenebek will bring another."

Emma panicked and shook her head. She realized she had taken off her bra and forgotten to put it back on. And where was Misrak, the other cook? It had been at least a week. She had meant to ask. "Where has Misrak been? Is she sick?"

Mariam inspired. He wore his button-up shirt with the huge pocket. It was bad news. Misrak would die soon.

Isaac spoke. "Oh, she iz very sick."

"Really? Why didn't someone tell me? I need to see her."

Barra coughed. "It is a ghost. There will be no cure. She will die soon." He moved to light the lantern.

"What?" asked Emma. "Die soon? What's wrong with her?" She recalled the little boy Mamoosh. He'd had a ghost in his leg, but he had lived. "Good God, tell me."

Afewerki spoke. "It is what they are saying. Her breast has turned to black, and she is suffering. She cannot to leave the bed."

"Jesus Christ, why didn't you tell me?" asked Emma. "She could have cancer. She needs to go to Addis. She has kids."

"The priest haz spoken. It will be true, the ghost," said Isaac. His wire-frame glasses gave him authority.

Emma stood. "Afewerki, we have to go see her now. I have to see her."

Zenebek stooped and entered the hut. There was still enjera on the platter. She needed to be home with her children. Why were they taking so long to eat?

Barra snapped at her in Amharic. He ordered her to bring fresh enjera and wot. He told her what Emma had done.

"Ishi," said Zenebek, and she withdrew.

No one seemed to be listening to Emma.

"We will pray for her children, no?" asked Barra.

"Yeah, we'll pray, but I need to see her. Afewerki!" She moved toward the flap in the hut. Afewerki stood to follow her.

Outside the hut, Emma felt naked. "Take me to her house, please."

Afewerki mumbled and took the lead. He wore a light blue jacket that the dimming light made purple. Emma passed the cookhouse, smelling smoke. Already, thousands of stars littered the sky. Zenebek emerged with a new platter of food for the team.

"Why didn't anybody tell me?" asked Emma.

Irigit gave them a big smile as he opened the gate.

Into the lanes they went. Emma followed Afewerki, keeping a few steps back. She heard the cries of "Ferenj!" but did not react. Her sister had had breast cancer, but she had lived. *Ghost? In her breast?*

Afewerki stopped to tie his shoe as they passed through the village center and then continued. Misrak lived near the old Polish airfield in a small enclave of simple huts with her husband and three children.

After about five minutes, they approached the crude gate to the compound. A bundle of thorns blocked the entrance. Inside were five goats and two oxen. Afewerki called out, "Hallo!"

"Hallo!" came the cry of a man sitting beneath the hut's straw overhang. He cradled an old rifle. He rose to let them in.

Emma paused to let Afewerki explain their presence. Misrak's husband dressed in the rags of a farmer, and he removed his tattered hat. A month's worth of beard covered his face. He led them to the hut.

Emma entered first, so dark, and she paused, not sure of how to proceed. Afewerki bumped into her from behind, and she stumbled forward, coming to the edge of the cold fire pit.

"Is there a candle?" asked Emma. "Misrak?"

Afewerki inquired, and there was none. A soft moan came from the bed against the wall, whispers of small children, and dogs fighting in the distance.

Emma could see the outlines of things. She saw three children standing together as if for a family portrait. She could not distinguish their faces. A large basket, it seemed, hung from the mud-daubed wall. She focused on the moan and saw the crude bed. "Misrak?" She moved closer and touched the bed's edge. Misrak cowered beneath a blanket. Emma kneeled and found Misrak's hand, which gripped hers.

"How long has she been sick?"

"By two weeks," said Afewerki.

"Misrak, we will help you. You must let us help you. Afewerki, tell her." She smelled fear, dung, and something oddly sweet.

Afewerki spoke, followed by a few words from Misrak.

She was crying.

"What does she say?" asked Emma.

Afewerki paused. "She may be pregnant, and the baby will die."

"Damn." Misrak's body beneath the blanket was emerging. Her face now glowed faintly, dry in the darkness, her eyes. "How many months is she pregnant?"

"She is saying three."

Emma caressed Misrak's calloused hand. "I need a GD flashlight." She blew her hair from her eyes. Outside, an ox lowed. "Afewerki, her breast is black?"

"Ow, and her arm is swollen. This one." He pointed to his left arm.

"Is she in pain?"

"Yes, very much."

"Oh, Misrak," said Emma. "Tomorrow, before clinic, we will come. Okay? Tell her."

"Ishi, Emma," and he told her.

With little moans amid her quiet crying, Misrak watched them leave. Her husband followed to close the thorn gate. He spoke to Afewerki.

"He is saying who will cook the food? No one is eating now except to buy from the neighbors." He led Emma into the wide, rocky path. The sky had purpled, now magically lit with millions of stars.

"Afewerki?"

"Yes, Emma."

"I need a drink."

"What is it?" Dogs barking, invisible to them. The faint sound of an AM radio.

"Alcohol. I need some alcohol." Emma caught herself

from crying. She took a deep breath. So much had happened, and when would it end?

"This is bad idea," said Afewerki. "Only the men are drinking now."

"I don't care. Take me there."

Horace drove the twenty minutes from the lake house near Palmerdale to Kristin's. Dora fiddled with a Kleenex in her lap. The tornado had spared their house. It was a miracle, Dora said.

"Hey, look back when you change lanes." Dora's frosty black hair looked ultra-neat. She wore brown polyester pants with a yellow top and a turtle brooch.

Horace frowned. His hearing aid squealed. "You know I can't turn my head." He wore his comfy jumpsuit from JCPenney. He didn't care that the legs were too short.

"Well, at least stay in the lane."

Horace growled. Kristin's mom had called. She hadn't invited them over, but had said that Reece had fallen down the stairs. Horace and Dora suspected that Reece was not entirely welcome there.

"You don't think him falling will aggravate his bullet wound, do you? Poor boy."

"He's hard-headed for sure. We told him there were plenty of colored folks to help right here." Horace shook his head. Reece was stubborn, but his heart was in the right place. "Where do I turn?"

"Are you lost? I don't know where to turn. I hate that he's been missing church. Lord, look at that car on top of that sign, like someone just picked it up and set it down. Sawn trees filled the sides of the road. The McDonald's on the side of the hill was gone. "I know her house is in Roebuck. Her daddy works at City Hall. Maybe someone at a gas station will know." She jabbed her hair with a metal pick.

"Are you kidding? Half these people around here are from out of state. They barely know where their own house is." He made a sound like a tire going flat. "I doubt if they'd know who the President is. That road there goes on over to Trussville."

"You should've gotten the address."

"I did get the address. I just don't know how to get there, Dora. And apparently neither do you." He was thinking about the gristmill back at the home place in Cullman County.

"Don't call me Dora."

Horace pulled into a Shell station. "I guess we'll have to call."

"We need some bread. See what it costs."

"Hell."

With her door closed, Kristin sat in bed with Reece. Leaning against the headboard, he felt naked in his hospital gown.

"Can you get me some pajamas? I don't need this gown. It shows my butt."

"Yeah, but a cute butt," said Kristin.

Reece suddenly wanted to make out with her. It would be exciting to be on her bed with her parents in the house. They had yet to do it, but why not now? Life was short and could be even shorter. He put his arm around her and kissed her curls.

She turned her head and brushed noses with him. She looked at the reddened bullet wounds. He should be dead. She knew in her heart that Emma had a thing for him. But she wasn't sure about Reece. She faced him and kissed him on the lips.

"That was nice." He wondered if his breath was still bad. He kissed her back and slid his tongue across her lips.

Kristin melted into his side and put her leg across his. "I want to have your baby." She closed her eyes. She was a virgin and imagined Reece exploding inside her. How would it feel?

Reece stumbled for a reply. He suddenly thought of Emma. God, he was comparing her breasts to Kristin's, and Emma was winning. "Would you breastfeed it? I mean him, or her?"

Kristin pulled back. "What? Why does that matter, especially now?" She wanted to grab his penis and push her mouth down over it. She knew her period would start in a day or two. "You're a dummy sometimes."

"No, come back. You feel so good."

The doorbell rang.

Kristin peeled away from Reece and stood. She straightened her blouse. She had just been ready to put his hand in there. God, she needed touching. "That's them."

Reece tried to sit up, but his stomach buckled. "I'm sorry."

"No worries. We have plenty of time."

Edwin rapped on her door. "Kristin, can you get the door if you are able?" He'd washed his face with a hot cloth and soap and felt better.

Kristin opened her door with a smirk, but then closed it. She had wanted him to see her making out with Reece on the bed. What could he do? Gert headed down the stairs to the door.

"Well, hello!" said Gert. "So, you found us."

A few raindrops began to fall.

"I built a deck on this street a few years back. I recognized the cemetery on the way up the hill," said Horace.

Gert realized she was holding the door open and letting out the air conditioning. "Come on in. Reece will be glad to see you." She hoped they would put him in the back seat and take him home. She looked up the stairs to see if Edwin would emerge.

Horace urged Dora up the short flight of stairs, the one Reece had fallen down. The TV was on.

"This is very clean," said Dora. She wondered if Gert washed the curtains every two weeks like she did.

They stood in a cluster.

"Uh, Reece is in Kristin's room."

Kristin looked at herself in the mirror and opened her door. "Hey! He's in here." She stood there with her hands folded.

"That's sweet of you to let Reece have your room," said Dora.

Horace wondered where her dad was. Walter whined, scratching at the back door. Horace bumped into Gert. "Excuse me." He felt like he was dancing with her.

Reece waited, and there was Dora. "Hey, Granny." He tried pushing up on his elbow and fell back. "Kristin's mom pushed me down the stairs, and I peed myself. So it's good news."

"I did not!" said Gert. She laughed the laugh, but frowned.

Horace moved to the foot of the bed and squeezed against the dresser. "Hey, Son." He reached down and pinched his foot.

Dora sat on Kristin's makeup stool with her huge purse

in her lap. "Are you, okay? When did you start walking? I couldn't believe it when I heard it."

"Maybe one more head knock and I'll be normal again. I crawled up the stairs."

"Your head is greasy," said Dora.

"Haven't had a bath in a few days, not since the tornado," said Reece.

Kristin stood in the doorway. She felt guilty about his appearance. "We'll get him cleaned up now that he can move around."

Dora eyed her. "You done gained some weight. You're so skinny. Looks good on you."

Reece laughed. "She's a whale."

"Hey," said Kristin. Had she gained weight? "Jesus."

"She's a pretty girl," said Horace, although she was too skinny.

"Thank you," said Kristin.

"And where are you sleeping?" Dora heard a door open, looked back, and glimpsed Kristin's dad. She'd only met him once, accidentally at Walmart.

"Here, on the floor, so I can keep an eye on him," said Kristin with some regret. Did her voice crack?

Gert had moved to the kitchen. She peeked in the oven at the stuffed bell peppers. Edwin stood there with his arms folded, frowning. He seemed desperate.

"Go say hello," said Gert with a frown.

"They're not staying for dinner, are they?" asked Edwin. He'd changed out of his slacks and shirt to loose jeans and a "Victory is Mine" t-shirt from the recent revival at church. He still wore his thin black polyester socks. His feet were always cold.

"Surely, they won't stay for dinner. I don't think so. Go say hello!"

Edwin shuffled his feet and went there. Kristin framed the doorway. He touched her shoulder. She moved so he could see in.

"Hello, everybody." Edwin waved at each one and moved one step closer. "Reece fell down the stairs."

"He's better, though," said Dora. "He's gonna be okay. God's looking out for him. I wish he could come back to his old bedroom."

"He's fine," said Kristin. "Mom takes care of him during the day."

"Well, that's sweet," said Dora.

"We appreciate it," said Horace.

Reece wondered how long Kristin would expect him to stay there. He'd much rather be back at the lake with his grandparents. "I'm feeling more solid. I'll be walking in a few days. I know it. Driving, too."

"Where's your glasses?" asked Horace.

"Back in Ethiopia, I suppose," said Reece. "My vision seems better, though."

"Let's head to the den," said Edwin.

They headed that way with Kristin supporting Reece.

"You're a bigwig at City Hall, I hear," said Horace.

"I'm a clerk, to the chief clerk," said Edwin.

"Oh," said Horace. He pursed his lips as if drinking lemonade. He needed to pee. His prostate was enlarged, and he never felt completely empty.

"You need a chair?" asked Reece.

"Right," said Edwin. He went to get a chair for Horace from the dining room. His stomach griped, smelling the bell peppers. He was missing the news. Walter whined on the deck. He opened the back door, and Walter ran in, squirming his body, sniffing the floor, his long ears drooping. He ran straight to Dora.

"No!" said Dora.

"Hey!" said Reece.

"Reece?" asked Kristin. She pulled Walter off Dora and put him in the hall. "Uh, would you guys like to stay for dinner?"

Edwin wondered what he had done for God to try him in this way.

Emma followed Afewerki along the narrow, rocky path, back toward the village center. She heard loud talking. The last time she'd had alcohol, she'd come around on a stranger's kitchen floor. God had forgiven her, protected her, and she'd promised Him that she would never drink again.

"It is here," said Afewerki. "The men will be angry."

"I don't care. What do they serve? Any American drinks?" She trembled. Misrak could die. There was HIV in Godo. Where was God? *Drinking?*

"Perhaps areke. It is very strong. I will not drink."

"What? You must drink. You must drink with me."

"God does not like."

"God doesn't like people either."

"Emma," said Afewerki.

"Afewerki," said Emma. "Go inside. I have money."

"Ishi," and he pushed through the grain bags that hung as the door.

The room went quiet, except for the AM radio playing Amharic music from Addis. There was an accordion, a flute, and the single-string masinqo beneath the voice of a woman. It sounded Middle Eastern to Emma. There were no chairs or tables, just a crude bench lining the mud walls plastered with pages from old Icelandic magazines. It smelled of sour mash, cloves, and garlic.

"It is areke." Afewerki knew everyone in the bar. This would be his first visit.

The barmaid, a young girl of seventeen, stood petrified.

There was no more seating. She smiled and continued to pour areke into empty orange cups. One man, standing in the middle on the left, motioned for Emma to come and sit. He took off his ragged hat and held it across his heart.

"You must sit," said Afewerki. "I will stand." He felt sick.

Emma made for her spot on the bench and sat. Her shoulders touched those next to her. The men squirmed, and soon she had six inches on both sides. She remembered she wasn't wearing a bra, and that made her nipples go hard. *Jesus.* She glanced down at her scrub top and there they were. She tried to think of something disgusting, perhaps a dog getting hit by a car. The room felt warm, lit by a kerosene lantern. Gradually, she relaxed.

The barmaid brought a cup to Afewerki. He frowned. She asked if she should serve the ferenj. "Ow," he said, much to her amazement. She remembered the Icelandic nurses drinking and sleeping with the men. She took the colorful pot and poured a drink for the ferenj.

Emma took her cup. "Amenseganalo."

"Yiqirta," said the barmaid. She had a two-year-old at home. She hoped that Emma's presence would not make her late to feed him.

Afewerki wanted to stand near Emma, but that would put him in the middle of the room. He moved in front of the tiny bar made of bamboo. He would have to drink his areke because everyone was watching.

Emma smelled the garlic in her cup, and she nearly puked. Sour garlic. She held her breath and drank half. Rather than swallow, she let it drain down her throat. It burned. She felt a hot flash in her chest. She thought about Reece's hands inside her shirt and then the very loud *pop pop* of the pistol. *Shit.* Kristin thought she had a crush on him.

"Loving will protect us from danger," said the song. Afewerki tried to focus on the lyrics. But he wasn't in the spotlight. Emma was. Everyone watched her. Some of them had even heard the rumor that she had seen a patient with HIV and had already begun to speculate that perhaps she had given it to her, or maybe the ferenj who was shot in the head, Ipa, Rice.

A farmer slipped out the door.

Emma nodded her head from side to side. She thought it must be noon in Alabama and wondered if Reece was okay. Did he think of her, even if he was unresponsive? She took a sip of the areke, savored it, and gagged on the strong garlic flavor. Light laughter filled the room. Suddenly, she felt vulnerable and looked to Afewerki for support. Anything could happen. She took another swig.

The older man on her right had eight children. He was wondering if her breasts were as white as her face. He would love to see. He called to the barmaid and ordered another drink for Emma. His wife's breasts were flat with long, hairy nipples. The rumor was that the ferenj was a virgin.

Emma felt the areke. She needed to pee and hit on a memory. She'd been driving through Hueytown. Traffic had slowed near a major intersection. A woman was there, wringing her hands beside her Ford Taurus. She was tall and thin with a worried look. Emma pulled off onto the median. She parked and looked two lanes over at the woman, who seemed to be a puppet. Traffic was slow, and she threaded her way across to the woman.

"What's wrong?" Emma gazed at the light-blue car stopped just under the traffic signal. Traffic was bending around it, flowing and then coalescing. The woman seemed as if she was trying not to exhale smoke.

"I think I hit something." She coughed.

Emma looked. She bent over and looked. Nothing. Traffic eddied around the car, only stopping when the light turned red. She put her hands on her hips. She walked to the other side of the car, and there it was, a massive pit bull hung up in the wheel well, blood dripping from its mouth.

"What?" Emma jolted from her dream. The barmaid was pouring into her cup. The man to her right had stood and was dancing a jig of sorts. He motioned for her to join him. Electricity and loud murmuring filled the room. *What to do?* The old joke was that Baptists couldn't have sex standing up because it might lead to dancing. "What time is it?" she said to the room, and it was a good guess that no one knew.

"You must not." Afewerki wanted to sit next to Emma, but was afraid the farmer who had stood would start a fight. The yawning of the radio made him anxious, and he wished to be in his bed, his white hen roosting overhead.

Emma downed her areke, essentially a double shot of 90-proof alcohol. Her throat and chest burned, but then the warmth extended to her arms and stomach. She felt a slight chill. Dancing would warm her up. She stood and hitched her scrub pants and swayed to the frantic music, moving her feet slowly, very conscious of her loose bosom. A roar of approval came from the packed crowd of twenty-one.

"Merda," said Afewerki. This was too much like the Icelandic nurses, Eydis and Svana, who regularly got drunk in the bars and slept with the farmers, usually married. He walked forward and made himself dance, wanting to dance with Emma alone, but now he must protect her. He stood planted to the floor, hands in his pockets, swaying just a bit.

Now she was in the middle of three farmers, all with full cups of sloshing areke. It was cheaper to buy a full cup. The farmers all wore tattered shorts with wide legs and ragged shirts made of tough cotton fabric. Cheering filled the room. A new song came on, suitable for dancing the traditional eskista. One man with a goatee begged the barmaid to dance and teach the ferenj.

Blushing, she approached Emma and took her hands to lead her to the middle of the tight room. She moved her shoulders and hips, swaying her long dress with her hands.

Emma looked back at Afewerki, who was frowning. She began to copy the barmaid, her breasts bouncing beneath her top. Emma stood a foot taller and could see the barmaid's tight braids coated with butter. She noticed a bald spot and then a scar on her arm that looked like a burn. A love was pouring through her. Emma felt as if her life had led her to this moment, this place. The music's pace picked up, and so did the dance. Half of the farmers were up, clapping their hands, moving their feet. Shadows crossed shadows from the kerosene lantern sitting on the tiny bar, behind which were a dozen bottles of areke flavored with garlic, cloves, and even roasted coffee beans.

"Simish man naw?" What is your name? asked Emma.

She stumbled a bit.

The barmaid's eyes widened. The ferenj was speaking her language. "Desta," she said.

"Desta!" said Emma. She wanted more areke. A light sweat flooded her body. The dance was making her breathless. There was a hand on her shoulder, and she turned to face a young farmer with reddened eyes. His white teeth glistened. *Why not?*

Holding his hat, the farmer grooved on Emma. He wanted to touch her hair. Everyone wanted to touch her. Emma's feet no longer moved, just her body. She still held the empty orange cup. She turned to find Desta, but another man had replaced her.

"Desta!"

Afewerki tried to stay on Emma's periphery, one farmer away from her. The dancing turned into jostling. Desta returned, pouring drinks, trying to keep track of who owed what. The bar owner would make her pay for any losses. Why did the ferenj have to come and cause such a ruckus? Desta stopped in front of the radio. The bottle in her hand fell to the mud floor, areke spilling. She saw a bright yellow light. She could hear the music but did not know if she was still standing, and then it happened. Always her worst nightmare, especially with drunk men around. On the floor, Desta convulsed, caught up in a grand mal seizure.

Desta was divorced and not unattractive. Her eyes rolled back in her head, and she trembled from head to foot, her dirty dress above her knees. Emma bobbed her head to the music, pressed on all sides, but something had happened. She wasn't sure. She turned, and a hand was on her breast. She knocked it away and moved for-ward. There was a circle of men unconcerned with her. The hand was back on her breast. She turned and slapped a man six inches shorter than she was. She'd forgotten about Afewerki. Where was Desta? She had a bad feeling. The music seemed to be a love song now, a pining, almost a whining.

One farmer pulled up Desta's dress, while another dropped his pants even as she continued to seize. Most had been drinking for hours, watching Desta, imagining, as she kept their cups full. Emma pushed forward and saw a man with an erect penis standing over Desta. He was dropping to his knees. Desta gasped for breath, her eyes jerking. What had happened?

"Yellum!" Emma, screaming. Nothing seemed real. She was drunker than she thought. She began to windmill her arms, striking anyone in her path. Afewerki followed be-hind her, ready to catch her. She fell on top of the man kneeling beside Desta and began to strangle him from be-hind. He stood, his pants around his feet, and fell. Emma landed on top of Desta and covered her with her body, weeping, weeping for home, weeping for Reece, weeping for all good people from whom God chose to look away.

Kristin's sister, Robyn, also a nurse, arrived at six-thirty, just in time for dinner. She worked with private patients in their homes. She was taller than Kristin, more rounded, and her cheeks creased when she smiled. She smelled stuffed bell peppers when she walked in, but whose car was in the driveway? She'd barely been able to park. She walked up the stairs, and there was an elderly couple in the den on the couch. She'd never met them before, but she guessed they were Reece's grandparents. Her mom was standing in the entry to the dining room like a sentinel. Edwin sat in his recliner, but he was not reclined. That was different.

"Hey!" said Robyn. There was silence. The TV was on mute with the news playing. She'd modeled a bathing suit in front of Reece in the den before he'd gone to Ethiopia. She was pretty sure that he'd been turned on.

"You must be Robin," said Dora. She was glad to break the silence.

"It's Robyn," said Robyn.

"Ruh-bean?" asked Dora.

"That's right."

"Oh," said Dora.

"It's a pleasure," said Horace.

"Robyn's a nurse," said Gert. She wadded her hands together. There were only four bell peppers. She would have to halve them.

"A nurse," said Horace. "Reece is a nurse."

"Everybody's a nurse." Robyn laughed, followed by a

titter in the room.

The phone rang, and it was the prayer chain from church. Thankful, Gert took the phone into the kitchen, stretching the long cord. Edwin watched the silent TV, trying to decipher the news. He saw airplanes and then President Reagan. "I suppose when missionaries are being shot, it's a sign of our Lord's coming." He gripped the arms of his recliner.

Horace looked at Dora. Dora looked at Horace. They were believers but had not connected Reece with the end of time.

"Honey, what's for dinner?" asked Edwin in a loud voice. He already knew. "Honey?"

Gert put her hand over the receiver. "Shush! It's the prayer chain." An elderly woman at church had been diagnosed with pancreatic cancer and given one month to live. God worked in mysterious ways.

Robyn saw the futility of the situation and excused herself. She assumed Kristin was in the basement with Reece and went to her room down the hall. He was more trouble than the dog Walter.

Kristin heard her sister's door close. "I'll be right back." She went across the hall and knocked. "Hey, it's me. Reece had to pee, and he's resting on the bed."

"Hold up," said Robyn. She opened the door. "Hey."

"Hey, yourself. Can you help me bring Reece into the den?"

"What? He can't walk."

"He's in my room. He crawled up the stairs today, while I was at work."

"Really?" asked Robyn. "Okay...Are his grandparents

staying for dinner?"

"Yeah, I think so. He can walk if we help him. He fell and gashed his head."

"Jesus."

"Yeah, right."

"Let me brush my teeth first," said Robyn.

Kristin returned to her room. It seemed like dead silence emanated from the den. "Hey, let's go into the den with your grandparents. Robyn's gonna help. She's home."

"Okay, but only if I can have some of those damn bell peppers. It's all I can smell."

"Sure."

"Knock knock," said Robyn. She surveyed Reece sprawled on the bed. "What's up, champ?"

"Hey," said Reece.

"Let's do this," said Kristin.

"Okey dokey," said Robyn.

"Yee ha," said Reece. He let Kristin sit him up and swing his legs over the side of the bed. "Dizzy."

"Sit there a minute," said Kristin. "You need a bath."

"Yeah, kind of rank. The tornado is to blame."

"Ha!" said Robyn. "You ready?" She had his left arm, and Kristin had his right. "Push up."

Reece stood, and he could feel cold air on his backside. "Tie my gown in back if you can. Don't want to start a riot."

"Mom needs to see your buns," said Kristin. She laughed.

"Yeah, she'll leave Edwin for sure," said Reece.

Robyn laughed. Reece started to laugh. Everyone laughed, and down went Reece to the floor, wadding into a ball. He laughed deep, and so did they. Reece couldn't catch his breath. He felt like he was in church, and the preacher had farted.

"Oh!" he said. He guffawed. He felt a release. All the pain and suffering, the dying children, the damn roosters, the spicy food that made his ass burn, the motherfucking Hyena who had shot him. He gasped for breath, releasing a universe of frustration.

For another minute, they laughed, doubled over. Kristin wanted to just lay him out and spread her body on top of his. She wanted to have his baby and now.

"Sweet Jesus," said Reece. He took deep breaths. "I can't breathe."

"Brother," said Robyn, recovering. "You, okay down there?"

"Yeah."

She and Kristin positioned themselves to help him stand. "On three," said Kristin. "One, two, three!" and up he came, a bit wobbly.

"Whew, that was great," said Reece. "I needed that. I thought maybe I was going to stroke."

"Okay, straight faces," said Kristin.

"Baby steps," said Robyn.

Reece felt their support. He couldn't do it without them. Together, they entered the hall and squeezed through the doorway into the den. Late afternoon sunlight filled the room.

"Hey y'all!" said Reece.

"Hey, son," said Horace. He was wedged on the couch with Dora, and he couldn't get up, but Dora did.

"Look at you," said Dora. "You need to shave. Here, put him here."

Reece shuffled and fell back onto the couch. He felt like a king. "Hey, you need a chair."

"I'll get one," said Kristin.

There was silence.

"I've been shot in the head," said Reece. "Talk among yourselves."

Edwin frowned.

"The bell peppers are ready," said Gert. She just wanted everyone to leave, to have her house to herself.

"There's not enough room at the table," said Edwin.

"We can eat in here." Kristin knew her mom hated that.

"I'm a starved lion," said Reece. "What flavor Ensure do you have, liver?"

No one laughed.

Gert busied herself in the kitchen, cutting the bell peppers in half. There were baked beans and loaf bread, too. Without asking, she fixed everyone a glass of ice water.

Edwin fidgeted. He felt that as man of the house, he should coordinate the conversation. "Reece, tell us about how the Lord works in Ethiopia."

Reece laughed. "What happens when a baby starves to death? How do you explain that?"

The room went dead serious. Horace had lived through the Great Depression and knew about hunger firsthand. The thought of a child needing food made his knees go weak.

Edwin spoke carefully. "It's hard to judge God, not knowing what his ultimate will is."

Reece felt entirely at ease. This was child's play. "What are a dying baby's last thoughts? What about the mother?"

"Reece?" Kristin could feel the storm brewing. She desperately wanted her dad to accept him.

Horace spoke. "One of my baby brothers died. I held his hand in the coffin. He was buried in the only shirt I owned, but that's the least I could have done."

Gert wrung her hands. "I'll just bring everyone a plate. How's that?" The dog was scratching at the door to get out. She busied herself in the kitchen, wishing for relief, anything.

The room went silent, except for Reece, who started laughing. He bent over double, chest to knees, and laughed. Tears wet his eyes. Visions of the people of Godo. The clinic. Tapeworms and trachoma. Epilepsy and burns. Emma, working her ass off. The homeless women in the shelter. Dr. Guthrie and his tight shirts. The priest digging a church into the rock. A man beating a donkey. He wept. He couldn't stop. The tears flowed like a pretty stream, blurring his vision of the brown carpet. He said, "Fuck," but no one heard him.

Gert brought paper plates in wicker-basket holders. She stood there with her arms extended. "Who likes bell peppers?" she asked.

With Emma lying across Desta, heaving with grief, the men left the bar one by one, perplexed, ashamed, and angry. Many went without paying their tabs, thinking it a lucky day.

Desta settled into the throes of a post-seizure delirium, foam in the corners of her mouth, her tongue bloodied. She could not afford to have another child, her first thought.

"Emma," said Afewerki, amazed and exhausted. The ferenj wore him out, killing him, it seemed.

The radio station had faded—static and moaning with snatches of guitar, voices, and what seemed to be the laughter of children. The red light of the kerosene lantern made everything clear. Something had happened. A miracle, perhaps. What if Emma had never traveled to Ethiopia? How would that have changed the night? For better, for worse?

"No one invited me here." Emma knelt, cradling Desta's head. She gazed at Desta's pretty face, her eyes searching for meaning.

"We must go," said Afewerki.

"We have to take her home," said Emma.

Afewerki knew it was pointless to argue, but he did anyway. "The bar owner will be here soon. He will take care. She must count the money."

Emma couldn't believe what she was hearing. "No way! She just had a grand mal seizure. She should be on medication. Those men wanted to rape her. So, where does she live? Tell me!"

Desta tried to sit up. She saw Afewerki. Where was she? Someone was holding her. She feared the worst and cried. Everything looked yellow.

"Desta. Desta," said Emma. The butter from Desta's hair was staining Emma's shirt. Emma looked around the room. Three men remained, looking on in amusement, drinking their areke. One poured himself a drink. "Afewerki, tell the men to leave their money and go home. Desta says that the bar is closed." She caught herself, woozy.

Afewerki mumbled the decree. No one moved at first, but then the men left one by one. Only one remained. He wanted to practice his English.

"Is goot?" he said.

Emma ignored him. The radio yawned, and then the kerosene lantern sputtered.

"We must light the candle," said Afewerki. The lantern fizzled in a cough and a final leap of light. "What a hell." Afewerki waited for his eyes to adjust. His night vision was excellent, as it was among most of the people there. It amazed him that Emma could not see in the darkness.

"Afewerki?"

"I am looking for the match." He made his way to the bar and ran his hand across the top. He felt a corncob stopper and some change.

The bar owner, speaking loudly, entered. He paused for a moment, going from starlight to darkness. He asked about Desta in a growl. Was it true that she had told the men to leave?

Afewerki lit a candle and told him the story. Desta could sit now, whimpering like a little girl. She could not lose her job. Her family would starve. She needed to breast-feed her youngest. Why had God cursed her?

"Afewerki, help me," said Emma. "Help her stand. We have to get her out of here." She could barely see. "What does this guy want?"

"He is the bar—"

The bar owner slapped Desta's face, and Desta moaned.

Had that happened? Emma held tight to Desta. "Hell no! Afewerki!"

Afewerki raised his voice at the bar owner, angry but cautious. He said that the Baptist Mission would pay for the unpaid tabs. No problem. Chicorilla.

The bar owner spat on the wall. He was tall and muscular. He told Afewerki he would come for the money the next day, and Desta would work the next day, or he would find another girl. She must have done something terrible for God to punish her with seizures.

Afewerki just nodded.

"Let's get outside," said Emma, "before this lunatic gets his balls crushed."

"Ai yi," said Afewerki.

Emma led Desta through the door. Outside, the stars flooded the village. The dark shapes of huts. The smell of dying fires. The bray of a donkey. Dogs fighting.

"Follow me," said Afewerki, and he led the way to Desta's tiny hut. He wondered if he would have to pay for the alcohol.

Emma walked arm in arm with Desta, amazed that she had recovered so quickly. "I can't believe that bastard slapped her. How often does she have seizures?"

"She says one time per month." He yawned. "She has

fallen into the fire only once, so God is watching her."

"That's good news, I suppose." Emma navigated the rocks in the path. Little orange glows came from huts they passed, candles.

Afewerki wondered how that could be good news. He worked his way down a narrow lane, his arms outstretched to keep from hitting the fences on either side. He stepped into a hole. "Damn!" His shoes would not last forever like the ferenjis'.

"You, okay?" She held Desta's shoulders. She smelled the butter in her hair, the unwashed body, the dress that had absorbed so much sweat only to dry again in the thin air of Godo.

Afewerki limped a bit. "I am okay." Perhaps Emma would let him walk her back to her house. Maybe she would fix him a cup of hot tea. The air was cool and getting colder. He wondered what God looked like and shook his head.

Emma and Desta followed. Desta stopped and called to Afewerki. He had passed the tiny hut that had no enclosing fence. Her husband was away, making charcoal to sell along the road between AK and Addis Ababa. She only saw him once every few weeks. Her oldest daughter took care of the children while she was at the bar, but only Desta could feed the baby.

Desta shrugged away from Emma, embarrassed at seeming helpless. She could hear the whimper of her little girl and a soft voice from within. Her heart quickened, and she called out for the ragged board door to be opened.

Inside was a cave of darkness. Desta spoke in whispers. Her daughter, little Jazarah, beloved princess. Already, she had two small braids of hair. With the sting of the slap fading, Desta sat on the narrow homemade bed and felt for her daughter. A moan and Jazarah cried.

"Oh." Emma could not see a damn thing, but she could feel the heat of others in the round room. She thought she might fall, still buzzed from the areke, and squatted. "Afewerki, will she be safe tonight? I can't see."

"Yes, she is safe. Shall we go?" He still tasted the areke and wanted to spit.

"Tell her to come visit us if she needs anything," said Emma.

"She will beg," said Afewerki.

"Tell her anyway."

Afewerki told her. He could hear the sucking sounds of the little girl and made a face. Her other children, a small boy and the oldest daughter, sat huddled in the corner with a blanket over their shoulders.

"Amenseganalo," said Desta in a breath.

"Chicorilla," said Emma. "Okay, let's go. I'm blind in here."

Afewerki laughed. The ferenji manifested weakness in so many ways, it seemed. "Shall we go to the compound?" He ducked outside, waiting for Emma to follow. He heard her bump into the door.

"Dang."

He reached in and took her by the elbow, leading her into brilliant starlight. He shivered. "It is cold."

"Thank you," said Emma. "I'll follow you. You don't have to go back with me, though. I can find the way."

Afewerki laughed. "Oh no, you will fall from the cliff. I must take you." He'd decided to go back along a different path, one that did not pass the areke bar. It would take them twice as long, but he would have more time with her.

Emma felt silly and laughed as well. "Okay."

For five minutes, they walked, and then Afewerki halted. He could hear a wheezing and the sound of tearing and quiet snapping. *Hyenas.*

Horace gazed at his half of a stuffed bell pepper. Bell peppers gave him heartburn. "Looks delicious." He didn't have a fork. No one had a fork. Within a few minutes, everyone had their plates and ice water. Kristin passed out plastic forks.

Walter whined at the back door. Robyn opened the door and then the storm door.

"I wouldn't do that, honey," said Edwin, reclining with his plate on his stomach.

"Just let him in," said Kristin. "He needs to see his daddy."

Reece made a tiny face, and Walter bounded into the room. He went for Dora and jumped onto her knees.

"No!" said Dora. She spilled ice water on her plate.

Walter yapped and went for Horace.

"Walter!" Kristin put her plate on the floor, and he dove right in, snapping at the hamburger stuffing.

Gert winced and wrung her hands. It was just getting worse by the minute.

"I'll put him in my room. Daddy, what do you have to say?" Kristin looked at Reece.

"Uh, bad boy." He reached and petted Walter's head.

Kristin led him away, holding his collar.

"That your dog?" asked Horace to Edwin. He picked the stuffing out of the bell pepper and mixed it with his beans.

"That's Kristin's dog. Cost three hundred and fifty dollars."

Horace's eyes got big. They'd had a black Cocker Spaniel years ago, but it had been free. That was more than he'd made in two weeks at the pipe shop back in the fifties.

Dora struggled to cut her bell pepper with the plastic fork, as did everyone else. "Horace killed poor old Blackie. Backed over him with the car."

"Well, he lived for a couple of hours," said Horace.

Reece had heard the story before. He held up his plate and took a direct bite of his bell pepper. It was divine. Juice ran down his stubbly chin. His plate tilted, and the beans were dripping off.

"Let me help," said Robyn. She put down her plate on the coffee table, sat on the couch arm, and took his plate. "Need a damn knife."

"Robyn!" said Gert. "Watch your language."

Robyn smirked and took Reece's plate to the kitchen. She cut up his bell pepper into bites.

Back in the den, Kristin wanted to feed Reece. "No," said Robyn. "I've been a nurse longer than you have, so nyah."

Kristin went to the kitchen to make a new plate. There was half of a bell pepper left. "Anybody want more bell pepper?" she said from the kitchen. No one replied.

"God, give it to me, baby," said Reece. He chewed and swallowed. "Oh, that is good." He felt free, as if he had nothing to lose. Being shot in the head had taken away his anxiety. Anything could happen, but why worry about it? He just wanted to enjoy his life. Before going to Ethiopia, he had been depressed and despondent at times. That seemed to have gone away.

Kristin watched Robyn feed Reece. "Slow down, Nurse Ratched. He'll choke."

"And then I'll do CPR." Robyn laughed.

Horace and Dora ate in silence, wondering if Gert or Edwin would have anything to say. Pretty soon, it was just the sound of Reece groaning with pleasure and the dog scratching on Kristin's door.

"What about that tornado?" asked Horace. "Looks like your neighborhood was spared."

That was a source of pride for Edwin. He felt that it had something to do with his relationship with God and maybe Gert's as well.

"It was a warning, I think," said Edwin. He put his feet back on the floor.

Reece choked a bit. "That was a hell of a warning. Took the roof right off the hospital. Killed how many? Two hundred, three hundred? Leveled churches."

Edwin's pulse quickened. "It could have been even worse, without God's mercy. He could have taken us all."

"Maybe there's not room for all of us in hell." His appetite was dwindling.

"Reece," said Dora.

"I'm not going to hell," said Edwin. "I assume that everyone in this room has accepted Christ as their personal savior."

"Yeah, but then I got shot in the head," said Reece.

Horace chewed his food. The bread stuck to his teeth.

"And then a damn tornado nearly sucked me out of bed."

Gert couldn't take it anymore and retreated to wash dishes.

"Perhaps God is testing you." Edwin touched his hair, still neat with hairspray.

"He's doing a good job," said Reece. "What's next, rectal cancer? Maybe I'll develop an allergy to oxygen."

Kristin stood by the couch, with Robyn still on the couch arm. Robyn put a bite of beans to Reece's mouth. He shook his head no. "Tagabjalo," he said, meaning he was satisfied.

"God gave his Son for us. Remember that. He loves us," said Edwin.

"So, fathers should kill their children," said Reece. He was getting a headache. He burped bell pepper. His stomach wasn't used to regular food yet.

Edwin blushed. The weather was on. It was James Spin. He'd survived the tornado and was broadcasting from a station in Huntsville. His face was stitched together, and he wore a borrowed suit. Everyone had thought he was dead when the TV station exploded during the tornado, broadcasting live.

Everyone gravitated their attention to the silent TV, Mr. Spin gesticulating, pushing the warm air with his hands against the full-screen satellite image of white clouds moving from south to north.

"He's a little crazy," said Reece. "Look at those cuts on his face."

"Yeah," said Kristin.

"Gets a little too excited about bad weather." Reece looked at his fingernails. They were long and needed cutting.

"Son, we'd better be on our way," said Horace. "Kristin, bring him out to the house when you can. Granny here'll make some dinner."

Edwin and Gert looked surprised. Wasn't Reece going with them?

"Sure," said Kristin. "He needs to see the lake."

"We'll be seeing you," said Gert. "Let me get your plates."

"It's so nice to see you again," said Edwin. The news was over, and *Inside Edition* was about to air. He grimaced. James Spin was one of his heroes.

With Horace and Dora gone, Reece said he wanted to go on the deck. He was tired of four walls. Robyn and Kristin walked him outside and sat him on a hard plastic chair next to the small baby pool that held Kristin's pet squirrel. Back in Ethiopia, Reece had been unable to conjure this place. In Godo, he'd been on another planet. Now it was reversed. Did Godo even exist? *Emma.* She was real. It was six in Alabama, but two in the morning in Ethiopia. Emma was sleeping in her tiny house. At night, she made hot tea for the guard. Sometimes he sang, keeping her awake.

"Reece?" asked Kristin. "You there?"

"Yeah." Reece watched a squirrel in the backyard. It stood, ran, stood. He laughed. "I need to cut my fingernails."

"Yeah, we can do that," said Robyn.

A black crow landed on the deck rail and sat there, growling through its beak, and flew off.

"Black crow," said Reece.

Robyn was bored, tired from her private duty shift. "I'm going to get a shower. You're doing great, Reece. Keep it up."

"See ya. Yeah, I'm getting tired. My stomach muscles hurt. Maybe I should lie down."

"Back in bed?" asked Kristin. The shadows from the

pine trees slanted across the backyard. They seemed longer than usual. A small plane droned overhead, sounding like a lawnmower.

"Yeah, I'm exhausted." His eyes looked heavy. "When I can walk, I need to head back out to the lake. I don't think your parents want me here. God, my eyes."

Kristin knew it was true. "Don't mind them. They're fine." She had Reece back and didn't want to let him go. "You're all mine now." She leaned over and kissed his cheek. "Hey."

Reece turned his head and kissed her. "I'm done for the day."

Afewerki held up his hand. "It is hyena," he whispered.

"The Hyena?" asked Emma.

"No, it is the animal that eats the animals. Listen."

Ripping, squishy sounds. Panting.

"Jesus," said Emma. "Don't they laugh? What are they doing?" She peered ahead but could see only the wide lane outlined in the starlight.

"Only when you are dead do they laugh. They are eating, perhaps a donkey."

"What do we do?"

"Let us come near to see. Sometimes they are afraid and will go."

"Oh Lord," said Emma. "Okay, let's see."

Afewerki walked forward. The noise seemed sixty feet away, near the path. He tried to fathom how many there might be. Perhaps one or two, and they could scare them away from the path. He felt a chill on the back of his neck.

Emma followed a few paces back, keeping his light blue shirt as her focus. The snorting sounds grew louder. A hyena yipped.

"There are two or three," said Afewerki.

Dragging sounds, breathing.

"We don't have a gun." Emma felt cold in the chill. She shivered.

Afewerki turned and put his finger to his lips. He motioned for her to stop. "You must stay here," he whispered. He picked up a rock, wishing that he had a hand grenade. Emma's presence gave him courage. He crept closer, disappearing into the gloom except for the glow of his shirt.

Emma shook. She stood still, then crouched. The snorting had stopped, replaced by deep growls. There were no huts nearby, just a large fig tree off to the left. A steady breeze washed over her, like air conditioning. The world seemed to have stopped.

Afewerki could see their eyes, six in all. They had stopped tearing at the carcass and growled low, baring their yellowed fangs. He heard the heavy breathing, but it wasn't the hyenas. He squinted, and he saw it. The carcass raised its head, and then it fell with a dull *whump* onto the dirt. The hyenas were eating a donkey alive. He found another rock. He aimed and threw, hitting nothing. The hyenas skulked back and then began their hideous laugh, broad shoulders ready to launch. One disappeared to the right, slouching. Afewerki guessed its intent and back-pedaled, turned, and then trotted back to Emma. He was sweating. He tripped and fell.

"Shit!" said Emma. He'd stumbled over her.

"We must go back!" He helped her to stand. "We must run. It is coming."

Emma turned and faced the darkness, the rocky path, and tried to run. She tripped and turned her ankle. "Afewerki!" He was behind her.

Afewerki turned and stared. There was more yipping, calling one to the other. He hoped the other two would stay with the donkey. "You are hurt?"

"My ankle," said Emma. She hopped.

Afewerki held her elbow and walked with her, looking back. He saw the eyes off to the left, perhaps twenty feet away. He still had the rock and threw it hard. The hyena yelped and fell over backward. The dying donkey brayed one last time, more of a scream. The hyena charged them. Afewerki reached blindly and picked up a large rock, normally too heavy to throw. He let Emma fall to the ground. The hyena slunk forward, stopped, digging in its front paws, daring them to move, huge teeth bared. Afewerki waited with the rock over his head. He was ready to die, but what would happen to Emma? There was a yip and short howl. The hyena looked back, growled, turned, and was gone.

"Emma, you are hurt," said Afewerki. "We must go." He glanced back and helped her to stand.

"Jesus, what's next?" asked Emma. She put weight on her right foot and limped forward.

"You can walk?"

"Sort of."

They would need to retrace their tracks to Desta's house and then return the way they had come. "It is my fault," he said.

"Not your fault," said Emma. She hobbled along as fast as she could. She could feel the swelling and tightness. "How many were there?"

"They were six eyes, eating the donkey. He was not dead, the donkey."

Emma's chest tightened at the thought. "Can someone go and shoot it?"

"Perhaps he is dead now. It is the way of life." He held her elbow. "Do you need to carry?"

"Carry me? No way. I can walk. I can't see, but I can walk." She winced. "Can I put my arm around your shoulder? That will work better."

"Yes, here." He smelled her sweat. She felt very soft and heavier than he thought. He tried to think of something to say. "This is the house of Desta." A faint light glimmered through the cracks in the wall.

"Right."

They passed between two huts and heard a growl. Emma stumbled. Afewerki grabbed her.

"Emma! Wusha!" he said. The dog barked and snapped from within the compound, as if killing an elephant.

"Abet!" came a loud voice from within the hut there.

Afewerki called out an apology. "We are to wake the village," he said.

Emma laughed. "What time is it? Seven, eight?"

Afewerki felt like a million dollars. "Yes, perhaps eight or nine. The moon, you see." A giant moon rose off to the right.

Emma looked. She hadn't noticed that she could see now. It was the moon. Reece might as well be on the moon. "I still need some alcohol." She had felt welcome at the bar, but then Desta had seized. What if she hadn't been there? Had that happened before? She should be drunk by now, stumbling home to sleep like the dead. Instead, she was wide awake, her mind racing.

"The bar is clos-ed," said Afewerki.

"There has to be another bar," said Emma. "I know there is." She followed him a few paces back, the moon nice and bright.

Afewerki thought. "My father has some drink made from warka, the fig. It is sour. I can get some if you like. My uncle is making it. He will sell to me for just one birr per bottle."

Emma liked figs. Her mother kept a small fig tree on the carport. "Fig wine? Sure, we can drink it back at my place." She didn't expect to get plastered from wine. She didn't like wine anyway. Maybe it would slow her mind and help her sleep.

They passed through the village center, empty, and then stopped at his family's compound. He called out for his father, who camped beneath the hut overhang, cradling his ancient rifle.

"Ho!" his father said.

Afewerki watched his father approach and open the gate into the fenced compound. Inside, the oxen stood still, penned in with thorns. The goats slept in a stall beside the large tukul. The animals stirred, nervous at the movement around them. His father saw Emma, smiled, and nodded his head.

Within a few minutes, with two bottles of fig spirits in hand, Afewerki and Emma made the uphill climb, bore left, and banged on the compound gate. Inside, Irigit called out, alarmed. Once inside, Afewerki felt that all would be well. He had been anxious about Emma in the bar with the farmers.

Barra, Mariam, and Isaac all came to their doors to see if they had returned. Had they gone to a bar?

Barra came outside. "You have been drinking? It is dangerous, no? The people will talk against us."

Afewerki mumbled, trying to make the bottles inconspicuous.

Emma felt perturbed. "We're just getting started. Would you care to join us? We have some fig wine."

Afewerki's heart sank at that. He stood stock still, as if

about to be vaporized.

"The fig wines?" Barra's voice accused her. "It is very strong, no?"

"The stronger the better," said Emma, hoping to escape the spotlight. "You're welcome to join us." She pushed her metal door inward, scraping the concrete floor. She could see the pilot light on her little fridge, heard its gentle hissing.

"Good night!" said Barra.

Afewerki stood outside, a bottle in each hand weighing him down. His stomach felt uneasy. He sensed that something was about to happen.

After Kristin positioned Reece in her bed, she closed her door and then, to his surprise, snuggled up next to him in a pair of silk pajamas. Sex wasn't the furthest thing from his mind, but he knew she was just taking care of him, making him feel comfortable. He wanted to sleep, but listened patiently as she detailed the drama at work, the extra patients from the tornado, the staffing shortage. She scratched his back, and he fell into a deep sleep with her by his side, and awoke to find her gone. What time was it? It was daylight. Another day with Gert seemed not so onerous as uncomfortable, not quite as bad as being shot in the head. "I'm lucky," he said aloud to the room."

Kristin hadn't clocked in yet and made the mistake of going onto the unit instead of hanging out in the break room. One of the patients she'd been taking care of had filled her bed with liquid diarrhea.

"Kristin!" said Larry. "A little help with the missus here?"

Shift change. Doctors charted. Nurses hurried from room to room, emptying and measuring urine outputs, only wishing for a few minutes to chart before reporting to the incoming shift. The twelve beds formed a horseshoe around the central monitoring and nurses' station. Only three beds at the bend of the U had narrow windows up high. Bright fluorescent light flooded the unit, dispelling shadows and notions of time.

Kristin rolled her eyes, walked in, snapped on a pair of

gloves, and took her position.

"Let me get a pan of hot water," said Larry.

Kristin choked on the smell. "Hey, Mrs. Jersey. It's me, Kristin. You're in a mess, but we'll get you fixed up in no time."

Mrs. Jersey's eyes searched hers. The ventilator breathed for her twelve times a minute. Kristin glanced at the ECG monitor, 126 beats per minute. The last recorded blood pressure was 80 over 50, too low to keep her kidneys perfusing and producing urine like they should. Kristin shivered.

Larry squirted liquid soap into the pan of water. "Ready?"

"Yeah." Kristin bent Mrs. Jersey's left knee and then turned her onto her side. Larry rolled the soiled sheet and pad and tucked it under her.

"Might as well get started," said Larry. He made quick work of cleaning her up and rubbed some lotion onto her back.

"Any V-tach last night?" asked Kristin.

"Nope," said Larry. "Restarted her IV around four. Rowena bathed her at six, but here we go, right?" He placed a new sheet and pad.

Kristin let Larry roll Mrs. Jersey to his side. She removed the dirty sheets and pulled the clean ones through. "Needs a diaper." Kristin could imagine this happening over and over.

"Yeah, but the doc says no diapers."

Kristin rolled her eyes. She wondered that Reece no longer needed a diaper. He could nearly stand by himself. "Once a woman, twice a baby." She mentally pinched herself. It was too easy to think the patients weren't listening.

"Much thanks," said Larry. "How's the Reece man doing?" He'd worked with Reece for a couple of years before he went to Ethiopia.

"Thanks for asking. He's starting to walk. He crawled up the stairs yesterday and then fell back down and banged his head on the door."

"He okay?" Larry fiddled with the IV lines, straightening them.

"Yeah, as far as I can tell. No insurance, so he's stuck at my house, but that's fine by me." Kristin repositioned Ms. Jersey's head on the pillow. "Gee whiz, I'm already tired." She hadn't slept well, never having slept with Reece before. She knew her parents would be furious.

"Sorry," said Larry. "Want to do report now?"

Kristin looked at the clock, six-thirty. "Sure." She walked over and swiped her ID to clock in. She glanced at the patient board. She had the crazy lady, Dunlop, in twelve and a new patient, Reeves, in two. Apparently, he was a circuit court judge. She followed Larry out of the room, and Dr. Phillips stood there, staring at her. He was young, a marathoner, a resident, and had sent her flowers on her birthday. She waved. He waved and smiled. Larry noticed but moved on to his other patient.

Hungry, Reece pondered. *What to do?* He decided to wait until Edwin went to work before he tried to get the attention of Gert. Heck, maybe he could walk today. He surveyed the room. Two tall windows to his right looked over the driveway. In front of the bed was a large dresser with a fancy mirror, a large closet to the right. Lotions and photos, mostly of him and Kristin, cluttered the dresser. She kept lotion in her purse and in the glove box of her car, too.

At the dining-room table, Edwin finished his oatmeal and a hard-boiled egg. "Do you think she slept with him?"

Gert circled the table. "She wouldn't do that. She's been raised better than that." She looked out the bay window into the fenced back yard. She would have to feed Kristin's pet squirrel and the dog. Would she have to cook Reece breakfast, too?

"Just call me if he gets out of hand. I think maybe he's lost some of his marbles. You know, the gunshot."

"I hope not," said Gert. "We've got to get him back to his grandparents, though. I would hate for Kristin to wind up pregnant."

Edwin coughed. Was that even possible? He hadn't thought about that. Robyn was the one who talked about sex, not Kristin.

Gert tidied up the sink, scouring the drain and then rinsing. She knew that she would have to remind him to brush his teeth. "Don't forget to brush your teeth."

Edwin grunted and went to do that. He paused by Kristin's door, listening.

After Edwin left, Gert couldn't get settled. She fed the squirrel and Walter. Usually, she would read her Bible, crochet, and then clean the house. She boiled extra egg to make egg salad for her lunch. She couldn't stop thinking about Reece and paced from room to room.

Reece needed to pee. He had a plastic urinal, but decided to visit the bathroom in the hall. He let his legs hang over the side of the bed and went to his elbows. Going from side to side, he sat up, and his vision went blank. He caught himself and jammed his feet into the light pink carpet. "Jesus." He leaned over and planted his elbows on his knees. His stomach was so weak.

The door was just four feet away. He stood, took a big step, and hit the door with his face. He grabbed the knob, and his knees buckled. He caught himself. He could feel hot drops of urine go down his leg. "Hell."

In the hall, Gert jumped at the noise. She turned and pretended to look at the thermostat. A door was opening?

Grabbing the door frame, Reece saw Gert. She wore stretch pants and house shoes. "Going to the bathroom."

"Oh!" said Gert. She turned as if surprised. "It's just there." Reece's hair looked wild. The gown fluttered around his knees.

Reece felt his heart racing. He could use help. "Yeah." He wanted to say that if she got out of the way, he could get there. "If you..."

Gert pressed herself to the wall and moved away like a spider. Reece watched her disappear into her bedroom. He gauged the distance to the bathroom, another four feet. He let go of the door frame to test his mettle. He wobbled and pressed his shoulder to the wall. One giant step and he was through the door. He reached for the far wall, careful of the photos there. He knocked one sideways. At least he wasn't walking seventy-five feet to an outhouse that had a toilet seat cemented into the floor.

Gert watched from her bedroom, just out of sight. She felt a slight thrill in her entrails. Would he fall in the hall? Would he make it to the bathroom and fall, hitting his head on the tile? Her mother was a lawyer and had wanted her to go into business with her. Maybe she should have. Was Reece the best that Kristin could do? The thrill turned to a burn.

Reece fell toward the sink and vanity, going to his knees. He really had to pee. He crawled to the commode on the cold tile floor and gripped it. The bolts holding the toilet to the floor were rusted, as if someone had peed on them more than once. He gave up trying to stand and raised up, still on his knees, choking his penis with one hand. He barely could aim into the bowl, being just an inch or so too low. He let it rip and exhaled. He'd been holding his breath. "Yes."

Gert heard pee hitting the water. She wrung her hands. Her yarn basket and needles sat on the made-up bed. She felt an urge to go to the kitchen. She would make instant pudding. She had plenty of milk. At the bathroom, she glanced in and saw Reece on his knees with his butt shining. She closed her eyes and lurched forward.

Reece flushed, lowered his gown, and pushed himself upward. He was standing, wavering, but standing. He moved a step sideways in front of the mirror. What he saw shocked him. His eyes looked crossed. He examined both scars on his head. They seemed a bit angry and red. A week's worth of beard carpeted his thin face. *Scraggly.* His arms looked like pale, hairy toothpicks. "Damn. And that's with the light off."

He turned to plant his hand against the wall and make his way out. He hit the shower curtain instead and fell headfirst into the tub. His shoulder hit the tile wall. It seemed to take forever to come to rest. He lay still, letting the pain register. "Damn!" He tried to scoot back and hit his head on the faucet. His butt skin stuck to the dry tub.

Gert processed the noise. She held a box of chocolate pudding mix. The milk was on the counter beside the electric stove. "You, okay?" She listened. She thought she heard a curse word. "Oh my."

Reece sat in the tub, his knees bent. Maybe he should just get a bath, make lemonade. "Why the hell not?" He tried to untie the gown around his neck. It seemed to be in a knot. He leaned back, letting the tub spout hit him right in the spine. Now he could use both hands. The dog barked outside. He couldn't see the knot, and his fingers didn't seem to be working right. "Hey! Hey!"

Gert heard him calling. Still holding the pudding box, she walked to the bathroom and peeked in. Reece wasn't there. She looked into Kristin's bedroom.

"In the tub!"

Gert felt her stomach churn and stepped inside, ready to close her eyes.

"Need help getting this knot untied?" asked Reece. "Going to take a bath."

"Did you get in there?"

"I fell in here, and now I'm going to take a bath. Just need to get this gown off."

Gert put the pudding box on the vanity. "Oh." She glanced to make sure his gown covered him. She would need to lean over him to see the knot. She pushed the shower curtain back. God, she wanted to crochet, make some pudding, anything but this. "Lean your head forward." She noticed his greasy hair and smelled his armpits. It took her just a few seconds. "There."

"Thanks. Can you put a towel where I can reach it?"

"Sure." Gert felt dizzy and went for the towel.

Reece let the gown fall onto his lap. He would need to turn around so he could work the water.

Gert laid the towel on the floor next to the tub. "Be careful." She felt that a significant hurdle had been crossed. She wondered if her stretch pants were too tight. Robyn had informed her just the other day about what a camel toe was. Robyn would be the one to get pregnant, and where did she learn such things? Gert hurried out of the bathroom, closing the door. Maybe he would drown? And she asked God to forgive her.

Reece grabbed the handle of the wall soap dish and gripped the tub edge with his other hand. His butt made screeching sounds as he balled up and tried to do a slow spinning 180. He breathed hard, grunting, but made it. What would Emma think of him right now? He laughed, laughed harder, and then coughed himself to a stop. He looked around, and there was a bar of soap but no shampoo. Not a problem, and he turned on the hot water, which was ice cold.

After report on her two patients from the outgoing nurses, Kristin got to work. She found her charts and checked to make sure there were no new orders. There were meds galore and baths to give. X-ray stood by to check the position of a nasogastric tube in room two. "Sitting up, Mr. Reeves," said Kristin. She put her arm behind his shoulders. He grunted, his face reddening. He'd been vomiting bile. The tech slipped a cold and hard X-ray panel behind his back and then moved into position.

"Ow, that's cold!" said Reeves. He was indeed a circuit

court judge. "God dammit!"

Kristin hurried from the room to protect her ovaries. The doctors had made their rounds on Reeves, and she could see a resident writing in his chart. Already, she didn't like the judge. She moved to Ms. Dunlop in twelve, a hardcore schizophrenic who'd had a massive coronary. According to her attending physician, she should be dead. Less than 30 percent of her heart muscle functioned.

"Good morning, Ms. Dunlop," said Kristin. Ms. Dunlop's broad face and deep eyes looked cartoonish. Her bangs were straight and short, her hair dark brown. Kristin checked the loose restraints on her wrists. She seemed to be doing something with her hands.

"Good...morning," said Ms. Dunlop. Her monotone voice creaked from decades of Thorazine, lithium, and Haldol. She moved her head like a turtle, looking over the side of the bed. She was running credit card receipts at Loveman's where she used to work in her twenties, before her descent into madness.

"How are you?" asked Kristin.

"I'm running credit receipts. I work at Loveman's. Do you have a sandwich?" Her fingers fluttered as if playing a piano.

Kristin checked the ECG monitor, heart rate 88. "Going to check your temperature. Can you hold this under your tongue?" She shook down the mercury and slipped the cold thermometer into her mouth. Ms. Dunlop mouthed it, jaw moving up and down ever so softly. Kristin did her best to hold the thermometer under her tongue. Ms. Dunlop kept looking over the side of the bed, the thermometer slipping out. Kristin put her hand on Ms. Dunlop's forehead, clammy and tepid. She didn't bother to look at the thermometer and wrote down 98.2. "Gonna get your blood pressure. What are you looking at on the floor?"

Ms. Dunlop smacked her lips. "I dropped something."

"What did you drop?"

"I dropped a ba-na-na. It's yellow."

"Oh." Kristin pumped the cuff and listened for the *thud thuds*. Ninety over sixty-four. Only the dopamine drip kept it that high. She wondered if her mom would make Reece some breakfast. She watched the rise and fall of Ms. Dunlop's chest, counting her respirations. Twenty-six per minute. The IV beeped. "Are you hungry?"

"I dropped my ba-na-na. Do you have a sandwich?"

Kristin checked the feeding tube in her nose. "I can give you a can of Ensure through your feeding tube. It's in your nose. You can't eat just yet. Would you like some ice chips?"

"I am running the credit receipts. I work at Loveman's. I am hungry." She smacked her lips. No one came to visit her.

"Have a drink of water." Kristin put the straw in her mouth.

Ms. Dunlop took tiny sips and smacked her dry lips. "I need to run the credit card receipts."

Kristin straightened her sheet. "Be back soon, okay?" She scooted to the nursing station and located Reeves' chart. She checked the flagged order. She was to manually aspirate gastric contents once every hour after X-ray verification of tube placement. Why not put the tube to continuous suction? She shook her head. *Busy work.* She initialed the order and looked up. "Dr. Phillips."

"It's Brad, dumbo." His short hair parted on the left. His neck was cleanly shaved, his ears prominent.

"Dumbo?"

"Sorry. Gorgeous?" He clicked a pen in his hand. He scanned her chest. He liked small breasts.

"Good Lord." Kristin blushed. Brad wasn't bad looking. He was a bit shorter and stocky, unlike Reece, who was gangly and taller. Her mother dreamed of her meeting and marrying a doctor, not another nurse.

The unit burst with energy—IV beeps, ventilator alarms, ECG warnings, bright fluorescent lights, attending physicians with their packs of residents and interns. The corner room set up for fluoroscopy had been converted to hold two patient beds since the tornado. A Code Blue on the fifth floor came over the intercom. A handful of doctors adjusted their ties and ran for the elevators. Randy, the nurse on call for Code Blues, grabbed the tackle box and followed.

Kristin walked over to the med cart to check the drug sheets on her patients. Brad followed. He loved women in scrubs. It could be why he wanted to be a doctor.

"I've got a pool at the condo. You should come over." He knew about Reece, something about being injured in Africa. He was just a nurse, though, paid by the hour like a plumber. He fiddled with the business end of his Littman stethoscope.

"Brad. Dr. Phillips. I'm engaged." She pulled out the med drawer for Reeves and retrieved his a.m. drugs. He'd had a mild heart attack, undergone a heart catheterization, but then had started vomiting bile and was still complaining of chest pain.

Brad watched her walk away, imagining her naked. He had a dozen patients to cover and shook his head, thankful that he wasn't on call that night. The coke helped, but he needed some real sleep at least once a week.

"Hey, Mr. Reeves," said Kristin. "Gonna get your vitals. Got your meds here. You want water or juice?"

"It's Judge Reeves!" He was seething. "How can I swallow pills with this goddamn tube in my throat? And why does everyone wear these tacky, baggy clothes? You do not inspire confidence, young woman."

Kristin stepped back. "You can swallow with this water. Just try, please?" She held out the plastic cup with his pills for high blood pressure and a giant Carafate pill to coat his stomach. Now, the lack of continuous suction through his NG tube made sense to her. "Oh," she said.

"What are these? I don't recognize these pills, and that purple one is like a football. How am I supposed to swallow that?" His face popped red and angry, his ears clotted with hot blood. His neat gray hair lay flat, his face square and rigid. There was something of the little boy in him. "And why did you say, 'Oh'?"

"I'll push the purple one down your tube. No problem. It's just to soothe your stomach. But try and swallow this one." He made her lower back hurt. She needed to do her shift physicals and line up bed baths. The IV bag for Dunlop in twelve needed to be swapped out. *Beep-beep, beep-beep.* She heard the alarm from across the bright unit. She looked out and saw Larry heading into twelve. He would take care of it for her.

"I asked you a question, young lady. And what is your name? You didn't even introduce yourself. Your badge is backwards. Turn it so I can see who you are. How do I even know that you work here, wearing those baggy clothes like a homeless person?"

Kristin crushed the Carafate and mixed it with water. She hit the call button, and the unit clerk answered. "Nadine, check with X-ray to see if Reeve's NG tube is in place, please?"

"It's Judge Reeves! I was elected by the people, and have been elected by the people for the past twenty-four years."

"Right, Judge Reeves," said Kristin. "I'm Kristin, and I've worked here for three years. See?" She showed him her badge.

"Don't get cheeky with me, young lady. If we were in court, I'd have you tossed out."

Kristin delayed her response. "That's all well and good, but you've had a heart attack and now it's being complicated by your gall bladder. I'm going to take care of you for the next seven hours. Is that clear?" She held out the shiny gel cap for him to swallow. "Take it, please."

"I want to see my doctor. You are rude, and I don't trust you." He tried to think of his doctor's name. His throat burned, and his chest hurt.

"He was just here. Dr. Cinegas."

The judge looked confused. "He was?"

"Yes. Someone should be back through after lunch to check on you." She noted his pulse and respirations and moved to check his blood pressure. "Going to check your blood pressure."

"I refuse!" said the judge. "Where the hell am I anyway?"

"You're in the coronary care unit at Carraway in Birmingham, Alabama."

"Oh," said the judge. He looked around the small room, bewildered. "There's a spider on the wall." He pointed at a tiny hole where a nail had been.

Kristin took a piece of silk tape and covered the hole. She would get his blood pressure later. She wouldn't be surprised if he had a freaking stroke.

Emma had a thought. "Afewerki. Send Irigit to stay the night with Desta. I'm worried that the men will find her there tonight."

"Ah, but the children will keep them away." Afewerki sighed and placed the fig wine on the table. The room was warm. A lone candle by Emma's bed lit the room. "Ishi." He stepped outside and called Irigit.

Emma wondered if she should eat something before drinking again. She was in her tiny house, though. If she drank too much, she could just lie down. The snaking clinic lines seemed a million miles away. The dimness gave her room a softness, a generic feel. She could almost imagine that she was at home, in the den with just the TV for light. She wondered how Reece was doing. The gunshots from that night burst in her head, and she winced. If she had pulled him toward the bed, he would still be there. Her nipples went hard. *Damn.*

Afewerki came back inside. "Shall I close to the door?"

"Yeah, sure, keep out the cold." She slipped on a jacket and zipped it. "Help me pull the table to the bed. I'll sit on the bed, and you can have the chair." She felt that getting drunk was becoming a chore, and the time passing as a weight. She pushed images of the clinic from her mind. She had jumped from the helicopter, had she not? The urge to drink ramped up. Was she clinically depressed? Did she need meds? Maybe Valium would help. It helped the young girls who married the old men.

With the table next to her bed, she bobbed on the

squeaky mattress and springs. She hadn't done her devotional since the helicopter incident. She hadn't made it past two or three people on her prayer list, but Reece was right there at the top. She was praying that Kristin would find someone else. She shook her head, filled with emotional cobwebs.

Afewerki sat in the chair with his hands folded in his lap. He wore his Exxon ballcap and a heavy brown sweater. He had trimmed his mustache that morning. "You want?"

"Yeah, pour me a stiff one?"

"What?"

"Give me a big portion of the wine."

"It is not the wine, but like the alcohol. It is made from the wurka, the fig."

"Oh hell, give me a lot." She pointed to the halfway mark on her orange plastic mug.

"Ishi." He pulled the corncob stopper and poured hers and then a small amount for himself. "Lehtaynachen."

"Cheers," said Emma.

They each sipped as if the spirit were rare. Emma's eyes grew wide. Afewerki frowned.

"Yikes," said Emma. "That's strong, and a little sour."

"Yes," said Afewerki. He knew Emma was not wearing a bra. He felt that his heart was on fire.

Emma took another swallow. She could feel the alcohol burning in her stomach and wending its way farther. She needed to forget, to remember. An image of her father appeared, the bastard. She took another drink, and the spirit made her cough. Her throat felt dry as if by a coal.

"You are okay?" asked Afewerki.

Emma swallowed saliva several times. "Yes." Her voice croaked.

"Ah, you must to be slow." He took another sip and knew that the others were talking, speculating, especially Barra. He might tell the Hyena. The whole village would know. He felt exposed, as if on a slide under a microscope. He put his hands on his lap, then withdrew them.

Emma watched Afewerki fumble with his hands. He looked everywhere except at her. "Is the Hyena still bragging that he shot Reece?" She took a more moderate sip. There was just a hint of fig, but not fig newtons like she had expected.

Afewerki paused. "He is frightened now that he will be jailed. He is saying that the ferenj has committed suicide, to kill himself with the gun."

"What?" asked Emma. "That's insane. He shot himself? What about the bullet holes in the wall?"

"The people are not seeing them, so they may wonder." He didn't want to say what he was thinking, what else he had heard.

"And they believe that lying thief, murderer? He'd steal a blanket from a baby!" She pushed her cup against the bottle, an old Awash wine bottle. "Jesus H. Christ, himself."

"Emma, to be careful." His eyes felt heavy, his heart thudding.

"Why would he say such a thing, other than to protect himself?"

Afewerki searched for words. "He is saying that the ferenji want to kill themselves. He knows…"

Emma took a drink and winced. "The helicopter. Jumping out. Yeah, right, the bastard. He could've had two ferenji deaths on his hands." She felt hollow, drained, and guilty on all charges. "I will get drunk tonight. I make that promise." She raised her cup. "What is it you say? Lay-tay..."

"Lehtaynachen," said Afewerki. "I am sorry. It was the devil. You have done many good things. The Hyena is fearing for his job."

"Good things, yeah. So, Lehtaynachen! Drink. Drink!"

Afewerki drained his cup and squinched his face. Did he want to stay and drink? What would be the result? He would stay as long as Emma wanted him to. "Now you must, to drink." He thought back to the Icelanders, Svana with the black hair, Eydis with the white hair, and Dr. Thorsson with the red. They drank every night to get drunk. It had been fun but frightening at times. Dr. Thorsson had said that he did not believe in God, that he believed in people, and what was the difference anyway? Volcanoes, ice.

Emma was feeling on the edge of something important. "Afewerki? Are you dreaming?"

"Yes, but no. Just to remember the Icelanders."

"Ha! Because they liked to drink?"

"No! They are like you, coming to help the people."

"Helping the people," said Emma. She drank. "Do the people really need help? You have the government clinic and traditional healers. What the hell do they need me for?"

"No, you must be proud." He drank.

"Heck, the Hyena could just shoot me right now. What would it matter?" She thought about a cigarette, how that would be nice. She wasn't a smoker per se, but would have one now and then. "Why doesn't anyone smoke here? Cigarettes?"

Afewerki laughed. "It is expensive. Only those in the cities are smoking. The smell is terrible."

"But the men like to drink."

"Yes, the women also, but they drink the beer only and sometimes the tejj."

Emma thought about the women of Godo. They needed hard liquor. She thought about the last time she'd had sex, a guy from church. They'd sort of been a couple, but she'd avoided him after their rendezvous in his apartment. He'd been so damn shy about everything. It had taken him hours to get naked. The orange cups were everywhere. What country had donated the cups? She would forever tie the cups to the famine. "Are you going to pour me some more?" She pushed her cup toward him. "Fig liquor."

"Certo," said Afewerki. He poured another half cup. His was empty as well, and he refilled.

Something hit the tin roof with a report. Emma stood. Afewerki looked toward the door. He could hear laughing from outside.

"Someone is throwing the stone," he said. "To agitate."

"Bucka!" Emma yelled. She sat back on the sagging cot. "Damn clowns. Trying to have a damn drink."

Afewerki laughed. He knew that the other guys were jealous, desperate to know what was going on. "Pay no mind," he said, a phrase he'd learned from Dr. Guthrie.

"Ah, I want to tear my hair out!" Emma hung her head. "Reece could be dead, and we wouldn't know it."

The mention of Reece sobered Afewerki. He seemed like a ghost, having only been in Godo for what, a month maybe two? He tried to remember what he looked like, tall and thin with a sharp nose. He'd liked Reece, but what could he do? Reece had been shot and sent back to the United States. No doubt, he was probably okay. Many were praying for him. "God is taking care."

A sudden blanket of sadness enveloped her. Emma wanted to break down and wail. She gulped the liquor and gagged. Tears brimmed at the ready, burning. "Why me, why him?" Her shoulders sank, and she dropped her cup with a thud on the table. She looked at the unvarnished wood, with its water rings and blob stains. There were no paper towels in Godo. Smooth stones served as toilet paper for most. The tiny house slumbered dead silent except for the hiss of the propane fridge. Dogs gnashing teeth in the distance, cruel sounds. God in heaven, laughing, running his finger down a chalkboard.

Afewerki thought. How to choose his words? "It is the devil." It was the best he could do. And at some point, didn't she need to move on? "You are very good in the clinic. You are helping many people."

"Kids with scabies, tape worms...headaches...mule kicks, burns..." Emma swallowed thin saliva. She thought about the Bible, a book. The book was closed in her mind, cemented shut. "People eating the berries of the black nightshade because they have no food. Walking on...razor blades. Swimming in...peanut butter." She was feeling ill but free. *The Hyena.* The drip of water from a faucet. She missed that. She gazed at Afewerki, her interpreter, a good man, a human being, and not unattractive.

Reece ran the yellow soap across his body. He felt so unco-ordinated. The water was getting higher and hotter, so he reached and turned it off. Taken with the moment, he determined to enjoy it. He was in his fiancée's bathtub. He'd been shot in the head. He was in Birmingham, Alabama. There had been a terrific tornado just a few days ago. He was alive! The clean water felt super, and he could feel his testicles floating. He felt like breaking into song, maybe some Wham! or Larry Norman. Kristin's parents didn't want him there, but so what?

He soaped his face and rinsed. One thing he had missed in Ethiopia was a hot bath. "Singing in the rain, just singing in the rain...Wrecked up like a deuce and something something..." He felt like a million dollars, high as a kite. He was alive and taking a hot bath by himself. He was in the tub that Kristin used, where she got naked. He felt a stirring, a rush of air through his body, and breathed deep. He smelled soap, good old soap.

He slid down in the tub, holding onto the soap dish. He let the water creep up his chest and his neck, and then he went under, blowing bubbles. He came back up, dripping and smiling. A light flashed, and his vision went dark. Briefly, he was back in Ethiopia, a smell of smoke and milk. His eyes burned. It seemed to him that he could taste the bullet as it passed through his temples, like chewing tin foil with chicken salad on it. Soap was in his eyes, and he gagged on soapy water. Was he under the water? He couldn't tell and panicked. He made a loud noise and pushed his torso out of the water with his legs. What had happened? He splashed water on his face to clear the soap as his vision returned. He heard knocking.

"You, okay?" asked Gert.

Reece tried to speak, but couldn't for a moment.

"You, okay?" Gert wrung her hands. The phone was ringing.

"Yeah! Okay." He coughed on tub water. "Just having a stroke! Or a seizure!" He coughed and then laughed. "Chicorilla!"

"Che Guevara?" Where had she heard that before? She ran for the phone.

Reece lounged in the water until it began to cool. He couldn't decide what he would do next. He had a feeling that he had to make every moment count, that he would enjoy the moments, savor them like ice cream. He considered that Emma had saved his life. She was a wellspring of good energy, as real as real could be. He thought he could remember his hands on her breasts, but couldn't be sure. A gloom set in. Should he tell Kristin? He knew she wanted to know what had happened that night, but what to say? She would cry and then tell her mother. Her mother would tell Edwin. They would surmise that God had punished Reece for his sinfulness. Maybe it was true. He was starving, and his focus shifted—Little Debbie snack cakes, peanut butter bars, even a heaping tablespoon of sugar sounded good, or maybe potato chips. A cigar, too.

It was the prayer chain as she expected. Most of the calls seemed to come between ten and noon. Gert listened. Maxine Caldwell's grandson had developed a severe case of itching. She wrote down the information, nodding to herself. Cancer, itching, what did it matter? God was all ears. *Reece?* What was he doing? Even he was on the prayer chain, and it seemed to be working.

Reece crawled out of the tub and dried off, sitting down in front of the toilet. He noticed how flabby and pale his chest was. His arms looked somewhat tan, ending just above his elbows. The sun had been very hot in Godo, even though the nights were downright cold. He ran his hand across his stubbly face. His dirty gown lay on the floor, stamped with the logo of UAB Hospitals. Surely, he could wear something in Kristin's room. His stomach rumbled.

Gert hung up the phone and thought about dinner. *What about chicken and dumplings?* She opened the freezer and found a pack of chicken thighs. *Perfect.* She pulled down the flour and baking powder for the dumplings. Where was the salt? Her mom put black pepper in the dumplings, but that was where the similarities ended. She stepped into the den and listened for noise from the bathroom. Nothing.

Reece wrapped the towel around his waist as best he could. Not only was he hungry, but he was thirsty, too. In Godo, he could drink only filtered water stored in the heavy Icelandic IV bottles with the red rubber stoppers. Suddenly, he thought about returning. *Why not?* He would get better, fly back, and *Bam!* back in the clinic with Emma. A breathiness filled his chest. *Why not?* He had made a pledge to God, given his life to mission work at Palmerdale Baptist Church, where his grandparents were members. Maybe being shot was just a new beginning? What would his grandparents say? They would scream,

"No way!" He thought about his parents. Killed at a Luby's in Killeen, Texas. Yeah, they would have approved, but he wasn't sure why. Maybe they would have invoked the mystery of God's will. *Probably so.*

Reece grabbed the edge of the vanity. He counted to three and pushed up with his weak legs. Shaking from head to toe, he stood. There was a toothbrush, probably Kristin's. It took him a few minutes, but he brushed his teeth. His hair looked wild in the mirror. He couldn't stop looking at himself. In Ethiopia, little kids died from hunger. In the US, fat people paid good money to lose weight. He spat foam and watched it swirl down the drain.

Gert filled a pot with hot water to thaw the chicken thighs. She was cooking for five instead of four and had to remember that. Into a large plastic bowl went flour, baking powder, salt, and milk for the dumplings. She heard the bathroom door open, rustling sounds. Her stomach tightened.

Standing, Reece staggered into the hallway. He paused to look at the school pictures of Kristin and Robyn on the wall. Kristin looked so damn cute, her cheeks with a hint of blush, innocence personified. He stumbled and put a hand to each wall, bracing himself. His legs trembled, vibrating with the effort. He needed food, fuel. He guessed he had lost thirty pounds. He listened, complete silence.

Stirring the flour mixture with a wooden spoon, Gert felt like a robot. The dough didn't need to be too thick, just enough to push off a spoon into hot broth. Definite sounds in the hallway.

Reece staggered his way to the den doorway. The house was carved into distinct spaces. His legs gave way, and he sank to his knees, leaning on his outstretched arms. If he had to crawl to the kitchen, so be it. He passed the couch, headed for Edwin's recliner with the dining room/kitchen just beyond.

Gert mustered and peeked around the corner. There he was, on hands and knees, coming toward her like a cockroach, wearing only a towel.

Reece looked up and saw Gert staring at him. "Hey, what's for breakfast?" His arms shook. He'd forgotten to look for clothes in Kristin's room.

Gert thought. "What do you want?"

"Anything. An egg, eggs, toast, butter. Anything." He sat back on his legs and felt the blood pumping.

Gert could see that his hair was thinning on top. Edwin's hair was as thick as a cow's tail, and he was twice Reece's age. "I'll boil a couple of eggs and make some toast."

"Boil a dozen," said Reece, his head hanging. He laughed.

"I don't have a dozen."

"I was joking." His head felt strange, like it was wired for unknown business.

Gert tugged at her flower-print blouse. "Maybe get on the couch? Can you do that?"

"Okay." He turned back for the rayon-covered couch. "It's yellow and orange, with brown streaks." He remembered having a cushion fight with Kristin there one night. She'd let him straddle her and kiss her all over, with her clothes on.

The phone rang again.

"Hello." Gert tugged the cord and walked back into the kitchen. She listened. Maxine Caldwell's grandson's itching had become worse. She imagined him scratching his arms, bringing blood, and winced.

Kristin stooped to retie her shoelace. The energy of the unit rumbled through her. No matter how tired she felt, there were so many things to do that she had no time to think of herself. The judge in room two was still a pain in the ass. The night nurse had warned her. Mrs. Dunlop in twelve, though, was a genuine curiosity, bonkers but a sweet woman.

Kristin grabbed a rolling chair and sat to chart her initial assessments. Traffic buzzed in and out through the automatic double doors. The patient who had coded needed a bed in CCU, but they were full. There was talk of moving a stable patient to the floor. No one wanted a new admit, though, with all the work involved. Her friend Kirksy pulled in next to her, charting as well. Kirksy was tiny, wearing blue scrubs. She wore her long brown hair in a ponytail.

"How goes it with Reece?"

Kristin scribbled on the chart. She looked up. "He's at the house with my mom right now. He fell down the stairs yesterday."

"Holy cow, he's walking?"

"More like crawling, but he can almost stand up on his own." She wondered what sort of adventure he might have that day.

"Still engaged, right?" The black pen looked large in her small hand.

"Yep." Kristin looked Kirksy in the eyes, big eyes with lots of mascara. She slept around with the doctors. "Why?"

"You know. Dr. Phillips?"

"Oh, him, Brad. Yeah, he called me dumbo this morning."

Kirksy scrawled her initials and flipped the chart shut. "I don't know. He's pretty damn cute. You might want to branch out and see what happens."

"I can't believe you said that." Kristin glanced into twelve. A lab tech was in to draw blood from Mrs. Dunlop. The head of the bed inclined at forty-five degrees. Her stockinged feet poked beyond the sheet.

"Well, he's a great kisser. I can tell you that."

"Jesus," said Kristin.

"We made out in the bathroom in the break room. He wanted to do it standing up, but I told him to fuck off. I just needed something to wake me up. You should go for it. What's Reece going to do about it?"

"Kirksy, you're not helping at all. I love Reece." She stood, impatient to get Ms. Dunlop bathed. She had assigned the judge to the nursing assistant, Rowena, although he could probably bathe himself. "And he loves me."

Kirksy shook her head. "Yeah, but is he the same person after being shot like that? He's got to have some permanent damage. Will he ever be able to work again?"

"Now you sound like my dad," said Kristin.

"V-tach in two!" the monitor tech yelled.

"Shit." Kirksy jumped up.

Kristin ran into the room with Kirksy. The judge was conscious, his eyes bleary. She glanced at the bedside ECG and saw the giant waves. Kristin lowered the head of the bed. The judge tried to talk but couldn't.

"Thump him," said Kirksy.

Kristin yanked up his gown, exposing his chest. He was turning a light shade of blue. A few people gathered in the doorway. "I'm going to hit your chest, Mr. Reeves." She forgot to call him Judge. She positioned her fist a foot above his sternum and brought it down as hard as she could. The judge gasped, and his eyes rolled back in his head.

"Good one," said Kirksy.

Kristin glanced at the ECG, normal sinus rhythm. The precordial thump had worked. There was a smattering of applause. "Damn." She loved Reece, and he loved her.

The judge's eyes focused. "Why...am I flat on...my back? Raise me...immediately!"

"Hold on." Kristin pushed the button. "You just had a run of V-tach." She wanted to say that she had blasted his chest. That he should thank her.

"A what, young lady? Why am I dizzy?" He gripped the rails of the bed. "I smell burned popcorn!"

Kristin laughed, watching the monitor. She would need to let the resident know what had happened. Dr. Phillips himself. "You had an arrhythmia, your heart was beating out of control, but you're fine now. How do you feel?"

"Where is my wife? I want my wife," said the judge.

"Visiting hours are at ten, about an hour and a half. You want me to check the waiting room?"

"Check for what?" asked the judge.

"I'm leaving ya," said Kirksy.

"For your wife," said Kristin.

"My wife passed away. I live alone."

"I'm sorry to hear that."

"Why are you wearing such baggy, wrinkled clothes?

Is this a homeless shelter? Where am I?" The judge's red face strained. His eyes strained. His knuckles shone white, gripping the bed rails.

Kristin told him where he was. She noticed that she had broken a sweat, checked his vitals, and put in a page for Dr. Phillips. She went to the linen cart and gathered sheets and towels for Mrs. Dunlop's bath. She turned the water to hot, testing it with her fingers. "Mrs. Dunlop—"

The room intercom. "Dr. Phillips for you, Kristin," said Betty, the unit clerk who smoked two packs a day, Virginia Slims.

Kristin turned off the water, *Brad,* and went to the long desk. She just wanted to spend some time with Mrs. Dunlop. She told him about the V-tach with the judge. He ordered a twelve-lead ECG, a bolus of Lidocaine, and an electrolyte profile. He wanted to know what the NG output was, and she didn't know. He sounded annoyed. She dropped the flagged chart with Betty, ran to the supply room, and rigged up the bolus.

"Hey," said Kristin to Mrs. Dunlop. The judge had asked her a million questions and insulted her several times. *Like water off a duck's back,* she had thought to herself.

"Do you have a sandwich?" asked Mrs. Dunlop. Her lips slid one over the other, and she smacked them.

Afewerki did his duty and poured more liquor for Emma. He glanced at the table beside her bed. There was a Bible, a book, a red radio, the candle flickering, a picture of her mother. He imagined what it would be like if he traveled to the United States and left his family. He closed his eyes and said a quick prayer for Reece.

Emma looked at her cup. Was it full, half full, or empty? She swayed to a Beatles tune in her head. She needed to eat something, but there was nothing to eat except some canned cheese. The thought made her nauseous. She put her hands on her knees and gazed at Afewerki. "You are a good man." She wondered if he would rub her neck, her temples. She just needed to be touched.

Afewerki processed her words. He was steeped in his own culture of semina werk, the wax and gold. Words were merely wax covering gold. No one ever said what they meant, but rather the meanings must be discovered. What did she mean by "good man?" Did she mean he was an evil man?

Emma took a sip. Her tongue burned, and she put her head on the sharp edge of the table. She felt that the cot would swallow her. Maybe she would wake up in her bed back in Alabama. She would be able to visit Reece. Would he recognize her? She wanted to write him a letter, but what good would that do? She looked at her hands, imagining a ring on her finger.

Outside, Barra whistled, sitting on a stool near the gate in the fence. Afewerki looked at the top of Emma's head.

Her hair was brownish-blonde and thick. What did it feel like? Was it soft? He remembered the Icelandic nurses. Svana's hair had been black and short, with Eydis's more like Emma's, but whiter. "Are you sick?"

"No." She lifted her head. Something was missing. She needed music to drink. "Let's turn on the radio."

"Yes, it is very quiet."

The radio clicked on with a buzz. Only the AM stations worked. She turned the dial until she hit something, pop music in French. "Not bad." She turned it up a bit. The music was cheerful and upbeat. She drank and frowned. She was buzzed. "Drink!" She held out her glass for a toast. "This is for Reece. May he fully recover."

Afewerki took a sip and nodded his head. "Yes, God willing. The bottle is becoming empty." He tapped his fingers. "This music is from Djibouti."

"Let's kill it," said Emma. She took the bottle and filled his cup, and then filled hers.

"What does it mean?"

"What does what mean?

"To kill, you say."

Emma laughed. "To drink this bottle, to kill it." She held up the empty bottle. "It is dead."

"We have killed it," said Afewerki. "I see." He laughed a nervous laugh.

A new song. "This is good for dancing. Come on!" Emma took a big gulp and coughed. She stood, coughing, bent over.

Afewerki frowned. "You must be careful." He looked at his cup. Should he help her? What could he do?

"Whoa," said Emma. "Come on." She began to sway

and move her feet. A rock hit the roof. "Hey! What is wrong with them?"

Afewerki stood. He looked down at his pants, nervous. "They are like the children." He stood with his hands in his pockets. Shadows bobbed on the wall and ceiling. The little house did not smell of smoke like those of the villagers. It had no smell at all, maybe dust.

Emma swayed, holding her cup with two hands. She danced with her head down, watching her feet. She kicked the table leg and stumbled.

"To be careful," said Afewerki. He steadied her with his hand.

Emma's cup sloshed on the sleeve of her jacket. She kept dancing, looking into Afewerki's eyes. He looked helpless, concerned. She felt numb and gazed at the floor. Just beyond Afewerki was the stained cement, Reece's blood. She breathed out and took a gulp of liquor. She staggered and squeezed her eyes shut. Afewerki's hand was on her biceps. Her eyes stung, and hot tears drained from them. She dropped the cup, spilling the liquid onto the floor.

"Emma." Afewerki lost his grip on her. She was squatting, taking deep breaths. "Emma." He lowered her to the floor. The music bopped along.

Emma sobbed. She looked like a sad monkey on its haunches. "It's too much!" She bawled, grabbing her knees and rocking. Tears wet her pants. An immense pressure in her head released. "Dear God." She was drowning in tears and sat back against the cot, wiping at them with her forearms. She felt hot, then cold, and struggled to catch her breath. "Reece," she said.

Afewerki stood over her. *What to say?* She was taking

off her jacket and trying to stand. "Shall I help you?" He put his cup on the table, glad to be rid of it.

Emma held out her hand, and Afewerki pulled her up. She threw the jacket on the bed and stood there, face drenched. She felt sick as her vision flooded to black. Salty saliva flooded her mouth. She gained her balance and pushed past Afewerki, holding back the sea.

Afewerki followed. The door screeched open, and Emma was outside, bent over. She threw up, over and over. He stood in the doorway watching, unable to bear the smell of vomit. He could see the others standing in their darkened doorways, watching. Barra whistled.

The grass in front of her glistened and stank. Emma tried to stand. She cramped and bent back over. "Dammit." She felt she wasn't finished crying and maybe not finished throwing up. She wanted to die. Maybe she would see the Hyena and slap his face. He would shoot her, and that would be that. She stood and walked away from the mess. She felt better and worse at the same time. The air was chilly and dry. She could feel it washing her lungs.

"Afewerki, where does the Hyena live?" God, she wanted to fall down and die.

In a delirious limbo, Reece sat on the couch, waiting for Kristin to get home. Over and over, he imagined the bullet slicing through a chink in the mud walls and piercing his skull. He glanced at the clock to the left of the fat TV: 3:12. Kristin's shift ended at three, but there was report, charting, and driving time. If it was a hectic day, it could be five before she walked through the door. Gert bustled in the kitchen, cooking something, pots and pans rattling. He had to pee and bad.

Gert just could not get comfortable with Reece in the house. She was an only child. Her mother was an only child. The chicken and dumplings bubbled on the stove. The Rice-A-Roni, she would start at five, and dinner would be at five-thirty. Reece was just sitting on the couch like a mannequin, like he was waiting his turn to bowl. Was he calling her?

"Gert," said Reece for the second time. He had to go, but didn't want to fall, plus he needed practice walking. He knew that Gert was in the kitchen. Normally, he would have avoided Gert like the plague, but his "accident" had changed things. Heck, it didn't matter anymore. She could be the freaking president, and he wouldn't care. What was right was right. People helped people.

Gert held the Rice-A-Roni box like an amulet against evil. He was calling her name. *Cream cheese on a cracker!* She smoothed her plaid, short-sleeve shirt and walked to the wide entrance into the den. He sat on the couch with his head down. His hair looked crazy. The cat, Wallace, licked his fur on the carpet in front of the TV.

"Hello!" Maybe he should just jump up and walk by himself, but he was afraid that he would slip and tumble down the stairs on his way. His eyes strained. He needed a big glass of ice water, too. "Gert?"

Watching him, Gert flinched at the sound of her name. Wringing her hands, she stepped into the den. Hopefully, he just wanted a drink. "Hey." It came out as a whisper.

Reece put his chin into his hands, arms braced on his elbows. He glanced right and saw Gert. "Hey. Can you give me a hand?"

"A hand with what?" Maybe he wanted to hitchhike to his grandparents' house. She held her breath.

"Can you walk me to the bathroom?" Reece tried to feel shame, but couldn't. If she had to wipe him, what would it matter?

Oh Jesus. Gert looked at the clock on the wall. Kristin would be home soon. "Can you wait?"

"Not really," said Reece. "Just walk me to the door. That's all." He sat up and flopped back onto the cushion. His bladder ached. He craved fried shrimp.

Gert walked toward him like a moth to the flame. She stopped and reevaluated the situation. Nothing. "Here," she said. Her hands were on her hips.

Reece gazed at her bangs, her pants, her blouse, her house shoes. He felt like a big spider and held his arms out to her. "Just help me stand. I can walk, I think."

"Okay." She stepped closer. His arms reached for her. She stepped back and took his hands. He was pulling on her. Surprised at his strength, she stumbled forward.

Reece felt himself falling backward. "Hell," and he

tumbled onto the couch with Gert on top of him.

Gert struggled, whimpering. She was sitting beside Reece, squeezed against him. She began laughing. Reece, startled, turned his head. Was she laughing? He'd never heard her laugh before.

"You need a good spanking." He felt so tired, so weary, so about to piss on the couch.

Gert sobered. What was she doing? "Here." She pushed forward and stood. "Put your arm around my shoulder."

Reece grabbed on and pushed up. Gert pulled. Reece stood, knock-kneed. "Oh boy." Gert led him to the bathroom, and he followed, putting one foot in front of the other. He opened his eyes and looked to his left at Gert. She was sweating, frowning, straining. He wanted to kiss her. "Can I kiss you?"

Gert laughed, then frowned. "No." She struggled along with him. Down the hall they went.

Reece felt his heart racing, but he felt good. He felt stronger by the minute. He imagined being shot, and then he was down, his spirit hovering above his body on the floor of Emma's tiny house. He considered the implications. How to explain it? Slowly, God was slipping away. He supposed it had begun even before he left for Ethiopia. The bathroom door stood open. "You think Mary was a virgin when she gave birth?" He grabbed the doorknob and pressed his other hand to the wall.

Gert slipped out from underneath and stepped back. "What?"

"If she were a virgin, then when she gave birth, that took away her virginity. So, technically, she lost her virginity to Jesus." He imagined little Jesus sliding out into the hay.

Gert took another step back, silent. Reece was babbling. She watched him make it inside. Good Lord, he wasn't even going to close the door. She should have turned away, but she was like a deer in headlights. He teetered and caught himself on the vanity and scooted sideways to the toilet. She could see his butt peeking out from the towel. He was too thin. Fascinated, she watched him plop down on the commode, groaning and panting for breath. He looked at her, and that was when she turned away, breathless.

He let it go and peed like a racehorse. He felt something warm on his leg. Shit! He was peeing on himself. He stopped the flow, tucked it down, and continued. He felt alive and glad, his pee burbling into the toilet. He would appreciate the small things from now on. He would enjoy every minute. "You're a good woman!" he said to the bathroom. Did he mean Gert? Did he mean Kristin, or maybe Emma? What about his grandmother, his mother? "Here's to everybody!" He smiled and felt warm and tingly, but his feet were cold on the tile.

Gert looked at the stove clock. He'd been in the bathroom for a while, but there was no sound. She wanted to go to her own bathroom, but didn't want to walk by Reece with the door open. She peeked at the dumplings and folded her arms. She blew on her bangs.

Reece wondered how long it had been since he'd had a bowel movement. At least not since leaving the hospital. He thought about that. His insides kind of felt dead. He thought about the stuffed bell peppers, and his mouth watered. He was famished and could smell the food cooking.

He flushed and struggled to stand. He took special care not to fall into the tub. His shoulder still hurt. He felt stronger and shuffled to the hall, supporting himself with the vanity and the wall. He decided to sit outside on the back deck to wait for Kristin, and a thrill ran down to his toes. *Sunshine!* Into the hall he went, bracing against the wall. He banged the large photo of Robyn crooked and stopped to straighten it. There was the piano, and he hung a left into the den. He needed to rest and bent over, hands on knees. He could feel Gert's eyes on him.

"Going...to the deck," he said. Gert stood at the back door, opening it. "Thanks."

"You're, uh, welcome. The dog will jump on you." She pushed on the screen door and held it open. Reece drew close and paused in the doorway. He tried not to breathe on her, thinking his breath was bad. "Mucho obligato," he said.

Walter scrambled up the deck steps, his nubby tail wagging, his big ears flopping. He sniffed Reece's legs and feet.

"Down, tiger." He lunged sideways for the deck rail and caught himself, sending a big pine splinter into his palm. "Ach!"

Gert watched him maneuver sideways, holding to the rail until he reached a deck chair and fell into it, then she retreated to the kitchen. Why was life so difficult?

Reece examined his hand. Some blood there. He needed some tweezers, maybe a pair of pliers. He tried to bite the end of the splinter. Walter snuffled at his feet, his tail beating the air. Reece patted his head and looked out over the back yard, the light and dark greens, the pine trees through which the sun poked. Pine straw littered the deck, which was stained to resemble redwood. Kristin's pet squirrel, Harvey, lounged in the plastic swimming pool under the overhang. His back legs were paralyzed, and he dragged himself around in circles, making scratching noises.

Quiet filled the backyard, peaceful, just the faint sound of a jet in the distance. He thought about Godo, so far away, eight thousand miles, the Horn of Africa. He'd wanted to visit the stone churches at Lalibela and see the aardvarks in the Awash River Valley. And then there was Emma. She had saved his life. Was she still at the clinic? Had they shut down the feeding station? He'd expected to have a letter from Emma, asking about how he was doing. Maybe she was mailing them to his grandparents. What if Kristin was keeping the letters? The back door opened.

"Hey!" said Kristin. "Wow, it's so good to see you outside." She wore scrubs and street shoes.

Reece felt her hand tussling his hair. "Hey, glad you're here. Pull up a cha-chair."

"Did you just stutter?"

"Yeah, sorry about that."

"Don't apologize." She pulled up a folding chair laced with polyester webbing. She reached and held his pale hand. "I have to ask you a question."

Reece looked at her. "Shoot." He laughed.

"That's not funny."

"Guess not. I need to get some clothes on. I'm feeling kind of naked in this towel."

"Are you warm enough? It's pretty warm out here."

"Yeah, warm enough. Sun on my legs."

Kristin felt a lump in her throat. She squeezed his hand. "So, are we still engaged? I mean...are we? Has anything changed? A lot has happened."

The first thing that came to his mind was Emma. "Well, I've started to think that I'm damaged goods…" He looked away.

"Don't say that. It's a miracle that you're here. But look at how well you're doing. You'll probably be back to work before you know it."

"Yeah, I hadn't thought about that, but yeah." He leaned forward, elbows to knees. He examined his hands. He felt dehydrated.

"So, we're still engaged, right?" Kristin smiled, her eyes twinkling.

Emma shivered in her jacket. "Take me to his house. I want to see him!"

"Dear God," said Afewerki. "We must not go there. He will shoot."

"Who cares?" asked Emma.

Mariam and Isaac wandered over, standing back. "What iz it?" Isaac folded his hands. "You are sick, no?"

"Yeah, I'm sick," said Emma. "This whole thing is sick." She felt strange standing there, the taste of vomit in her mouth.

"She is wanting to visit the Hyena," mumbled Afewerki.

Mariam inspired. Isaac frowned. "No, no, is bad thing. Why it iz?" asked Isaac.

"He shot Reece, and nothing is being done about it. He should be punished, right? I'll punish his sorry ass." She clenched her fists. She hiccupped and gagged.

Barra's door opened, and he emerged in a housecoat given to him by Dr. Guthrie.

"He is a bad man," said Afewerki. "We must not go there."

"God will punish," said Isaac. Mariam nodded.

Barra approached with his dress shoes on. "You have been drinking, no? Is not good?"

Emma stared at Barra. He seemed a little ridiculous in his robe with the belt tied. Did he think he was at the Hilton?

Afewerki shook his head no and looked down. "We will visit him tomorrow. The night is very dangerous."

"You give him money, don't you?" asked Emma. "How much? And why the hell are we giving him money?"

"Oh, too many alcohols." Barra's eyes had grown wide, shining in the moonlight.

"We must do this thing," said Afewerki. "To stay, we must bribe."

Barra looked from face to face. "We are to pay him rent. It is the agreement. He will throw us if we do not pay."

"And what does he do with that money? Buy guns and bullets...damn rockets?" Even with the jacket, she shivered. Her head was clearing by the minute, but she could feel her blood boiling. She wanted to hit something. "And you don't have to be so damn friendly with him, right? You cannot give him any more money. I forbid it!"

Mariam and Isaac looked frightened.

"Emma," said Afewerki.

Barra removed his hands from his robe pockets. The robe was very soft and warm. "He will throw us. Dr. Guthrie is the one to decide this."

"To hell with everybody. I'll go find him myself." Emma looked down at her feet, and she was still wearing shoes. She realized that she had no idea which way to go. She only knew where his office was. She could hear faint music coming from her house. "Let's burn down his office. Afewerki?"

"Ai yi yi." Afewerki watched Emma walking to the gate. "Emma!"

"She will cause many troubles." Barra went back to his room. He kept a hand grenade there for protection.

"Emma, no." Afewerki ran to Emma and took her wrist. Ketow was there with his rifle, looking bewildered. What was going on?

Emma let Afewerki stop her and yelled at the top of her lungs, a piercing scream.

Ketow nearly jumped from his skin. He looked to Afewerki for answers.

Afewerki put his arms around Emma, squeezing her from behind. She struggled and broke free.

"Dammit, take me to his house, now!" She faced him and saw the fear in his eyes, the compassion as well, and perhaps something else. She began to melt. She walked to the gate and hit it with her fist. The steel sheeting, cold and hard, scraped her knuckles.

"How much are we giving him, the Hyena?" She shivered.

"Perhaps fifty birr per month," said Afewerki.

"Is that all?" asked Emma. She felt somewhat better. "But he steals oil from us, and we let him."

Afewerki knew it was true. "Yes, but to stay, to help the people, we must do these things. It is the only way."

Emma suddenly felt exhausted. "Tomorrow will be a better day, right?" Reece had said something to that effect. It was something that his grandfather said. Simple but true. It had to be true. She turned to her house. "Good night."

"Good night, Emma."

Afewerki watched her cross the yard and then close her door.

Emma slept like the dead, dreaming of barbecue. She awoke to doves sliding down the roof. She lay on her back, staring at the pitched ceiling. She was wearing a jacket, which felt wrong. She tasted sour liquor on her breath and remembered throwing up. What else had happened? What day was it? *Maybe Wednesday.* She threw back the blankets and felt cold and hungry. Had she written in her diary? She fumbled the notebook and glanced. She hadn't written a thing since Reece had been shot. "I will be okay," she said to the room.

In front of her stove, she said it again. "I will be okay." She turned on the large front eye and then the two smaller eyes in the back. She smelled the gas and leaned over to feel the heat. She remembered Desta and hoped that she had made it through the night. And Misrak, she would need to visit her. Misrak needed to go to Addis. It had to be cancer. And what about the young girl, Mariam, who could be infected with HIV? *Jesus,* and then there was Reece hanging in the balance. The heat was scorching her face, and she moved back. Someone knocked.

Emma opened the door, and it was Afewerki wearing his Exxon ballcap.

"Hey," she said. She only had one thing on her mind. "Are we going to see the Hyena?" She felt determined, stubborn, defeated.

Afewerki looked surprised. "Let us forget the night. It is no good. The people are waiting at the clinic."

"Damn." She had nearly forgotten about the clinic. "What time is it?"

"It is one hour past the time." He shuffled his feet. "Today, maybe Terry will come. I think he will come."

"Maybe he'll have some mail." She brightened at the thought. "Is there any breakfast left?"

"Ah, Zenebek has leav-ed. It is finished."

Emma thought. "How about one of those MREs at your

place? Maybe that pork patty?"

Afewerki made a face. Pork was unclean, worse than eating a monkey. "You can eat, but you must not tell anyone. They will complain."

After she had changed and washed her face and hands, Emma walked with Afewerki to his house, greeting villagers along the way, giving them her lopsided smile. She recognized almost everyone, including the teen boy with the red-banded straw hat. She'd treated him for worms more than once. She wondered if worms were just a natural part of things, and who was she to interfere?

They passed into the compound, and there was no smoke coming through the door or the top of the roof. "Let's say hello to your mother," said Emma.

"She is feeling badly today," said Afewerki. This had happened before.

"Oh no. Let me see her." She peered in and heard a soft moan. She walked in and let her eyes adjust. His mother lay on the floor with a piece of twisted cloth in her mouth. Emma drew closer and kneeled. "Mendeno?"

"She is sick by two days. She is passing the stone through her urine."

"Kidney stones, my goodness. That's so painful. Her face is covered with sweat. Is she biting the cloth for the pain?" She reached down to feel her pulse. "Rapid. Afewerki, we can help her. She needs IV fluids and pain meds."

"She cannot go to the clinic."

"To hell with the clinic! Go and bring back three liters of normal saline, an IV kit, tubing, alcohol swabs, and some tape. And bring ten codeine tablets from the tin." She turned back to his mom. "What is her name again?"

"Abebe, like the flower. Shall I go?"

"Yes, go. Tell the people at the clinic we'll be there in half an hour. Bring Zenebek here so that she can take care of her while we're gone."

"But she must cook and wash the clothes," said Afewerki.

"Not today. She's here today, at least until you can come back. What about your dad?"

"He is with the farmers. He is talking them. He will come for dinner."

"Of course he will. She can't cook, though." She remembered Misrak, and then Desta, and then Mariam. "What a hell!"

Afewerki ducked out to the clinic and passed into the lane. Through a fence, he could see his father drinking talla with a small group of men. It was his routine, as the meher rains had not been sufficient to plow and plant. The villagers were getting restless, ready for the worst to happen. It was mid-August, and the steady rains should have started in June or July. People were not as alarmed, though, since the Mission was there with grain.

He shook hands with the village's agriculture minister, who always wore an old, light-blue polyester suit, and then began the steep downhill jaunt to the clinic. He noticed how windy it was, which was strange. In the distance, he could hear it, the helicopter. Terry was coming. He hurried, passing the long line of patients piled against the fence, many sitting on large stones. He turned and shouted to them that it would be soon when the ferenj would arrive, and to be calm. No one responded, eyes shaded, slapping at flies. Their time would come, no doubt. What to do other than wait?

Inside the compound, he found Isaac, who had the key to the clinic. He took an empty grain bag and loaded it with supplies for Emma. The ten codeine tablets he put in his pocket. He decided to wait for Terry, but changed his mind and trotted up the hill.

Terry zoomed over the main village and did a slow turn to begin his descent. Everything looked brown, except for the large trees. He had some news about Reece, about Birmingham, and wondered how Emma would take it. He was convinced that she'd jumped because of Reece, that she had a crush on him, and felt responsible for the shooting. It was still the primary subject of conversation back in Addis. He knew that the Mission would pull the plug soon. He already had another assignment lined up in Tanzania with Helimission.

Isaac and Barra watched Terry coax the machine to the landing pad. Dust and loose plastic flew into the air. They waved as usual, wincing at the loud noise. The net to carry out the dozens of empty oil tins was in the passenger compartment. Isaac hunched over and ran for the net as the copter idled down.

Back at his parents' house, Afewerki flushed the IV line and held it ready for Emma as she started the IV. He wondered if Emma was making too much of a fuss.

Emma applied the tourniquet and slapped for a vein. She opened the IV packet with her teeth, tape strips ready. In slipped the catheter, blood flashed back, and she plugged in the saline. She thought about the shelter at the top of the hill. She hadn't visited since jumping from the helicopter, and a pang of guilt pierced her. So many things to worry about. She needed help! When the Icelandic team had been in Godo, there had been three of them.

"Okay." Emma adjusted the drip to run in a liter over two hours. There was no place to hang the bag, though. "Did you tell Zenebek to come?"

"No, but I will go. Can you hold?"

Emma patted Abebe's shoulder and stood, taking the bottle. "Make sure your mom knows to protect the IV and not to adjust the flow. Okay?"

"Ishi," and he spoke to his mother, who looked on with a grimace.

"Bataam taruno," said Emma to Abebe. Emma looked around for a place to hang the IV. Since Abebe was on the floor, the rickety bed frame would work. With one hand, she reached and dragged the bed toward her. She reached the bottle under the bed and brought it up to the corner of the leather webbing. "Perfect."

Terry jumped out with the mailbag. He walked with Isaac, who was dragging the net into the clear. The clinic door was open, but there was no Emma or Afewerki. Barra came out of the warehouse with a big smile.

"Hello, my brazzer." Isaac shook hands with Terry. He imagined that Terry was wealthy. He had a beautiful wife and worked for the Swiss and the Americans.

"Hey," said Terry. He shook Barra's hand. "Where's Emma?"

"Ah, we do not know. Afewerki has come to take some medicines away. Perhaps she is with him?"

"I can wait a while. I have your mail here." He handed the bag to Barra, who reached in for the small bundle of letters. Two were for Emma, the rest for the team. A gun fired in the distance, young men scaring the girls coming up from Sokoro spring with pots of water on their backs.

"I will give her," said Barra.

"You are rugged," said Isaac. He'd just learned the new word.

Terry laughed. "Rugged?"

"Yes, like the adventure man." Isaac smiled.

"I suppose," said Terry. "Let's spread the net and pile on the oil cans."

Barra sprang into action. Three daily laborers loitered in the shade of the warehouse. He barked orders at them, and they broke into a run. Barra was their enjera and wot. They made three birr per day working for the Mission. Terry wanted to help, but that would insult the men.

Terry stepped into the dim warehouse and surveyed the piles of Canadian and US wheat and sorghum. Barra and Isaac followed. He wondered if he had already made his last grain drop. It would be up to the Mission and the RRC. The party had to end at some point.

"How is Emma doing?" He rumpled his thick brown hair. He wore tire sandals and cargo shorts.

Isaac looked at Barra and raised his eyebrows.

"She is very angry, I think," said Barra.

"Really? About what?"

"The Hyena makes her to be angry," said Isaac.

"Right. I don't blame her. Is she doing okay in the clinic?"

"Yes," said Barra. "But the peoples are murmuring. She has tried to kill herself. She may have the buda they are saying."

"Hmm, evil eye." Terry pushed some stones with his

sandal. "But the people are still coming to the clinic, right?"

"Of course, what can they do?" asked Barra. "It is free."

After Afewerki returned with Zenebek, he and Emma headed to the clinic.

"Have you heard anything from the shelter?" asked Emma.

"I am checking there yesterday. All is fine, except for the diarrhea." He made a sour face. "The smell is terrible."

"In the shelter?"

"Inside and near the shintabet. Very bad."

The wind whipped them as they walked. The sun was dry, hard, and warm. Two little girls took Emma's hands. "Ferenj," they whispered with big smiles. Emma admired their braided hair with beads at the ends.

"Emma!" said Terry as she stepped into the compound. He waved and walked toward her. "Good to see you."

"Hey, good looking." Emma blushed. "Did I just say that?" She hugged him. He smelled sweaty. "What about this wind?"

"Yeah, it just blew in, it seems, or it's coming and going." He shook Afewerki's hand. "How are you?"

"It is fine, God willing," said Afewerki.

"Good enough." Terry considered himself a Christian but was not religious. "Couple of letters for you. Gave them to Barra. He's in the warehouse. Clinic going well?"

Emma thought about the line of forty or so sitting outside the compound. "Jesus, I've got to get to work. I'm late this morning."

"Heard some news from Birmingham. Big tornado went

through and hit the hospital there. Two or three hundred people died."

Emma's eyes grew wide. "No way. Any word on Reece?"

"Nothing new. Dr. Guthrie said he would make a phone call. He knew you'd be interested, plus he's from there. I've never seen a tornado. You?"

"Oh yeah. Like a cloud gone psycho. I've only seen one from a distance, but it scared the bejesus out of me. Kind of got me worried about this wind." Her scrub top pressed against her skin, the sleeves flapping.

"No tornadoes out here, I think. Afewerki, have you ever seen a tornado?"

Afewerki looked puzzled. "No, what is it?"

"It's a funnel cloud that touches the ground, destroys everything in its path."

"We have no such thing, but there are sometimes the small winds in the dust."

"Yeah, like that, except very powerful," said Terry.

"My goodness," said Afewerki. He tried to imagine it.

"But really, we've got to get to work. Can't keep these patients waiting any longer."

"Okay, not a problem." Terry looked, and the net was piled high with oil cans. Isaac was pulling the net together at the top using a heavy hook with a catch.

"Okay, see you," said Emma. "But let me know what you find out about the tornado. Will you be back on Saturday?"

"Not sure." He didn't want to be the bearer of bad news—that the feeding program was being scaled down in preparation for closing the station in Godo.

Reece racked his brains for an answer. Were they still engaged? No one had called it off, so he guessed the answer was yes.

"Yes, we're engaged." He looked at Kristin. She seemed so damn innocent. He smiled. Did she understand anything about what he had gone through?

"Well, first comes love, and then comes marriage," said Kristin.

Reece didn't finish the rhyme. What was he getting into? Her parents hated him. What he wanted was to run to the airport and fly back to Ethiopia. He looked out over the backyard. It sloped from right to left. The pine straw seemed to be the one thing that connected him to this place. He wanted a piece to chew on.

"Why so quiet?" asked Kristin. "Let's go inside and sit on the couch. I can scratch your back."

The thought of having his back scratched seemed thrilling. It would feel great. "Yeah, sure. Help me stand? Maybe rub my freaking tailbone." He smiled, and the day seemed bright.

Reece hobbled inside, holding onto Kristin's arm. He felt woozy, and his eyes adjusted to the dimness. The couch looked inviting, and he turned and fell onto it with a dull *whump*. "Smell something cooking."

Kristin thought. "Tonight is dumplings." She knew her mother could hear her. "Lean up and I'll scratch your back."

Reece widened his eyes to clear the cobwebs and leaned

forward. He could feel the skin stretched across his spine. "Oh, mama."

Kristin ran her fingernails back and forth.

"Dear Jesus," said Reece. "That feels so good. Go up and down the spine." He thought he would faint from pleasure.

"You're silly." Kristin thought about their honeymoon, losing her virginity. Her sister Robyn had explained everything, including the mess at the end. Her mom had given her the talk and just told her it was quick and to keep her eyes closed. She raked hard down his spine.

"Oh!" said Reece. "That hurt but do it again."

Kristin obliged. Reece moaned and put his face in his hands.

In the kitchen, Gert's stomach muscles tightened. They were being too loud, but what to do? She glanced at the clock. Edwin would be home soon. Maybe they would give it a rest then. She opened and closed the oven, letting the door slam. She blew on her brown bangs. Never in her life had she imagined such a complicated situation.

"Here, let me get behind you," said Kristin.

Reece scooted up a bit, renting the edge of the couch. Kristin eased behind him, encompassing him with her long, thin legs. She massaged his neck.

Reece winced with pleasure. How could he not love Kristin? God, he could just die. *Emma.* He pushed Emma out of his thoughts. Kristin's hands were on him. She was what mattered. He went back to the tornado, the wind, the sucking sounds, the roar, his heavy hospital bed moving back and forth as if attracted by a giant magnet. There had been no screams that he could remember. He pitched forward and fell between his legs, doing a complete somersault on the floor and losing his towel.

"Hey! You, okay?" She was ready to have his baby right then and there.

"I'm sorry," said Reece. He covered himself. A sudden emptiness filled him. People on the hospital floor he had been on had died, and he was still alive. He'd been shot in the head, and he was still alive. What was the point? What mattered? Did anything matter but the moment?

"Dang, that was impressive," said Kristin.

Gert peered around the corner. She was afraid they were having sex. "What happened?" She held a spatula like a sledgehammer.

"Oh, nothing," said Kristin. "He did a flip on the floor. Pretty amazing."

"I should be in the circus." He wanted to laugh, but couldn't. "I bit my tongue, ouch."

"Here." Kristin planted her foot between his legs and extended her hand. "On three. One, two, three!" She pulled, and Reece tried to stand. He made it halfway up and sprawled back on the couch with all his glory on display.

Reece laughed. "Sorry about that."

Gert had seen it all and fled back to the kitchen, murmuring a childhood song, "Down came the rain and washed the spider out..."

"I'm a beast." He took Kristin's hands and pulled her toward him. She fell on top of him, and they kissed.

The front door opened and shut. Reece tried to sit up but couldn't. Kristin rolled over onto the couch, giggling. Their mouths fit together perfectly. He loved the feel of her tongue in his mouth, reaching for his tonsils, tonsil hockey.

"Hey guys." Robyn gave them a naughty look. "For shame, what is going on here?"

"We're having fellowship." He remembered all the fellowship dinners he'd had at church, usually spaghetti.

Kristin laughed. "Yeah, what he says." She wanted to rip her clothes off. "How's the world of private nursing?"

"Not bad. Just playing a lot of checkers and pushing him around his backyard. He's a rich old fart, something to do with insurance. Here seems more exciting, though."

"Maybe you'll get married," said Kristin. "Here, help me get him up on the cushion."

They each took an armpit and on three lifted Reece to a sitting position. Reece went for it and pulled them down, just a big knot of people laughing on the couch.

"This is great." He was getting an eyeful, being tickled by Robyn.

"Hey!" said Kristin. She put an arm around his neck. "He's mine, dear sister."

"Oops," said Robyn. "My boob slipped out." She untucked her scrub top and adjusted her bra. "You're a bad boy!"

Gert wanted badly to intervene, but couldn't bring herself to look into the den. She tapped the spatula on the counter and then remembered to take her vitamin, which she did.

"Ah, life." Reece leaned against Kristin with his hand on her thigh. "But I need to get back to work." He wondered how much he owed the hospital, probably thousands.

"Maybe you can sell boiled peanuts at the gas station,"

said Kristin.

Reece laughed. "I would probably like that, except for the selling part."

"I'm going to change." Robyn reached down and pinched Reece's cheek.

"Ow." He tried to grab her arm but missed. He turned and went for Kristin's knees. Kristin screamed and squirmed on the couch, fighting him off, laughing.

Gert couldn't stand it any longer and walked into the den with her hands on her hips. "Your dad will be home soon. Can you help me make a chopped salad?"

Reece pulled his hands away from Kristin. He'd forgotten about Gert. "I'd be glad to."

"No, I mean Kristin."

"Silly boy," said Kristin. "Yeah, sure, but shouldn't we wait? It'll be all wilted."

Gert frowned. Kristin was right. "I'll put it in the fridge." She noticed the light in the den, how everything had a maple tinge. She thought about how she'd wanted to be an artist, how her mother had discouraged her.

"Be right back. Gotta chop some lettuce." Kristin ached, ready to devour Reece. It was meant to be, right?

The day crawled at a steady pace without lunch. The most interesting patient was a woman who claimed to have been impregnated during a dream of being attacked in the night. The man had been fat with fangs like a hyena. She wanted an abortion, but there was nothing that Emma could do except to give her vitamins.

Around five, the final patient, number sixty-five. Emma's lower back ached from stooping over, leaning to look into ears and eyes.

A middle-aged man was sweating to soak a mattress. He shuffled to the clinic door, and Afewerki helped him up the step. The man breathed deep and slow, nodding with each breath. He shuddered. He wore the farmer's pants of thick, patched cloth and wide leg openings. His shirt was from an old military outfit, Russian in origin.

Emma first looked into his eyes, which were yellow and bruised with thick bursts of capillaries. "Mendeno?"

The man leaned his head against the wall. After a moment, he spoke, and Afewerki nodded as if in agreement. Emma noticed his dry skin, the bruises and cuts on his legs.

"He has been to the kolla, the low places, and he is having malaria. His fever will come and then come again."

Emma wished that she had the equipment to do a blood smear and verify the diagnosis. "How long has he been sick?"

"By twenty days."

"Wow, let's give him some ORS now and chloroquine.

Was anyone else traveling with him?"

"One other woman, his sister, but she has died."

"What? Good Lord. Scratch the ORS, and let's do an IV of D-five normal saline. We'll get him started with a chloroquine injection."

"Ishi," said Afewerki. He explained to the man what would happen.

The man moaned and slumped on the bench, which tipped forward and crashed to the floor. The man's teeth chattered, and his eyes rolled back.

"Well, damn." Emma watched Afewerki put the bench back in place. The man was kneeling with his head bowed, as if in prayer. She and Afewerki lifted him onto the bench. "Hold him while I get the thermometer."

Emma slid the thermometer beneath the man's armpit and pressed it there. She glanced at her watch, and the second hand wasn't moving. "When did his sister die? Are they from here?"

Afewerki knew the man. "He lives near." He asked the man about his sister, but he did not respond.

"He smells sweet," said Emma. "Like perfume."

"It is the incense, the itan," said Afewerki. "He thinks it is to cure him."

The man slumped sideways, and Afewerki caught him.

Emma prepared the injection, pushing the air from the syringe. "Lean him over." She pushed down the dirty pants, swabbed with alcohol, and plunged the needle into his buttock. "Now for the IV. Oh, fu—hell!" She had jabbed herself in the thigh. "Hold him."

Emma looked back at Afewerki as she unhitched her jeans and pushed them down to find the puncture. Just a small dot of redness, but she attacked it with an alcohol swab and pressed to make it bleed.

Afewerki tried not to look, but could only stare at Emma's underwear, the pale skin with veins. The man mumbled.

"Jesus Christ, I've never ever stuck myself before," said Emma. Her face glowed pale. "What was I doing?"

"You must to throw the needle away," said Afewerki.

Emma realized she was still holding it and pushed it into the used needle container. She felt her heart beating a hundred miles an hour as if she had committed a great crime. She gathered her wits, hiked her pants, and fetched a bottle of D_5NS from the shelf. "Yikes." She flushed the line, had Afewerki hold the bottle, and fished for a vein on the man's dehydrated arm.

With the IV flowing. Emma stood back, realizing what she had done. It seemed as if tears wanted to flow, but she only experienced a tremendous pressure in her eyes and a painful emptiness in her chest.

"How fast to let the IV flow?" asked Afewerki, holding the bottle at chest level. The fluid ran pell-mell into the man's vein.

"Oh." She adjusted the drip rate to allow the liter to run in over an hour. "Fudge, the thermometer." It was still there, stuck under his armpit. She held it up to the light. "One hundred and four. Dang. Needs paracetamol as well. That's why he's so out of it."

"Ishi," said Afewerki. He tried to get the man to understand him, that he needed to swallow some pills.

The man nodded, but his eyes looked wild.

"We'll crush it and give it to him with some water."

After the man had swallowed most of the liquid, he seemed somewhat better and looked around like a newborn baby, eying Emma and Afewerki.

Suddenly, Emma remembered the shelter, and she needed to visit Misrak as well. And then there was Afewerki's mom. She'd run by to hang a fresh bottle of fluids, but by now the IV would be clotted off. The liters of fluid would help her pass the stones, though. "Can he stay at the shelter tonight?"

"The women will complain," said Afewerki.

"He can stay in the little storage shed there. The guard can keep an eye on him."

"If you wish." Afewerki was dead tired and starving. He imagined the others gathered in the dining hut, waiting for them.

"Let's get some help and walk him up there."

Afewerki went outside and called into the warehouse. No one answered. It would have to be the guard, and he called him over.

With Afewerki on one side and the guard on the other, the man stood, wobbling. Emma held the IV fluid at head level. Outside, the wind blew brisk and roared in her ears. She thought of the beach at Gulf Shores back in Alabama. Her sister worked at the state park there. She imagined walking down the beach with Reece, their first kiss in the stiff ocean breeze. She shivered, the wind sending a chill through her.

Up the steep slope they labored, bearing to the right and winding to the highest reaches of Godo, past the Orthodox church and to the long shelter with its tin roof that reminded Emma of a large chicken house. Villagers paused as they passed, putting their hands to their mouths. Even they could tell the man was afflicted with a high fever, perhaps malaria, the dreaded woba. She smelled human waste, stronger than she had ever experienced, even with the wind. She worried that she was neglecting the women there, who had no place else to call home.

Afewerki shouted to the guard to unlock the storage shed. Inside was a quintal of teff used to feed the women and a pile of nails. With a dozen grain bags, Afewerki made a bed for the man who plopped to the ground, turned to his side, and moaned.

Emma saw the lack of an IV pole. Why didn't countries donate IV poles? "Afewerki, the guard will need to hold this bottle until it runs out. Tell him, we'll be back in an hour to take out the IV."

Afewerki did so. "Emma, it is time to eat."

"First, we need to check on the women." She looked at the shelter guard holding the IV bottle like a ticking bomb and laughed. The laughter overtook her, and she doubled over.

Afewerki frowned. "What is it? We must eat soon." He remembered that Zenebek had been ordered to stay with his mother, and that there would be no dinner. His heart sank. Emma would want to go there as well.

"Okay, wow, let's do it," said Emma, leading the way outside in the wind, which now felt truly cold. God, she just needed Reece standing over her, his hands on her shoulders.

Outside, in a stiff breeze, the two dozen women and their children stood in two groups, waiting to see what would happen next. They had already chosen one of the women, Tigist, a small, wiry mother of four, to speak for them.

Afewerki and Emma approached the groups, and Tigist put her hands on her hips. It was now or never. They needed more food, and the shelter was full of fleas. And why did they not have a wall around the shintabet to keep the old guard from watching them while they peed and defecated?

Afewerki scratched his head as he listened and relayed the information to Emma.

"Not enough food?" asked Emma. "What should we do?"

"Perhaps the old man is not giving enough," said Afewerki. "He must be watch-ed."

"Well dang," said Emma. "Can you make sure that they receive enough food? What more do they need? There's a whole bag of teff in the shed."

"She is saying they need some fruits, some mooze, the banana for the little ones."

"Of course they do. We need to do that tomorrow. Can you find some bananas and maybe some oranges?"

"Yes, Emma. And they are complaining that they have no lentils for the wot."

Emma felt a bit dizzy. She had fallen down on the job of caring for these women. "Nega, tomorrow, we will take care of these things. Tell them." She walked toward Tigist and held out her hand as an apology. Tigist bowed her head and flashed a toothy smile. A murmur spread through the crowd, and the children, held captive by the spectacle, suddenly began to stir and make noise.

"There are many fleas in the shelter," said Afewerki.

"Lord," said Emma. She peered into the dark and dank building. Large mats of grain bags stuffed with corn shucks lined the dirt floor. The smell was of smoke and diarrhea. "Tomorrow, we have to do something."

As if in response, a furious straight-line wind swooped down. The pitched roof of the shelter groaned and, with finality, ripped free, lifted, and fell over to the other side with a deafening crash. The wind whooped and howled. Emma stooped and walked back toward Afewerki. She felt that her clothes would tear from her body and that all was lost.

Reece, dressed in a pair of old sweats, was watching the local news when Edwin came home. Where was Kristin? Edwin, short and stocky with rolled shoulders much like Gert's, strolled into the den with his jacket over his arm. His eyes on the TV, he overlooked Reece on the couch.

"Hello, sir!" said Reece.

Edwin jumped. "Criminy!"

"Criminal?"

"No, criminy."

"Hominy?"

"Hey, honey." Gert looked like a little girl in her puffy-sleeve blouse. She held a wooden spoon. She'd decided to make a chocolate pie with pudding mix.

Edwin glared at Reece. "Hey, dear." He wasn't in a joking mood. The main news was over with, just sports and weather to go, then national news, and then more local news. Edwin adjusted his attitude, trying to set the example. "How was your day, Reece?"

"Bonkers, I suppose. Watch this." He leaned as far forward as he could, put his hands to his knees, and grunted into a simian standing position. "Come dance with me."

Edwin just wanted to plop into his recliner and watch the news with smells of cooking from the kitchen. "Honey, can you get me a glass of water?"

"How about a cocktail?" asked Reece. He plopped onto the couch.

Edwin smirked. He was an alcohol virgin. He'd even abstained during his time in Korea. Gert referred to him as her rock. "Water is good for the kidneys."

"You got me there," said Reece. "You know, just about everyone in the village drank some form of alcohol."

Edwin listened to high school football previews. "That so. Probably not very educated." He backed up to the recliner and sat.

"Educated? What does that have to do with it?" Reece laughed.

Edwin felt that Reece was mocking him. "Everyone knows that alcohol is bad for you, especially your liver."

"I didn't see any bad livers while I was there. I think I ate some goat liver by accident."

"Daddy!" Kristin floated into the room. She'd pulled her hair back and washed off her makeup. Her face looked thin.

"Hey, darling," said Edwin. "How was your day?"

"Busy, busy. Had a jerk for a patient, a judge. I did as little as I could to stay out of the room. No wonder he has health problems."

"God is punishing him," said Reece. He made bug eyes at the room.

"Is he a Christian?" asked Edwin. "Perhaps he's just not in his right mind." A commercial for body wash. He turned his eyes away.

"If he is, he's the rudest Christian on planet Earth."

"At least he didn't shoot you in the head," said Reece.

Edwin grimaced.

"Sheesh," said Kristin.

"Sorry," said Reece. "A judge. Huh."

"Had a run of V-tach and I got to thump him, though."

"Well then, high five."

They slapped palms.

"What goes around comes around," said Reece.

Edwin saw his opportunity. "Why do you suppose God let this Hyena fellow shoot you like that?" He'd been pondering this for weeks, wondering what sort of wickedness Reece had committed. "God's will is mysterious."

"Daddy!"

"No, no, let me think." Reece thought. Maybe it was because he had been lusting after Emma. Had he not been shot in her house? It was all a fog. Had they made out? He wasn't sure. "Since I've been through all of this, God seems to be a little willy-nilly. What about the people killed by the tornado, some of them young children? Does God strike children dead because they played with matches, stole a crayon?"

The weather was on. Another week of 90-plus without rain.

"We must learn to have faith in God's plan for each person. He calls us home when we are needed."

"Why does he need so many children? Why starve them first? Why suck them hundreds of feet into the air and toss them down like a bag of blue aquarium gravel? Why not just let them pass in their sleep?" Reece felt his chest pounding.

Edwin smiled. "God's will is mysterious. We're not meant to understand, only to have faith."

"To hell with that," said Reece.

"Reece?" Kristin shook her head no. She saw her mom peeking around the corner, also shaking her head no.

"Were you speaking to me?" Edwin couldn't decide if he should stand or not. He needed to pee. Water or talk of water always made him pee.

Reece looked around the den. It was as big as Emma's tiny house in Godo. He remembered the little fridge and stove, her cot. A commercial for Vaseline Intensive Care Lotion. He tuned out the words. A woman wrote *Dry* on her hand with her fingernail. He remembered the day his parents died at Luby's. They had all three cowered beneath a table. He had been spared. He'd told no one, but he'd pissed his pants that day.

"Reece?" asked Kristin.

"Yeah. I'm here." He looked at Edwin, sitting back in his recliner. His hair was neat and trim. What was the point of arguing with him? His tear ducts went hot, threatening to spill. "Maybe let's go on the deck. How about it?"

"We just have to get the vertical right before we can work on the horizontal," said Edwin, making motions with his right hand.

"Lovely," said Reece. "Help me up."

Reece stood with a little help. He was getting stronger by the minute. Maybe he would walk to his grandparents' house on the lake. That would be fun. He limped to the door with his hand on Kristin's shoulder. He held to his sweatpants.

"You're gaining ground." Kristin looked closely at the wound on his right temple. "Looks like little threads in the scar on your head."

"Maybe from the gauze." Reece followed her through the door and held onto the rail on the deck. "Let me stand for a while, strengthen my legs." The sun had passed over the house on its way to set, leaving the deck in full shade. "Not too hot." A gnat buzzed his face.

Kristin went over to say hello to Harvey. "Hey, buddy." Harvey crawled along the bottom of the plastic pool, pulling himself with his front legs and long claws. "Let me get him some fresh water and a treat."

"Right," said Reece. "The horizontal with the vertical." He let go and made a cross in the air. He pondered the neighbor's yard across the chain-link fence.

Kristin brought water and five pecan halves for Harvey. "Here you go, little buddy." She pulled the piece of fence across the pool. "You know, Reece, that when we get married, Harvey will be your son."

Reece shivered. "Hadn't thought of that. Will he take my name?"

"Of course he will."

"That sounds super."

"You don't sound excited," said Kristin.

"I don't? But don't I look excited?" He let go of the rail and waved his arms in the air. "Oh shit." He buckled, squatted, and fell over backwards.

"Reece!" Kristin scrambled to help him up. He was laughing. "What, you're okay, I can tell." She could see his member through the sweatpants she'd made him put on. "Got to get you some underwear from Walmart, big boy."

Reece looked up at Kristin. She seemed to be twenty feet tall, standing over him. Trees loomed behind her, a bright blue sky above, a couple of swallows flitting there. He tried to look up her scrub top and felt a bit frisky.

"This deck is hard." He rolled on his side and pushed himself up. "A little help." Together they stood and headed back inside. "I need to water the horse."

"Do what?"

"Write in the snow."

Back inside, the national news played, something about a Navy spy.

"Drain the mighty python."

Edwin flinched, gripping the sides of his recliner like a pulpit.

"I get it," said Kristin. "Let's go." In front of Edwin, she grabbed his butt and squeezed.

Edwin coughed. "Young lady?"

"Dinner's ready in five minutes," said Gert. "Help us, dear Jesus." She tried to catch Edwin's eye, but he was focused on the TV.

Within minutes, the wind calmed to a brisk breeze. The roof had just folded over. What to do? The women shrieked and slapped one another. Afewerki headed downhill to fetch help, and it took only half an hour for eighteen men to appear, some with poles.

Emma waited to see what would happen. She recognized the carpenter who worked for the Mission. He tipped his hat and examined the building. She wanted to make sure that the women had a roof over their heads and that they had enough food for the night. She walked to the crooked cookhouse with a tin roof. Smoke eked through the cracks. Inside, three women squatted around a fire. A large pot bubbled, a wot without meat, lentils, or peas, just an oily, fiery pepper sauce. The women stood and wiped their hands on their dresses.

Emma looked for an enjera basket. "Enjera?" she said.

"Yellum," said one. Her head was shaved, and she was very short. She looked at the dirt floor as if ashamed.

"For God's sake," said Emma. "What the hell?" She stepped back outside, looking for Afewerki. There was teff, so why no enjera? The men tackling the roof caught her attention. It had happened so quickly.

With poles, four men grunting and straining pushed the flipped roof up a few feet. Another, on the shoulders of a friend, scrambled onto the roof into the gap. If the poles slipped, he would be crushed. He inserted himself as a wedge and pushed with his back, his sandals slipping. The roof inched upward. The men with the poles pushed with all their might. Someone with a crude ladder came running. Two more men clambered onto the roof and joined the other in pushing as hard as they could. Emma feared the worst. The men with the poles had pushed as far as they could and were yelling. The three men on the roof were on their own. Their calves popped with the strain, and one slipped and fell. The roof pushed down the other two, but the fallen man leaped up and retook his place. Another man scrambled up with a pole. He jammed it between the rising panel of roof and the roof he was standing on. The three men rested a moment, and then, with a mighty heave, the roof section went vertical. They had no more leverage. Emma closed her eyes, waited, waited, and then heard a mighty crash. She opened her eyes, and the men were celebrating. She clapped her hands. "Bataam taruno!"

Emma trotted downhill, the light golden, fading at the end of the day. She passed the church and wound her way to the compound. The gate stood ajar. Inside, everyone was grouped around the cookhouse, eating. The carcass of a goat lay in the grass, skinned. Irigit stood over it with his gun, grinning and eating a large chunk of steaming liver.

"What the...Hey, guys."

"Hello, it iz you," said Isaac, his face smeared with grease, his hand dripping with fluid. "We have kill-ed the goat. Zenebek is busy." He laughed.

"Afewerki?" She saw him inside. There was a large pot over hot coals, steaming.

"We are eating the goat from the inside," he said, holding a piece of boiled intestine.

"Oh," said Emma. "The roof blew over, but it's fixed."

"You would like some?" asked Barra. His smile slid with greasy liquid.

"No, thank you." She hadn't eaten since that morning and could not remember what she had eaten. "Is there enjera in the basket, Afewerki?"

"There is." He loosened the lid, revealing a dozen or so of the large flat breads.

Emma felt lost, lightheaded. "We need to take the enjera to the shelter. They have none."

Afewerki frowned. "Zenebek will anger."

"I nearly forgot about your mother. We have to check on her and then on Misrak. Isaac or Mariam, please take this enjera to the women at the shelter."

Isaac looked to Afewerki and then to Barra. "Iz okay?"

"Of course it's okay!" Emma flushed crimson. She brought it down a notch. "We can make more, right?"

"Ishi, Emma," said Isaac. "I will take."

"Afewerki, the guard is holding that bottle of IV fluid for the guy with malaria. Can you run up and check on that?" She needed someone to go with her to see Afewerki's mother, Abebe. Mariam's English was not so good, and that left Barra.

Afewerki fished the goat's tongue from the pot and broke it in half, giving a portion to Mariam, the gursha. Both murmured.

"Barra, come with me, can you, to check on Afewerki's mom?" She sweated in the hot room, standing in the waft of smoke. She couldn't take it anymore and stepped outside.

"Yes, yes, I will come," said Barra. "I must wash." He

held out his hand as evidence and stepped over to the water barrel.

"Afewerki, the old man at the shelter, make sure the liter goes in. We'll give him another tomorrow. Plus, he needs to take another dose of chloroquine by mouth tonight."

"Do you have?" asked Afewerki. He was not smiling.

"Dang, we didn't bring it from the clinic. You'll need to get it."

Before taking the enjera basket, Isaac took the clinic padlock key from his neck and gave it to Afewerki. "Here, my brother."

"Ishi," said Afewerki, and he left with Isaac.

"Okay, let us go now, before the dark." Barra always looked fresh, even after dining on entrails.

Emma slipped through the gate and led the way, looking down to avoid twisting her sore ankle. "Ferenj!" came from every compound they passed, little boys home after a day of herding, little girls from hauling pots of water.

"So, you are not to be angry?" Barra caught up with Emma and walked beside her.

Emma thought. "Well, I'm angry that the Hyena gets money even after he shot Reece."

"Ah, but we have not seen him do this thing. It is rumor, as you say." He smiled.

Emma shook her head. "Who shot him then?" She rounded the corner, headed downhill for a bit, and then back to the right.

"No one is knowing. He will be catch-ed, no? God will catch him and punish. It will happen."

"How do you know it was a man?"

Barra looked surprised. "A woman does not have the

gun."

The gate to Afewerki's family compound was closed. Barra called out, and one of Afewerki's younger brothers let them in. The oxen fidgeted inside their pen of thorns, the goats gathered in a crude shed beside the hut. No smoke filtered through the roof, and Emma peered into the darkness. "Hello!"

A low moan. Emma stepped carefully toward the middle. She let her eyes adjust until she could see Abebe sitting on the floor, her back against the hut's low stone wall. She stooped over and put her hand on Abebe's forehead, cool and clammy.

"Is she okay?" asked Emma.

Barra spoke to Abebe. "She is pain in her urine, but she can walk."

Emma looked for the IV. The bottle was on the floor. The IV would be clotted. She exposed Abebe's arm, the crook where the IV was, and pulled out the catheter. She pulled a wrinkled alcohol swab from her shirt pocket and swabbed the entry site, folding Abebe's arm. "Tell her to keep her arm folded for a few minutes."

Barra told her, and Abebe whispered. "The fire has become cold," said Barra.

"Tell her, we will come again in the morning. Does she need more pain medicine? Has she eaten?"

Barra said, "She is thirsty. That is all."

"Does she even have a blanket?" She'll be cold, especially with no fire.

"She has the dress," said Barra.

"We give out blankets all the time. How come she doesn't have one?"

"Maybe she is selling it?" asked Barra. He chuckled.

"Okay, we need to get a blanket from the warehouse for her tonight, in fact, get two blankets, no, three. And bring a few packs of famine biscuits. Is there water?"

"The water is gone. No one has brought today," said Barra.

Emma wanted to scream. "I'll go get some water, and you get the blankets. Ishi?"

"Ishi, yes, yes," said Barra. He left in a hurry.

Emma patted Abebe's leg. "Chicorilla. I'll be back with water. Wuha." She made the motion of drinking, and Abebe seemed to understand.

It took her just a few minutes to retrieve a cold bottle of water, an Icelandic IV bottle, for Abebe. There were a couple of daily laborers there helping to eat the offal of the goat. Nothing would go to waste. Back with Abebe, she gave her the bottle, and Abebe dropped it, shocked by the cold, spilling water on the dirt floor.

"Oh!" said Emma, and she retrieved it for her.

This time Emma held the bottle to Abebe's lips, and she sipped, making a face as if the water hurt.

"Biridi," said Abebe.

Emma thought of Helen Keller. "Yes, cold!"

Abebe took the bottle and drank slow, licking her dry lips. "Amenseganalo," she said in a whisper.

"Minem aydelem." Emma sensed a lull in the action, a moment to savor. Her hunger and thirst marched to her attention, and she stood. Where was Barra with the blankets? She decided not to wait, praying that he would deliver them. She had some spaghetti and a can of tomato sauce. "Okay, good night," said Emma. "Ciao." She hadn't noticed, but Afewerki's two brothers had entered and sat on the homemade bed. She knew they were hungry as well, but what could she do? And then Barra was coming into the hut, carrying the blankets and a grain bag with a dozen packets of biscuits.

After giving Abebe the blankets and passing out the biscuits, they left, walking in silence to the compound. The early stars prickled the sky, and the wind had abated to a light breeze. Dogs barking, not yet fighting as if for life and death.

The silence between them gelled. Emma once again thought about just knocking back a few shots and then passing out on her squeaky cot. She needed food, though.

"You have brothers and sisters, no?" asked Barra.

Emma remembered she was not alone. "Six sisters and one brother."

"The family is big one!" Barra laughed.

"I guess so. How about you?"

"I am having four sisters. Just one man, and it is me."

"Lots of sisters like me."

"Yes, many."

The gate was closed, and Barra called out. Irigit welcomed them with his toothy grin and nappy hat. He was full of goat.

Emma waved at the small crowd around the cookhouse and went to her tiny house. *Misrak. Damn.* She thought about Misrak lying in her hut, dying from breast cancer, her children taking care of her, she hoped. The thought of turning back to go and check on her seemed like pushing a tank wedged in thick red clay. She couldn't do it. Maybe she could send Afewerki, but she felt that he was tired and needed to eat. God, if only Reece were there to help her. She pushed her door open and listened for the hiss of the fridge.

Edwin held Gert's hand as he said the blessing. The Rice-A-Roni was calling his name, and not so much the dumplings.

"Dear, dear Lord, we thank you for blessing us this day with this food before us. We ask your blessing on the cook and thank you for guiding her hands."

Reece was famished, his eyes wide, staring at the dumplings. He looked at Edwin's moist face, his mouth moving with the prayer. He imagined chewing a dumpling and did a practice swallow, but farted instead.

Edwin paused.

"My bad," said Reece.

Kristin laughed, and Gert frowned bullets.

"Uh, we thank you for all of these things, amen." He gazed at Gert. She gazed back at him—the impossibility of the situation.

Kristin couldn't stop laughing. "Do you need...a shovel?" She wiped tears from her eyes.

Gert huffed. "Who wants dumplings?"

"Need a front-end loader." Reece liked to see Kristin laugh. Her smile covered her face. "Good thing I put on underwear." Kristin had nabbed a pair of Edwin's for him.

The dining room was small, an extension of the kitchen with a dull-green linoleum floor. The table sat four. Edwin helped himself to the Rice-A-Roni. He acknowledged Gert as she spooned chicken and dumplings onto his plate.

"Where's Robyn?" asked Edwin.

"She has a date tonight, a church date. I think they're

going to eat somewhere after." Kristin took a deep breath. Then she made the mistake of looking at Reece, who was making a face.

He burst out laughing, and so did Kristin.

Edwin chewed his food. Gert busied herself with her cloth napkin, wondering when it would stop. Gradually, they brought it down and took their first bites of food. Reece gobbled his dumplings.

"Chicken in there," said Reece. "That is superb."

"Um, thank you," said Gert.

"No, thank you." Reece nearly choked, bringing Kristin down with him, laughing his guts out. God, it felt good, and then he gagged and heaved. He panicked and sat up straight. It was coming, and he was paralyzed.

"Oh no!" said Kristin, panting for air. "You, okay?"

Reece put his hands on the table and sucked in. He let it out. "I'm okay. I'm okay."

Robyn walked into the den wearing jeans and a bra. "What's the commotion in here?"

Edwin's jaw dropped. "Robyn! The very idea! You're dang near naked." He held his fork like a daisy. He got in a good scowl with Gert, who was shaking her head and pushing her rice around.

"Robyn, what's the deal?" asked Kristin. She glared.

Reece tried not to smile. "Looking good, there," he said. "Do you come here often?"

"Stop flirting with my sister," said Kristin.

Robyn put her hands over her bra. "So sorry to upset the apple cart. It's just a bra. Reece is a nurse, right? The human body?"

"Yeah," said Reece. "I like the human body." Robyn's

jeans fit tight. She was wearing little white socks. Her breasts looked bigger than Kristin's.

"Robyn, go!" Kristin stood, her fists clenched.

"Yes, please go," said Gert. She chewed. There were dishes to wash, clothes to fold.

"No," said Robyn. She let her hands fall. She thrust out her chest, turned, and wiggled her butt.

Kristin was on her like a cat. She raked her nails down her back, and Robyn shrieked. Her bra had come undone, lifted, and hung from her shoulders. She pushed Kristin, her nipples burning holes in the air, and stomped away to her room.

Kristin's face looked dead serious. Her curls seemed like question marks. "Well, did you like it?" She tapped Reece on the back of the head. "I can't believe her."

"Anyone want more Rice-A-Roni?" asked Gert. "There's a little left."

"My appetite has been whetted," said Reece.

"Reece, stop it," said Kristin. "I mean it. It's not funny anymore."

"Did any of you hear about the volcano that let off poisonous gas and killed about two thousand people?" asked Edwin.

"Where was it?" asked Reece. He took a drink of his unsweetened iced tea.

"I think it was in Africa," said Edwin.

"What country?" asked Reece.

"I'm not sure," said Edwin. "Does it matter?" He fumbled the dumpling spoon.

"Do you need help, little baby?" asked Gert. She smiled and scooped dumplings onto his plate.

"Don't call me little baby," said Edwin. "Maybe Reece would like some more."

"Sure," said Reece. He looked at Kristin's plate, which was still half full. "Kristin?"

"I'm good." She blew out a long breath. Would they get married? Maybe he would marry Robyn and her floppy boobs. "Reece, what are we gonna do?"

Reece waited for someone to say something. Maybe it was a rhetorical question. Nothing, just chewing and forks hitting the plates with little tings. "Hey, what if I help with the dishes?"

"You can't do that," said Gert. "Plus, it's my kitchen. Kristin can help."

"No, really, if I sit on a barstool."

"Reece," said Kristin. He was changing the subject. "I mean it. What are we going to do? Are you going to just stay in my bedroom forever? Are you going back to your grandparents? Are we..." The we was quite long.

Edwin glanced at Gert, and she glanced at him.

"Don't you want me in your bedroom forever?" asked Reece.

"She needs her own bedroom," said Edwin.

"Until she's married," said Gert.

"Geez, let me decide. It's my bedroom," said Kristin.

"It's my house," said Edwin.

Reece swallowed the last of his Rice-A-Roni and wiped his mouth with the cloth napkin. "That was delicious. Do I smell pie?"

Gert looked startled. "I'm chilling a chocolate pie with pudding mix. It's in the fridge. Probably still runny."

"I guess I smelled it in the fridge—superpowers from

being shot in the head."

"Reece, you're driving me crazy!" Her period had just started, and she felt ugly, like she didn't have any friends.

"I think pie will do us all some good." Reece smiled at Kristin, and she pouted back at him. "You're still my little snickerdoodle, though. Right?" A pain shot through his head and out through his left eye. He winced and held his breath for a second.

"You, okay?"

Reece wasn't sure who had spoken. "Yeah, just a stabbing pain in my head. I should be fine, soon."

Kristin watched Gert bring the chocolate pie. There was no meringue or whipped cream, just the pudding in a shell. She felt something under the table, Reece's foot against her leg. She pushed it away.

"Stop it," she said.

"I'm sorry." He felt that he should blurt out that he loved her, but couldn't do it. Was it because he didn't love her? He wasn't sure. Had being shot changed his life? Had Ethiopia changed his life? Had Emma changed his life? And the general answer was undeniably yes...or maybe. "You're cute when you're angry." He waited for the pie, coming to him in a bowl with a spoon. "Oh yeah, pie in a bowl, pie in a bowl. Can't wait to eat my pie in a bowl."

"It's Emma, isn't it?" she said.

Oh Lord, here we go. Reece took a bite of pie.

The pasta with the plain tomato paste and some salt passed as okay, but Emma still felt a rush of energy and well-being. Everything would be fine. It was just dark enough that she couldn't read, but with enough light that a candle would be weak. She walked a circle around her tiny room. She touched the plastic covering the walls of poles and mud. Her head felt light, but a chasm deep within held a heavy lead weight. She imagined she was so tired that she wouldn't be able to sleep. When that happened, the next day was a nightmare of nodding off, eyes straining to focus. She thought about the can of generic Valium in the clinic. It said five thousand tablets on the label. Why didn't she keep a few in the house for such an occasion?

She had not kept up with her prayer list or devotional since Reece had been shot. She decided she would catch up, but first she warmed a pan of water on the stove and washed her face, neck, and chest. The rag felt good on her skin. The water dried quickly, giving her a chill. She wanted to look in a mirror to see if her breasts were even. She always imagined that one hung differently than the other, depending on how she held her shoulders.

Standing near her bed, she massaged her breast and pinched her nipple, eyes closed. She felt dizzy and imagined Reece on the bed. She would just lie down beside him and let his hands go where they may. She sighed and then remembered the prayer list, which included fifty or so souls. But first, she lit the candle on the table, sat on her bed, and took up the devotional. The entries were dated by month and day, but she randomly chose. "I am accountable to God for the way I control my body under His authority," she read aloud. She remembered that she wasn't wearing a bra or shirt and put down the book.

The words made her feel extra weary, as if she would fall. "God help me." She laid back on the cot, her eyes closing. She needed to go over her prayer list. *Misrak.* She decided to pray for Misrak, and then for Abebe, and then for Mariam, the young woman who could have HIV. She prayed for the women at the shelter and the man there with malaria. She prayed that the old guard at the shelter would give teff to the women so that they could grind it and make enjera. In the distance, she imagined the *pop pop pop* of the gas-powered mill and fell into a fitful sleep, the candle's flame standing straight and tall. She dreamed of purple birds with a third vestigial wing and long claws.

It was one hour before the sun peeked through the mist. Afewerki's younger brothers lounged on the homemade bed. Each had one of the blankets brought by Barra for their mother. Usually, Abebe woke them to eat and sent them along their way with the goats. She also woke their father, who slept outside beneath the roof overhang with the Preduzece rifle. The oldest child, Tefari, slipped off the bed and found his mother lying on the floor, curled beneath a blanket. He whispered, and she did not stir. He looked back toward the bed and whispered again. Perhaps his father was outside, and he opened the door. He checked, but no one was there. In this case, his father would be at his uncle's house playing checkers, or so his mother had told him. Back inside, he whispered once again to his mother. "Enat?" Nothing.

Tefari went to the bed to wake his brother, nicknamed Ras. Ras tightened his hold on the blanket and shook his head.

"Ras!" He shook his brother.

"Abet?" He kept his eyes closed, hoping to sleep a few more minutes.

"Mother is ill. She is sleeping."

"Then it is not time to wake up."

"No, it is time. Listen."

A rooster crowed from the next compound.

"Ai yi," said Ras. "She is sick. The ferenj gave her medicine."

"Get up!" Tefari went back to his mother on the floor. What should he do? He squatted and touched her. She didn't move. "Enat? Enat?" He stood, dizzy. What to do? *Afewerki!* and he went into the compound past the twitching oxen to Afewerki's square house with the tin roof. He tapped on the door.

Afewerki was still wearing his jeans and sweater from the previous day. Was his mother up and about? What time was it?

Tefari spoke through the door. "Mother is sick. She is sleeping."

Afewerki rubbed his eyes and threw his feet to the cold dirt floor. Usually, Abebe was the first to wake, but she was passing kidney stones. She needed to rest. "Let her sleep!"

"Please come," said Tefari. Tears wet his eyes, and he needed to pee.

The hen over Afewerki's bed stirred, clucking. He went to the door and opened it. "Did you try to wake her?

Where is father?"

"Yes. Father is at uncle's."

"I see," said Afewerki. He knew what being at Uncle's meant. "Let us check." He donned his ballcap and followed Tefari inside the large hut. The roof was steeply pitched, very tall, one of the better huts in the village. His mother was on the floor. Right away, he felt it. He stood over her and called her name. "Abebe?" he whispered. He stooped and touched her face, which was cold. He panicked and stood, seeing Ras in bed with the blanket over his head. The fire had been out for two days. A fly buzzed. The roosters were crowing.

Emma slept poorly, tossing back and forth. She'd had to pee twice with the flashlight. She heard roosters crowing and knew that daylight would be soon. She slammed the side of her fist against the wall, sending down a shower of dust.

"Dammit!"

She took a deep breath. The day ahead seemed to run past her and pile on the floor like film flying from a spinning reel. She craved a bagel with cream cheese. God, she wanted one, two. Her eyes felt like pool balls, eight balls. She wanted to scream. Would anyone ever understand if she tried to explain? Outside, Irigit whistled.

Emma put the pillow over her face. Maybe she could suffocate herself. Within seconds, her head felt like a furnace. "Dammit!" It was a clinic day. No rest. She vowed to pocket some Valium for the coming night. She would sleep if it killed her. A thought struck her. Terry had brought her letters. Where were the letters? Maybe there was news about Reece. That gave her some hope for the day, for the moment."

She sat up and saw the open notebook, her prayer list. Another failure. But people were praying for her. Her church back in Alabama. Her mother. She imagined their expectations as unreasonable. How did they know what she was going through? What good would their uninformed prayers do anyway? Misrak, Abebe, Mariam, the man with malaria, the women at the shelter, the patients already making a line at the clinic. She wondered what it would feel like to shoot herself in the head. It would be quick and maybe no pain at all? Perhaps she would slap the Hyena after all and let him shoot her. *Death by Hyena.* A wave of nausea, and she hung her head.

A shot of cold air ran down Afewerki's spine. He kneeled beside his mother and pulled back the blanket. He pushed on her shoulder. He touched her face again, and it was ice cold. What could he do? He leaned back. He looked up at Tefari and over to the bed where Ras was peering at him from beneath the blanket, the colorful handmade blankets from the Mennonites in Canada. He could smell his body odor. His hands felt dry. He pulled the blanket back over her and stood.

"What is it?" asked Tefari. "She is sick?"

"You must go outside. Ras!" said Afewerki. "You must come outside."

"She is sick." Tefari huddled beneath his blanket and went to help Ras from the bed. "Come." And together they went out into the dull morning light.

He should go and tell Emma. She would know what to

do. He stumbled into the yard, dizzy. He realized he wasn't wearing shoes and went for them.

At the gate to the compound, he knocked. "Open!"

Irigit, smiling, opened the gate. His smile faded.

Afewerki looked to see if the others were up, but their doors were closed. Emma's house was a white rectangle. The door was made of corrugated tin. He knocked.

Emma was sitting in a chair. Someone was knocking. She looked at her hands and feet. At the door, she paused. The knock came again. "Yes."

"Emma, please open. It is Afewerki."

Emma unlatched the hasp and opened the door. Afewerki looked small and frightened. "What is it? Come in."

Afewerki stepped up. His ancient leather shoes were untied. He gazed around the tiny house. His eyes rested on the two small holes in the plastic over the stove.

"Afewerki, what is it?"

"It is Abebe, mother. She has died." He looked at Emma. What had he just said?

"No," said Emma. "Died? How? We must go and check on her. Come on, let's go." She jammed her feet into her hiking boots and tripped. "Damn!"

Afewerki followed her on an invisible leash. He stumbled over a stone. She was running. He was running. A small herd of goats blocked the path. Emma pushed through them, yelling.

She rushed into the hut and kneeled beside Abebe. She felt her forehead. She palpated her carotid artery, and the *thud thud* was very slow but there. Emma felt like an ice cube in a cup of hot coffee. "She's alive."

Afewerki had to squat. "What is it? What has happened?" He felt dizzy, a little bit crazy.

Emma shook Abebe, patted her cheeks, called her name. "Did she take the pain meds last night?"

"I did not give to her," said Afewerki.

"Ask your brothers." She continued to shake Abebe, and there was some movement.

Afewerki returned. "Yes, Tefari has given to her many pills last night. He gave them all."

"Oh, hell. She's overdosed on the codeine. That's my fault for leaving the pills like that. But she's breathing. Let's get her on the bed and off this cold floor."

"Ishi," said Afewerki.

Together they lifted Abebe and carried her to the bed, covering her with the blankets. She stirred slightly and made a strange noise.

"She's so cold. Is there another blanket?"

"Yes, I will bring," and Afewerki ran to his little house.

"Abebe, Abebe," said Emma. "Flower, flower..."

"Oh, I wish I was an Oscar Meyer wiener!" sang Reece.

"Stop it!" said Kristin.

"I'm a complete idiot," said Reece.

"No, you're not an idiot." Kristin growled.

Edwin and Gert frowned. Edwin poked at a grain of rice on his plate. Reece needed to get his horizontal in line with his vertical. He imagined the cross.

"Love is not a game." Gert couldn't believe what she'd said and recoiled as if placing her hand in a bowl of warm water.

"Well, what the H does that mean?" asked Kristin, elbows on the table, her fingers laced.

"Kristin. That's no way to speak to your mother," said Edwin. "But, she's right."

Reece ate a bite of pudding pie from his bowl. He ate another bite and another. He was starved. What was Gert trying to say? He cut his eyes at Kristin, who was looking at the brass light fixture hanging over the small table.

"Maybe Mr. Reece here should declare his intentions," said Kristin. "Instead of beating around the bush and singing like a wiener." She looked at her left hand, the engagement ring there. It was not that impressive, just a small diamond.

"Good Lord." Reece felt his intestines clamping, his stomach gurgling. He fumbled for words. "What would you have me do? I'm just lucky to be here. A piece of lead went through my head. A tornado nearly sucked me out of bed." He paused. "My mother's hair is red...Here, I am, not dead."

"What is this, a game?" asked Kristin.

"No."

"Gotta go." Robyn stood in the den. "Gonna meet Ryan at the Sizzler."

"Mmm, steak and church," said Reece. "Tell Ryan I said *moo.*"

"Reece, you don't even know Ryan," said Kristin.

"I met him in Ethiopia, on a bus. He was wearing a little black hat and had a hand grenade pinned to his sweater."

"What?" asked Robyn. "You're a barrel of monkeys." She held her Bible and her purse.

"Just kidding," said Reece. "Did I need to say that?" He looked at Edwin and then Gert, and he had not.

"Goodbye, Robyn," said Kristin. She said it like *Robin* to irritate her.

"Have fun, dear," said Edwin. "Take notes," and he laughed. The pastor at Robyn's church had a doctorate in theology.

"Bye y'all." Robyn was on her way.

"I think she'll do for a sister-in-law," said Reece.

"What?" asked Kristin. "Did I hear that?" She took a sip of tea.

"What about me?" asked Edwin. "Will I make a good father-in-law?" He wanted more Rice-A-Roni, but it was finished. He laced his fingers and put his chin there.

Gert cleared some plates. All eyes fixed on Reece.

Reece pondered his options. "Of course. I'd like to put a trailer in your backyard, though, if you deem that suitable." He realized he was sweating. Why was life so disingenuous? Why was he so uncomfortable? He could just get up and walk out the door, walk to the airport. But how would he buy a ticket? He was flat busted. How much did he owe the hospital? What had the Mission paid for? Had he not been evacuated from Addis Ababa on a jet? Who had paid that bill?

Kristin's brief surge of optimism faded. Her plate was still full of Rice-A-Roni. "Okay, hilarious, Mr. I've-been-shot. Don't you want to write a letter to Emma? Maybe ask her what you should do? She saved your life after all, right?"

Reece sobered. Emma had saved his life, and Afewerki, too. And maybe Isaac and Mariam. And perhaps even Barra. He had a vision of the Hyena, stumbling around with a pistol strapped to his thigh. Nothing was standing between the Hyena and Emma. He could just as well shoot up her house while she was sleeping or, *hell,* just walk into the clinic and blow her away.

"I don't know," said Reece. "She's a tough cookie. She'd just tell me to..."

"To what?" asked Kristin.

Edwin looked alarmed. He shook some salt onto his plate, licked his index finger.

"To hunt down the Hyena...and kick his ass," said Reece.

"That's great," said Kristin. "And to do that, you'll have to go back over there and probably shack up with her." She pushed her plate away and stared at Reece. What did she see in him anyway?

"Anybody want more pie?" asked Gert from the kitchen. "Three more slices left."

Against his better judgment, Reece said, "Sounds good to me." He was still hungry.

"Is that all you've got to say?" Kristin stood, ready to explode through the roof. "You're turning out to be something else."

"Kristin—"

"That's it!" Kristin pushed her chair back and went to the den, crying. She turned to look at the back of Reece, his broad shoulders, the faint bald spot beginning to show. She had willed him to be back home, and there he was, alive and somewhat well. What was her problem?

Reece tried to stand and sank back into the chair. He turned and saw her weeping in the middle of the den, the TV playing. There had been no TV in Godo, no electricity, no running water, no dens, no dining rooms, no Rice-A-Roni, no pudding pie in a bowl. He wondered how Edwin and Gert had met. He'd never heard the story.

He pressed his hands on the table and stood. The chair punched the backs of his knees. He locked them, sending the chair backward. "Kristin." He watched Edwin stand. He saw Gert. The light seemed dingy, orange. He tried to think of a word that rhymed with orange. Forage. Hourage. Dang-er.

Sobbing, Kristin felt her way into the hall and made it to her room.

"I've got this." Reece turned and walked like a yeti. He thought about having diarrhea and stumbling to the shintabet in Godo. God, that had been the worst, but he wished he were there again, squatting over the toilet seat cemented into the ground. It was a place where no one disturbed you. The raucous squeak of the door, and everyone knew what you were up to.

Reece, with his hands against his thighs, walked by

himself. A surge of joy energized his body. There was nothing he couldn't do. He visualized Kristin's bedroom door and took it one step at a time into the hall, down the hall, on the left. He banged the door with his head to keep from falling.

"Hey!" He listened. He remembered the Icelandic medical team and the glass IV bottles they had left. Where were the Icelanders now? He would like to meet them. "Kristin?" Gathering his strength, he tried the doorknob, turned it, and fell headlong into the room, tripping and falling on his face.

"Ha, God is punishing you," said Kristin, holding a box of tissues. She watched him turn over like a turtle.

On his back, he could see Kristin, her mascara running. "I'm sorry. I'm a dunce. What else do you want?"

Kristin took a deep breath. "I...I want to know that you still love me, darn it!" She put her hands on her hips. She wanted to kick him, drag him into the street, and leave him there. Maybe then he would wake up.

"Okay." She had nearly cursed, and he knew it was beyond serious. He clawed at the bedspread, seeking some traction to raise himself. He came to his knees. He felt a burning in his throat. He stood and flopped onto the bed.

"Get off my bed," said Kristin. "You can go back to the basement or, better yet, back to your grandparents."

"The basement smells like cat pee." He knew he was digging a deeper hole. "I'm sorry. Really. What else can I say? I do love you. I do. It will work out—"

"Work out! What does that mean? You mean all three of us will live happily ever after in a hut? That's just ridiculous." She thought about how small her room was with Reece in it.

"For God's sake, you don't understand what it was like over there. It makes me cringe. I suppose I had it easy being a ferenj, but the people, the people. It's hard to explain. Right now, kids are like, dying, from diarrhea, from ghosts in their legs. Emma works there by herself. Not many people could do that and for practically no pay."

"Yeah, just as I thought," said Kristin. She wanted to push him through the window into the driveway.

Reece lay on his side, looking up at her. "Okay, so I have feelings for Emma, but—"

"Reece Myers. Are we engaged or not? Who do you love? Me or her? Say it!"

Reece let his head fall back on the pink comforter. "I love you. We're engaged. That's all there is to it."

Kristin let her arms fall. He looked rather pitiful. His eyes were straining. He'd lost so much weight. His face was more angular, his hair an inch long. He seemed somewhat European, whatever that meant.

Reece let his body relax. He felt like he weighed a ton, but that the storm had passed.

"Just give me a couple of days, and I'll head back to my grandparents' place. I think it's stressing everybody out, me being here. Your parents don't approve. It'll be better that way. I'll be able to drive, maybe in a week. I can feel it. I'm getting better by the minute. Heck, I walked in here from the dining room. What do you think?"

Kristin could feel her heart beating. She suddenly felt drained and sat on the floor with him. "What if we went to counseling?"

"Counseling? A psychiatrist?"

"No, like a Christian counselor. Dad's been egging me

to do it. Maybe it's a good idea, considering." She touched Reece's hair, pushed her hand through it. "Did you wash your hair?" She smiled.

Reece took a deep breath. "What could it hurt, the counselor?"

"Reece. That wasn't the right answer."

"I mean, sure. Let's do it. It can't...I mean, maybe it will be a good thing." He imagined wandering into a cave, coming to a room with a narrow passage. The counselor would get them through. "Do you know someone?"

"Dad gave me the name of a guy. Can I call him?"

"Sure. As long as he's not a shrink. That would be weird. And let me sleep on the floor tonight. Or I'll sleep in the basement. No problem. Beats a mud hut."

"There you go again, thinking about Africa. Maybe I should have gone with you." Kristin wiped at the moisture in her eyes and laughed.

Reece sighed.

So early. So early. The day had already begun, and Emma was exhausted. Afewerki had fetched hot, spiced tea for his mother. She was alive but addled from the codeine. Emma imagined she would need to give her another liter or two of fluid to help her pass the stones. Now, she was on her way to see Misrak.

Emma followed Afewerki, nodding and greeting the villagers. She recognized them all. There was Omar, a farmer, batting at his donkey with a doolah. Afewerki stopped and made small talk. Omar was on his way to the warehouse to fetch a bale of dried cod from Norway. The bales of cod only took up space in the warehouse. No one knew how to cook dried cod, plus it took so much water. Omar planned to use it as firewood for his wife's still.

"We'll need to get Zenebek to come and cook for Misrak." Emma hit the toe of her hiking boot against a stone and stumbled.

"She will be angry," said Afewerki. Afewerki quick-smiled at a young woman who had visited the clinic many times, sometimes for diarrhea, most often for lotion.

"Maybe not angry. They must be friends. They cook and wash clothes together." Past the huts and fences of plants and sticks woven with briars, they walked. The sky oiled into a dull gray with low-hanging clouds. Emma could smell the water in them. Through a small herd of multicolored goats they passed, the goats ear to ear, fat eyes bulging with hope. The path emptied into the open, the old Polish airfield before them growing waist-high grass.

Emma recognized the dingy gate. She noted a thinning of the steep straw roof in places. A hen with three chicks ran inside, clucking, the chicks at their mother's heels like little magnets. No one was in the dirty yard. The rusted remains of half a steel barrel used to make talla sat empty. No smoke escaped through the doorway. Afewerki called out, and a thin girl in a dirty dress and no shoes came to the door, her eyes shy and wide. She was alone with her mother. Her sisters were out to fetch water, and her father was drinking tejj nearby.

Emma walked inside behind Afewerki, getting used to the darkness. She felt the coolness and shivered. The room smelled something like shoe polish mixed with vomit. She tried taking shallow breaths to adjust.

"Ai yi," said Misrak. She lay on the bed in her dress without a blanket or pillow, an empty gourd on the floor.

"Oh, baby." Emma stooped and ran her hand across Misrak's shoulder. "How is she?"

Afewerki asked. "She is very sick. She feels she is dying. She cannot to move this arm." He pointed to her left arm.

"Dang, I can't see in here. We need to get her near the door. Can she stand?"

"She cannot stand, she is saying. She cannot eat. She is vomiting the food."

"Damn, another IV for sure."

"We can carry the bed to there," said Afewerki. "Can you help?"

"Sure, at least we can scoot it. Let's do it."

With one at either end, they carried and pulled the bed across the dirt floor to the opening of light.

"There." Emma got a good look at Misrak's face, with

very dark skin, but ashen. She pulled down her eyelid, and it was white like paste. "I need to see her breast and arm. What's the best way?"

Afewerki mumbled to Misrak. "You must take up the dress. It is like the poncho."

"We'll need something to cover her with."

Afewerki found a grain bag with corncobs in it. He emptied it and laid it on the bed. Emma pulled up the dress to her hips and slid the grain bag over her groin.

"We need to roll her, okay? To get the dress up."

The dress slid up, and Emma did her best to keep her covered. The little girl watched with wide eyes. Emma lifted the dress over the left breast. "God."

Afewerki looked away. The swollen breast looked bruised, purple. Below her armpit, a wound oozed. The nipple seemed to disappear into the diseased flesh.

"How long has she had problems with this?"

"By two months," said Afewerki.

"We've got to get her to Addis. We can't wait for Terry. We need a jeep. How bad is her pain?"

"She is saying very bad."

"No doubt. Let's get an IV kit and some fluids from the clinic. Can she swallow pills?"

"No, she will vomit."

Misrak moaned and heaved. She turned her head and vomited clear liquid through the leather straps of the bed.

Afewerki stepped outside. Emma tried to cradle Misrak's head, pushing her toe into the pool of mucus. "We'll need a hundred milligrams of pethidine IM and maybe some promethazine for vomiting. Afewerki!"

"Yes, Emma." Afewerki held his breath, being sensitive

to unpleasant smells.

"Can you bring back the IV and the meds? I'll stay here with her. I hope she'll be okay. Tell her you're going for some medicine to make her feel better."

Afewerki did so and set off at a quick trot.

With Misrak taken care of and clinic in full swing, Afewerki kept alert for a jeep to take Misrak to AK and on to Addis. Perhaps Terry could fly her there. Emma knew she would need to be her own envoy to ensure that it happened. She packed a small bag with just a few things, ready to go at a moment's notice. The clinic would just have to be closed for a few days. The thought somehow excited her, a break from the routine, but for a worthy cause.

Emma examined a small boy cowering in the folds of his mother's dress. Afewerki would stay and take care of simple things that he could treat, like worms and simple diarrhea. Some of the villagers had taken to calling him doctor.

"She is asking for vitamins only," said Afewerki. "But she will sell them." He yawned. He thought it very unwise for Emma to travel alone.

"The boy is not sick? What am I doing? Why does she need vitamins?" She examined the woman's face, which was long with sagging cheekbones. Her front teeth protruded, and she was skinny. She wore a tiny metal disk on a thick black string around her neck, which showed just a hint of goiter.

"Ah, she is feeling weak. She wants to have the vitamins by injection."

"Oh hell, the murphy." Emma made a face at the little

boy and said, "Boo."

The little boy recoiled, gripping his mother's dress like a cat on a curtain. Emma laughed. The mother laughed and scolded the little boy, pushing his head to look at Emma. Outside, Barra sang a song in English, a song Emma knew from Vacation Bible School. "I'm going to let it shine!"

"Okay, vitamins it is, but no murphy, tell her. Just pills."

Afewerki told her, and her smile faded. She scolded the little boy and stood, ready to be on her way.

"That's it?" asked Emma. "Here, give her some biscuits at least."

Afewerki gave her two packets of famine biscuits, and the woman whispered her thanks, picking up the little boy and swinging him around on her back, seating him on the wide sash around her waist.

A young man stood at the door with news.

"The jeep has come," said Afewerki. "You must hurry."

"Yikes," said Emma. There were at least thirty left in line. "Okay, take care of the rest as you can. I'll be back as soon as possible. Close the clinic if you have to, but send out word. Make sure Misrak's kids get food while she's gone. " She washed her hands with soap and dried them on her jeans paired with a long-sleeve, gray t-shirt. "We'll need two men to carry her down to the jeep. Can the driver pull it up closer?"

"He will charge you," said Afewerki. "But as you wish." He stepped out and called for Barra, who dispatched two daily laborers to fetch Misrak, both used to carrying the heavy grain bags.

"Okay, good. Come with me to the jeep," she said, hoisting her backpack. At the last moment, she grabbed two vials of promethazine, two syringes with needles, and a handful of alcohol swabs, stuffing them into her pockets. She looked around and took a packet of famine biscuits and three packets of oral rehydration solution.

"It will be dangerous," said Afewerki.

"She will die otherwise."

"The jeep will bounce her."

"Brother, let's just go."

"Ishi," said Afewerki, following her through the gate into the wide, narrow lane. A few fat drops of rain began to fall.

Reece awoke, and the drop ceiling was very close. He realized he was back in the basement and sighed. He made up his mind to return to his grandparents' house. It would just be easier on everyone. He looked around for a clock. Kristin was probably already at work. He had to pee like a racehorse. "I can do this," he said to the bundles of yarn and plastic storage boxes in the room.

He pushed himself up and sat there dizzy. He lowered his legs over the side of the bed and let his feet touch the carpet. He was wearing underwear, a pair of Edwin's that hung loose. Gert would be upstairs doing what she did during the day. He knew that he freaked her out and felt bad. Ethiopia was eight hours ahead of Alabama. It was probably after dinner there, getting dark and cold as night fell. He tried to remember the taste of enjera, the spicy dorowot. It all seemed so distant. He was on his feet. He tested the strength in his thighs and decided to walk instead of crawl up the stairs.

Gert stood in the formal living room, biting her nails. She wanted to check on him, but was afraid. She didn't know why. Reece seemed to have come from another world, and he had. He was different than before. He'd only been gone for less than two months, though. He didn't even look American. He looked foreign, especially with his short, scraggly beard.

Reece took a few steps, wavering and pressing his hand to the thin, wood-paneled wall. He felt weak but steady and watched his feet move forward to the base of the stairs.

The cat walked by and looked up at him, not sure. "Hey, kitty." He couldn't remember Wallace's name. He looked up the carpeted stairs and gripped the wood rail, going up one stair at a time, resting after each. His grandparents' house was a single level, no stairs. There was a swing on a patio in the yard. He could sit there and look out across the road at the lake.

Gert walked into the kitchen and could smell the bananas. Time for banana bread, and she took down the baking powder. She would need two eggs, flour, butter, milk, cinnamon, and sugar, too. She knew Reece liked banana bread. It would be something easy to give him for a late breakfast. She reached in for the loaf pan and set it aside for oiling. *The oven.* She turned and set the oven to 350. Things were okay. He'd said something about going back to his grandparents.

Near the top of the stairs, Reece rested, catching his breath. He could hear noise in the kitchen. God, he had to pee, and he staggered to the bathroom, closing the door with a bang so that Gert would know he was up. The last time he peed, he'd had to kneel on the floor, but not this time. It felt good to hear his stream hitting the water. "Simple pleasures," he said to the wall.

Gert heard the door bang shut and assumed the worst. She put down the eggs and peeked into the den. She maneuvered to the hallway and listened to the toilet flush. He was up. Edwin had said to call if there was any trouble. Was he going to take a bath?

Reece needed to rest and put down the toilet seat. There was a *Southern Living* magazine on the back of the commode. He stopped at a piece about growing basil.

He'd never thought of basil as a food, just a spice in spaghetti sauce. He surveyed the vanity countertop, hairspray, toothpaste. He opened the drawer nearest him, and it was filled with mascara, blush, and brushes. Robyn wore more makeup than Kristin. "What am I doing?" He decided to make his move and call his grandparents. Had he agreed with Kristin that was the best thing to do? He couldn't remember. Suddenly, he felt trapped. He'd only met Kristin a few months before leaving for Ethiopia. He'd proposed to her a month before he'd left. Her house was still foreign to him, somebody else's house. Into the hall he went.

He stopped at the opening to the den. The phone looked like a toy on the wall. He felt that he should ask to use it. "Hello!"

Gert flinched. She dropped an eggshell into the wastebasket. She was wearing one of her favorite plaid button-ups, short-sleeved, with a pair of khakis. She adjusted her bra strap. "Hello!"

"Hey," said Reece.

"Hey," said Gert. "You're walking."

"Yeah, but I need to sit down." He wobbled to the worn couch and fell onto it, realizing that he might need help getting up.

Gert wrung her hands. From what she could gather, Reece might no longer be a believer. He had expressed doubts to Kristin. Plus, he was being wishy-washy about the engagement. She waited for him to say something else.

Reece could hear birds singing outside. Walter was probably on the deck sunning. "Can I use the phone?"

"Can you use the phone? I mean, sure. You can use the phone. Do you want me to dial it for you?"

"Yeah, sure. That would be great. It's 681-7314, my grandparents. Gonna see if they can...can maybe come and get me."

Gert fidgeted. "You sure? You're welcome to stay here."

"I'm pretty sure. I think they want me there. I can walk there. No sidewalks here."

"No sidewalk." Gert had never thought about there not being a sidewalk. She drove everywhere. "What was the number?" She pulled the handset off the wall mount, gave it to Reece, and pointed her index finger at the buttons.

"Thanks. It's 681-7314."

Gert pushed the buttons and stared at Reece.

The phone rang. "Hello," said his grandmother, Dora.

Reece looked at Gert looking at him. "Hey there. It's me."

"My goodness, Reece. Is something the matter?"

"No, no, all is well. I'm walking, getting better."

Gert realized she was staring and slipped back into the kitchen, listening to his every word.

Reece explained he wanted to come home, and when could they get him? Dora was all for it and said that she could come right away. Did she need to bring Horace? He was out pulling up the corn. Could he manage getting in the car, and he assured her he could.

Reece held the receiver in his hand, listening to the dial tone. He felt that a great weight had been lifted from his shoulders. He was starved, but Dora would stuff him with food. He tried to stand and fell back.

"Let me get that for you," said Gert. "Are you hungry? I'm making banana bread, but it'll be about an hour. I can make you some toast, maybe some cheese toast?"

"Mmm, that would be super. I can make it."

Gert frowned. "No, no. I'll do it." She couldn't wait to call Edwin and let him know Reece was leaving.

Dora fixed a glass of ice water and walked across the road to the garden. The sun was already hot, and she worried about Horace having a stroke. Smoke swirled from a pile of burning corn stalks. He sat beneath a lone black walnut tree that straddled the neighbor's property, hoe in hand, planted in the high grass like a staff.

"Hey!" She walked slow but steady.

Horace craned his neck. "Hey!" He looked country in his one-piece jumpsuit from J. C. Penney and a straw hat. He pushed his glasses up onto his nose.

"You'll never guess. Reece called. I'm going to bring him home. He's up and walking." She handed him the ice water.

"Walking? That son of a gun. Well, bring him on back. Maybe he'll get up on the roof and sweep off the pine straw."

Dora frowned. "Now don't get any ideas. You know he's been through it. Drink your water and give me the glass." She knew that otherwise she'd never see it again.

Horace gulped the cold water and slung the ice cubes into the grass. "Hits the spot. That's some good news." He started to stand.

"No, you stay here and watch that fire. I'll get him. Our boy's coming home." She felt a few tears pushing behind her eyes.

"Yeah," said Horace. "We shoulda never let him go off like that. But he's stubborn."

Dora waved him off and headed back across the road. She gathered her purse and keys and backed the blue Buick out of the driveway. She thought about how fast Reece had fallen for Kristin, and how she had seemed so clingy when they were dating. Horace said that Edwin was as stiff as a board and Gert as timid as a mouse. She wondered if Kristin knew that Reece was leaving. She felt that Kristin wouldn't let him go without a fight. She turned on the AC, hoping for the best.

In a steady rain, Emma and Afewerki ran downhill to the jeep turnaround. A crowd of ten or so huddled around the jeep, two with umbrellas, others with grain bags over their heads. Afewerki surged ahead. He'd had a daily laborer wait there, holding a place in line. He knew that the driver was waiting for the highest fares to rise to the top. The game was in his favor, especially with the rain and the ferenj needing a ride. Afewerki opened the door and told him that a sick woman was coming and that Emma would pay her way and that she would pay extra for him to drive into the village as far as he could go to pick her up.

The driver looked annoyed and argued with Afewerki about the price. The other riders would be angry, he said, and he would need one hundred birr for his trouble. Afewerki said no problem and ordered Emma into the passenger side. He fought his way through the small crowd and opened the door to much protest. He yelled and said the ferenj would need the back seat and that a very sick woman, Misrak, would sit with her. Normally, four people could sit in the back seat with two more behind and two in the front seat.

Emma pushed through and clambered in. Afewerki yelled at the others to wait until the jeep fetched Misrak, but no one listened, and they fought their way inside. The driver sat sullen and disinterested. With the doors closed and Emma now sharing the back seat with a lanky farmer, the driver shouted for everyone to give him the money.

"Sentino?" shouted Emma. The rain pounded the roof.

"Mato birr," said the driver.

Emma peeled off five wet twenties and handed them to him. The others paid twenty. Outside, five more still hoping for a ride, standing in the rain, arguing with Afewerki, who looked miserable. He shouted at them and motioned for the driver to move uphill.

The driver cranked the jeep and jerked around in a circle. His windshield wipers did not work, and he drove by looking at the edge of the lane to his left. Already, the road was mud and rocks. He put it into low and ground up the steep hill to the clinic and warehouse. Water rushed in muddy streams down the hill, which was even steeper and narrower at the top. He wiped at the fogging windshield with a dirty rag.

Misrak was expecting Afewerki and Emma, but not the two farmers who worked for the Mission. Her teeth chattered, and she moaned in protest as they pleaded with her. Barra had sent them, they said. Her three children cowered in the corner.

"We must do this," said the taller one named Alem. "The ferenj has ordered it."

"It is to cure your sickness," said the shorter one. He was Nigas. "We are strong and will not drop you."

Misrak pleaded in a high voice. She was still groggy from the pain medicine and had urinated in bed. She was embarrassed and confused. "No, no, no..."

The two men consorted and decided to take her by force. Alem moved behind to grasp her shoulders. Nigas took her legs. He smelled urine and made a sour face. "And, hulet, sost," and they lifted her from the bed. She began to cry and could only go limp.

"My arm!" said Misrak. Alem's hands pressed beneath her armpits.

She sagged between them, her butt on the floor. What to do? Alem puffed. She was slipping from his grasp, and they let her down to the dirt floor. Negas suggested they carry her on their shoulders like a sack of grain. They could take turns. "Ishi," said Alem. "You go first. I will lift her, and you go beneath."

Negas moved in as Misrak went vertical. He nor Alem had any idea of what her problem was. Negas took her arm and stood, his shoulder plowing into Misrak's tender breast. She screamed.

"Ai yi," said Negas, and he spun to exit.

"Come!" said Alem as they stepped into the downpour. Misrak had passed out from the pressure against her diseased breast. The rain beat down on her limp form, as Negas navigated the mud and rocks in his tire sandals. He huffed, and his muscular calves strained with his load. Onto a narrow footpath they went, headed for the village center.

The jeep whined uphill in four-wheel drive, the lowest gear. Emma could walk faster than they climbed. The windows fogged, and the smell of wet men filled the jeep. She would lean against the jeep's interior and cradle Misrak. If the ride didn't kill her, there would be help in Addis. Her mind wandered back to Alabama, to playing with her sisters. One of her older sisters had had a lumpectomy, and everyone had been scared about the outcome. There was just nothing she could do for cancer in Godo.

The driver veered left, the sides of the jeep scraping the fences on either side. He could only go as far as the administrative compound. Beyond the village center, there were no other roads. The jeep heaved and hawed, passed Afewerki's family compound, and entered a wide muddy clearing. The driver ordered his front, outermost passenger to see what he could see. The door opened, and he jumped out, cowering in the cold and wet. He scanned the flooded market area and crammed his way back inside the jeep.

"Yellum," he said.

The driver frowned. He needed to be on his way. He was wasting fuel. He pulled around, ready to head back if the sick woman did not appear soon.

"No, no, bucka!" Emma feared he was leaving.

The driver spouted a string of curse words and groaned the jeep to a stop.

Negas humped Misrak from his shoulder to that of Alem. Sweat and rain mixed on his face. They were almost there. He feared that maybe Misrak was dead. She was not making any noise.

Alem strained under his load and moved forward with long strides. He thought about how strange his life was since the ferenji had come to Godo. His wife was very proud that he was working with the Mission, and he could buy sugar cane for his children as a treat. He loped along with the load of Misrak.

The jeep driver, as a last resort, blew his horn. The jeep was over thirty years old, but had a new horn. He didn't like to use it very often, trying to preserve its essence. There was a pounding on the hood. He opened his door, and there they were, the woman on the farmer's shoulder. He was smiling.

"Inside!" the driver shouted. He pushed his seat forward, wincing in the cold rain.

Horrified, Emma watched as Alem dumped Misrak into the back seat on top of her. Misrak was out cold, her jaw trembling. She smelled of smoke and urine. The farmer beside her pressed himself to the side of the jeep to give her room. "Help me! Dammit!"

The man reached and pulled Misrak's legs into the cramped backseat space. Emma pushed her upright, cradling her in her arms. Misrak moaned a deep moan like the wail of a wolf. The seat came crashing back against her as the driver piled into his seat, cursing. This was more than he had bargained for.

"Haya birr," said the driver. He looked back at Emma. Emma didn't hear him.

"Doctor, haya birr." He thought she was a doctor.

"What?" asked Emma. She couldn't believe he wanted more money. "Well, hell." She shoved her hand in her pocket, retrieved the soaked wad of birr, and shoved two tens his way. "Bucka! Andiamo!"

The driver took the money and laughed. The ferenj was speaking his language and Italian too. He revved the engine, spun the wheels, and began the slow crawl to Alem Ketema, twenty-six miles away.

Misrak opened her eyes, felt a great pain in her chest, and faded once again.

Dora pulled into the driveway, left the keys in the ignition, and pushed the heavy door open. It didn't take Gert long to answer the door, as if she had been standing there.

"Hey. Long time no see," said Gert. She laughed a little laugh.

From the dining room, Reece heard Dora's voice. "Hey, Granny!" He took half a piece of cheese toast and crammed it into his mouth.

"So, he's walking? Is he telling the truth?" Dora wore jeans from Sears and a lavender t-shirt with a gold chain necklace. Her hair was combed and not yet fixed for church, which she would do on Saturday.

"He's walking slow." Gert stood with Dora in the tiny foyer between floors.

Dora slipped past her, eager to see Reece. "Where are you, boy?"

"In here!" Reece stood to greet her, wearing his hospital gown, but with underwear.

"Well, I declare," said Dora. "Look at you." She gave him a side hug. "Have you had lunch? You sure are skinny, boy."

"Had breakfast, cheese toast. Watch me walk." He walked into the living room, staying close to the wall.

"My, my," said Dora. "You know we've been praying for you."

"Can I get you something to eat?" asked Gert.

Dora looked alarmed. "I left a rice pudding in the oven. We've got to get back and quick. Reece, come on. You got any clothes here?"

"No, just this. No stuff, just the bare bones of life." He laughed.

"We were going to come and get some of his clothes. Kristin was." Gert frowned just a little.

"It doesn't matter," said Reece. "I'll call Kristin when she gets home." He stood there a few seconds, wondering if he should hug Gert. "I appreciate everything you've done. Really."

"That's what we're here for," said Gert. "Kristin's going to be surprised."

"Yeah, I figure, but I've...well, you know..."

Gert willed the phone to ring. She put one hand in her pocket. "Well, goodbye."

"He'll be back. He'll be driving soon," said Dora.

"I can drive now," said Reece.

"Oh no. I'm not doing that." Dora laughed. "Come on. Don't just stand there and waste your strength."

"Yeah," said Reece, and he kind of staggered to the stairs.

Once in the car, Reece sighed. He had one thing on his mind: a filet of fish sandwich and French fries. The Buick seemed to swallow him. The seat was soft and long. "Can we stop by Mac-Donalds?"

"No, boy, that rice pudding'll burn the house down. I'll cook you up something better than Mac-Donalds. I'm gonna make you some salmon patties and green beans."

Reece watched the scenery go by. "Mmm." Everything he saw seemed to be a kind of miracle: the pine trees, the houses, the street signs, the traffic. He thought about the crazy little blue Fiat taxis in Addis Ababa and the giant Marxist billboard in Revolution Square. "Workers of the world unite," he said to himself. And then there was Emma. Her family lived south of Birmingham, not over forty-five minutes away. Maybe he would go and see her mother and eat some of the famous barbecue.

"What are you mumbling about, son?" She powered up the window and punched on the AC.

"Just thinking." He turned his head as they passed a tiny white house. A little boy was holding a beer can and standing inside a bucket in the driveway. A string of homes destroyed by the tornado. He anticipated the turn at the gas station in Clay and kept his eyes open for the rooster farm where Dora veered right to head out to the lake. They had bought the house after Horace retired from ACIPCO, a pipe factory in Birmingham. Horace had added a large living room and boxed in the small front porch as a bedroom for Reece after his parents were killed. That had been six years ago.

"And there he is, staked out beside the garden," said Reece. Wisps of smoke curled from the burn pile in the middle of the garden. "Have you already put up the corn?"

"Lord, we have another batch to go. You know how he is about his corn."

"Still have tomatoes?"

"Lord, yes. We give 'em away."

Dora pulled the Buick into the driveway. Reece thought back to the dark morning he had been whisked away by Kristin to the airport, leaving them standing there looking lost.

"It's good to be home." Reece took in the detached garage, painted with redwood stain to match the house.

He knew how the garage door sounded when lowered, a steady screech. The old Citation was inside, the car he drove before Ethiopia. He could see the white deep freezer, where the corn would go, and the okra and the green beans. The RV sat in the pine straw off to his right. A four-cylinder Toyota engine powered it and could barely make the hills in the Smoky Mountains. He knew there was an 8-track tape of John Denver. *Grandma's Feather Bed.* Sunshine on my shoulders *(gives me sunburn)*. He felt tears and fought them.

Reece popped the lock and swung out his legs.

"You need help?" asked Dora.

"Heck no." He grabbed the roof and pulled. He smelled the lake and the pine straw. He listened and heard the slight breeze in the tall pines. The sky shimmered a brilliant blue with clouds that he recognized. He decided to walk down to the garden, taking deep breaths.

Dora watched him. "The pudding!"

Reece arched his back and staggered backward. "Whoa." He could see Horace coming across the road, straw hat on. He was in one of his jumper suits with short sleeves. Reece examined the step down from the cement driveway to the grass littered with pine straw. He took a deep breath and did it without falling, but then he kind of went into a walk and then a run. He ran headlong into a pine tree, hitting it with his upper body, and thumped backward onto his butt.

"Hey, boy!" Horace quickened his walk and reached Reece, sitting on the ground. "You sure you should be up like that?"

Reece held out a hand, and Horace grabbed it, pulling hard. Reece went to his knees. "I got it. Just pull some more." He stood, feeling like he was squatting a thousand pounds.

"Go and sit, son. Take it easy." He led Reece to the swing beside the marble patio, leftovers from a construction job.

"Whoo," said Reece. He fell onto the metal bench swing. "Thanks."

Horace pulled up a folding chair. "You gotta take it slow now."

"I know. But I'm feeling stronger by the minute."

Horace gazed at Reece. He'd almost given up hope of ever seeing him alive again. Tragedy just seemed to nip at his heels. He wondered about Kristin. He thought he understood love. He'd first laid eyes on Dora when she was twelve and he was twenty-two. "Kristin know you're here? I guess she does."

"Nope."

"You shoulda told her, probably." Horace scratched his knee.

"How did you bloody your arm?"

"Dang tomato basket. My skin's getting thin, bleeds easy. Is she at work?"

Reece nodded. He pushed the swing with his feet. "We talked about it."

"Talking and doing are two different things."

The screen door banged shut, and Dora walked up. "Pudding's a little brown on top. How about our boy here?"

"Looking swell," said Horace. "Lucky boy, that's for sure." He wanted to ask Reece if he had headaches from the bullet passing through.

"Did you put raisins in it?" asked Reece. He loved rice

pudding, but not the raisins.

"Well dang," said Dora. "I didn't know you were coming. You can pick 'em out."

"You get headaches? From that bullet?"

Reece laughed. Edwin had asked him the same thing. "No, just dizzy when I stand up. I feel like I can see better, like everything is really clear, like a clean glass of water."

"You want to talk about it? The accident and all?" Horace folded his hands on his lap. No one knew the whole story.

"I don't really remember getting shot. I was in Emma's house, the nurse there. The town administrator, we called him the Hyena, shot through the wall. He couldn't see me, so he got lucky."

"Maybe he was aiming for the other lady," said Horace.

"He had to be drunk. Maybe he wanted us both dead. He had a gold front tooth, a real bastard." Reece's mind wandered. He didn't want to talk about it.

"What happened to Emma, the nurse? Surely, she didn't stay there," said Dora. She sat in the swing beside him.

"Yep, she stayed, as far as I know. I need to write her a letter. There are no phones in the village."

"You've got to be kidding," said Horace. "Is she loco?"

Reece smiled. "Nope, just a machine. She's something else, not afraid of anything as far as I could tell."

"Was she pretty?" asked Dora.

Reece thought about her dirty blonde hair, her hips, and her breasts. She had that lopsided smile that killed him. "Yeah, she's pretty."

"Was she a white girl or a black girl?" asked Horace. He twiddled his thumbs.

"She was jet black and she's gonna have my baby." Reece looked over Horace's shoulder at the twinkling green lake.

"Aw, go on." Horace laughed, but he wanted to know. Where he came from, you were either white or black, and it mattered, or at least it used to back in the old days.

"We were the only two white folks in the village, unless Terry or Dr. Guthrie flew in. Dang, I'm super hungry."

"Goodness. I forgot," said Dora. "You want me to bring you some pudding?"

"Let me come inside. I need to see the inside, sit at the table in my chair." He'd been dreaming about his place at the table and what he would eat there: cabbage, collard greens, country-fried steak, biscuits, eggs. He found his footing and stood up slow. "My back hurts from lying in bed so long."

Horace stood, ready to catch him. "I say you should of worked it out with Kristin first. She can be a hothead."

"His mother was a hothead," said Dora.

Reece winced and nodded, heading for the back door.

By the time the jeep had pounded its way from Godo to AK, Misrak looked like a corpse. She had vomited twice, entered a delirium, and stopped breathing for a full minute. Emma was thoroughly jolted and exhausted, and decided they would need to rest right away, even if Terry could fly her to Addis that day. She didn't even know if he was in AK. The driver pulled into the town center, the rain coming down in torrents.

"Baptist Mission," said Emma to the driver. It was half a mile down the road near the edge of the cliff.

The driver scowled and pulled around the stone circle. His jeep stank of urine and vomit. Ferenji were too much trouble, but they were rich. "Ishi," he said. He pushed his luck and slowed. "Amist birr?" He wanted another five birr.

Emma came out of her seat. "No! Yellum! Bucka! This woman is going to die, dammit. Andiamo!" She thought about choking him.

"Okay, okay!" His eyes were wide, and he was shaking his head, trying to follow the washed-out road in the rain. "Tsk, tsk, tsk," and he took a deep breath. He thought about the girl he would sleep with that night at the hotel, but he was not feeling particularly well. The previous night, he had soaked his bed with sweat.

Emma watched through the side window to make sure he was taking them to the Mission compound. They passed a wide rocky field where the men and boys played soccer with makeshift balls. And then they were there, outside the gate. The driver beeped his horn three times, calculating how many horn blasts he might have left. Everything was subject to break and cost money to fix. Within a minute, a bedraggled guard swung the gate in and motioned them inside. Where was the helicopter? Emma cursed. Terry wasn't there, but his wife Lisa would be and the two Ethiopians on staff, Alene and Daniachew. Maybe there would be food.

Emma waited to see if anyone would come out to help her. She told the driver to blow the horn again and made a pushing motion with her hand. He looked at her as if she were crazy. Emma leaned over him and pressed the button screwed into the dashboard. The horn blared, and the driver jerked her hand away.

Lisa thought she'd heard a horn, but then she heard the long blast. It could be anything. She wasn't sure if Alene and Daniachew were still around, and she donned her Helimission slicker, slid into her unlaced hiking boots, and opened the door to her two-room "house" built into the side of the grain warehouse. There was a jeep, and she stepped along a raised stone path, shielding her face from the rain. The door opened. She hoped it wasn't a woman giving birth. That had happened before.

Emma yelled at the driver to help her, but he sat sullen, watching the other ferenj approach. Emma stepped into the downpour and yelled. "Lisa! I need help!"

Lisa ran. "What is it?" She peered into the mud-covered jeep and saw a woman sprawled in the backseat. "Okay, let's get her to the guesthouse!"

Thankful, Emma wiped a tear from her wet face. "Can you get her legs? I'll get the other end. We can do it!"

Misrak moaned. Emma had given her an injection of promethazine during the journey, and she was groggy. Together, they extricated Misrak from the jeep and nearly dropped her in the mud. "Fuck!" said Emma.

With Misrak's butt hitting the path, Emma and Lisa struggled toward the tin-sheeted guesthouse. The rain on Misrak's face woke her, and she sputtered, yelling at the pain in her arm and breast. They half-dragged her to the door, but it was padlocked. "Shit!" said Lisa. She lowered Misrak onto the soaked ground and, without speaking, ran to get the key. Grasping Misrak beneath her arms, Emma looked up into the sky. She glanced down at Misrak's pained face. Would she make it? Could anyone ever endure such hardship? She wanted to scream, and she did.

Lisa returned and fumbled with the lock, throwing it to the ground. Once inside, they dragged Misrak onto a narrow bed made of rough boards with a thin mattress and a thick layer of Mennonite blankets. Misrak moaned, breathing in gulps.

"You're okay, you're okay," said Emma. "Let's get the dress off and get her under some covers. She needs a bath."

They undressed her and made her as comfortable as possible, propping her head with a thin pillow. The rain drilled the roof, making it hard to hear. Emma took a deep breath and sat on the other bed. She put her face into her hands, wanting to cry.

Lisa came to her side. "Gosh, are you okay? You look awful. And what's wrong with her? She looks terrible. What's wrong with her breast?"

"Cancer. She's one of the cooks, Misrak. I've got to get her to Addis. Where's Terry?" She was whispering.

"What?"

"Where's Terry?"

"He flew to Rabel this morning. Probably waiting out the rain, I'm sure. Yeah, we'll get her to Addis. Don't you worry about that." Lisa's Canadian accent soothed Emma.

"Yeah, good. She needs to eat and drink, but she's vomiting. I'll need to get some supplies and give her some IV fluid. Some pain meds, too. I'm surprised she made the jeep ride. It was absolutely horrible." Thinking about it nauseated her. She thought about her bedroom back in Alabama, the tiny chest of drawers that had been a hand-me-down, the framed photos there of her sisters and mother.

"Baby, you need some hot tea and cookies. I made them this morning, oatmeal. Do you need something else, dry clothes?"

"Yeah, that would be great." Emma shivered, and she watched her breath coalesce into fog. She looked over at Misrak, seeming dead beneath the blankets.

"You stay here."

Emma watched Lisa leave, feeling overwhelmed with gratitude. God had brought them all together on this hellacious day, but for what, she wasn't sure. She stood, shaking, and checked Misrak's carotid pulse, only fifty-two and not very strong. "Misrak?" She placed her hand on her forehead, and it was cold. Misrak moaned in reply, whispering the names of her children.

Emma looked around the small room, just two beds and a small table made from particleboard, left over from the pallets used in grain drops early in the famine. Nothing had gone to waste. The floor was cement. The walls, corrugated tin. There was no window, but one of the roof panels was translucent, letting in clouded light. She said a brief prayer for Misrak and decided to join Lisa.

Back into the rain she went, and she didn't bother to knock. Lisa stood at the propane stove, boiling water for tea. The room looked tidy and warm with colorful wall hangings of woven straw and cloth. There was even a faded rug, and she stepped onto it, feeling transported.

"Here." Lisa put the cookies onto the small dining table, also made from particleboard and covered with a plaid tablecloth.

Emma took one and held it like a stone. "Thanks."

"I've got some clothes over here."

A rope line strung with jeans and shirts on hangers drooped across the bed.

"Let me get you a sweater, though." She opened a cheap trunk with brass hinges. "How about this? Famine fashion."

Emma laughed. Embroidered into the thick material was "Happi 1984!" "Not good with spelling, huh?"

"Nope, but it's like wearing a heater."

Shivering, Emma stripped down buck naked. "Got any panties?"

Lisa looked at Emma and laughed. She fumbled in a box and handed her a pair. "Got hearts on it. And take those jeans on the end. They should fit."

"We're about the same size, except you're better looking. You always look good." She slipped into the jeans and donned the sweater, which smelled like hay.

"Stop," said Lisa. "You look a little better. Eat a cookie."

"Oh yeah," and she found the cookie on the table. She

ate one and then three. "Scrumptious."

"Sit down. I'll get the tea ready." She thought about how Emma had tried to jump out of the helicopter. How Reece had been shot. She hadn't had a chance to get to know him. There were rumors, but she wasn't sure if they were true.

"I'll need to get back with Misrak, then get some supplies from the warehouse."

"Okay, let's just take the tea there, and then you can dig around the warehouse. I'll stay with her. Gosh, she looks really out of it."

"She's one sick lady, cancer or no cancer." She slid her cold feet into her wet tennis shoes. "I'll see you there."

Lisa watched her go, hunched against the rain as she opened the door. What if Reece hadn't been shot? What if he came back? Maybe there was something between them. That would be so cool, a wedding in AK or maybe in Godo. She waited for the water to boil. It always took longer than she was used to with the altitude.

Emma ran and pulled the door open to Misrak's room. Right away, something was not right.

Where there had been screams and the loud pop of gun-fire, now there was shouting and hustle. Reece kept his position, eyes closed, ready to feel a hot bullet slam into his skull. He smelled fireworks and warm food. He opened his eyes, and his hand was on a plate in some mashed potatoes and brown gravy. He tried to decipher the noise, and knew that he was a coward, and that he had failed in the moment. He could feel wind, as if lying beside a highway with diesel trucks flying by. He counted to fifty. No more loud pops. He would have to lift his head and look.

He hit his head on the underside of the round table. Still, his eyes were closed. He heard weeping and wailing, more shouts as if the room were filling with humanity. First, he saw his father, sprawled, and then beneath him his mother balled into a knot. He touched his dad's leg and then shook it. He wanted to look around the dining room, but couldn't, his eyes glued to his parents. There was blood.

"Dad," he said. He crawled. "Dad? Mom?"

He could see the bloody hole and maybe brains and retched. On hands and knees, he dry heaved. He had barely touched his plate. He went back to a crouch and began to cry, an uncontrollable sob. He looked around, and others were on hands and knees. He saw a policeman with a shotgun. He saw the Ford Ranger with a pile of tables and chairs in front. There was broccoli on the windshield. Still, he sobbed. What had happened?

Reece put his hands to his knees and stood, shaking so

hard he could barely breathe. His eyes ached. His heart wanted to leap from his chest, and he cut his weeping with a switch. The place was a wreck, glass everywhere. Someone was asking him a question, a man he didn't know. He was obese and wearing a red necktie. Blood soaked his white shirt. Reece couldn't hear him. He had to get out and looked around for the door. For a full minute, he just stood there, stymied as to which way to go. His feet seemed frozen.

There was activity farther back. Cops in a circle. Maybe he would find the car and drive home. He decided to do that and picked his way through the mess. He remembered the keys and had to go back. He felt sick. Keys in hand, he stepped through the shattered windows where the truck had come through. *Why? Why today? Why at Luby's?* Had a soldier from Fort Hood done this? There was a music store nearby that sold Gibson guitars. He liked to look at them, imagining that he would play one someday, be a rock star. He'd bought a ZZ Top album there, what, just a week ago? He had his first job ever, delivering pizzas for Domino's, and his first real money. He tried to think if he had to work that night. *Nothing.* What had happened?

The sun baked a rare clear sky. One thing he hated about Central Texas was the weeks of cloud cover with stiff winds. The asphalt parking lot radiated heat. He walked, looking for the Mercury Bobcat. It was bronze, a hatchback. He wandered from one row to the next. Where was it? He reached the end of the parking lot. Traffic flowed on the expressway as if all was well with the world, but he could hear sirens, and soon the first ambulance swerved into the parking lot with a firetruck on its heels. He turned back and took a different route through the parked cars, or did he? *Nothing.* A cop was talking to him, asking him if he was okay, and he said, "Yeah."

Reece walked, a song playing in his head, a disco tune.

Full of rice pudding, French fries, and skillet burgers, Reece groaned. He just wanted to sit in the recliner and look at a *National Geographic.* "I'm gonna be sick, but that was so good." It suddenly occurred to him that his parents had been shot in the head and so had he, but he had lived. Why was that? He drank another swallow of cold tea.

Dora beamed, and Horace took thirds of the rice pudding.

"You go rest," said Dora.

"I'll wash the dishes," said Reece.

"No, you go rest. Sit in the recliner."

"Whatever you say."

"Help him," said Dora.

"I don't need help. I'm fine." He hobbled his way to the blue recliner, backed up to it, and fell. "Oof!" From the corner of the den, he could see the TV, the kitchen, and the doors to the two bathrooms and his bedroom. The old gas heater sat between the kitchen and the den. A bookshelf to his left held *National Geographics.* The clock over the TV had a fake pendulum that swung back and forth about eighty times per minute. It was just past two, and Kristin would get off work at three. He dreaded calling her.

Reece grabbed the yellow mag on the end, and it had a picture of the Statue of Liberty on the cover. He flipped through the pages. "Maybe I should call Kristin before she leaves work."

Dora, at the sink, rolled her eyes. Reece was her grandson, and no woman could tell him what to do except for her. "She'll get over it."

Horace cleared his throat. "You might do that, son. Save yourself some trouble."

"Horace, he needs to be independent."

"Well, they are engaged."

"Well, they ain't married, are they?" asked Dora.

Reece cringed. "Okay, I'll do it. She can come out here, and I'll be able to drive soon, maybe tomorrow."

"You can't drive, Reece. You've been shot in the head," said Dora.

"Maybe I'll be an even better driver. Everything looks so clear, like glass. I'm gonna call her right now." He'd lost his glasses in Ethiopia but had an old pair that seemed to work.

He reached over and grabbed the phonebook from the shelf and looked up the number to Carraway Hospital. The tiny numbers seemed to move on the page. He picked up the phone on the lamp table to his right and dialed.

"Uh, yes, can you connect me with CCU?"

The phone rang, and someone answered, probably the unit secretary.

"Hey, can I possibly speak to Kristin Glover? This is her fiancée."

"Hey there, Reece. This is Eudora. I'll see if I can get her. It's so good to hear your voice."

Reece had nearly forgotten that he'd worked there for two years. He slapped his palm against his thigh. It's where he had met Kristin. She had been a student nurse in CCU and then had taken a job there. *Eudora, Eudora.*

"Oh, hey. Eudora. Yeah, it's me."

"You doing okay? I heard about the accident. Everyone

here's been thinking about you. Kristin kept us up to date. She's the best."

"Right. Yeah, it's been kind of rough, getting better, though." He remembered that Eudora had a pet horse. She lived on a farm in Shelby County. "And how's the horse?" He cleared his throat. He could hear vague noises, IV pumps and ventilators.

"Peanut is fabulous. He gets lots of apples, you know, the fall harvest. Lots of apples. Hold on, and I'll get her for you. Good to talk with you."

"You too." Reece waited. He held the phone tight against his face. The pendulum on the clock over the TV was ridiculous. It kept swinging by virtue of a magnet, having nothing to do with the accepted units of time. He waited, perhaps two minutes. His throat felt dry. He coughed.

"Hey!" said Kristin. "Can't talk long, but what's up?" She tapped a pen on a chart, Ms. Dunlop's chart, her favorite patient ever. She was weird like a sea cucumber and had no idea that her heart was a mass of dead muscle.

"Hey!" Reece thought back to when his dad had been transferred to Germany. His parents had not explained to him that there would be a new language. He couldn't read any of the signs in the shops. Nothing had made sense. "You working hard?"

"Duh! Yeah right, what's up?"

Reece paused. "Hey, just wanted to call and let you know, uh, that I've, uh, moved back out to my grandparents' place." He winced and closed his eyes. He'd never had a beer and was thinking that maybe it was about time.

Kristin looked at the new order on Ms. Dunlop's chart. She would need to give her a bolus of potassium. Ms.

Dunlop thought she was still running credit card receipts at Loveman's and chewed on her sheet like a sandwich.

"Oh no. How did that happen?" asked Kristin. "I mean, how did you get there?"

"I called them. I walked this morning, really walked. I just need to get out of your parents' hair. You know. It makes them uncomfortable."

"Did they come and get you?"

"Yeah, Granny drove out. She made a rice pudding. I mean, your mother made me cheese toast before I left, so that's cool and all." Reece felt like he was falling down a coal chute.

"Got it, okay." She imagined Reece fishing off the pier, grinning from ear to ear.

"Yeah, well, I think I can drive in a day or so. But you can come out any time. I'm not going anywhere. Right?"

Kristin had to go. She needed to get ready for shift change, get her patients' intakes and outputs, do her charting, and tidy up the rooms. Thankfully, Larry, the charge nurse, had given the rude judge to someone else. The judge was such a royal asshole, but in exchange she'd taken first admit, a sixteen-year-old hit head-on by a coal truck. His leg had been nearly detached, and his head was the size of a small watermelon. On her shift alone, he'd received ten pints of blood. It was endless. The bleeding wouldn't stop. She knew he would die, but the parents had brought in several framed photos and placed them around the room. They were hoping for a miracle.

Kristin growled into the phone. "I've got to go." She waited for a reply.

"Ishi," said Reece. "I mean okay. Yeah, that's cool. I'll

talk to you later."

Kristin hung up without a word. She had to get another hematocrit on the kid, but already knew from the drainage bag that he'd need another pint of blood.

Reece hung up the phone and tapped his fingers on the magazine. "Well, that's that."

Emma left the door open. Beside Misrak, she kneeled.

"Misrak?"

Was she breathing? She couldn't tell. She put her fingers on Misrak's carotid, which seemed to be vibrating instead of pulsing.

"Misrak! Hey!"

Misrak seemed dead. Emma pinched Misrak's nose, lifted her jaw, and gave her two quick breaths. She leaned in and compressed her chest fifteen times. She couldn't remember the correct ratio, but it seemed right. *Two more breaths. Fifteen compressions.* Misrak's chest rebounded with each downward stroke. Nothing. She blew in hard, making herself dizzy, and popped back up for more compressions. Nothing.

Down she went again, mouth to mouth. She alternated between kneeling and leaning over. Misrak vomited into Emma's mouth. Emma spun backward and fell, spewing the bile. It tasted like burned meat and hot sauce. Emma regained her balance. The vomit was pooled in Misrak's mouth. If she aspirated the liquid, that would be the end. Emma forced Misrak's head to the side, jammed two fingers in her mouth, and cleared the mess. Was she trying to sit up? And she was, with wild dilated eyes flashing.

Emma leaned back on her knees. Misrak gagged, choking, coming off the bed with each deep heave. Emma let her flail. There was nothing she could do.

Misrak arched her back and breathed deep, staccato, very slow. Just when Emma thought she had stopped, Misrak sucked in another ragged breath. The seconds seemed like minutes. The pounding of the rain on the metal roof formed a sound cocoon. Emma imagined a vast space, the Superdome. Would Misrak live or die? Who had the power to decide? Misrak's breathing hastened, but with stops and starts. Her eyes closed as if from relief.

In came Lisa with two orange plastic mugs of hot tea with yellow sugar. "Emma!" She tried to fathom the scenario. Misrak seemed possessed, the whites of her eyes. Was Emma praying?

Emma heard her name. The world was not as large as it appeared to be, and she was thankful for Lisa. She would be able to share this experience, unlike Reece being shot, having been the lone witness.

"She stopped breathing," said Emma.

Lisa could feel the heat wasting from the plastic cups. "What can I do?"

"Nothing," said Emma. She watched Misrak's chest rise and fall, rise and fall, like nothing had happened, like all was well. "Tea." Emma needed relief, whatever she could have at that moment. She was ready to mainline heroin.

"Tea, right here." Lisa shaped Emma's hand around the orange cup. "You need it. Drink."

Emma held the cup with both hands and sipped. It was sweet and good and washed away the vomit taste. The tea felt warm in her mouth but hot in her throat and stomach. *Misrak's three children.* Someone would need to cook for them, and the husband, too. She hoped Afewerki would take care of that. He was a good man.

"Lord, let's get an IV in her," said Emma. "Can you stay with her? I'll need a flashlight for the warehouse, though."

The supplies were stacked in piles. Only Daniachew and Alene knew what was what.

"Yeah, for sure," said Lisa. "What a kerfuffle."

"A what?" asked Emma.

"You know, like a commotion."

"Oh, a kusplutterment." Her mom said that.

Lisa laughed. "Yeah, that, too."

Misrak's breathing regulated into a more normal rhythm. She was blinking her eyes.

"Hey," said Emma. She smoothed back Misrak's hair. "You're gonna be okay. Chicorilla."

Misrak mumbled and sighed. Grimaced. Where was she? Where were her children? She remembered the jeep, being held by the ferenj, the woman called Emma. She tried to say the name. It came out as just "Muh."

"Here, let me light a candle. It's getting a little gray in here," said Emma.

"Matches are there." Lisa swapped the black rope of her long ponytail from one side to the other.

With the candle lit, Emma was ready to hit the ware-house. "The flashlight."

"Right," said Lisa. "I'll be right back."

Emma knelt again beside Misrak. What else could she do? She found Misrak's hand beneath the blankets and held it until Lisa returned with the flashlight.

"Great," said Emma. "Be right back." She stepped into the rain and hurried to the warehouse, and the side door was locked. "Hell." There was no overhang to block the rain. She stumbled and splashed her way to the main opening, a huge double door. There was no lock, and she slid the latch. She couldn't tell if it swung in or out. Her hair was soaked, and she felt the cold of the rain through her clothes. She pushed, and the door moved a foot, just enough to squeeze in. "Thank the Lord."

Silhouettes of vast stacks of grain, thirty bags high, greeted her. She beamed the flashlight around and located the medical supplies: boxes of pills, IV fluids, and bandages. She aimed her flashlight at large boxes stacked three high. IV fluid in bottles, all of it from Iceland. She hunted a mixture of saline with dextrose, D_5NS, and pulled out two bottles. She had no idea where the IV kits might be or the IV tubing, and began a methodical search. There were boxes of penicillin G for infections and niclosamide for tapeworms. Cases of oral rehydration salts. Boxes of syringes and sutures. The cement floor radiated the cold. In her sweater, she shivered, wet from rain and sweat.

After ten minutes, with supplies in a grain bag, Emma ran back to the guest room. "Hey, she okay?"

Lisa sat in a rickety chair beside Misrak. "Yeah, she's trying to talk, but can't understand her. You get the stuff?"

"Got it," said Emma. "Needed to find a feeding tube, but couldn't. Maybe she'll be able to eat in a day or so." She imagined getting drunk with Lisa. Terry and Lisa weren't Baptists, weren't religious, but very nice people, nonetheless. "Got any alcohol?"

"What?" asked Lisa. Terry liked to drink the local hooch, but she didn't. It was usually too smoky or too strong for her taste. "Drink?"

Emma laughed. "Yeah, to funnel like water. I'm a wreck. A drink or two won't hurt."

Lisa brightened. "Sure, we have some katikala. Terry claims it's the best liquor he's ever had. He likes to compare different batches from different ladies in AK. It's not my forte, but it will get the job done. Yeah, we should have a few, tell some stories."

Emma nodded her head, searching for a vein. She told Misrak there would be a stick and slid in the IV. Lisa held the bottle of fluid. "Plug her in." Lisa, hand shaking, inserted the end of the tubing into the IV.

Emma taped it down, covering the site with a folded 4x4. "Good work there, Lisa." There was no IV pole, the bane of her existence at times. "We'll need to rig this, maybe hang it from the rafter."

"I have a coat hanger. Will that work?"

"Should," said Emma. "I'll hold the bottle."

Lisa opened the door, hesitated, and leapt into the rain.

Emma decided to give Misrak another dose of promethazine. It seemed to sedate her just as much as an opioid and would reduce vomiting. Emma's stomach rumbled. She'd not had breakfast or lunch, and it was just an hour till dinner. If it stopped raining, they could walk into town and eat at the hotel there. Maybe some tibs, some goat or sheep with enjera. Her mouth watered. But could she leave Misrak? She felt foolish. Of course, she couldn't. Misrak had stopped breathing for God's sake. Misrak was looking at her. Emma felt guilty.

The door slammed, and Lisa had the coat hanger. She bent one end to drape over the rafter and the other to hold the bottle inside a plastic hanger. It was a bit high, but it worked.

"Want to eat some food before we get trashed?" asked Lisa.

"Lord," said Emma. "I feel selfish. I need to stay here.

Maybe just some eggs and a piece of bread?"

"I can do that," said Lisa. "I doubt that Terry will fly back today. It's starting to get dark, plus the rain. He would have been here by now."

Within half an hour, Lisa returned with scrambled eggs and toast. She also had fetched the bottle of katikala, untouched. They ate more or less in silence, taking their time, glancing at Misrak, who was in a deep sleep, snoring. Emma had bolused her with 12.5 mg of promethazine. The bottle of D$_5$NS was half empty, dripping, dripping. The rain had slackened, but was still peppering the tin roof, creating a hum.

Emma sat on the empty bed, and Lisa sat on the wooden chair.

"Thanks a million," said Emma. "I was starved."

"No biggie," said Lisa. She had lots of questions for Emma, about Reece, about that night when he was shot. There had been no detailed TV news report or breaking news flash to fill in the details. Everything was rumor. She chewed the last bit of her toast and put her plate on the crude bedside table.

"So, have you heard from Reece?"

"Not yet."

Emma felt a wash of relief. She desperately needed to talk with someone about the whole situation. Dr. Guthrie had listened to her while she was with Reece at Black Lion Hospital, but he hadn't asked the right questions. She felt that Lisa would do a better job. She sipped from an orange cup of water. She leaned forward, elbows to knees. Her breasts felt tight in her damp bra. She shivered and pulled a blanket around her shoulders.

"You feel like talking about it?"

Emma brightened. "I think I need to. But let's have a drink. Just for the heck of it."

"Want to just drink from the bottle? Manly."

"Sure. That'll be new. Maybe we'll have a knife fight, too."

"Ha," said Lisa. She pulled the corncob stopper from the plain brown bottle. "Let's do it," and she took a swig. "Oh, that smoke. Tastes kind of like Scotch. I like the flavored areke better."

Emma took the bottle. She thought back to the night with Afewerki in the bar, when the men had tried to rape Desta. She let the clear liquid pour into her mouth, and it burned her gums. "Shoo!" and she swallowed as fast as she could. She squinched her eyes. "Yowzah!" The burn extended into her chest.

Lisa looked on. Emma was strong but not indestructible. Everyone had their edge, their abyss. "Tell me what happened," said Lisa. "That night when he was shot."

Emma thought. Should she tell Lisa everything? *Why not?* "Well, Reece had given up his bed to this guy with a rotting leg. Reece needed a place to sleep, so I said he could sleep on my floor. We had dinner. I wanted to bathe, but he came in right after we ate. There was still some light out, like a light purple. I went ahead and lit a candle. We didn't talk much at first. Kind of awkward. I guess the Hyena was making his way to the compound next door, the government clinic. I don't think he had any idea that Reece was there. He was after me." She reached for the bottle on the floor.

"Damn, but why would he want to kill you? Maybe he

was trying to scare you. He sounds like a lunatic."

"He hates women for one thing. He's raped every woman he can get his hands on. Maybe that was his way to get close to me." Emma swigged. "This is hard to drink."

"It gets easier," said Lisa. "But I think if I were born a woman here, I would have to kill someone myself."

"No doubt," said Emma. "Anyway, Reece was just sitting there, and I was just sitting there. I asked him to rub my neck. I was in the chair. His hands felt so freaking good. I thought I was going to, you know, right then and there."

"Sounds nice. You'd been there for months by yourself. He spoke English. He was familiar. He had great hands. You must have been on cloud nine."

"Cloud nine, yeah." She dipped her head. "Was I moaning? I don't remember. At least not out loud." She tipped the bottle and let another mouthful flow in. She coughed. She felt warmer. "I wish there was a heater in here."

"You want to get under the covers?"

"Not yet. This blanket is enough for now." She closed her eyes. "His hands were on my neck, slipping down, you know. I was about to fall out of the chair. I was so relaxed. He leaned over and let his hands slide down. His hands were there. It felt so good." She stopped.

"Wow," said Lisa.

"And then *Blam! Blam!* He fell to the floor. I thought he was joking. I thought maybe it was all a big joke. That someone had lit a couple of firecrackers. It took me a second to open my eyes, like I was waking up on a cold morning to a lousy alarm clock. And he was on the floor, gasping, and the blood, my God, the blood…"

Reece decided to walk down to the lake, to stop halfway at the black walnut where Horace sat, and then rest before heading to the pier. When he was younger and spent summers with them, he liked to fish for bass with his Jitterbug and Tiny Torpedo.

"What do you think you're doing?" asked Dora. She was washing the dishes, wearing green rubber gloves.

Reece paused at the dining room table, holding onto the back of a chair. "Down to the lake. Gotta see it. Thanks for lunch. I'll get to where I can wash dishes pretty soon."

"You're like an old man walking, boy. You be careful. Don't overdo it. And for Pete's sake, don't fall in the lake."

"Yeah, that would be great. Take a bath." He walked around the table and made his way to the laundry room and the back door. His first romantic encounter with Kristin had been on the lake. He'd taken her to a Japanese restaurant, and then they'd wound up sprawled in a flat-bottomed boat floating in the cattails, talking past midnight. He had felt electric.

The screen door slammed behind him. The houses nearby were arranged around a U-shaped road that intersected the main road. The community pool was off to the left, about two hundred feet down the road that went around the lake. He remembered swimming in the pool when he was five. The rough bottom made his feet bleed. He'd had many a massive sunburn at the pool.

He walked through the yard, going from tree to tree to rest and balance himself. A car passed, and he waved. He crossed the road and cut toward the black walnut. The sun blazed his head, his arms. For the first time in weeks, he wore clothes instead of being half-naked in a hospital gown. He staggered happy along a row of irises. He'd cut the grass below the road hundreds of times, always painting the irises with the deck of the riding mower.

He focused on the two folding chairs at the tree, seeing the neighbor, Elbert Sykes, there. He was Horace's gardening soul mate. They grew their gardens side by side, pumped water from the lake to irrigate their crops of tomatoes, beans, squash, potatoes, and corn. Sykes' pump was electric, and Horace's was two-stroke.

"Hey, boy!" Mr. Sykes' gravelly voice boomed. His nickname was Boss, and he'd been a supervisor at a valve company for forty-three years.

Reece conserved his breath until he reached the tree. "Hey...Mr. Sykes...Long time no see." He fell into Horace's folding chair strung with polyester webbing.

"Lord, Lord, Reece, I thought I would never see you again. You, okay?"

"Oh," said Reece. He took a few deep breaths. "Yeah. Came out here this morning."

"We'll have to go fishing for some bluegill. What do you think?"

Reece tried to imagine fishing, casting the rod with the red-and-white float, a lead weight, and a red worm on the hook. "I'd like that, sure. How are you? It's been about, what, three months?" Time had ceased to have much meaning. He wasn't sure if he'd been in Ethiopia for a week or ten years.

"Your Dora and Horace were sure worried about you,

boy. Over there in Africa." He'd never been out of the South.

"Yeah, but it's not so bad, real rugged and scenic, like the Grand Canyon, or from what I've seen of it."

"Are the people black?" asked Elbert.

Reece laughed. "Some are black, but most are like kind of golden, an unusual color. The women are really pretty."

Elbert raised his eyebrows. He'd been with a couple of black women, but not any golden women. "You don't say." He looked out over his garden, the cattails and lake beyond. "Were there any white people?"

"In the city, Addis Ababa, there were. But in the village, there was only one other white person, a nurse, Emma." Reece felt a knot in his throat.

"A woman? What was she doing there?"

"She's a nurse, like me. A real tough nut, cute." He imagined Emma yelling at the Hyena and smiled.

"Well, highway to hell."

Reece laughed. "She's still there, even after that bastard shot me. I think."

"She needs to be careful," said Elbert. He wiped sweat from his forehead with a handkerchief.

"No doubt," said Reece. "I'm headed to the pier, if I can get out of this chair."

"Yeah, go on. I bet you missed it."

"I did," said Reece. "Talk to you soon."

"You know where I'm at," said Elbert.

"Right." Reece pushed down and stood, gauging the sixty feet to the pier, which was T-shaped with one rough bench.

Reece felt like a zombie, but kept on. He came to the

step and planted his hand against his knee. On the deck, he could see into the still and greeny water, minnows flitting, moss sending out slimy tendrils. Something splashed, probably a small bass. He limped to the end of the pier and sat on the bench. A turtle ducked its head. The water rippled from kick-up breezes. He could barely see the end of the lake off to his right, about a mile away. To his left, the lake curved back. Across the lake were piers and houses with a steep hillside climbing several hundred feet behind. He had swum across the lake occasionally, a good half mile.

Everything pulsed green and alive, with 100 percent humidity. The sun beat down on him, making his back and face sweat. He remembered writing a note and putting it inside a small glass bottle, throwing it as far as he could. What would Emma think of the lake? He imagined her there beside him for a moment and then thought of Kristin. "Damn." He wanted to punch himself.

He sat there for half an hour, but soon needed to pee, and it wasn't dark enough to pee in the lake. It was a long walk back to the house. Hell, he had shorts on and a t-shirt. Why not just get in the lake, cool off, and pee in there? The water at the end of the pier would be up to his nipples. Normally, he didn't like the muck, but what the hell? He kicked off his tennis shoes. He looked back and saw that Horace had joined Mr. Sykes. To the edge of the pier he walked, hesitated, and then just stepped off, plunging into the mire. Clouds of silt billowed up around him. The warm water smelled like fish and mud.

Reece laughed. Why not just take a swim, maybe dog paddle or float on his back? He tried to lift his foot, but it wouldn't budge. He tried the other foot. *Stuck.* He could feel little fish nibbling at the hairs on his legs. He brought his arm up, and it was covered with slimy moss. Then he remembered the leeches and tried to twist back to the pier. "Damn." Water splashed in his mouth, and he spit. There were giant carp in the lake, yellowish and big as logs, and snakes, too. The mud around his legs seemed like cement. He went ahead and peed.

Horace and Elbert held their hoes like staffs, talking about honey.

"You been up to Blount County lately?" asked Elbert.

"Just passed through, headed up to the homeplace."

"There's a fella outside of Cleveland sells some real good honey. His bees feed on clover and honeysuckle. Real sweet like, extra sweet even."

Horace wanted to know how much it was. He looked at the pier and didn't see Reece.

"He'll sell it to an old timer like you for about five dollars a pint. What's the matter?"

Horace stood. "Where in hell did Reece get off to?"

Elbert shaded his eyes with his hand. "Well, hell, you don't think he fell in, do you?"

"Better go look," said Horace, and he walked that way at a brisk clip with Elbert not far behind.

Horace hopped onto the pier. His heart went a little cold.

"Hey!" Reece could hear somebody on the pier.

Horace went to the end, and there was Reece chest-deep in the water. "What in blue blazes are you doing, boy? You can barely walk. Did you fall in?"

"Did he fall in?" asked Elbert. Maybe Reece was a little

nuts after all, being shot in the head and all.

"I jumped in. I'm stuck." Reece laughed. "I can't get up." The sun glowered overhead, hot on his face.

"Gonna be a pile of leeches on you, boy," said Elbert.

Horace couldn't squat, and went to his hands and knees, and then sat with his legs dangling over the side. He reached out to tag Reece, but he was just out of reach, except for the hair on the back of his head. "Hey, Elbert, get me the boat oar."

Elbert growled his approval. The flat-bottomed boat lay flipped over on the bank with the oar underneath. Careful of snakes, he turned the boat over and grabbed the oar.

Horace took the oar and dropped it onto Reece's shoulder. "See if you can pull yourself this way."

Reece pulled on the oar, focusing on freeing his right leg. The mud sucked at his foot. He could feel Horace pulling like tug-of-war. "Pull," said Horace. Reece yanked and heard a *Ploosh!* Elbert was laughing. Reece turned his head, and Horace stood in the water, missing his glasses.

"I guess it was meant to be," said Horace. "Elbert, you coming in? Lost my damn glasses."

"I'm sorry," said Reece. "More trouble than I'm worth. Get me unstuck and I'll find your glasses."

Horace grabbed Reece around the waist and pulled. "Get one leg out, can you?"

Reece struggled and wiggled his right foot, and it came free. "Got one out!" He searched the bottom for a rock or something solid to push against, but there was nothing. "Pull again. I'll twist."

It took a few pulls, but his left leg wrenched free from the blackish goo. He spat lake water. He turned, stepping lightly on the muddy bottom. Horace was right there, and he wasn't smiling.

"Go ahead and get out, and I'll find your glasses," said Reece.

"You sure?"

"I think I can." Reece watched Horace wade through the moss to the cattails. The water around Reece was clotted with clouds of brown and black. He took a deep breath and went down, searching with his hands. The top layer of mud seemed to slide under his hand, and he floated up buoyant. He heard someone yelling and looked up, water in his eyes.

"Reece!" It was Dora. "Get out of there! Horace, what the dickens! He can't be swimming like that. Reece, get out of there before you drown, right now!"

Reece began to feel a little cold. "Gotta find his glasses. Just hold on. I'm okay."

"Horace! Did you send him in there to find your glasses? Are you crazy?"

"Hold on, now. He fell in, and then I fell in and lost my glasses. Just simmer down. Ain't nobody died." He noticed a black leech on his arm and wiped at it.

"Reece, you come out right now," said Dora. "He can just buy some new glasses."

"I'll let y'all crazy people sort it out," said Elbert, and he headed back to the garden.

Reece sucked in a breath and went down. His hand gripped something in the mud, an old fish basket, and he held onto it. He searched with his other hand. His breath gave out, but there they were, a pair of glasses. He popped up and took a deep breath. He held up the glasses. "Got 'em!"

"Boy, you come on out." Dora had her arms folded, watching Reece slog to the cattails, through, and to the grassy bank.

Reece looked up at the sky and then down at his muddy arms and legs. He saw a leech and then another one. He slid his hands across his muddy legs and felt sick.

With the candle, the katikala, the rain, the warm blanket, and Lisa, Emma felt at peace. Misrak snored lightly, and the first bottle of IV fluid had just finished. Emma had told Lisa just about everything, even about her dad coming on to her, groping her when she was twelve.

Lisa shifted in the chair. Emma wanted to know how she and Terry had met, but Lisa had one final burning question.

"So, I was volunteering, doing maintenance on a hiking trail in Newfoundland, a place called Gros Morne, and he just came by hiking along by himself. It was June. I was sweating, a real mess, and so was he."

"Hmm, a sweaty man in the woods." Emma looked at the half-empty bottle of katikala and felt just a tiny bit sick.

"Don't remind me," said Lisa. "Anyway, we stopped to have lunch, and this other guy suggested that Terry join us, and he did."

"Wow, did he pull some ambrosia out of his backpack and feed it to you with his fingers?"

Lisa smiled. "Maybe it was olives. And I licked his fingers." She grinned. "God, he was so cute in his hiking shorts. He had a big beard then and longer hair. But we didn't even talk. He finished eating and headed off into the woods."

"What happened after that?"

"We worked until about five and then hiked up to a shelter to spend the night. It was only about a mile off, and he was there."

"I'll bet he knew you guys would come there," said Emma. "He saw you and died inside."

"You know, you're right. He confessed later that he'd stopped ahead of schedule, hoping we'd catch up."

"Then what happened?"

"I wanted to sleep in my tent. I don't like the hard floor in the shelters. Anyway, he had staked out the best level spot with his tent, and that kind of pissed me off. I asked him about it."

"Ha!"

"Yeah, he got this confused look and started apologizing."

"And then you wound up sleeping in his tent that night." Emma clapped her hands.

"Well, duh. But how did you know? I don't look slutty, do I?"

"Heck no," said Emma. "You saw what you wanted and went for it. Good for you."

"I guess I did, but we didn't have sex, but got pretty close."

"That makes me think of Reece. I loved his legs." She wanted to bang her head against the wall.

"Yeah, he was cute, kind of lanky."

"Not enough beef for you?" Emma reached for the bottle. The warm liquid coated her mouth, and a rush of nausea ran down her spine. She swallowed. "Ugh."

"We don't have to drink the whole bottle, you know." Lisa pulled her fleece coat tighter around her body. Should she ask Emma the million-dollar question? "Did you love him?"

Emma looked at the dusty floor. She looked at the drip

chamber of Misrak's IV, 60 ccs per minute. Lisa was gorgeous. Terry was a hunk. They had a perfect life, living on the edge together, a grand adventure that they could talk about years from now. She eyed her wrist. She'd thought about ending it that way, with a scalpel from the clinic.

"Love him? Now or then?" Was the answer the same?

"I should have asked, '*Do* you love him?' You seem to really care for him."

Emma looked somewhat fierce in the candlelight, sure of herself in a place that she belonged, *right?* She had proven her mettle but had also shown a darker side. Who was she? Emma wanted another swallow of katikala, but the thought made her queasy. Maybe she hadn't loved Reece the night he was shot. "Yeah, I think I really do now."

Lisa nodded as the rain continued to drum on the metal roof. "You guys connected, had some amazing experiences together. You saved his life that night."

"Maybe." Emma remembered the two letters she had brought and had not read. Would they make her feel better or worse? One was from Kristin, and the other was from his grandparents.

"I can't imagine seeing Terry hurt like that. You must have been devastated."

Emma nodded and ran her hands through her oily hair. "We just hit it off, you know, like we'd always known one another. He was great in the clinic, and he was there when the damn Hyena came calling."

"I just don't see how you even stood up to him, the Hyena. What a horrible nickname. Emma, you are one strong woman. You deserved to have someone like Reece with you. The Hyena took that away, and..." Lisa felt tears. "I can't imagine what you've gone through."

Emma glanced at Misrak. "Everyone has their hell. Just look at Misrak. She may not live to see her kids again. What if she dies in Addis, without her kids there? That will be my fault. You just can't win in this place. I'm not even sure if God exists anymore."

Lisa pulled her chair next to the bed and took Emma's hand, which was warm. "Life is complex. You're in a very complex situation, taking risks that not many would take."

Emma looked at Lisa's hand in her own. Would a bullet come crashing through the wall and take her as well? "Maybe God is punishing me. Maybe he's just a crank who gets his kicks tormenting people."

"Emma, that's not true. You have to keep your faith, right? Who knows what great things will happen? You'll see Reece again, maybe sooner than you think."

"What do you mean? What do you know that I don't? Are they closing the station? Is that why Terry hasn't brought more grain? Dr. Guthrie hinted at it."

"I'm not supposed to say, I think." Lisa wanted to kick herself. She squeezed Emma's hand, but Emma pulled away.

"So, I'm right?" asked Emma. "Guthrie is closing the station, and I'll be the last to know? Is that it?" She wanted to get mad, but it was slow in coming. She felt she was slurring her words, and she was.

"Emma, I only hear what I hear, but it does seem like they'll be closing down the feeding stations, but I'm not sure about the clinics. Maybe they will stay open. It's just what Terry tells me. But maybe that would give you a chance to go home and visit, see Reece."

Emma thought about that. A fleeting thought of them coming back to Ethiopia together. But that seemed impossible. He could be dead or a permanent vegetable. "All good things must come to an end, I suppose." She withdrew her hand from Lisa's. "It would just be nice to know what's going on around here. The other feeding stations have radios. I've never understood why we don't have one."

Emma stood, woozy, and stretched. "Hold on." She went to Misrak's side and put her hand beneath her dress, feeling the wet. She smelled her hand, urine. Misrak's eyes were cut to slits, her breathing heavy. "She's peeing, which is good. We'll need to get her some dry clothes, give her a bath in the morning." She walked in a tight circle. "I feel kind of drunk."

"Me, a little bit, too," said Lisa.

"Hey, let me check something while you're here. A letter. From his fiancée."

"Really? You sure?"

"Yeah." Emma went through her small overnight bag and found the two letters. She took the one from Kristin and sat, scooting closer to the candle, which dripped wax onto the bedside table and then onto the floor. She took another swig of katikala and coughed.

"Want me to read it?" asked Lisa.

"That would be nice." Emma tore open the end and pulled out a single notebook page with writing on both sides.

Lisa took the letter and read. "It's dated August 16, about three weeks ago." She read halfway down the page. "Reece is at the hospital in Birmingham. Hey, she says that he's started to move his eyes and his fingers."

Emma choked, and she put her head into her hands, tears leaking onto her hot face.

Lisa paused. "You, okay?"

Emma collected herself, took a deep breath.

"His grandparents come every day." Lisa skimmed the back page. "Wow." She put down the letter and went to sit beside Emma on the bed. "It's okay."

Emma felt silly. So, he could move his fingers and eyes. Was that it? But it also seemed like a miracle. She hiccupped. "What else?"

"Well...basically, she's talking about how they're engaged, but she's not sure what will happen. She wants to know if anything happened between the two of you, anything she should know about."

"Dang, why did he have to be freaking engaged?" Emma pressed her lips together. "I already told you what happened. We were connecting, and then the bullets. I would have slept with him that night, no doubt. I needed to, wanted to. And I think he was, well, the same."

"She's put her phone number here. Wants you to call her if you can."

"You're kidding?" asked Emma. A sudden surge of energy pressed through her. "That's kind of bold. Does she think I'll just give her a call and make everything okay? She has no idea. She couldn't possibly understand." She wiped her face with her shirt. "Is that it?"

Lisa said, "Basically, yeah. But she kind of sounds like she's at her wits' end about this. Her fiancée being shot, not knowing you, not knowing what really happened."

"Well, damn. I don't even know what happened. Who does she think she is?" She wanted to scream.

"Do you think you'll write her back?" Kristin's handwriting was very precise, very neat, methodical. In a way, she felt sorry for her.

"Huh, let's see what his grandparents have to say." She knew without looking that the letter would be written by his grandmother. She tore open the envelope, two pages written in a sprawling script. The letter was addressed to Emma, "the nurse at Godo."

Lisa held the letter, pages torn from a spiral-bound notebook, trying to decipher the difficult cursive handwriting. "It's dated just a few days later." She struggled through the first page.

Emma sat back on the bed, watching Lisa read. She could see Reece on his back in a hospital bed, his face covered with sweat, his lips dry and cracked, his sharp nose, his thick eyebrows, his eyes moving, following people in the room. She imagined there was a TV on, that he struggled to understand the soundless images.

Lisa cleared her throat. "Wow. Listen to this." She checked to see that Emma was listening. The rain seemed to be slacking, with the silence in the room growing louder. "There was a tornado in Birmingham."

"Yeah, Dr. Guthrie told me," said Emma. She knew it was that time of year. "What does she say?"

Lisa scanned the first page again and turned it over. "Holy cow, nearly three hundred were killed."

"Jesus. Dr. Guthrie was right. In Birmingham, three hundred?"

"Yeah, or in Alabama at least. The tornado hit the hospital, but Reece is alive. She says—it's hard to read here—that he had to go to Kristin's house because the room he was in was destroyed. Wow."

Emma tried to fathom the news. Which was worse, the tornado or him being at Kristin's house?

"She's writing you because he had just started talking, had mentioned your name, had said that she should write to you."

Emma sat up straight. "She said that?"

"Yeah, she did. She thanks you for saving his life, and then she just talks about how glad she'll be when he can walk, and hopes that you're safe. She says you should leave as quick as you can."

"Huh," said Emma. Misrak moaned, and Emma adjusted her IV to make it last through the night.

Dora marched behind Reece, who was holding onto Horace. She barked at Horace for letting Reece fall into the lake.

"Hold your horses," said Horace. "He jumped in."

"You hold your horses!" said Dora. "I ought to spank the both of you, just like kids. Why he could've drowned."

They passed the garden and reached the road. Reece was sucking for breath and had to stop.

"Hold up." Reece leaned on Horace and got his breath back.

"Look at him, can hardly breathe!" said Dora.

"I'm alright, Granny," said Reece. "Just...get me to the hose."

Horace helped him across the road and up to a chair beside the swing.

Reece fell onto the old metal chair. "Need the hose. Got leeches."

"Leeches?" asked Dora. She ran to the hose beside the back door.

"I'll do it," said Horace. He was winded himself. "Just settle down."

"Well, mister, you settle down. You'll be the death of us all," said Dora.

Horace held his words and turned on the faucet. He pulled the garden hose across the yard. "Gonna spray you down, boy."

Reece rubbed his arms and legs as the cold water hit him. He stood and let Horace spray him all over.

"Horace!" said Dora. "Leeches everywhere!"

Reece fell back onto the chair. A few leeches wiggled on his arms and a dozen or more on his legs. He grabbed at one, and it slipped through his fingers. He tried another.

"Need the pliers," said Horace, and he headed off to the garage.

"Maybe," said Reece. He didn't care. What were a few leeches, but they would have to come off.

Dora just stood there, hands on hips. "Young man, you may not go back to that lake, you understand? Did you fall in?"

Reece couldn't remember if he had fallen or jumped. "I guess I jumped in. But it's okay. It's my fault. What's for dinner? I'm starved."

"Dinner? I should have you locked up," said Dora.

Reece laughed. "I'm starving." He laughed loud and hard. *Could it get more ridiculous?*

Horace came back with needle-nose pliers.

"Oh," said Reece. "Can't use that. Need to scrape them off."

"I'll pull 'em off," said Horace.

"Not really," said Reece. "Can you get me a piece of plastic, like from an antifreeze jug or a milk jug? It's better to scrape than pull." Watching the leeches on his arm, they seemed to be doubling in size, sucking his blood.

"You sure?" asked Horace. "Let me just try one."

"It'll just break off," said Reece. "If I had my driver's license, I could use that."

Horace pulled out his wallet. "Here."

Reece took the card. He placed the edge at the mouth of a leech and pushed down and scraped. The leech slid off, and he knocked it to the ground. "See?"

"Reece, you get 'em off, right now," said Dora.

Reece laughed. "I will. I will. Just be patient." He scraped off another and then another. Within ten minutes, he had scraped off more than a dozen. Each site bled, giving him the look of a butchered carcass.

"Take off your shirt and pants," said Horace.

"Okay," said Dora. "I'll be inside. And by the way, we're having pork chops and mashed potatoes." Dora stormed to the house, feeling a little bit sick.

In his underwear, Reece stood. Horace took his driver's license and scraped one off his back and two from the backs of his thighs. The marble patio glistened with bloody leeches.

"Let me get a hot shower," said Reece. "Appreciate it."

"Hold on," said Horace, and he walked Reece to the house. "Confounded leeches."

After a hot, soapy shower, Reece looked into the steamed mirror. Little streams of blood trickled down his arms and legs. He found a tube of expired antibiotic ointment and dabbed the tiny wounds. Then, he wrapped himself in a towel and went to his little bedroom to dress, smelling the slow sizzle of pork chops on the stove.

"I'm alive!" he announced to the cozy den, Horace in his recliner nearly asleep.

"Huh?" said Horace.

Dora held a spatula in the run-on kitchen. "You go get your clothes on. Look at you still bleeding. You need some Band-Aids."

"Don't worry. I'll take care of it." In his bedroom, he

searched through his tiny closet for some jeans and a t-shirt. He wondered if he was eligible for the Purple Heart. He ambled into the den and fell onto the loveseat between Horace's recliner and the propane heater. The window AC unit hummed behind him, blowing just above his head. He had a clear view of Dora cooking. She was slicing yellow squash from the garden.

"Look at them spots on your arms, boy." Dora waved the spatula at him. "Leeches. Makes my skin crawl. You're liable to come down with a fever or some such."

The excitement was wearing off, and Reece began to think about Kristin, who would be arriving home soon. Should he invite her for dinner? Did they just need a day's break?

"You know you ought to invite Kristin for dinner," said Horace. "Seeing how you just up and left."

"I'm not sure," said Reece. "Maybe." He felt pampered sitting on the loveseat, freshly showered, lucky to be alive.

"She's got a little attitude, if you ask me." Dora wore a long-sleeve purple shirt even though it was in the nineties outside. Age spots covered her hands. "You know that other girl over there, the one you talked about that saved your life. Her name's Emma. Well, I wrote her like you asked me to. I just sent it to the same address I mailed your letters to." She turned the pork chops with a fresh pop of grease in the pan.

Reece thought about that. "You did? How long ago? I need to write her, maybe even today."

"A couple of weeks ago. Had to go to the post office for the stamps."

"Maybe I should invite Kristin over tonight. Is that okay?"

Dora tapped the skillet three times. "If you want to. Whatever's best. I don't know much about all this modern love. Seems like it can go one way or another."

Horace reached for the latest *National Geographic*. He'd already read it twice. He turned on the lamp and then slid a piece of an envelope inside his glasses to block the glare. "Smart move, I'd say."

"Maybe we'll go for a swim." Reece pressed his bare feet into the carpet and wiggled his toes.

Dora glared at him. "Don't you even talk like that. Swim, my behind." Her eyes flashed or sparkled depending on the angle.

Reece laughed and went to the heavy black phone mounted on the wall beside the dining table. He dialed her number and felt a bit surprised that he could remember it. *Oh God,* what if Gert answered? He braced himself.

Gert answered. "No, she's not here yet, running late, it seems."

"Okay. Just tell her I called. I wanted to see if she could come over for dinner." Reece twirled the phone cord around his fingers.

"I'll let her know. I did make lasagna for tonight, which she likes. But I'll tell her you called."

Reece held the phone for a moment before placing it back in the cradle. He wondered why she was late. Probably a late admit or maybe a code blue. Or possibly traffic. That happened. "Yeah, she'll call when she gets home," he said to the world.

It was three-thirty. Kristin rushed from room to room. The kid hit by the coal truck had died, his poor parents in a delirium of grief. She had to prep the body for the morgue, padding and wrapping it. Even after he died, he continued to ooze from his torn leg. He'd received thirty-six pints of blood in less than forty-eight hours. She'd had to basically let Ms. Dunlop run on autopilot, dashing in to check on her, and now she felt obliged to tidy up her room, give her a quick bath, and change her sheets. Evening shift was stretched thin as usual. She noticed Dr. Phillips hanging out at the nursing station. He winked at her.

She ignored him and yanked linens from the cart, grabbed towels and washcloths, and hurried back into Dunlop's room. Ms. Dunlop's restraints were loose, and she was hunched over, chewing on her top sheet with her gums.

"What'cha doing, honey?" asked Kristin.

Ms. Dunlop focused her giant eyes on Kristin. Her skin was milky. "I'm eating a sandwich."

"Are you hungry? I can get you some food. Would you like a milkshake?" She hit the hot water and grabbed the liquid soap, shoved the bath basin under the stream.

"Yes, I would like a chocolate milkshake." She spoke like a slow-moving train. "I have to run the credit card receipts. I work at Loveman's."

"Yes, ma'am, I'll order that for you." She hit the call light. "Hey, order a chocolate milkshake for number twelve. Thanks."

"Will do," said Eudora.

"Need any help?" Dr. Phillips peeked around the curtain and stepped into the room. He was the same height as Kristin, maybe an inch shorter, stocky, but not fat. He made a point of having his dark hair trimmed once a week, hell or high water.

"Hey, Dr. Phillips. I mean, Brad. You can hold her on her side while I wash her back."

Kristin worked like a Swiss watch. She lowered the head of the bed and released the restraint on Ms. Dunlop's right arm. "Ready? Going to turn you and wash your back, Ms. Dunlop. Here we go."

"I'm eating a sandwich."

Brad held her while Kristin did her magic and lotioned her backside. While Dunlop was on her side, Kristin made half of the bed. "Roll her back to me and pull the sheets through."

"Very efficient," said Brad. "You're good."

"Thank you. Ms. Dunlop here is special. Aren't you, Ms. Dunlop?"

It took her about ten seconds to reply. "Yes. I'm eating a sandwich." She made chewing motions with her mouth.

"Milkshake's on the way." Kristin replaced Dunlop's gown and unfurled a crisp new sheet on top. "There. She's good, except for the new TED hose, which Carol will take care of. Your new nurse will be Carol, Ms. Dunlop. Okay? You're doing so good, and I'll see you tomorrow." She washed her hands, slightly out of breath. It hit her that Reece wouldn't be there when she got home.

Brad followed her out of the room. "You working Friday night?" He watched Kristin grab a chart and write. The other nurses and doctors were taking note.

"I need to focus here, if you don't mind. Plus, I am engaged, as you know." She looked at him. He was kind of like a teddy bear, and she smiled. "Maybe we can get coffee on break tomorrow?"

Brad's face registered that he'd scored a minor victory. "Yeah, I'm here pretty much twenty-four-seven. Coffee is always good." He also regularly booted himself with coke, but that wasn't important at the moment. All the residents and interns did coke, except for a precious few. He only worried about the cardiac implications, the stress that the drug placed on the heart.

"Great," said Emma. "But now I need to chart and get out of here."

"Where's the fire?" asked Brad.

"There isn't a fire. I just need to get away from here before I have a meltdown." She'd forgotten to empty Ms. Dunlop's urine drainage bag. "Damn," and she left Brad in her wake.

Emma awoke in a haze. She'd slept like the war dead. Where was she? She heard the thump of a helicopter. She had to catch it, but wasn't sure why. She leapt out of bed, glanced at Misrak, and opened the door. In her bare feet, she ran between the buildings to the helipad. She could see Terry inside. She waved at him and realized that he'd just landed and wasn't taking off. Lisa came up beside her with a big smile for her husband.

"Did you sleep well?" asked Lisa.

"Yeah, and then some," said Emma. Everything fell into place. Misrak was in bed. Emma needed to get her to Addis. Misrak was dying. "Let me check on Misrak, and then I'll come over. Okay?"

Lisa nodded and waited for Terry to shut down the engine.

The cobbled path of sharp rocks peeked just a few inches above the thick muck. A wind was sweeping down and through AK, seemingly to dry out the town. The cool air smelled clean, like clean dirt. Emma shivered and stepped from stone to stone. Inside, she went to Misrak's bed. The IV looked to have just finished dripping, and blood was backing up in the tubing. She switched out the empty for a new bottle and adjusted the drip rate to 60 ccs per minute, clearing the blood. Misrak's open eyes searched her own.

"Abet?" asked Emma.

Misrak whispered. "Wuha." She wanted water.

Emma stumbled over the bottle of katikala on the floor.

"Hell." She was surprised she didn't have a headache. Maybe katikala was her drink. She poured a cup of water from an Ambo bottle for Misrak. "Here, wuha."

Misrak raised up on her good arm and took the cup. She sipped and coughed and then drained it. She asked Emma where she was, but Emma couldn't understand.

"Do you need food?" asked Emma. "Enjera, mooze, arancia?"

"Ow," said Misrak. "Dabo." And that was a good sign.

"Ishi," said Emma. I'll get you some bread, dabo. No worries. You stay here, though, okay? I'll be back. Mel-less-ah-loo. Okay?" She patted her hand.

Misrak nodded, her face knotted.

Emma slipped on her hiking boots and went to see Terry and Lisa. The wind whipped her hair and cut through her thin jacket. She knocked on the sheet-metal door.

"Hey, come in," said Lisa. "You need a better coat."

"It'll warm up."

"Hey, Emma!" Terry gave her a big bear hug. His shoulder-length hair was a mess, but he still looked handsome, beard and all.

"Has Lisa told you?" asked Emma. The pressure of his hug lingered like colorful tissue paper.

"That you have a patient who needs to go to Addis?"

"Yeah, can you do that? Today? She works for us in Godo. Her breast looks awful. She's not long for this world if we wait. The jeep ride nearly killed her, so that's not an option."

"It's a matter of fuel. I need to make a run to Meranya today." He put his hands in his pockets, then withdrew them.

"Meranya? Why there?" asked Emma.

Terry glanced at Lisa. "Well, Lynn and Mary are pulling out, heading back to the States. They'll take a jeep from here."

"You've got to be joking. Am I always the last one to find out? Wasn't anyone going to tell me? You got any coffee, Lisa? I need coffee or tea. I'm sorry, whatever you have. It's just....What happened?"

Terry put his hands back in his pockets, rugged trousers made of burlap with big pockets. His thick sweater, the arms pushed up to his elbows. "They're shutting down the station, Emma. The famine is over."

Lisa busily heated water for tea. "It was bound to happen."

"Yeah, but the people are still hungry. What about the clinic? What about Godo?"

"Well," said Terry, "Guthrie should be talking to you about that soon enough. I only hear rumors, but I do know that Lisa and I'll be transferred to an operation in Tanzania soon, maybe within sixty days."

"Get out," said Emma. "Wow, the whole world is coming down. So, what happens to this place?"

"We don't know," said Lisa. "We haven't told Daniachew or Alene. I don't think I can. They'll be devastated."

As if on cue, there was a polite knock on the door. "Allo!" It was Daniachew.

Terry opened the door, and a gust whipped through the room, blowing out the flame on the tiny propane stove.

"It is to be much wind," said Daniachew. "Ah, it is Emma!"

"Hey!" said Emma.

Daniachew smiled from ear to ear. He was dark with a shaved head to keep away the lice, which he found revolting. He was somewhat peculiar, according to Terry, a real stickler for hygiene, but a good worker. "The tea is coming, no?" He rubbed his hands together.

"Yes, very windy. Come in. Have some tea," said Terry.

Emma hugged herself. She sat on a three-legged stool strapped with a leather seat. "I say that the guys in Meranya can wait a few days. We need to get Misrak in today. You have a radio, so that's not a problem, letting them know. Of course, I've never had a radio."

"Guthrie is expecting them in a day or two."

"So, he can just wait. They're alive and well, and Misrak is dying. Come with me and see for yourself if that will help. Lisa?"

"She's right," said Lisa. "She stopped breathing."

"Plus, she has three children." Emma sat with her hands folded beneath her chin. She wasn't budging. "You can have us there in an hour. And come to think of it, Daniachew can come with us. I'll need him to interpret, perhaps stay with her at the hospital so I can get back."

"Yes, to be going to Meranya?" asked Daniachew.

"No, to Addis," said Terry. "There is a woman who is sick."

"Who is dying," said Emma. "I'm worried it's spread to her nodes, maybe to her lungs."

Lisa watched the water sizzle in the pot, hot enough for weak tea. She dropped in tea bags and poured in a healthy dose of sugar and cloves.

Terry knew that Dr. Guthrie would disapprove. The Mission couldn't afford to fly patients in and have them treated in Addis. It tied up the helicopter and created problems with in-country travel permits, which were like an iron code. Terry was relatively free to fly to any of the Mission feeding stations and to Addis, and that was only because of Helimission's relationship with the country's Relief and Rehabilitation Commission, the RRC. The Baptists paid the operating costs of the flights, and Helimission paid Terry's salary, but all were accountable to the RRC, which had been coordinating the massive relief efforts. It was data gathered by the RRC through NGOs that showed there was no longer a need for the foreign presence in the highlands. Everyone was being kicked out now that the crisis was over.

Terry shook his head. "Okay, I get it. We have radio contact again at three p.m. Lisa can let Lynn and Mary know about the delay."

Emma stood and gave him a big hug. "I knew it. You won't be sorry. If anybody in Addis complains, I'll take the heat. No problem. But once we get her settled, I'll need a flight back to Godo. Maybe after you bring Lynn and Mary back."

Terry shook his head. "They're taking a jeep from here to Addis. I have to make what fuel I have last as long as possible. Although we don't want to leave behind a big bladder full of unused fuel."

Daniachew tried to follow the conversation. "What it is?"

"Terry's taking you and me to Addis, along with the patient. Will that work? Can you be gone for a few days?"

"It is not possible. I am working here, no?" Daniachew's eyes drifted to the gnarled rafters, the wind whistling there. He just did what Terry and Lisa asked him to do.

"Emma, you'll more than likely need Guthrie to go with you to the hospital. Only he can guarantee payment. They won't take her otherwise. We'll just have to call when we land and let him know the situation. He may tell you to bring her back to Godo." Terry took the orange mug of tea from Lisa and passed it to Emma. She handed it to Daniachew, who protested and passed it back to her.

Emma held the tea like a baseball and sipped, burning her lips. "Yikes. Okay, so you'll just take me and Misrak. Guthrie'll take us to the hospital. Done deal. When can we leave?"

Lisa passed cups of steaming tea to Terry and Daniachew. The room seemed tiny with the four of them there.

"I need to refuel myself and the machine. How about an hour? Maybe the wind will die down." It suddenly occurred to him that the last time she'd been in the helicopter, she'd jumped out. Guthrie had said afterward that she should only be allowed to travel by jeep. What if she tried it again? "Hey, I have an idea. Maybe Lisa can go with you for moral support. She needs a break anyway. Right, babe?"

Lisa folded her arms and stared at Terry.

"That would be great!" Emma was so used to doing everything alone, but any chance of company was very welcome. "What do you say?"

Lisa made a thoughtful face. "Sure, why not. Two girls on a mission. Shouldn't be gone for more than two or three days, right? Terry, you'll have to put the chickens up at night."

"Sure," said Terry. "Or Daniachew can help if I can't

make it back for some reason."

Daniachew wrinkled his nose. He didn't like animals, especially chickens. "Yes. Yes." He laughed.

"Hey," said Emma, "let me get back with Misrak. I'll need to clean her up. Oh, she wanted bread. Do you have any dabo?"

"No, but Daniachew can run into town and buy some buns. Here, I'll give you a birr." Lisa opened a small drawer in a bureau that doubled as the coffee and tea station. "And get yourself one, too."

Daniachew took the money, dreading the muddy walk into town, which would soil his clean shoes. "Okay, no problem." He would need to fetch his umbrella.

"This is great," said Emma. "Let me take some tea to Misrak."

"Okay," said Lisa.

A fist of wind walloped the building, and there was a definite scream beneath it all. The hair stood on Emma's arms, and she rushed for the door.

Gert turned off the oven, the cheese bubbling on top of the lasagna. "He called about an hour ago. Wanted to know if you'd go out there and eat dinner."

Kristin leaned against the wall, arms folded. She'd traveled to Ethiopia to see him after he was shot, and now he'd just left.

"Honey, don't feel pressured, but go if you want to."

Kristin laughed at the pull-push energy. One thing her mom was good at was sending conflicting messages. "A doctor asked me out today. This guy Brad."

Gert brightened. "Really? But you're engaged. What does he look like?"

Kristin rolled her eyes. "Dark hair, kind of muscled up, cute. Smart, I suppose. But he knows I'm engaged, so I don't appreciate him being so aggressive."

"Maybe you could just have coffee with him. It's not a bad idea to have friends who are doctors." The smell of hamburger and cheese permeated the room.

"Did Reece say what they were having for dinner? Maybe I'll eat here and then go see him." She saw the detergent by the sink and decided to wash her hands for good measure. She always worried about bringing some flesh-eating bacteria into the house.

"Probably some pork dish, knowing them." Gert laughed. "I'm just saying. How does he stand living with them? They're so old."

"He likes old people. His grandparents practically raised him, especially after the shooting. You know, in

Texas." Kristin thought about how impressed she'd been with his devotion to his grandparents. But then he'd up and left for Africa, leaving them behind, and he'd almost died there.

"But we're not spring chickens, your dad and me. Of course, I feel young. You have to feel young to stay young." She decided to take off her old-fashioned apron before Edwin came home. She looked at the clock on the stove. "Five o'clock."

"Oooh! I can't decide. Let me get a hot shower, and I'll let the water decide for me."

"You need to feed the animals. Don't forget."

Kristin looked around. "Uh oh, where's Wallace?" The cat always greeted her.

"Oh dear," said Gert. "The door to your room has been closed all day."

Kristin marched to her room and opened the door to find Wallace on the bed and a neat curly pile of cat feces on the carpet. He stood, arched, and jumped down, purring.

"Ick!" She rubbed his neck and went to the bathroom for toilet paper. At least it didn't smell so bad. She heard the front door open and close. "Hey, Daddy!" She flushed the toilet.

"Hey, honey!" said Edwin. "Mmm, I smell lasagna."

She met him at the top of the stairs and kissed his cheek. "Have a good day?"

"Reece is back at his grandparents, right?" He was trying to make a joke.

"Not so funny," said Kristin. "I've got a little cat mess to clean up. Need the carpet cleaner."

"Hey," said Gert.

"Hi, sweetie."

She took Edwin's tie, walked it to the bedroom, and placed it on the tie rack.

Edwin checked his watch against the clock over the TV, five-fifteen. Gert had turned it on, and the local news was halfway finished. He would watch it again at six after the national news. A tiny thrill ran from his tailbone to the indentation beneath his nose.

"There you are," said Kristin. Edwin, in his recliner, was classic, like corn chips. She tossed the paper towels into the trash and decided to call Reece. She washed her hands again. "Gonna call." The avocado push-button phone was mounted to the wall above Edwin's recliner.

She dragged the cord into the dining room and sat at the table. She hoped Reece would answer. The phone rang four times.

"Hello."

"Reece?"

"Hey! How are you?" Reece sat in the rolling table chair. It was comfortable, upholstered with cheap brown vinyl. Dora was looking in the fridge, assessing its contents.

"Okay, I guess." Kristin had relaxed, but then she was charged hearing his voice. The muscles in her lower back tightened. She wondered about the sound of her voice. Did she sound happy, sad?

"Have a good day?" Reece was squeezed between the bronze heater and the table, his spot, but it somehow felt smaller than usual.

"A crazy day." She relaxed, letting her feet go flat against the linoleum. She could see him with the phone to his ear.

"So, what happened? You're there."

Reece expected the question. "Uh…I was just in the way, probably freaking out your mom, and your dad. I just need my space, that's all. They need theirs." He noticed that he was rocking his head like a bobblehead bird, drinking, drinking.

"Did you pray about it?" asked Kristin.

"Well, yes and no." Reece felt cornered. He hadn't said a prayer since when? He marveled at the rawness of the fact. But what did it mean? "I mean, Gert is Gert and Edwin is Edwin. You know. It's their house, their little kingdom." Maybe that wasn't the right language.

"Okay, I get it. You're more comfortable there. I'd be the same way, except we're engaged. You should want to be with me."

"But, usually engaged people don't live together, right? You get married to live together." Reece slumped in his chair, sliding down, accentuating the curvature of his spine.

"Yeah, you're right. But still…"

"Come out for dinner. I'll walk with you down to the pier. We'll watch the bats eat bugs, fly like crazy birds."

Kristin felt the ice melting. "But I have to be back here by ten. Otherwise, I won't be able to get up at the crack of dawn." She looked, and Gert was watching, listening with hands on hips. The TV blared. Edwin was fully reclined. Wallace was rubbing against her leg. All felt right with the world.

"Not a problem," said Reece. "Just dinner and a walk to the lake. It's pork chops and fried squash and something else."

"I love you."

Reece tried not to cough. "I love you...too."

"Are you sure?"

"Of course, I'm sure." Reece felt an ice pick poised against his navel.

"Why do you love me?" Kristin felt powerful, like she was holding a loaded shotgun.

Reece thought. "I just love you, okay? I just do."

Kristin frowned. "Is that all?"

"No," said Reece. He was about to slide onto the floor and hoisted himself. "What can I say?"

"That you love me."

"Okay, I love you."

"Not, 'Okay, I love you' but 'I love you.'"

Reece felt like he was shooting an unreasonable rapid in a limp inner tube. Was this merely semantics, or was it the dialog of love? No one had trained him for this, and he felt he was failing miserably. Feeling that he was falling, he said, "I love you." He pressed the phone to his ear like an iron, and it hurt.

"That's better," said Kristin. She felt somewhat powerful that she had knocked an inch of nonsense from Reece's shoulders.

Reece felt he was covered in chicken skin. "Ishi. I mean, okay. So you're coming for dinner?" He was exhausted and wanted to sleep. "We have vanilla ice cream for dessert." He looked to Dora for confirmation, and she nodded her head.

"Sounds good," said Kristin. "See you soon."

"Bye," and Reece collapsed into a jelly heap. He maintained his weird shape and then, having trouble breathing, sat up straight, reached, and dropped the receiver onto its cradle. He felt he had run a marathon.

"Good job, son," said Horace.

"I'm not so sure," said Dora. The pork chops were done and soaking in a brown flour gravy. "Sounded too much like work to me."

Reece grunted. He knew she was right, but couldn't say it. Should he get a quick shower? *No,* he'd just had a shower. He looked at the red leech marks on his arms. That would freak her out. He felt somewhat better. "I need some fresh air." He stood with shaky legs.

"Horace, help him!" said Dora.

"No, I can do it." He waved off Horace. He waited for his vision to clear and made his way to the back door, tracing the wall with his hand.

"You be careful, boy," said Dora. She followed him to the laundry room. "Push on the latch there."

Reece stepped through the glassed screen door and then down onto the sidewalk. The swing, sitting in front of a slab of marble, was about twenty feet away. He imagined himself as a U-boat captain, looking through a periscope, and that the swing was his target. The soft pine straw prickled his bare feet. The lake was beyond the road, sparkling in the late afternoon sun. It seemed to call his name, and he wandered closer to the swing. Kristin was coming for dinner. At the marble, he grabbed the side of the A-frame swing and stood for a moment, catching his breath. The cabin to the left, across the road, had never looked more beautiful. It belonged to a chiropractor. Reece put his right foot forward and slipped. He was about to do the splits, but then froze the forward motion. His left foot caught and then shot ahead, throwing him onto his back, his head cracking against the white stone veined with gray.

The blast of air slowed Emma, but she ran for the guest room. Was there a fire? Had she left a candle burning? She splashed through thick mud, a slight rain wetting her face and hands. The light shone bright and furious, as if a day had dawned that would require a special darkness. She saw the body.

Misrak wept, lying naked in the muck beside the rock path. *Where are my children? Where am I? Where is the ferenj?* She had pissed herself.

Emma ran to her, Misrak howling, followed by Lisa with Terry and Daniachew behind. It was as if rare lightning had struck. Emma kneeled in the black slop of rain and dirt.

"You're okay," said Emma. She wiped the rain from Misrak's brow, her cheeks, her chin. "Xavier meskin, okay? Praise God." Emma wondered why she had said that. It sounded right, and she said it again, "Praise God. Xavier meskin."

"Ah, she is frightened," said Daniachew, pulling his jacket collar. He had acquired the bright red coat from a bundle of donated clothing strapped with steel tape. "She is asking where she is."

"Tell her she's safe. Let's get her back inside."

All moved in to help Misrak, who stood as if raised by four pillars. The wind streaked her tears, and she drew away, protecting her sore arm and breast. Inside, Emma checked the cot and found the mattress to be soaked with urine, the IV bottle still attached to the ceiling, dripping onto the floor.

"Put her in my bed," said Emma. Terry and Daniachew took over, and Alene arrived with a bright smile.

"I'll get her some clothes from the warehouse," said Lisa. "Daniachew, don't forget to get some bread."

"Ishi," and he left, glad to be away from the swell of sorrow.

Soon, Misrak wore loose men's suit pants and an acrylic sweater with a bizarre zigzag pattern, like the sewing machine had given up trying to make sense of the fabric. On her back again, she gazed around the room. She called out her oldest daughter's name.

"Alem Ketema," said Emma. "Your family is okay. We're going to Addis Ababa. Helicopter. You are very sick," and she pointed to her own breast.

Alene elaborated for Emma in Amharic.

"Yellum," said Misrak, and she said that her children needed her.

"But she will die, otherwise," said Emma.

Alene told Misrak, "Sometimes the mother bird must fly away. She will be stronger when she returns." The wind seemed to whistle in approval.

Misrak tried to sit up, but fell back with the pain.

"Can she drink water?" asked Emma. "She needs to drink."

"No, she is not thirsty."

"May need another IV."

Alene stood with his hands in his pockets. He liked the feel of the lining there, plus his hands were cold. He tried not to stare at Emma. He could only think that she had jumped from the helicopter and lived. Many were saying that she had fallen more than thirty meters, but had broken no bones. It seemed a miracle or perhaps, as some suggested, the work of the devil. He had never met a woman like her, trying to save this peasant woman who would most likely die anyway.

Within an hour, Terry had refueled the Bell 412 with three hundred gallons of aviation turbine and was ready to go. He should have waited until everyone was buckled in to power up, but he was in a hurry to get back and make the trip to Meranya. The rain had stopped, but the wind still kicked over the cliff edge in terrific gusts. It reminded him of flying conditions in the blustery mountains of Lesotho. Lisa had decided not to go and made a travel bag for Emma of homemade cookies, famine crackers, and wheat buns. "Be careful!" she shouted.

"Will do!" Emma stooped her way to the open door. Inside, two seats faced two seats, with the others removed for baggage and boxes. Misrak, who was strapped in and moaning, tried to keep her head erect. "Poor baby," said Emma. She pushed back Misrak's head, the skin warm and dry. The copter roared. Misrak's head flopped forward, her eyes dull from an injection of promethazine. Emma waved at Terry, who was looking over his shoulder, waiting for her to strap in opposite Misrak.

Emma grabbed her backpack and fished out a roll of wide silk tape. Terry was motioning for her to put on her headset. She yelled for him to hold on and strung a piece of tape across the top of Misrak's seat, pulling her head back against the headrest. She applied two more strips for good measure.

Buckled, Emma put on the bulky headset.

"Thumbs up? Ready?" asked Terry. His voice sounded as if it was coming through a Brillo pad.

Emma spoke, but forgot to push the inline talk button.

Terry brought the engine to 101 percent RPMs. Everyone was buckled and the doors locked. He estimated wind gusts to be nearly 25 kph. He waited for the orange cone to droop and nudged the craft upward, rotating toward the cliff edge. An avalanche of wind slewed into the copter, pushing them sideways and backwards only meters from the ground. "Motherfuck!" and Terry muscled the controls and dipped the nose, trying to go with the wind and climb above the turbulence.

Emma gasped. Briefly, she thought they were flying backwards, and they were. "What the hell!"

Like corkscrewing up to avoid a rock wall, Terry climbed and raced with the wind, AK spinning away below. He stabilized and rounded back for his southwest course to Addis Ababa. "You, okay?"

"Yeah, what the hell happened?"

"Wind got us. Anyway, all's well, right?" He worked his way to ten thousand feet, enough to clear every amba and mountain with room to spare.

"I thought we were a kite there for a minute!" said Emma, shouting into the microphone. She kept her eyes on Misrak, slumping a bit, the tape pulling her eyebrows up into a look of surprise.

Terry laughed. "Yeah, basically we were, but nobody had the string." Again, he checked the seatbelt light.

Emma glanced out the window, watching the patchwork quilt of browns and greens pass below. She could see a road with no one on it for miles and miles, and soon they crossed the swollen Jemma River and a wide, wide valley. Within thirty minutes, the land rushed up again and then down into the bowl that was Addis Ababa.

Terry approached Lideta airport, which was primarily used for military aircraft. The Polish Army had established a temporary but ship-shape camp there. The Mission was on good terms with the Polish, having worked with them in AK, receiving their airdrops in Godo and Gundo Meskel two years prior. He picked a patch of old runway, near a demolished tank, circled twice, and landed. Within seconds, a military jeep fitted with a 50-caliber gun approached and waited. The passenger, a young soldier nicknamed Fidel, recognized Terry, took off his hat, and approached.

Terry idled down and reached for the clipboard with his RRC papers. He had no idea what they said, but they were his magic travel passport, but always with a little angle. He pulled a 20-birr note from his wallet and waited for the rotors to spin down. "Emma, I'll come around and help. Hold on!"

Emma tore the tape holding Misrak's forehead. Misrak's eyes roamed the interior, through the windows, into Emma's eyes. Emma regretted not dressing her better. She looked crazy in the suit pants and zigzag sweater.

"Shintabet," said Misrak. She gagged.

"Oh Lord," said Emma. The door opened behind her, and Terry hopped up. "She needs the toilet."

Terry frowned. Was this why he flew helicopters? "Okay, let's just get her out first. There's a jeep that'll take you to the Polish camp at the other end. She'll have to wait."

Emma couldn't think of the word for wait. "Tigist," she

said, a girl's name meaning patience. "Tigist, okay. Shint-abet?"

Misrak mumbled and just stared at her. "Ishi," she said, and felt herself lifted. She was moving toward a door, and the ground was far away. She moaned, fearing they would drop her.

Fidel had stamped the papers with purple ink and pocketed the birr. This woman looked horrible, barely able to stand, her face swollen, her clothes an abomination. He guided them with stiff forearms to the bench seat on the back of the jeep.

Emma piled on with Misrak, cradling her. She looked to Terry for help. "What's next?"

"I can't leave the machine, have to go. At the camp, ask for Kapitan Jozef. He speaks English, a little English. He can call Guthrie for you. You'll be fine, real friendly people." He spoke to Fidel, "Kapitan Jozef?" He pointed to Emma.

"Ishi, ishi, Kapitan Jozef." He gave Terry a winning smile and hopped up front with the driver, and away they went, the tires throwing up grit and gravel.

Emma watched Terry recede and gazed at the cracked runway, as if cut with a giant knife. The sky looked like souse meat. She searched for the sun, but nothing gave it away.

The jeep puttered up to the encampment of tight, dark-green tents. An elevated wooden path snaked down the exact middle. There seemed to be no one about. Emma could hear the helicopter revving, but could no longer see it.

"Okay, come." Fidel waited for them to stand and then

realized help was needed. He shouted to the driver, who popped up with a toothy grin. "Wait," said Fidel, and he stepped onto the boardwalk and ventured down three tents. He scratched on the fabric instead of knocking, and the large, heavyset flight sergeant known simply as Luka opened the built-in wooden door. Fidel asked for the Kapitan, but Luka only shrugged. "What is it?" he asked in Polish. "The lady is sick," said Fidel in Amharic. He pointed down the walkway.

Luka knew where the Kapitan was but wanted first crack at whatever Fidel had summoned. He was lonely in Addis and spent hours listening to old 78s on a wind-up record player. "Let us see." He smoothed down buttons over his enormous stomach and checked his shiny boots.

Emma watched the large man in green fatigues approach. She was standing in front of Misrak, holding her up. The man seemed to have a happy face, like he was used to eating lots of ice cream. She waved, not knowing why.

"Hmm, what is this?" Luka spoke only Polish. He tipped his gray felt hat to Emma and frowned at Misrak. Perhaps he would need the Kapitan after all. "Luka," he said. Maybe this one could dance?

"Luka? Emma. I need to get this woman to Black Lion Hospital. I need to call Dr. Guthrie at the Baptist Mission." She let that sink in. Misrak moaned, cleared her throat, and spit, but it caught on her lips and stayed there.

"Ah, Baptysów." Luka nodded. He motioned for Emma to follow. "Come."

Fidel barked at the driver who helped Emma with Misrak. He was speaking to Misrak, asking her if she had typhus. He would run if she did. Between them, Misrak hobbled, looking like a wounded freak. Down they stepped and through the door into Luka's pristine tent. There was a dining room table, three wooden chairs, the old phonograph, a cot, and an antique sideboard with dishes.

"Here," Luka said in Polish.

Emma lowered Misrak onto the stiff chair, wanting to lay her down on the cot covered with a green wool blanket. "Ishi, mama. You're okay. Almost there." She watched the driver exit and was left with Luka looming over her.

"She is sick," said Luka. "Vodka, shai?"

"Shai. Amenseganolo. For this one." She pointed at Misrak.

Like magic, Luka went to the sideboard. There was a kettle on a hot plate. He took a delicate china cup and drew off a cup of steaming tea, which he handed to Emma.

Emma placed it on the table to cool.

"And you?" asked Luka.

Emma thought she understood. "Okay, shai. Amenseganolo."

Luka precisely tippled another pour into a matching cup. He made a frog noise and then placed each cup on top of a white saucer. He clapped his hands and cranked the phonograph ten times. The record wobbled as it spun in the dim light. Luka let the needle down to a loud hiss followed by rambunctious polka music. His face lit up into a grin. Maybe the pretty one would dance, but first he had to find the Kapitan. "Ah, mi scusi," he said. Emma smiled and laughed. Polka music, an accordion and a tuba. The door closed behind him. "Shinatabet," said Misrak.

Reece was stunned, his brain jolted. All he could say was, "Hey!" Looking up through the swaying pines, the baby-blue sky seemed attached to the tops. He eased his right leg from beneath his body. The marble cooled his back, and he placed his palms down and traced where the slabs joined. He looked over to the green swing. He remembered his mom and dad sitting there like statues all those years ago. A man, a neighbor, had walked by smoking a cigarette, and his dad had chewed him out. His mother was allergic. *For Pete's sake!* And then that crazy guy stalking through Luby's, firing every five seconds, shooting people in the head. He imagined the baby blue of the sky melting into purple and then the chocolate of space. There had to be life out there, on other planets, visitors to Earth. He remembered the nightmares from his childhood, the being that plagued his room late at night. How he'd felt helpless, how he'd never once tried to get into his parents' bed, as if they were somehow behind the terror. God, he had dreaded nightfall, and still he heard his heartbeat at night, footsteps on the carpet.

"I've fallen," he said to the trees. He supposed he could just stay there until Kristin arrived. Maybe she would take pity on him, but his back hurt, and he felt nauseous from whacking his head. He wondered if rain that had fallen in the lake below the road had ever touched Godo, maybe a tear that had evaporated into the sky. He put his hands in his jeans' pockets to see how that would feel.

It took a minute, but he stood and sat heavy on the metal

swing. His mind wandered back to Africa, flying into Ethiopia from Nairobi. The stewardesses had been numerous and lovely to look at. He tried to remember a smell but couldn't. A mushroom of thought slowed time. Dr. Guthrie had met him at the airport in Addis Ababa. They'd had a warm soda in a small café. *Warm soda.* Herds of goats in the streets. Men with wheelbarrows full of oranges. Huge burlap sacks of potatoes. A definite smell of musty concrete. He'd had his hands on her breasts, Emma's breasts for God's sake. He remembered, and he squirmed. He'd slid his hands down her scrub top through the large arm openings. She wasn't wearing a bra.

Kristin tapped the horn. Reece twitched, fathoming the disconnect, and turned and waved. She parked in the driveway behind him. He put his arm onto the back of the swing and turned, smiling, he thought. He wasn't sure. He repositioned his face with the muscles there. Hoping to get it right.

"Hey, brought you an egg roll."

She looked pretty in shorts and a bright yellow t-shirt. Her legs were pencil-thin, with narrow hips and shoulders. He'd never tried to touch her breasts, just pressure through her clothes.

"Really?" He loved egg rolls. He'd only had his first Chinese food about a year ago with his friend George. They'd both ordered sweet and sour chicken with the sticky red sauce. It hadn't seemed very Chinese, but it was good like breaded fried chicken should be. "Thanks. Have a seat." He patted the swing.

"I am so tired."

"Rough day?"

"The usual. Standing, running. Are your eyes a little crossed?"

"Maybe. I did just fall and hit my head." He put his hand on her thigh and squeezed.

"What? You don't need to be walking alone. You know that."

"Not as bad as the leeches, though." He grinned and told her about jumping into the lake.

Kristin looked disgusted. She examined the marks on his arms. "My God! Reece. Next, you'll walk in front of a car." She held the egg roll in a little paper sack stained with oil, stapled at the top.

"I doubt that. Maybe one will back over me, though." He laughed. "Maybe you, to get rid of me." His head hurt. "Dinner should be ready soon. Want to walk to the lake first?"

"Are you kidding me? You just fell in. Here, eat the egg roll."

"No, it'll spoil my dinner. Pork chops, fried squash. Maybe some chess pie, too."

"I made a special trip," said Kristin. "If Emma had brought you one, you'd eat it." She folded her hands in her lap.

Reece looked away.

"Well, that's a great answer," said Emma. "Maybe we'll go to the lake, and I'll push you in."

"Kristin, please. Forget about Emma."

"Has she written you any more letters?" She hunched her shoulders.

"I have no idea. Not yet anyway. I'll let you know if she does." His cheeks flushed just a bit.

"You do that, okay? Promise? I don't want her sending you letters. I think she's unstable."

Reece rolled his eyes. "Why do you think that?"

"I don't know. Just an impression from the hospital when I visited you. I had to borrow the money from my parents for the plane ticket."

Reece winced. "I'll pay them back. I should be able to get back to work soon."

Kristin laughed. "Are you kidding me? You can barely walk."

"Never underestimate the power of a Frigidaire."

"What is that supposed to mean?"

The screen door to the laundry room slammed. "Hey, dinner's about done." Dora had her hands on her hips. "Hey there, Kristin." She moved toward them.

"Hey, Granny." Kristin still cringed every time she said Granny. She had a meemaw. "We're coming."

Dora nodded and stepped back inside.

"What did the tired squirrel in the refrigerator say?" asked Reece. "This is my Westinghouse."

Kristin pulled her mouth sideways, a look Reece recognized.

"Are we married?" asked Reece.

"No, but we're engaged...at least I thought we were."

"For the love of God, of course we are. Let's go eat."

Kristin nodded. "That's good to hear. I love you, Reece." She put her face close to his.

Reece kissed her soft cheek.

"Oh God, on the cheek!" Kristin stood with effort. The paper sack fell onto the marble.

"I'll get it." Reece leaned over and fell to his knees. He

looked up at Kristin, her face couched in brown curls. He opened the bag and took a bite. "Want some?"

"It'll spoil my appetite," and she walked to the house.

At the table, Kristin told them about the rude judge and then about Mrs. Dunlop, the crazy lady she was taking care of. The dead boy hit by the coal truck was too depressing to mention.

"You see a lot, don't you?" said Horace. "One time, I was in my daddy's wagon. We came around the bend, and there was a dead baby in the ditch, just as dead and lifeless as could be."

"Horace, that's enough," said Dora. "We're eating."

Reece laughed and looked to see if Kristin was laughing.

Horace looked especially old telling that particular story. His thin gray hair was combed straight back, a horseshoe of bald in the front. He treated it to keep it from going white.

"That's a pretty yellow shirt," said Dora.

"And the squash is good," said Kristin.

"Gravy's good," said Reece. He put his hand to his forehead and arched back. "Jesus."

"Reece?" asked Dora, her fork midway to her mouth.

Reece imagined a lone steer being beaten to death with an iron bar. He made a squeaky noise. Was he still in the chair? He grabbed the air for balance and knocked over his sweet tea.

"Reece!" Kristin leaned over to keep him from sliding out of his swivel chair. His eyes quivered, and he arched for five long seconds.

Reece saw yellows and browns, rivers and canyons, a crowd of red fish swirling, birds swarming to a point, a poem of metal falling into a small wooden bowl.

Dressed in an unbuttoned greatcoat despite the heat, Kapitan Jozef peered into the tent. Luka stood behind him. Polka music, a young woman with dirty blonde hair, and another woman taking deep breaths, slumped in the chair. The music, and he knew Luka was trying to seduce the young one.

"What is this?" He spoke English.

Emma wanted to stand, but Misrak would fall from the chair. "Hey, hello, sir, my name is Emma. Is there a bathroom, shintabet?"

The Kapitan lifted the needle arm from the record. A brief silence. He turned and gave Luka a stony look. "Yes, you are with the Baptysów?"

Misrak's lips moved without sound.

"Correct," said Emma. "The Baptist Mission. I need to call Dr. Guthrie for a ride to Black Lion, the hospital."

The Kapitan spoke to Luka. "He will help you take her to the latrine. The phone is near, in my headquarters. You will come soon, no? Luka will show you."

"Yes," said Emma. "Sure. Thank you."

Misrak let out a slow and shrill moan. She looked like a collapsed balloon, her eyes closed. "Let's do this," said Emma, and she motioned for Luka.

In the latrine, Misrak had diarrhea and vomited bile. It was so far back to the tent that Emma convinced Luka to lean Misrak against a eucalyptus tree stripped of its lower branches. "She's a mess," said Emma, squatting beside her.

Luka hovered, wanting to help. The music had helped, he thought. He spoke a few encouraging words in Polish. Emma nodded but couldn't understand. She needed to wash her hands. For the first time, she noticed a wet spot over Misrak's breast near the armpit, as if something had ruptured, and it had. She mumbled a curse, challenging the devil to eat his own. She growled and then smiled at Luka, who loomed large over them like two or three men inside his uniform.

She told him that she was going to use the phone to call the "Baptist sows," to call Dr. Guthrie. Luka circled his large stomach with his hands and grunted okay to whatever she had said. He watched her stand and walk toward the tent of Kapitan Jozef. She looked back, and he saluted her.

The door was open, and Emma peered into the impeccable tent, even more tidy than Luka's. There was a single bed, a small desk, and four matching chairs. The phone sat on a rough wooden table. Did it work?

"You remind me of my sister," said the Kapitan. He stood with his hands behind his back.

"Thank you. I wish I could meet her."

"It is possible. She lives in Sweden."

"You said I could use the phone?"

"Hmm. Yes. Of course." He turned his back and looked out the open door of the tent.

The dial tone amazed Emma. She could just reach out and touch anyone in the world with a phone. She dialed zero and then the operator connected her to the Baptist Mission's main number. A male voice answered in Amharic. Emma could tell that the operator was still there listening.

"It's Emma, from Godo. I'm in Addis at the airfield and need to speak with Dr. Guthrie."

Tesfaw stumbled for a moment, piecing the puzzle together. "Ah, yes. Emma. You are visiting us?"

"No, I have a very sick woman. We need a ride to the hospital. Is Dr. Guthrie there?"

"Dr. Guzry is not here. He may be at his home. Yes. I will call him."

"Okay, great. Thank you. I'm at the base of the Polish Army at the airfield. Kapitan Jozef? The woman is very ill. She may die."

"My goodness," said Tesfaw. "At Lideta with the Kapitan. Yes, of course. I will tell to him. I will call and tell to him." The connection was a little cloudy.

"Okay, great, thank you, Tesfaw. I will wait here, okay? Tell him to come as soon as possible. It's urgent. He may be angry."

Tesfaw knew it was true. "Oh no, do not say that thing. He is coming for you, no, very soon, okay?"

Emma feared letting Tesfaw go, afraid that the magic connection was only temporary. "Okay, thank you and goodbye."

"You are welcome. Ciao." There was a click

A sound of breathing on the line, as if the phone were being held up to a vast empty room. "Okay." Emma placed the black receiver back on the tall handset and stared at it for a moment.

"All is good?" The Kapitan put two fingers between his collar and neck.

"Well, not really. The patient is very ill, with cancer. She needs a doctor, surgery, something I can't provide." There was silence, and Emma could hear a clock ticking even though she could not see it. *Misrak,* and she walked past the Kapitan.

Dr. Guthrie was elbow deep inside a cow's uterus when Rosie came outside with the news. Emma was in Addis, with a patient who needed to go to Black Lion Hospital. Guthrie was nearing the end of a clinic, held in his front yard, and frowned. What could it possibly be? He remembered the last patient flown out from Godo, a man with his intestine looped down inside his scrotum. That had cost them a pretty penny.

He finished clinic within the hour, washed up, and took the Toyota van out to Lideta, the military airport. His wallet held 500 birr to get the ball rolling on whatever catastrophe Emma had uncovered. He flashed his purple-stamped papers at the gate and drove beneath a lifted steel pole. This would be the first time she had flown with a patient to Addis, so it must be a doozy. He half-expected to see a torso separated from its legs or possibly just a head. He made a note to himself that he should be ashamed and hit the parking brake.

Squatting beside Misrak, Emma watched Dr. Guthrie appear over the tops of the tents. She stood. Her vision went black, and she bent over to catch herself. She'd only had a cup of tea and a small cup of water the entire day.

"Whoa, You, okay? The sick taking care of the sick?" asked Guthrie. He realized his pants were loose and his shirt was tight. It occurred to him that his body was changing shape, getting bigger up top and shrinking down below. He looked at his tennis shoes, which fit just fine.

Emma cleared her vision. "Yeah, but this lady here…"

Guthrie looked down at Misrak. She looked like death warmed over. "What's the problem?"

"Her breast turned black, swollen, and now it's weeping or something ruptured. It's under her armpit, too."

"Could be cancer."

"That's what I thought. She has three kids."

"We're not equipped to be taking folks from up-country. It's dang expensive, and even here, there's not much they can do. She would probably need to fly out to Nairobi if it's cancer."

"We have to try. I'll pay for it if that's what it takes." Emma's face flushed. She felt a pocket of air in her chest. "Three kids."

"That's not unusual. You know that."

"What does that mean? Just give up?" She put her hands on her hips.

"Heck, Emma." He folded his arms.

"Yeah, heck. She'll die soon if we don't help her. If she has to go to Nairobi, then so be it."

Guthrie shifted from one foot to the other. He put one hand in his pocket. "Let's get her to the hospital. See what they say."

Emma smiled. "Yeah, good. Okay. She needs us both to help her."

Guthrie untucked his shirt and grunted an affirmative, smelling the diarrhea. His whole life seemed to revolve around poop and pee.

Emma had an idea and looked at her watch. It was early morning back in Alabama. At the Mission, she would call and check on Reece. She had his grandparents' number.

The ceiling was white or gray. The floor was cold. Reece moved his eyes from face to face. He spoke, but it was gibberish.

"Reece?" Kristin sat cross-legged beside him on the kitchen linoleum. "You back?"

Horace and Dora sat in their swivel chairs, eyes on Reece on the floor.

"What?" asked Reece. His bottom felt warm and gushy.

"You had a seizure. You're back. You're okay." Kristin ran her fingers through his damp hair. "Do you know where you are?"

Reece could hear her, as if she were speaking into a microphone. "Sallad, Texas?"

"He lived in Texas," said Dora.

"You're at the lake with your grandparents, in their house. You had a seizure."

"Amabala?"

"Yeah, Alabama, not Ethiopia. You're home?"

"I've been shot," said Reece.

"You were, but not just now." Kristin couldn't decide if she wanted to laugh or cry.

Reece closed his eyes, could feel sleep calling him. A warmth cloaked him, a deep and thick sleeping bag, dark within. "Fudge everybody," he said. "Sleep." He turned on his side.

"Reece!" said Kristin. What was she supposed to do, get him a pillow and a blanket?

As if in response, Reece said, "Pig in a blanket." He was

recalling fifth grade, December, moving to Fort Knox. He was the new kid, as usual. The lunch line had been long, and the menu in chalk had announced the day's entrée as pig in a blanket. He'd had no clue what he was about to be served, but then there it was, a piece of hot dog inside some kind of biscuit. "Pig in a goddamn blanket."

"Reece!" Kristin looked at Dora for support and went to her knees.

"I can't believe it," said Reece. "All these years. Water over the dam." There was the Big Bang, or was there? There was something before the Big Bang, and what could it be?

"Can he stand up?" Horace was glued to his chair, watching the events unfold in slow motion.

"He's talking funny." Dora marveled at Kristin, trained to help others. "I'm sure glad you're here, darling."

"Hey, try to sit up, slow. Try it," said Kristin. Would this be her future, forever taking care of him?

"Yadda, yadda, yadda." Reece pushed up on an elbow and turned to his side. Little lights danced, and he stared at the brown built-in stove. The same middle school. A punk had shoved his tray across the table onto Reece's, knocking his Jell-O from its molded space. There were words and then punches. Reece wanted the little bastard to die, but then his homeroom teacher had appeared. Reece punched him in the stomach and then ran from the building in a rage. Everybody, it seemed, wanted to fuck with him.

"Son, let her help you," said Horace. He was standing now. "Can I help?"

Things sort of clicked, and Reece bent his knees, turned

over, and crawled to Horace's recliner, using it to stand. He was dizzy and sat, head in his hands. He thought about how the dogs fought at night in Godo, how it sounded like murder, like the end of the world. Emma was there, caring for the sick. He had been there. *Damn.*

"He said he fell outside and hit his head," said Kristin. "Look at me." She peered into his eyes, comparing the pupils. She took his wrist and felt his fast and thready pulse. "You really shouldn't let him walk by himself."

"Well," said Dora. "I can't stop him. He walked to the lake by himself."

"You could, if you wanted to," said Kristin. Her cheeks colored. Could no one help her?

Horace cleared his throat and coughed, waiting for the moment to pass.

"Don't blame them," said Reece.

"I'm not blaming anyone," said Kristin.

"Sounds like it." Reece wanted to laugh and did.

Kristin sighed. "What's so funny?" She stood over Reece, like a mother eagle shading her young from a hot sun. "And what's that smell? Did you?"

"Hell," said Reece. He frowned, dismayed, defeated, incontinent. "I did, but I don't need help in case you're wondering."

"Fine, have it your way." Kristin looked to Dora for support, but she was scraping a skillet in the sink, head down. Horace twiddled his thumbs.

Reece forced himself to stand. He felt the sag in his underwear and walked funny to the bathroom, but he needed new underwear. "Can somebody bring me a pair of underwear?" He gazed into the bathroom, talking to it.

"I'll get 'em," said Dora. "You go on in." She rinsed the skillet and dried it, set it on the stove.

After his second shower of the day, Reece sat on the love-seat with Kristin. She had her hand up his shirt, scratching his back. Horace and Dora had retired to their respective bedrooms, but the door was still open, and their snores resonated off the wood-paneled walls. A single lamp barely lit the room, and the TV was on with the sound low, a *Mission: Impossible* rerun.

"You like that, don't you?" Her jeans were tight, and her t-shirt untucked, shoes pushed off beneath the oval coffee table.

"Yeah. Go in the middle, up and down." He arched his back to get the most from her nails on his skin.

"Did Emma scratch your back?"

Reece coughed and rolled his closed eyes. He wore his comfy blue shorts and an old white scrub top that had a dive flag painted on the back.

"So, she did, didn't she?" She pulled her hand away.

Reece groaned. "No, she did not." He wanted to say that it would have been just fine if she had. "Can you scratch over my right shoulder blade?" He moved his shoulder up and down.

"No more scratching until you look at me and tell me exactly what you did do with Emma." She pulled her legs up in the chair, cross-legged, and folded her arms. "Hey."

"I was just going to sleep on her floor. I gave my bed to the guy with the rotten leg. I was just lying there, and she…" He felt like he'd swallowed a piece of unchewed meat.

"And she what? Why can't you look at me? Reece?" She leaned up. "No more back scratching then."

It was now or never. "She said her neck was stiff and asked if I could rub it." He turned and looked at Kristin.

"Oh my God. I knew it. She had a crush on you." Kristin licked her lips. "So, did you do it?"

Reece shook his head. "Okay, so I did. I freaking rubbed her neck. The guy I gave my bed to had no meat on his tibia and fibula, just a mound of jelly around his ankle."

"That's so gross, but you wanted to rub her neck. And then what happened? You might as well tell me."

"Well, a bullet went through my skull. How about that for a climax?" He sat back, not looking at her.

Kristin melted just a bit. "Really?"

"Okay, I may have touched her breasts. I don't remember. She wasn't wearing a bra, and everything was just so tense and chaotic."

"Her breasts! Talk about karma," said Kristin. "If you'd been on the floor where you belonged, the bullet would have missed you. Right? I can't believe this."

"What happened happened. I'm sorry. I really am."

"You should have told me this sooner. I mean, how am I supposed to trust you? We're engaged, or at least I thought we were, and you go off to another country, to Africa for God's sake, and start fooling around with another woman. Jeez."

Horace stumbled from his bedroom into the little den, wearing his underwear. He saw them on the loveseat. "Oh!" He retreated for his pants.

"He pees about a dozen times at night," said Reece. "Prostate."

"Has he had it checked out?"

"Yeah. He's had to have a catheter—"

Kristin slapped his leg. "Don't change the subject, Albert Einstein."

"Albert Einstein?"

"You know what I mean. Don't play dumb. I can't believe it. And to think I trusted you."

"Okay, call it karma, call it even. I think I've paid."

Horace, with his pants on, closed the bathroom door. Reece listened to the weak trickle of urine splashing into the bowl.

"Are we engaged? Are we getting married?"

"Yes, of course. Nothing's changed. I keep saying that."

"Yeah, but you left, then you were shot, then the tornado. You're covered with leech bites, you had a seizure, crapped your pants, and now you tell me you cheated on me. What's next? Sex with a stripper?"

Reece laughed. "Covered with leech bites. That sounds so ridiculous, but it's true." He kept laughing.

"And I brought you a dingdang egg roll. You didn't get any leeches on your you-know-what, did you? Crapped your pants." Kristin fought the smile, began laughing.

Horace hurried from the bathroom back to the bedroom, glad that they were having a good time.

Reece doubled over, laughing. Tears came to his eyes. His face felt wet.

Kristin threw back her head, laughing, exhaling. "You bastard. You S.O.B." Her laugh halted, and she teared up. "I need to leave. I have to get up and go to work. Think about this on the way home." She wiped her eyes. "You dummy, I love you."

Reece had stopped laughing, but still, one last laugh crept out. He caught his breath and steadied himself. He knew what he had to do. "I love you, too."

The phone rang, odd at that hour, and Reece answered.

Darkness with winks of light to the side, Emma sat silent in the van as it rolled across the potholed roads of Mekanisa, the neighborhood of the Baptist Mission. They crossed a bridge, and Emma held her breath. The runoff from the Awash winery spilling down the hill in rivulets smelled like puked vinegar. She would never get used to it.

"Geez, how do the people stand it?" asked Emma. The van navigated a deep pool of muddy water, yawning in and out.

"You can get used to anything," said Guthrie. His forearms bristled as he steered. He just wanted to get home and sleep. It had taken them until nearly midnight to get Misrak admitted to the hospital, and then there would be a hefty bill.

Emma rolled with the van as it roamed over large holes in the road. Back in Alabama, it would be four in the afternoon. She could get up as early as six and call Reece. She set a mental alarm clock. "Can I sleep at your place tonight? I need to make a phone call early." There was no phone in the guesthouse. Phone calls back home from lonely missionaries could bankrupt the Mission.

Guthrie nodded and said, "Yeah, sure. Livvy'll take care of you. The boys are back at boarding school, so plenty of room. Gonna call your mom?"

"Um, not really." Should she call Reece? She was the reason he'd been shot, or was it just fate, or God's will? Or maybe the devil, a freaking accident. "Gonna call Reece at his grandparents' house."

Guthrie suspected, as did everyone else, that Reece was why she had jumped from the copter.

"Have you heard anything new?" asked Emma.

"Just about the tornado, from friends back home." Guthrie flashed his lights at a pack of men walking in the middle of the road.

"Yeah, Terry told me. Said it hit UAB Hospitals, where Reece was. Couldn't have been too much damage, right?"

"Well, it killed hundreds, so must have been an F-5. Alabama gets 'em every few years." He turned the van into his long dirt driveway. His house didn't have a wall around it, a gate, or a guard. The people needed his services and spared him any mischief.

Emma wrapped her head around the tornado. "Surely, he's back home by now. I just know it."

Guthrie coughed and put it into park. "Emma, he was shot in the head. I wish that it could be good news, but you have to be realistic."

"Yeah, I was there. But the bullet went through a wall first. Maybe..."

"And it still went through his head. I really don't see how he's alive. It's God is all I can say. He had some cash in the bank, if you know what I mean."

"Cash in the bank?"

"You know, credit, savings. He's obviously within God's favor."

"Credit? But he was shot. How is that credit?" Emma reached to push the button on her seatbelt, but she'd never buckled.

Guthrie laughed. "He should be dead, but he's alive."

"Why would God let him be shot, though? If he has

credit."

Guthrie sensed a standoff. "He's blessed to be alive. That's all I can say." He hit the emergency brake, even though the ground was flat. The van's engine fan kicked on.

Emma opened her door and heard the hum of a dark ghetto. The leper hospital was just half a mile away. Dogs yipping, but not tearing one another apart, the murmur of a hundred thousand voices.

Livvy met them at the door wearing a man's brown robe with a belt tie. "Look who hung the moon. I'm sure glad to see you." She looked at her husband as he walked to the kitchen and then at Emma. "Hey there, stranger." Curlers poked her hairnet.

"Tired as a dog," said Emma.

"I wish I'd have known you were coming. Would have had a room ready."

Emma waved her off. "I can sleep on the floor if I have to."

"None of that for sure. Who do you think I am?"

Without thinking, Emma said, "The queen bee." She laughed to herself. "Sorry."

"That's a good one," said Livvy. "Need anything to eat, drink? Cookies, tea?"

"Just a giant glass of water would be great, and maybe a cookie or two."

Livvy moved to the kitchen, and Emma led herself into the dark living room with its cheap paneling and plethora of family photos. She arched back with her hands to her kidneys and groaned. She did the math, and it would be ten p.m. in Alabama if she called at six a.m. That seemed the right thing to do. She was too tired to even try at the moment. She eased herself onto a plaid couch covered with an orange-and-brown afghan. She thought about her mother working at Duck's Barbecue, her asshole dad who lived not so far away in a trailer. Thoughts of Green Hill Baptist Church played among images of Reece in a hospital bed. She hadn't been able to keep up with her prayer list, but she had made a point to pray for Reece. Would he answer the phone? His grandparents would be in bed. He'd be there in their house, maybe watching TV, and he'd get the phone on the fifth ring. She replayed his voice in her head, not Southern but understated and a bit monotone.

"Goodness, Emma," said Livvy. "You have more adventures than anybody." She set the water and cookies on the homemade coffee table.

"I haven't been shot yet. Surprise." She ran both hands through her oily hair. Her left hand seemed a bit bigger than her right. Was that normal?

"Please don't even joke about that," said Livvy.

"The Hyena is crazy. I'm probably next on his list. Maybe he was trying to hit me instead of Reece." The thought pressed her into the couch.

"We think he was just drunk. He could have unloaded the whole gun, but he only shot twice."

It occurred to Emma that others were thinking it through, reaching conclusions. She gulped her water and wasted a cookie in one bite. "Too drunk, I suppose, to get it right."

"Look, it's way past my bedtime, and Norbert's already in bed. Let's talk in the morning. What do you say? I'll get a clean pillowcase for the bedroom."

"No need," said Emma. "Just point the way."

The next morning, the roosters woke Emma. She fumbled for her watch under the pillow and tried to read it. It was too dark, so she knew she had some time to just lie there before she called Reece. She practiced saying *Hello, Hey Reece. Reece! Reece?* Life was short, very short. She had to pee and unfurled herself from the comfy blankets and sheet. The air chilled her. The twin bed belonged to Guthrie's oldest son, a freshman in high school in Nairobi. A framed puzzle of a dinosaur hung on the wall. A walnut-stained wooden dresser held two trophies, but otherwise the room was plain, kind of empty. She imagined that her life's momentum was zero.

She checked her watch in the bathroom. Four-thirty. Maybe she should go ahead and call. She decided to wait at least until five-thirty and then slid back beneath the covers. She remembered Misrak, how frightened she had been on the open ward with a dozen other patients in iron-framed beds painted white. *The clinic in Godo.* The people would have to wait, but Afewerki could take care of the minor aches and pains, the worms, and dog bites. *Who am I?* She felt that she had let down the entire universe, especially when she had jumped from the helicopter. She replayed the scene. The helicopter to her had seemed to be spinning out of control, the door unrelenting, but then *wham,* she was on the ground. She rolled her shoulder, still feeling the soreness there. What did people think of her? Was she crazy? She felt a little crazy, no doubt about that, like at times a bucket was over her head as she ran an obstacle course. And Reece had understood. He was the only one who would ever have a clue. She imagined dialing the phone. Maybe a jovial "Hey!" would be best.

Emma laid there, turning every few minutes, twisting the sheet and blankets. She was warm and comfortable, but her mind raced. Sunlight began to weep through the thin curtains, and she imagined a full moon rising back in Alabama. She pulled the top blanket over her head and smelled her body, her sweat, her anxiety. *Need a shower.*

She dreamed of rice pudding and woke an hour later, time to call Reece. She felt lethargic, ecstatic maybe. She felt like running a marathon, becoming a ball of dough. Her heart beat regular and loud. Now was the time to call. Still in her clothes from the previous day, she stretched and yawned. She half expected the Guthrie's oldest son to crawl from beneath the bed and perhaps pop a balloon. She decided she needed to wash her face with cold water first and did. The hand towel squeaked on its rack. She peered into the mirror over the sink. Her eyes seemed smaller, her eyelashes less full. Was she shrinking? The finest blonde down of a mustache fuzzed her upper lip.

The phone was in the living room with the vaulted ceiling, the brown paneling, and family photos. She held a letter with the number, opened her door, and went there. *Holy cow,* Dr. Guthrie was up and drinking coffee. He seemed like a sleuth, silent, sipping, wearing reading glasses, a book on his lap. Were his eyes closed?

"Hey there." Emma screwed her face sideways.

Guthrie flinched. "Oh, yeah, well, hey." He examined the book in his hands. "Up early?"

"Yeah." The phone was on an end table beside the

couch. She went there and sat down, crossed her legs, and realized she needed to pee. "Would you mind if I make that call to Reece?"

"You know the rules. We'll bill you for it. Tesfaw will." He pushed his feet down and raised the recliner.

"Whatever," said Emma. "It's a shot in the dark anyway. He could still be in the hospital, but his grandmother said he was coming around, moving his hands."

"I'm curious to see how he's doing, too. Do you need privacy?" He clasped his hands over his slight belly.

Emma thought. "No, no problem." She looked at the phone. There was magic in it. She would ask the operator to dial a number, and someone eight thousand miles away would answer and talk to her.

"You, okay?"

"Just thinking." She read the number on the paper to herself. Area code 205. "Well, here goes."

Guthrie laughed. "Livvy should be up soon. Make us some eggs and toast."

Emma put the phone to her ear and dialed zero for the operator. The intervening silence reminded her of an empty hallway. "Uh, yes, ow, United States, please. Yes. Two zero five, six eight one, seven three one four. Amenseganolo." Seconds passed, and then a ring that seemed to go on forever.

Reece squeezed Kristin's thigh, stood, dropped into Horace's recliner, and answered the phone. Right away, he knew the call was from far away, something about the hush and silence, a kind of invisible roar. He gazed at Kristin on the loveseat. The window AC unit kicked in, adding a hum to the room.

"Hello?"

"Reece? Oh my God. Reece?"

A slow procession of facts assembled in Reece's mind. He stared at Kristin.

"What?" asked Kristin.

"Yeah, hello?" He wanted to say her name.

"It's me, Emma. Say my name, you crazy person. Are you actually talking, answering the phone?"

"Who is it?" asked Kristin.

Reece felt like he was inside the barrel of a loaded gun. Who should he respond to? "It's you. Emma. Oh my God, and hey there."

"Emma?" asked Kristin. "Emma from Africa?"

"Yeah, I'm in Addis at Dr. Guthrie's house. He's right here. How are you? I can't believe you answered the phone."

"I'm okay. The leeches tried to eat me today, but otherwise okay." Reece considered reaching out his hand and touching her. He needed hours and hours to explain everything. He could see her face, Guthrie's face, the living room with the paneling, a smell of homemade crackers. Kristin folded her arms across her chest, uncrossing her legs. The deep green of her eyes.

"Reece? Leeches? Did you jump in the lake?" Her voice sounded like it was in a tin can.

"Yes, I did. Crazy, huh? I can't believe you're on the phone. Must be early there?" If he ever needed a drink, now was the time. He nodded his head at Kristin to indicate that it was indeed Emma from Africa. He put his hand over the receiver but then couldn't speak.

"Wow, I heard there was a tornado."

"Yeah, nearly got me. Destroyed the top floors of Spain-Wallace Towers. I had a nursing assistant there named Debbie Dee. She had cold sores in the corners of her mouth, but she got me out of bed, stretched my legs..." Reece watched Kristin lean even farther over, her mouth pinched.

"Reece! I can't take this." Kristin stood and put her hands on her hips. She could hear his grandparents snoring, the *whum* of the air conditioner. She envisioned the lake below the road as a black hole. "I'm leaving!"

Reece put his hand over the receiver. "No, don't leave. Hold on." He seemed to be floating on a giant potato chip down the Yangtze River.

"It's so good to hear your voice. I didn't think it was possible after what happened. And then the tornado."

"And don't forget the leeches," said Reece. He was standing, shaking his head at Kristin, pointing for her to sit down.

"Reece. Oh, you are so, so bad," said Kristin.

"Sit, just wait." He grimaced like a clown at a funeral home. He felt like a magnet in a black hole.

"Reece?" asked Emma.

Reece sat in Horace's recliner. It was made as cheap as they come, but worked, reclined like it should, although the leg reach was a bit short. "Emma, uh, I'm here with Kristin. We had dinner here, pork chops."

There was a silence of twelve seconds. "Yeah, Kristin. How is she?"

Reece felt a bit relieved. "She's great, doing just fine. Brought me an egg roll in a paper sack tonight. Yeah, we're here at the lake."

A silence of ten seconds. "I guess that's great. Are you..."

"Yeah, we're just here. I had a seizure today. How about that?" Reece realized his ear hurt, pressing the phone so hard against it.

"Jesus, leeches and a seizure? Maybe you should stay in bed for a few days."

"Yeah."

Kristin hung on his every word, staring at Reece through microscope eyes.

"Is she spending the night?" Emma wondered at the intermittent beeping tone every minute or so, typical of international calls from Ethiopia.

Reece delayed his response. He made a vague face gesture to Kristin. "No, no. We had dinner. Fried squash and pork chops."

"I'm sorry about what happened. I feel like maybe it was my fault, even though the Hyena pulled the trigger."

"What? Your fault. No way. It was his fault, the Hyena. I can't believe his name is the Hyena." He laughed. "Has he shown his face since?"

Kristin sat back on the loveseat, arms folded, legs crossed.

"Yeah, but he hasn't caused any trouble. Laying low, I suppose. I miss you in the clinic."

Reece swallowed. *The clinic.* "Yeah, the clinic was a trip. It seems like a million miles away." And it did. "I wish I could help."

"God's will and all that," said Emma.

Reece glanced at the TV, a commercial for dog food, chunky morsels. "Yeah, that's a topic for sure." He imagined Emma in her tight jeans and loose scrub top. Her breasts had filled his hands, and then *Bang!* He realized he was tense and then relaxed, first his neck and then his face and lower back.

"So why do you think it happened?" asked Emma.

"What do you mean?"

"You being shot, dummy."

"I don't know, alcohol, drugs. Jealousy. He's a crazy character."

Kristin stood again, then sat, pursing her lips. She wanted to break something. "Give me the phone. Reece?"

Reece made his eyes big. "Emma, hold on." He gave Kristin a begging look. "Please, I love you. Right? She's just checking on me."

"She knows we're engaged, unless maybe you told her otherwise. Give me the phone." She held out her hand.

"No," said Reece. His face flushed, his heart pounding. He went back to Emma. "Sorry, so maybe we should talk later."

"Oooh!" Kristin pulled back her brown curls, stretching the skin on her face. "That does it. You *want* to talk to her."

"Emma, hold on." Reece covered the receiver. "Yes, I do," he said in a hoarse whisper. What's wrong with that?

She works in that clinic by herself."

"Reece? Is she mad at you? Because of me?" asked Emma to an emptiness. Guthrie was pretending to look at a book by the fireplace. Livvy was in the kitchen, hanging on every word.

Kristin stood and stamped her foot on the faded carpet. "What? I couldn't work in a clinic by myself?"

"Oh Lord," said Reece. "No, it's—"

"You think she's prettier than me? Don't you?"

Reece gripped the phone. "What the hell? You said that, not me." He went back to Emma, feeling the fragility of their connection over two continents. "Uh, I should probably go for now."

"No, wait. I flew down here with a patient. Do you remember Misrak, the cook? She has breast cancer. I've been wanting to hear your voice, to see how you were doing, to make sure you were still alive."

Kristin moved to the kitchen by the stove, hands on her hips. She could see into Dora's bedroom and knew that she was listening. Whose side was she on?

"Emma—"

"The way you say her name..." Kristin moved to the door that led into the front living room. She held her keys in her hand like a grenade.

"Kristin, please," said Reece. "Emma, give me Dr. Guthrie's number. I'll call you in an hour. He picked a pen from a mug sitting on the bookshelf. There was a scrap of envelope.

Kristin watched Reece writing on the envelope. He was going to call Emma after she left. She stormed into the laundry room and couldn't unlock the back door, and then she did.

"Reece," said Emma. "Promise that you'll call me back."

"Okay, sure. No problem. I need to go for now."

"I...love you..." Emma felt the blood drain from her upper body as she said it, a vacuum of Arctic air in her limbs, a hollowness behind her eyes, as if falling.

An electric charge hit Reece in the chest. He imagined a broken watch, imagining Emma bending over a child in the clinic, looking into his ear with an otoscope. "Wow..." he said.

Emma dropped the phone onto the cradle. She hadn't been able to stand the silence after Reece's "Wow." She felt liberated, though, as if a torpedo had missed her life-boat by inches. She'd said it, though, gone out on a limb and said it. To her, the "Wow" was all she needed. She loved Reece and felt that he had reciprocated, that he'd been circumspect with Kristin. She imagined physically fighting Kristin for Reece and winning. Grabbing her hair, throwing her to the ground. She shuddered and realized she was staring into space with Dr. Guthrie watching her.

"That was him?" asked Guthrie.

Emma coughed. "In the flesh. He's walking around, jumped into the lake, got bit by leeches, and then had a seizure. But he sounds good, maybe kind of tired."

Livvy came in with a tray of sugar cookies and a pot of spiced tea. "This'll hold us till breakfast." She wore a long cotton housecoat with roses on it and fuzzy gold slippers. "That's amazing about Reece. I can't believe it."

"There's been a lot of prayers, mind you." Guthrie took two cookies and poured himself a cup of tea.

Emma felt energized. She felt like she needed to go on a long walk, maybe down to the leprosy center and back. The baseline of depression seemed down around her ankles, easy to step over. "He said he'd call back in an hour." She nibbled a cookie and felt the sugar rush through her body.

"He is, though, one lucky character." Guthrie ate two more cookies. "Gonna get fat."

"You already are, mister," said Livvy. "Save some room for eggs and toast, though."

"So why did God let Reece get shot? It doesn't make sense. He was doing good work. He'd given his bed to a man with a rotten leg." Emma sat on the green plaid couch with her cookie and tea in a china cup.

"And that man's in the hospital along with Misrak, remember that. Who knows what causes what? Without Reece, that man would not have had a chance. Without you, Misrak would probably be history. The only thing pretty in the Bible is heaven and maybe the Queen of Sheba."

Emma thought about how ugly Ethiopia could be, the hunger, the worms, the flies, the fighting dogs, the hyenas, and then the wretched Hyena himself. But then there were the smiles, the vistas, the huge fig trees, the market alive with spices and potatoes, the pretty young girls with perfect front teeth.

Livvy rattled a skillet in the kitchen, placing it on an eye. She felt that God gave each person a gift, and it was that person's purpose to exhibit that gift and not to question the good or the bad. Her gift was extreme patience. In the end, God would prevail, no doubt. She stepped into the hall. "How many eggs, y'all? Two apiece?"

Emma said, "Two is fine, scrambled or fried."

Guthrie said, "Make mine three, scrambled, and use that leftover beef tallow to fry them in." He rubbed his hands together. "Warm enough for you?"

"Sure." Emma was a bit chilled but okay. It was September, and dropped into the forties at night, warming into the seventies.

Livvy sliced six pieces of homemade white bread and

buttered them, placing them to the side on a baking sheet. The steel skillet was warming, the white butter melting. She hummed, "God is so Good...God is so good...He's so good, to, me." The eggs she got to work on, and she hit the bowl with a splash of raw milk and dashes of salt and black pepper.

"Well, he did survive, and he seems to be back on his feet without any kind of permanent damage," said Emma. "That's a miracle, right?" She imagined the foyer of a cheap motel, a slotted stand with brochures of local attractions. *See Rock City!* Reece had said something about his parents honeymooning in Chattanooga and that maybe he was conceived there. She'd never been and tried to imagine it. Was it a cave with rocks? And what about Ruby Falls? Was that in the same place?

Guthrie took the last cookie, poured more tea. The day was going to be busy with cattle clinics in his front yard and plenty of ivermectin to go around. "Better give me four pieces of toast, honey!"

Livvy grumbled, but sliced two more pieces.

"Tell me. Did you and Reece work in the same hospital back in Alabama? I can't remember," said Guthrie.

"No, I worked at UAB in infectious disease. He was at Carraway in CCU. Kristin, his fiancée, worked there, too."

"Oh," said Guthrie. "So, it's none of my business, but I heard you say that you loved him." He slurped down his tea.

Emma blushed. "Yeah. I think we had something, a real connection, working in the clinic. It's hard to describe, kind of like bonding. I felt like he understood me, what my problems were. Seeing a hundred patients a day will drive you insane by yourself. I think I would have gone nuts had he not shown up. At first, I was told his name was Rice. I thought maybe he was going to be from Vietnam."

Guthrie cleared his throat and laughed. "He's still engaged, though, right? Or has that changed?" He leaned over and loosened the laces on his scruffy dress shoes.

"Yeah, but..." Emma screwed up her face. She felt like throwing a gang sign, but didn't know any. "He was pressured into getting engaged, as far as I can tell. He said he was at a McDonald's eating a filet-of-fish sandwich, the ring in his pocket, going back and forth. He said he felt guilty about leaving her and coming over here, so he asked her to marry him, but then he wondered if he'd made a mistake."

"Good Lord, had to get McDonald's mixed up in it." Guthrie smiled and laughed. "Sounds pretty tricky to me. You better be careful, you know, and not get hurt." He remembered Emma jumping from the helicopter. She was damaged and bore watching.

The scrambled eggs cooked quick and fluffy, and Livvy dumped them into a ceramic bowl. Just then, the broiler beeped on her dark brown stove. She rubbed her hands together and opened the door. The toast needed a few more seconds, and she watched with the door cracked as the toast browned around the smears of bubbling butter. "Ready!" said Livvy. "Gets cold quick."

"Yo, yo, yo and a bowl of eggs." Guthrie wore worn dress pants and a blue short-sleeve shirt with a pocket, too tight as usual. He moved to the neat dining room with its 1950s laminated table and six red, vinyl chairs held together with screws and bent steel tubing. He took the chair at the head of the table.

Emma wondered at the lack of music in the house, although Livvy was humming in the kitchen. She needed some music about now, something to sink her teeth into, maybe some Dire Straits. Afewerki, back in Godo, liked them, had a tape, and how he'd gotten it, she had no clue. Just that refrain, "So far away from you." Made her think of Reece. Just a simple plane ride, though, and she could be in Birmingham. What was stopping her? The clinic, no doubt, and the people. She wasn't one to disappoint. She found herself in the dining room with Guthrie and took a chair.

Livvy brought in three glasses of water with lemon. She returned with a plate of perfect toast, then the bowl of fluffy scrambled eggs. Emma wondered if she would say, "Soup's On."

"Soup's on," said Livvy. "Eat up." She returned to the kitchen to do some dish soaking and make coffee.

"Livvy! Get in here and eat like the normal people," said Guthrie. He grinned.

"I agree," said Emma. "But maybe give her some leeway. She's got a system."

Guthrie looked up. "Yeah, she just needs not to be the martyr and eat. Livvy!"

"Coming, coming, hold your horses." Livvy made sure her housecoat was belted and brought in a small plate for herself. She took a scoop of eggs and a piece of toast. She wanted to stand, but sat since Emma was there.

"Emma here told Reece she loved him." He devoured a piece of buttery toast. "What do you think?"

"Oh my," said Livvy. "Yeah, I could hear." She poked at

her eggs, wondering if she should get the Merti ketchup.

Emma pushed back from the table. This was between her and Reece. "It goes both ways, so why should I be silent? We have a crazy bond. If he'd not been shot, we'd have been married in Godo. I'm sure of it."

Guthrie felt a little remorse. "It's just been drama and surprise this past few weeks. What could happen next?"

"I could leave and go back to Alabama." Emma looked Guthrie in the eyes, took a bite of eggs, a bite of toast, a drink of water.

"Emma, please, although the situation is changing. I hadn't wanted to tell you this for a couple weeks, but the Baptist Mission is being forced to pull out of the countryside, out of Shewa Province. Our time there is limited."

"No more clinic?" asked Emma. "No more food distribution?"

"The data shows that children are gaining weight, that food supply is secure, that our presence is no longer needed. And when the grain stops coming, the people will throw us out. It's happened before and is happening now in Meranya. You might as well know. It's probably best for you to go back one more time, gather your things, and say your goodbyes. The team there will bring the work to a halt and distribute the remaining supplies."

"What about the employees, the daily laborers, the cooks, Afewerki, Isaac, Mariam, and Barra?"

"We'll help the core team find new jobs in Addis. We'll have to do our best with the cooks, guards, and daily laborers. It's hard to say. But it will take us a couple of months to close it down. We'll figure it out as we go along."

"Geez, it just doesn't seem fair, such short notice. What

will happen to me? Back to the States?"

Livvy poked her eggs. "But you've done such a great job here, and you'll be able to check in with Reece."

"The RRC has determined that the famine is truly over based on weight/height percentiles of children."

"What about the diseases, though, the worms, malaria, goiter, scabies, diarrhea," said Emma.

"The government clinic will remain, so there will be something. On occasion, we'll be invited back to do vaccine clinics for people and cattle, but they want our stations closed, especially the priests."

"So, I get a final trip back to settle my affairs and say goodbye to everyone." She hadn't touched her food.

That's right," said Guthrie. "Unless you just want to stay here."

"And what about Misrak? You're not going to ship her back to Godo to die, are you?"

"Look, Emma, we're out to do what's right even though it's hard. We were fortunate to be allowed into the countryside. We were allowed because of the dire situation. Now that the situation has settled down, we are no longer welcome."

Emma bit a perfect half-circle in her toast, and her mouth watered. "Yeah, I need to go back and say my goodbyes, especially to the team. I don't care so much about my stuff. I'll just give it away."

Livvy spoke. "You might want to think about a lottery system for your stuff. Have them draw numbers for your sleeping bag, for example, otherwise you could generate bad feelings."

"That makes sense, want to be fair, and I have quite

a few things to give away. Maybe I'll just leave Ethiopia wearing a grain sack." She laughed.

Guthrie took big bites of eggs and toast, smearing it with homemade grape jelly, a gift from home. "That sounds like a plan. There's no helicopter today, but Craig is in Addis and will be headed back to Meranya by jeep in the morning. He can detour and drop you in Godo, and then Terry can fly you back to Addis."

Emma remembered Craig. He lived in Meranya with his wife...*What was her name?* Craig suffered from systemic alopecia, completely hairless, smooth. He was a civil engineer, a great builder of bridges and roads, and deeply dedicated to his wife, who seemed most times to be at a complete loss, as if she were in a dream.

"Okay," said Emma, feeling the next chapter of a big adventure, returning home to Alabama. She shuddered at the delight and despair. "I have today to putter around before heading back to Godo with Craig, right?"

"Yep. He's in the guesthouse. You should walk over and let him know the situation."

"Will do." Emma chowed down the rest of her eggs and nibbled the toast like a beaver. She drank her water. An orange Fanta she craved, and she knew Reece was to call back, but when? She estimated half an hour had passed and found herself sitting next to the avocado phone, sipping hot coffee.

Kristin sat in her Toyota for ten minutes with the engine running at the only gas station in Clay, halfway to her house. There was a pay phone there. The car smelled like the egg roll she'd brought Reece from the mall. He'd once brought her daisies on the back of his bike, her favorite flowers. He'd wanted her to sell the car since she owed money on it. His Chevy Citation was paid off and had more cargo area, although it was the ugliest car she had ever seen.

Kristin looked at the dashboard clock, and ten minutes had passed. She wanted to hear what round two between Reece and this Emma consisted of. Maybe the truth would come out, maybe he would ditch her long distance. That would be best, and she couldn't imagine otherwise. Was he a man or a mouse? It was obvious what the right thing to do was.

Had enough time passed to call? A grain of sand seemed like an hour. She rolled her window down, reached in a quarter, and punched his number. She knew the phone rang loud, both on the wall and on the lamp table between the recliners. The night was dark, with a sky of bright stars.

In her bed, with a pair of underwear over her hair, Dora heard the phone ring and wondered why Reece did not answer. She was sufficiently asleep not to care, but awake enough to process the noise. Horace snored, out like a light.

Kristin dialed the number again, and it was busy this time. Reece was back on the line with Emma. *Dammit.* She imagined walking down a waxed bowling alley, slipping and falling. Reece had said there was bowling in Addis Ababa, that young boys stood above the pins and set them up by hand. She let the busy signal go for a good minute, trying to imagine what was being said. She had told Reece she loved him, and he had said the same. Since he'd been back to the States, he seemed to want to say things vaguely or in riddles: "If I didn't love you, I wouldn't be here." What did that mean? It seemed like code between two drug dealers.

For Christ's sake, she would just have to drive back, go inside, and hear it from the horse's mouth. Within ten minutes, she was back. Kristin popped in a piece of peppermint gum and stood outside the back door. The house was still lit. Elephant-ear lilies waved in the slight breeze. She wondered why the garage was built so close to the house, perhaps five feet between them. Without knocking, she opened the back door and entered the laundry room. There, she knocked, hesitated.

Dora was back up, pacing and doing things that could wait, such as changing the towels in the bathrooms and tying up the trash to be taken outside. All this love triangle business had her on edge. She heard the knock and knew it was her. She opened the laundry-room door with a blank stare, as if opening a can of tomatoes. "You want to come back in?"

Kristin passed through the corner of the living room and walked into the kitchen. Reece was on the phone. She felt like reaching down and ripping up the carpet, slamming holes into the paneling with a hammer. She said, "Hey."

"Hold on, she's back." Reece put his hand over the receiver. "Just let me get through a simple conversation, and we'll be through. You're right here, and she's in Africa. The line could go at any minute."

Kristin was through with patience and niceties. "Do you love her? Tell her if you do. It's no skin off my nose. In fact, I'll be able to breathe and move on." She picked up the phone by the table, holding it at chest level.

Dora retreated to her bedroom.

Reece looked pale, beyond reach. "It's not that easy, Kristin. I worked with you in CCU at Carraway, and I think we bonded. But then there was Ethiopia, working in the clinic with Emma, and we bonded over the insanity. And then I was shot in her place. Yeah, I wanted to have sex with her, and then a bullet whizzed through my brain. Maybe God was punishing me, or perhaps he was drawing us closer together. Does that make any sense? You there, Emma?"

"I'm here. What's the holdup?" said Emma.

Reece felt trapped. He put his hand over the phone. "I still care for her, but I love you more, most. What else can I say?"

Kristin put the phone to her ear.

Reece shook his head no. "Kristin, no. This is private."

"Emma," said Kristin.

Reece shook his head, listening for Emma's response.

"That you, Kristin? It's good to hear from you. Sounds like Reece is being a real handful." Emma wished Guthrie and Livvy would leave the room, but they seemed content sitting there.

"Why are you calling my fiancée? It's enough that you hit on him over there, and now you're doing the same thing by phone. He loves me, says he loves me, and he doesn't need you confusing the situation." Her voice trembled, and she felt that she would lift from the floor like she did in her dreams.

Reece said, "Hey, let's—"

Emma said, "Whoa, hold on." She wanted to say that she jumped from the helicopter for Reece, and what had Kristin done other than whine in her letters to him? "Nobody's married yet, right? Seems like a fair game to me." A curtain of certainty draped her. She felt that she had the upper hand, but she was stuck in Ethiopia for the time being.

"Nobody's married yet," said Reece.

"What is that supposed to mean!" said Kristin. "I mean, good God, are you saying that you can't decide between me and Emma?"

Reece scratched his head. There was a tiny blackhead there, and he saw blood on his fingernail.

"Reece!" Kristin shouted at him from across the room. "Do something, say something!"

"Hell, you'll wake the dead. Don't shout, for Pete's sake." His vision clouded yellow, and his head fell back. He dropped the phone on his lap, his hands and feet twitching.

Kristin hung up her phone. "Reece," she hissed. She was on her knees, watching his eyes dart back and forth. She took the phone from Reece's lap, said, "Goodbye," and cut the connection. She held her hand to his cool forehead and could only watch as he trembled in the recliner. His breathing was irregular but steady. She checked his carotids, which were bounding. "Reece?"

Reece opened his eyes, seeing yellow. Kristin was kneeling beside him, holding his hands. "What?" He gazed around the room at the kitchen, the TV, the loveseat, the AC unit in the window humming. "I'm cold."

Kristin let him go and slid onto the loveseat. "You had a seizure."

"A seizure...yeah. But...was I on the phone?"

"You were professing your love to Emma, if you want to know." She felt cold and rubbed her arms.

"No way, what? Did you hang up?" Reece sat up straight. He felt queasy.

"Yes, I hung up, and she doesn't need to call here ever again." She shook her finger at him.

Reece took a deep breath. "That's crazy. She has news. Maybe they've arrested the Hyena. You can't do that, forbid me to talk with her."

"But I will, mister. You've got a choice to make. We're engaged, Reece, to be married. That girl just latched onto you because there was no one else."

"What about Terry, the pilot, or Dr. Guthrie?"

"So, you're saying that she had a choice, and she chose you. That's even worse."

Reece reached to adjust his ballcap, but he wasn't wearing one. "I have no idea what you're talking about. Did I wake up in the wrong universe?"

"Is that what you want. Go to another universe and hook up with Emma? Let me know how that works out." Kristin puffed the curls away from her face and crossed her long legs.

"Look, it's getting late. You have to work early, right, and I'm exhausted. I walked more today than I have in the past week. Can we just call a truce here and sort this out maybe tomorrow?"

Kristin grunted. "A truce? How about you just say you love me and help me set up a wedding date, unless that doesn't jive with your truce. And so, did you tell her that you loved her while I was gone? You had plenty of time." She took a deep breath. The oval coffee table was too close to her legs, and she pushed it out, knocking over a knick-knack.

"I should be taking something for these seizures. I'm getting worried. I feel numb and tingly." He stretched out his arms and flexed his fingers. "You know I could've been an invalid. Would you have still wanted me then?"

"Yes...I'm concerned about your seizures, although they seem mild. You need to get in and have another CT scan to make sure no fluid is building up."

"But what if I were paralyzed, in a wheelchair, incontinent? What would you do? Would you be worrying about Emma?"

Kristin smiled. "If I married you, it would be for better or worse. Plus, you're not paralyzed, except maybe in your brain."

Reece pushed up on the arms of the recliner.

"What do you need?" asked Kristin. She stood. "Can I help?"

"Nope, just getting a glass of water." He walked, but felt as though he was gliding on skis. He took down a jelly jar and filled it with tap water. He let the water float in his mouth and then swallowed. He yawned. "Want to go sit in the swing and talk? We're keeping them awake. How about a nip of wine?"

Kristin stared at him. "Is that something else you learned to do in Africa? Drink? You know I don't drink, and neither do your grandparents. Don't act crazy."

"Is that a yes?" He reached over the brown fridge and opened the cabinet door. He fetched down a cheap jug of Mogen David blackberry wine that Horace kept to help him sleep. "It's sweet."

"Wine tastes terrible, and you don't need any." She grabbed the bottle.

"No," said Reece. "If you make me drop it, I swear."

"You swear what? Would you hit me?"

Reece shouldered into the fridge. "For Christ's sake, no. Just be cool for a second. Probably less than ten percent alcohol. I tasted moonshine in Godo."

"Now you're a drinker? Wait till my parents hear about this."

"Look, I'm going out to the swing with this wine and a glass. I'm asking you to come outside and talk. Is that a sin?"

"Yes, it is." She folded her arms. "But, okay, let's do it, but I do have to leave soon."

Outside, he smelled the lake, pine straw, and the engine heat from the Toyota. A full moon carpeted the ground with a hue of granite. The pine needles felt nice against his feet.

In the swing, Reece pushed them back and forth, holding the jug. He unscrewed the lid and poured a full glass. His thighs felt cold against the metal. He glanced at Kristin, who was looking up in protest, and drained half of the glass. "Yikes." The wine was old and a bit sour. "Try some?"

"I thought I said no. And are you supposed to drink that fast?"

"I'm a big boy now, been shot in the head, faced down an F-5 tornado, and leeches." He wanted to laugh, but only felt sad.

"Remember when we snuggled in the boat and drifted in the cattails?"

"Let's do it again. That was nice." He drained the glass and smirked.

"Tell me one thing you hated about Ethiopia." She was helping him push the swing. "Put your arm around me."

"Hold up." He reached down and poured another full glass. "Maybe I should start smoking. Did you know I like cigars?" He put his arm behind her, resting it on the swing.

"Oh God, that would do it. Cigars? Do I even know you?"

"That's a good question. I feel so different now, like I've had major brain surgery and the wires have been crossed."

"I think you need brain surgery." She smiled at him with her big green eyes.

He took a drink and let his arm drop on her narrow shoulders. His hand hung off the side, and he toyed with her sleeve. "Wow, this is perfect."

"Almost," said Kristin. "It would be if you were mine."

Reece could see the hurt in her face and scooted closer. "Look, I love you. We're engaged." He reached in to kiss her cheek, and she let him. She turned and kissed his lips.

"That wine stinks, but I've missed you so much. You have no idea." She melted toward him. "You were gone for nearly two months, the longest days of my life."

Reece downed the wine and let the glass drop. It broke

on the marble slab. "Hell." He started to reach for the pieces, but Kristin pulled him closer. She put her mouth on his, and they kissed for real.

"Giving me chill bumps."

"Giving me bumps all over." He pulled her legs over his and kissed her hard, opening her mouth.

"I want some of that wine," said Kristin. "It seems to work magic."

"Do we have to stop?"

"No, just pause it. Pour me some."

"Glass is broken." Reece lifted the jug and took a swig. "Here, straight from the pot."

"This is heavy." She smelled and then had a drink. "Yuck. Tastes like sour candy."

"Drink some more until you feel warm."

"What, are you like a pusher?"

Reece smiled. "I'm a wolf in sheep's clothing."

"The devil in disguise."

"You know it. Let's lie down on the pine straw." He took a lengthy swig.

On the ground, they lay beside one another, propped on elbows. Reece ran his fingers through her long brown curls. Their hands began to touch and explore, and Reece felt the wine and the pleasure of her body. In the bright moonlight, they coupled and pressed together, pausing every few minutes to hit the wine. Reece's hand explored beneath her scrub top, touching her breasts through her bra. He was still a virgin, and as far as he knew, so was Kristin. He was aching to have sex, but had no condom. He wasn't even sure of how to proceed. Would this be his first time? With her hand rubbing his member through his jean shorts, he knew that it should be sooner than later.

Sitting on the bed, Emma tried to imagine what had happened. Obviously, Kristin had been on one line and Reece on the other, but the connection had been cut. What to think? Kristin was definitely on the offensive, and maybe that was okay. Emma imagined Kristin as angry and helpless. But she had a bond with Reece, one that Kristin would never have with him.

She gazed around the bedroom, a boy's bedroom. It felt cozy, but she was a guest and felt like an outsider in Guthrie's house. She decided to walk over to the Mission compound and see if Craig was around. She could only think of him as the hairless man. She donned her trusty blue jeans and a long-sleeve cotton pullover.

Livvy washed dishes in the kitchen, still in her housecoat. A dozen bobby pins held her short, graying hair in place. "Emma, what's the day like for you?" Her hands were red from the hot water.

"I'm going over to the compound." She looked through the large plate glass window in the living room. People crowded the road beyond the dirt driveway, going back and forth. "What's that semi-trailer doing on the road?"

Livvy wiped her hands. "Oh, that poor little girl who was killed, got run over. The driver took off, but the people unhooked the trailer and haven't seen him since. What did Reece have to say on the phone?" Livvy took a seat on a large stuffed chair. She enjoyed hearing about the drama, living vicariously through the young missionaries.

"He was at his grandparents' house, and Kristin was

there." She stood near the window, fingering the green curtain. "Said he'd jumped into the lake and a bunch of leeches got on him."

"Lord, Lord. He's a magnet for disaster. You know you should be careful with him, being engaged. I met his fiancée when she came to see about him. She seemed like a little lost bird."

"Yeah, I just can't imagine him with her. Too tame, you know." Emma felt small and alone. She looked down at her dirty tennis shoes. "I think she hung up on me."

"Will you try to see him once you're back in the States?" Livvy took up a pile of yarn from the floor and began to knit.

Emma toyed with the curtain. "If he wants me to. I'd like to see him. I mean, who am I going to talk to about this place?"

Livvy said, "Mm hmm."

"I'm going over to the compound and see what's going on."

"Be careful on the road."

"Thanks again for breakfast."

Emma stepped onto the dirt driveway. The air always seemed so clear, like looking through fine glass. She skirted the semi's trailer, walked past the rehab center for Cuban soldiers with its NO PHOTOGRAPHS sign, and soon came to the gate in a wash of men and women, some with baskets of grain balanced on their heads, others beating donkeys weighed down with eucalyptus branches.

The gate was opening, and it was Craig in the green Toyota jeep. "Hey, what are you doing?"

"Coming to see you about a ride tomorrow up to AK

and maybe Godo," said Emma.

"Cool. I should be back by mid-afternoon. Have to take this jeep in and have the steering aligned. It's all wonky."

"Yeah, sure." Emma took in his smooth skin. He wasn't wearing a hat, and his head seemed to be made of modeling clay. "How's your wife?" She couldn't remember her name.

"Eve is well, wants me to come home as soon as possible."

A woman wrapped in a shamma approached with her hand to an open mouth, begging for food or coins. The gate guard hurried out and told her to move along.

"Wait." Emma pulled fifty cents from her pocket. The woman took it and stumbled off backwards, watching the guard, who looked mighty displeased.

"Okay, I'm on my way." Craig put it in low and lurched into the crowd of people, driving as slow as possible.

Emma greeted the guard, who now flashed her a giant smile. She walked to the administrative building, which housed the printing press inside. She could hear the *ka-chunk ka-chunk* through the walls. The priests upcountry did not like the Baptist Bible, even though it was in Amharic. There was too much emphasis on the New Testament, and the Baptists left out books such as Tobit and Tegsats. But still, the press pressed on, day and night.

She could see the whitewashed guesthouse. The house beside the office belonged to the business manager and his family. Their home was notable for the huge piles of scrap and parts that were recycled into useful objects. Emma crossed a narrow grassy area inside the road that circled the compound in a long oval. She wondered what the director's wife, Teresa, was up to. Her husband Ben was away on business. Emma knocked on the door and heard a long roar. It had to be Claude, and it was. He bellowed and stamped his foot like a deranged bull.

"Hey, Claude. Is your mommy home?" Just more roaring noises.

"Hey there!" It was Teresa with her four-month-old, Kimo. "Come in. Don't mind Claude. He's just pretending. Always pretending." She sounded tired. "And have to keep this one fed." She held Kimo in a sling around her shoulder and neck. He punched the air with his tiny fists and did the fish mouth, looking for her nipple.

"A real cutie."

Claude was up against her legs, standing ramrod. Emma maneuvered around them and took a seat in the chaotic living room. Everything was at an angle as if being swept under. Claude followed her, staring into her face, sticking his tongue in and out like a snake.

"Claude! Don't mind him, Emma."

Claude said, "Beedly weedly beedly weedly."

Emma laughed. She looked around the room, an American feel. She would be home soon, back in the States. "You know they're shutting down the feeding stations?"

"I guess Dr. Guthrie told you. Yes, we have to pack up and leave. Kind of like turning off the faucet. Are you okay?"

"Yeah, I'm okay with it. Things come to an end, and I can see how much better the situation is. There's been rain, and the farmers are planting. The markets are always full of food."

"Maybe you'll get to see Reece."

"I'll definitely get to see him. I talked with him this morning, but his fiancée was there, and she hung up on me, so there's that ball of wax."

"Goodness." Teresa pulled up her light blouse, exposing her breast and large maroon nipple. Kimo struggled until he latched on and sucked as if he'd never eaten before. "Ouch." She drew her tube of brown hair to the side, off of Kimo's face.

Emma laughed. "He's got radar." She thought about Reece, how it would have been heaven for him to explore her breasts. Claude continued to walk in circles saying, "Beedly weedly beedly weedly."

"Do you think you should call him back?"

"No. It's late there now. Maybe I'll try again tonight."

"You're welcome to hang out here today," said Teresa. "I could use the company."

"No, I should get over to the hospital and check on Misrak before I head back tomorrow. Is there someone around who can drive me? You know I don't like to drive around here."

"I bet Tesfaw would take you, if you won't stay for long. I'll call him. He's in the office." She picked up the tan phone and dialed. Tesfaw said he could take her in perhaps one hour, which could mean two or three hours in Ethiopian time.

"Thanks," said Emma.

"Beedly weedly beedly weedly." Claude made cockroach feelers with his fingers.

"I can hang out here until Tesfaw's ready. If you don't mind."

"I'll get Berta to make us some tea. How about it?"

"Sure," said Emma.

Hearing her name, Berta emerged from the kitchen. "Abet?" She smiled at Emma and bowed her head. Emma was the crazy one who had jumped from the helicopter. Everyone knew.

"Berta, shai?" asked Teresa.

"Ishi," and Berta left to boil the water and make the tea.

Claude crawled up into Emma's lap and made purring noises.

"Claude, you're a character," said Emma. He looked like a little professor with his thick glasses. She rubbed his head, and he snapped at her like a Chihuahua.

"Claude," said Teresa. "Let's be nice."

"Beedly weedly." Claude licked Emma's hair.

"Claude! Emma, just make him get down if he's bothering you."

Emma was laughing. "He's fine." She let him lick her hair and kept her hands to herself.

Teresa wanted badly to ask Emma about the helicopter incident and wanted to hear more about the night Reece was shot. Ben had written up incident reports for both, but there were still unanswered questions. The area coordinator for East Africa had questioned Emma's mental health and urged the Mission to retire her as soon as possible. The famine had wound down, anyway.

Emma pondered the silence. "I haven't talked about this with anyone. The helicopter and all."

Kimo lost the nipple and looked around with a wild look in his eye. He found it again and sucked with gusto.

"Go on," said Teresa.

On top of Kristin, with her scrub top off, Reece came in his pants. He hated when that happened and wanted to change his underwear. He knew there would be a wet stain on his pants and was embarrassed. He rolled off her and onto his side, the pine straw sticking to his hands.

Kristin didn't move. She knew he'd come by the way he'd moaned, and his hips had moved. It wasn't the first time. She had promised herself and God that she would only have sex once married. There had been an abstinence class at her church, and she had a certificate in a drawer.

"What's wrong? You, okay?"

"Yeah, just got me so turned on, you know." He stroked her soft belly with his fingers. He ran them over her bra and then her face. He felt wet and sticky.

"I love you," said Kristin. The warm moon. The lake below the road. The stars. He was hers and hers alone.

Reece sighed and looked away. "I love you, too." A string pulled tight in his chest. Why was he so damn immature and afraid of what lay ahead? He'd survived being shot and knew in his heart that Emma was special, that he was more attracted to her than Kristin, that he was a fool, that he should be shot again to take away his doubts and fears.

"Really?" asked Kristin. "Why do you love me? And just me?"

"Jesus." He put his hand on her thigh and then toyed with the drawstring on her scrubs. "I just do."

"And not Emma? Let's go inside the camper. I'm starting to get a little freaked out, half naked out here." She sat up and grabbed her scrub top.

"Let's not talk about Emma. It's just us right now. Yeah, the camper. More comfortable in there." He stood and glanced down at the splotch on his jeans. Maybe Kristin was right. Maybe he should forget Emma. Kristin was right there, alive, in the flesh, and he was possibly about to have sex, real sex, with her. He helped her up and brushed pine straw from her shoulders.

"But it's so late. I don't know," said Kristin.

Reece felt stuck. "Just for half an hour. I'll put a tape in." He held her close as they crossed the driveway. A breeze. A dog howling in the distance. In the sky, a plane winking. "You're real. You're here."

He opened the door to the small RV, and she stepped up. Inside was dim and warm, the key in the ignition. Kristin sat on the narrow, cushioned bench seat, and Reece maneuvered into the cab. There was a tape in the player, but he couldn't tell what it was. He hoped it was *Dark Side of the Moon,* but suddenly it was John Denver singing about grandma's feather bed. *Why not?* He slipped back to Kristin and looked into her wide eyes. What should he do next?

"Thanks for that egg roll."

"Here." She put his hand on her bra. "Take it off."

Reece's erection was back, and he felt almost sick, kind of giddy. He reached behind her, and the bra fell away from her chest. He breathed deep. Why was he such a pussy? He was pretty sure that he was the only virgin guy left in the world. She bunched her shoulders, and the bra fell to her lap. It was the first time he'd seen her breasts, and they were small and beautiful with erect nipples. Without thinking, he kissed one and then the other. She took deep breaths. John Denver was describing the bed, "soft as a downy chick." The song struck Kristin as funny, and she laughed.

Reece didn't pause, caught up in the pulse of energy quickening his body. She leaned into him and cozied up on his lap. His hands went to her breasts, feeling the softness there as if it were forever. "Sorry about the music."

"Who cares about the music? Kiss me."

Reece bent over to kiss her, straining his neck. His hand moved to her pants, sliding down to her panties. He felt that he would come again and forced his mind into a corner, imagining a plastic chair, an orange plastic chair. He could already feel his hips wanting to move, to thrust. He thought he was melting.

Inside the house, the phone had rung, waking Dora but not Horace. It was Kristin's mom, worried about her not being home, and she had to work day shift. Wearing a hairnet and a silky nightgown, Dora set out to find Reece and Kristin to let them know that her mom was worried. In the tiny laundry room, she slipped on a dirty pair of Horace's garden shoes, which used to be a pair of church shoes.

Breathing, Reece scooched down beside Kristin, barely fitting on the bench seat. He grabbed the long back cushion and tossed it on the floor, giving them more room to spoon. His hand was just there, exploring, his mouth on hers. There was the music, but he no longer heard John singing, only feeling the life force of Kristin, absorbing her smell and warmth.

Dora opened the back door. The moon was bright. "Reece?" She thought she could hear music and stepped into the midnight chill. A whippoorwill called out. They weren't in the swing. Maybe they were down by the lake, sitting on the pier. She walked through the pines to the road and called out. "Reece! Reece!" She listened and turned back. She wasn't about to walk down there in her pajamas. Oh, the music, and she walked back to the driveway. "Reece?"

Kristin was pulling down her scrub bottoms. Reece was fumbling with his jeans, still with one hand in her pants. He looked at her, and her eyes were closed, her lips parted. There was a rapping sound, and Kristin pushed him away.

"Somebody's knocking."

"Shit," said Reece.

"Reece? You in there?" Dora knocked again.

"Uh, yeah, we're here." Reece looked to see if his pants were undone.

"Kristin's mom called, worried about her. She should come in and call her. Okay?" She figured it was best not to open the door. "You hear me?"

"Okay, we'll be there in a minute. Thanks!" He counted to ten. "Well, the eyes of God are upon us." He sat up.

Kristin frowned. "I can't believe she called out here like that. Like she has to know everything. Reece, we almost did it. I'm sorry. Are you okay?"

"Yeah, but you need to call your mom. Christ. Let me turn off the music."

They stepped outside, and Reece moved into her for a hug, and they stood there for a moment. Once inside, Dora sat in the recliner, rocking it with her toes. She knew, but young people were young people, and with her hands, indicated she was headed back to bed.

"You know what?" asked Kristin. "I'm not calling her. I'm twenty-one years old, and she can deal with it."

"That's settled. Not so loud, though." He pointed to the bedrooms. Horace was snoring.

"You better call your mama," said Dora from her bed. "I know how mamas worry."

Kristin frowned. Reece nodded to the phone on the lamp table between the recliners. "Just to make everyone happy."

"I'm not interested in everyone being happy at the moment, just us. We're what matters." She spoke in a whisper.

"Already, your folks don't like me, so maybe just call."

"No, I won't. Let's go outside, okay?"

Reece followed Kristin and let the screen door close. He felt weary, sleepy. "Back to the camper?" He put his arm on her shoulder, but she pulled away.

"I'm not going to call, but I'll go now. That should make everyone happy. It is late." She yawned. "I can't believe how mobile you are. You're doing so great."

Reece yawned. "Yeah, I'll have to start looking for work, maybe."

"You know they'll take you back at Carraway. I'm sure of it. You might not get the day shift right away, which would suck. Jesus, my bra's in the camper."

Reece followed her and waited. "I love your fruits."

"My what?"

"Your boobs."

"Breasts."

"Yeah, those."

"They come with the package deal," said Kristin. She opened her car door. "Good night."

Reece leaned in and kissed her. "Good night. Don't let the bedbugs bite."

"You're as country as corn flakes. Bye."

"Bye," and Reece closed her door. His eyes hurt, and the sky wanted to spin. He walked to the garage and felt his way to the house, worried he was going to pass out.

Emma sipped the hot, sweet tea flavored with ginger. She was glad that Kimo was through feeding, so that she could focus on Teresa instead of his slurping and grunting. Claude dozed in her lap.

"Had you wanted to hurt yourself before Reece was shot?" asked Teresa. Her dad was a clinical psychologist.

Emma thought. "Yeah, when I was at Gundo Meskel with Jill and then Hattie, the thought kept bugging me. Everything was just so depressing. So many people dying. It was like an urge, not a voice, but a constant thought."

"And then you were alone at Godo before Reece came. That must have been awfully hard." Teresa cradled Kimo, rocking him to sleep.

"Yeah, especially when I was sick and had to keep working. I remember one day, seeing ninety patients, running to the shintabet every ten minutes, and then remembering that I needed to visit the shelter. I threw up in a biscuit tin. I really didn't think about killing myself, but that I would just die from exhaustion." Claude felt hot on her lap.

"You're a tough lady. As tough as they come."

"But I feel kind of broken, especially since Reece was shot." She slumped in the stuffed chair.

"That must have been a nightmare. Can you talk about it?"

"I guess so. I mean, I was attracted to him. And to be honest, he was attracted to me. It was just chance that he gave his bed to some guy with a rotten leg and was in my house. Otherwise, the bullets would have just passed through. He wouldn't have been there. The back wall of the house is just blank, no windows. No way to see in. Why would God allow such a thing?" Emma let her head drop and then snapped it back. She wanted a cigarette, a shot of katikala, a hit of Valium.

Teresa nodded. "This is not a situation that is easy to understand. You guys must have really bonded in the clinic."

Emma leaned forward. Her hair covered her face. She wanted to push Claude onto the floor. "Exactly. Like we were partners, of course, with Afewerki, a real team, the three of us. It was great, the back and forth, Reece's accent. He knew exactly where I was from, had been there."

"You both have that Alabama twang," said Teresa. "God, that must have been a trial. Did you...see him get shot?"

Emma closed her eyes. What should she say? Reece had been engaged at the time and still was as far as she knew. She felt like the forbidden fruit or maybe like Eve. "I was sitting down. He was standing behind me. Two shots. He fell sideways, hit the table, crumpled to the floor, blood shooting everywhere..."

"I'm so sorry. I can't imagine."

"Yeah, neither can I. It's beyond imagination. It just happened, like a clock striking midnight, right on cue, bang, you're dead."

"Wow." Teresa patted Kimo on the back. "Would you like to pray? Maybe for understanding, for his continued recovery." Kimo belched and hiccupped. "Good boy," and she rocked him in her chair.

"Not right now. Thanks, though. I'm not sure that anyone is listening." Emma noticed Berta peeking into the room every few minutes, a look of concern on her face.

"It can seem that way sometimes. Can I just pray for you?"

"Maybe not now. I'm fine." Emma gripped the arms of her chair. Holding Claude was becoming a chore, but he was sleeping or appeared to be.

"Just for my sake, okay? Don't be so humble."

"Humble?"

"I think humility is your gift, but you can be too humble," said Teresa. "Let us help you. Let God step in."

Berta came in with the kettle. Emma waved her away, and Berta poured more tea for Teresa. She kept the house going, did the washing, even ironed the sheets. Was the ferenj dangerous?

"Maybe I can put Claude on his bed?" asked Emma. Her legs were going to sleep, and she wanted to take a long walk, or maybe she just wanted to lie down and sleep, or die.

"Yeah, just put him on the couch. Sorry about that. He likes you."

Emma struggled to stand, cradling Claude like a fireplace log.

"Sit back down, and let's pray," said Teresa.

Emma rolled her eyes and sat, putting her head in her hands. She listened as Teresa prayed, but she didn't hear the words. Teresa said, "Amen."

"Amen," said Emma, standing. "I probably need to take a walk, clear the cobwebs. Thanks for the tea."

Teresa nodded. "You know you've lost weight. That's a cute top, though."

"No doubt, and thanks," said Emma. "I'll check in with

Tesfaw about the ride to the hospital."

"Okay. Be careful on the road. Don't get run over."

Emma wandered across the dirt oval to the main office. She found Tesfaw, and he said to come back in an hour. Outside, she passed through the gate onto the crazy dirt road with bathtub-size potholes. She could head left toward Guthrie's or right, which would lead her to the leprosy hospital, ALERT. Looking down to keep from falling, she fell in behind a spindly man carrying a huge plastic jerry container. His dusty calves popped with vein ropes. His shoes seemed to have exploded around his feet, and she wondered how they stayed on. She could smell his sweat and work and heard the calls of "Ferenj!" but ignored them.

There was a juice bar ahead, and she determined that to be her destination. She imagined Reece with her, how good his company would be. She laughed and then frowned, half believing that he was beside her. A woman passed with two crates of empty soda bottles balanced on her head. Emma counted her blessings in half a second of commiseration. There were so many different lots in life, some fair and otherwise. She thought about the old monk carving his church into the rock and wondered that he'd visited Reece in the hospital in Addis. Reece's parents, both shot in the head at a cafeteria in Texas, and then the same for him. *Rotten, absolutely rotten.* She paused. The juice bar was behind her. She had passed it. A Mercedes G Wagon approached, one of the Save the Children vehicles. Emma stepped to the side and watched the vehicle pass. *The juice bar,* and she looked for the sign that just said, "Birke." To her left and right were shack after shack, one holding up its neighbor and so on, all with rusted sheet metal roofing. She stooped to enter the dim, cool room that held a small rickety bar and a large steel juice squeezer. There was no one there, except a young girl, and she let out a yell that made Emma jump.

A young woman with a headscarf popped in from the back, smiling with large, gapped teeth, all pearly white.

"Tenesteling." Emma suddenly felt parched, as if it had been years since she'd had orange juice. "Arancia."

The young woman put her smile away and cut three oranges in half. Into the juicer went each half, shooting pulpy liquid into a glass like a cow giving milk. The glass looked heavy and had a handle like a beer stein. Emma placed a birr on the bar and took her change. A young man appeared from the back. He walked up behind the woman and grabbed her hips. She turned and hit him. He cursed and backed off, smiling.

Emma tasted the sweet juice. It was the best juice she'd ever had in her entire life. She licked her lips and drank slow and hard, finishing it in three swallows. The juice felt heavy in her stomach and cool. "Ciao," she said and left, parting the cloth that hung over the door. Donkeys and then goats, she let them pass before moving on. Little streets entered the lane. A dusty Lada taxi crept down the road, the driver beeping his horn. Emma paused and watched him pass. He had a huge afro and that glassy look of someone high on qat. He was just a part of things, a part of how things were in Ethiopia. And that was okay, more than okay. She kicked a large rock and fell forward, her breasts leaping in her bra. "Jiminy crickets." She laughed, stepped off the road beside a ramshackle house, and adjusted her bosom. *My bosom.* She laughed again. Others were watching and smiling, except an old man with a ball-peen hammer. He was nailing a sign that said *Welcome* in Polish to his son's house. He'd traded four Coke bottles for the sign in the Mercato. His son was a paraplegic and confined to bed with massive sores on his hips. He chattered at Emma, as if accusing her and all Americanos of his troubles. He just wanted to drink tejj but had to take care of his son, his wife, and three other children.

Emma sized him up, listening to his words. "Mendeno, baba?"

The man fumbled his hammer and hitched his baggy pants. *What the devil?* The ferenj could speak Amharic. He yelled at her that his son was dying.

Emma winced, but understood that he was frustrated beyond all means. It was in his voice and in his eyes, brown and liquid, folded into his face, which expressed a kind of dumb hurt. "Asa yeen," she said. "Show me."

The man stopped at that and put the hammer into his large shirt pocket, the handle clipping his chin. How long had it been since his wife had died in childbirth? Twenty years? And what was her name? Abebe, of course. Flower. Her face rushed from his memory, spurred by this ferenj.

"Nah," he said. "Come." It would be good for her to see his misery.

"Okay," said Emma. She remembered how good the juice had been.

She followed him to the side of the house. There was no door, just a wire at eye level where a curtain might go. Inside was a kind of living room with a crude couch made of scraps. A dozen flies played Pong with the walls. There were old boots and a TV with a smashed screen. Emma followed him into the next room, and the smell, a smell of something dead mixed with what? Maybe iron filings or maybe wet wood. She cringed, and a chill ran down her sternum and into her stomach. The old man was talking and gesturing at the pallet on the floor on which lay a skeleton that moved its head and moaned a great, long "Ohh-hh." It, or rather he, was naked except for a dirty green towel that read "Hôtel."

"Dear God," said Emma. Images of the women at the shelter flashed through her mind. What would they do when the Mission pulled out? Emma squatted beside the skeleton man. He seemed to be young, his face smooth, his hair matted, his eyes bulging as wide as softballs. "Dear God." She took shallow breaths to stifle the stench of urine and feces. She looked up at the old man with the hammer in his shirt pocket. She noticed he had a pencil behind his ear.

The man's son whispered. "Anchee." "Hey, you." He said it again.

Emma's butt grazed the packed dirt floor. She pinched a corner of the towel and lifted to expose the left hip. As if launched, a fly zoomed into the saucer-sized wound that went to the bone. A rind of black, dead flesh ringed the hole. The exposed flesh below the rind looked like pink brains. Emma flashed to Misrak in the hospital. She had to get back in time to ride with Tesfaw. "Jesus." She guessed that the man couldn't move his legs, that he was paralyzed. She put her hand on his bony shoulder. "I'm so sorry." The father was talking behind her, above her, just words in passing. She needed to talk to Reece, to tell him about it.

Reece, for the first time since returning, prayed for guidance and clarity. Prayer, though, seemed blank since Ethiopia, and he had no desire to go to church. He went to bed, certain of his love for Kristin and their plans to marry. He needed a strategy and had to stick to it. What was right was right, and he fell asleep, sleeping like the dead.

His grandfather, making coffee, woke him around six-thirty. He closed his eyes, rolled to his back, and imagined doves screeching their claws down a tin roof. Here, in Alabama, his grandmother would make a big breakfast with Pillsbury biscuits, grits, eggs, and bacon, with hot coffee. There, in Ethiopia, he would have a plate of cold fit-fit, crumbled enjera soaked in sauce. There was there, and here was here. He tossed to his side and felt doomed, feeling it in his bones. He turned to his stomach, a measure of last resort, and that lasted for thirty seconds. What was it that he had to do? How could he satisfy Emma? She needed him. Did Kristin need him? Maybe she just wanted him. *Jesus!* The back screen door slammed. Horace was going to get the paper.

Reece thought he had settled things in his mind. He was engaged to Kristin. He forced himself to remember giving her the ring before he left for Ethiopia. Yes, he had done that and with real intent. His thoughts crashed into one another. He flopped onto his back and imagined himself screaming. Heck, just two or three weeks earlier, he hadn't even been able to sit up, and now he was walking, jumping into the lake. He had a lot, a lot, to be thankful for. He considered saying a prayer to count his blessings. The screen door slammed again. *The Birmingham News.* Not *The Ethiopian Herald.* The day before, there had been a hijacking, a Pan Am 747 headed to Pakistan. People had died. Biscuits from a cardboard tube that popped when you pressed it with a spoon or banged it on the counter's edge. The little dough boy. Like fingering a balloon.

Coffee. A cup of coffee. He focused on what he needed to do in the next hour. *Drink coffee. Eat breakfast. Get a shower?* No, he'd had two showers yesterday. He examined the red sores on his arms and legs and laughed. He imagined himself as a houseplant, chronically under-watered and raspy, and wished that Emma would call him back so that he might explain to her the complexity of the situation. Or did he simply just want to talk to her, to hear her voice?

He arched and flipped to his stomach, pulled a pillow over his head. He heard the door to his little bedroom close. Horace was about to turn on the TV and catch some *Country Boy Eddie.* Reece willed the phone to ring. But heck, why couldn't he call her? He had Dr. Guthrie's number. He could take matters into his own hands. But what matter was it that needed attention? He yanked off the pillow and let it fall to the floor. The TV blared. Coffee was brewing. He was in Alabama. He was engaged to Kristin.

He flipped over and threw back the covers, shivering. He imagined having a little ketchup with his eggs. Dora put milk into the eggs to make them fluffy. Yeah, he would mix it up and have ketchup with his eggs. He felt a tiny bit more certain of his day. And then he wanted to scream. *Fuck!* And then he recanted, asking forgiveness. And then he scolded himself for that.

What time was it in Ethiopia? He did the math. Probably three in the afternoon. At the hospital, Kristin was getting patient reports ready for shift change. Would he tell her if he called Emma? He remembered that the easy thing to do was often the worst option. However, everything should be open and transparent. He wondered if trauma from the bullet was creating his sense of confusion. He decided to get up, eat breakfast, and then call Emma. That would give him some time to percolate, to gel. He pressed his hand to the dark paneling and left a handprint there.

"Hey, boy," said Horace. He lounged in his recliner with a cup of Joe. "Sleep all right?"

Reece ran his hand through his hair, touched his oily nose. The den was tiny and cozy. "Yeah." Somebody was ringing a cowbell on *Country Boy Eddie*.

Dora was in front of the stove, a brown spatula in hand, cooking Jimmy Dean sausage patties with extra sage. "Hey, boy."

Reece knew she would scramble eggs in the leftover grease and smiled. He put his arms up and stretched as hard as he could.

"You're up early." Dora tapped the skillet and peeped into the oven at the biscuits.

"Yep." He passed her and found the orange juice in the fridge. He loved orange juice.

"Did Kristin get home okay last night?"

"I think so. It was late, but she would have called if she'd had a problem." He now felt guilty that he hadn't called to see if she made it home.

"You know, I don't think you should be talking to that

nurse over there," said Dora. "Just gets Kristin riled up, and there's no sense in that."

Reece sat at the table with its dark wood-veneer finish. The paneling in the kitchen was more of a maple, and the table clashed. "I don't know. Maybe you're right, but Emma most likely saved my life. She was right there, you know, when it happened. There's that connection..."

Horace snapped the newspaper, thoroughly comfortable in his routine. He turned up the volume on the TV and adjusted his hearing aid, which let out a squeal.

"You could lose Kristin. Is that what you want?" She flipped the sausage. "Horace! Turn that mess down. I couldn't hear a jet plane go over if it was to."

Reece laughed and made lower-the-volume movements with his hands. "Heck no. I guess. We're engaged."

Dora coughed. "You don't seem so sure. You need to do some soul searching and figure this out before you get bit."

Reece thought about making out with Kristin in the RV. He tried to remember being with Emma in her little house. It was all so fuzzy. He wasn't even sure what they had done, if anything. Had he touched her breasts? *Yes.* He went to the Mr. Coffee and poured into a green melamine cup. The heat felt good. He took his place on the loveseat and rocked it with his foot. A commercial for Alabama State Parks played on the TV.

"Should I call her?" asked Reece to the room.

Horace lowered the paper. "Call who, Kristin?"

"No, Emma, in Ethiopia. Kristin hung up on her last night."

"Emma?" asked Horace. "Was she a black girl?"

Reece laughed. "No, she was the other nurse in Godo.

She's white."

"Call her if you want to," said Horace.

"Horace," said Dora, "that's bad advice. Kristin is jealous of that Emma. Reece is engaged, remember?" She checked the oven.

Horace was already back to the paper, fiddling with his hearing aid.

"Maybe I should flip a coin." Reece fished in a glass bowl on the coffee table and pulled out a dull penny.

"You're pushing your luck, boy," said Dora.

Reece flipped the penny, snatched it, and slapped it on his wrist. It was heads. "Looks like the penny wants me to call her, so that makes two against one. I'll call after we eat. I'll have to find the number." He watched Dora take out the biscuits and put the sausage on a paper towel.

Emma knocked on the gate to the Mission compound. She'd left the old man and his paralyzed son fifty birr. That was all she could do. She was beyond taking on another human project. It was apparent the young man would die, and soon she guessed, and probably for the better.

The guard swung open the gate and smiled as wide as Lake Tana. He wore an old, mismatched suit coat and dress pants. His rifle leaned against a eucalyptus tree. Emma checked her watch and went to the office to see if Tesfaw was ready. He sat behind his desk, counting stacks of money, placing them into a safe. The two others in the room, both beautiful Ethiopian women, looked startled. This was the ferenj who had tried to kill herself. One coughed, and then the other coughed as well.

"We will go to Black Lion, no?" asked Tesfaw. He finished counting and placed all of the money into the safe. He stamped a half dozen receipts with purple ink. "You are ready, no?" He stood, using his crutches.

"Yeah, ready if you are, but let me run to the bathroom first."

"I will wait outside, in the van."

Tesfaw drove around the hospital looking for a parking space. He tried backing into a spot, but it was too small. He needed a drink. He decided to double park and just let Emma go inside while he waited. A horn blared and then another, but his face remained stolid.

"To get out here." Tesfaw was sweating and tugged at

his necktie. He pointed at the door handle.

"Yeah, sure." Cars flowed around them. Another horn and Emma jumped. "Dammit."

She made it to the sidewalk and looked at the buildings around her. She only knew of one way to navigate the hospital and walked to find the emergency room. The day was very warm with a stiff breeze that floated her hair. A truckload of soldiers with rifles passed. There were whistles and jeers. "White cunt!"

Emma had no idea what room Misrak was in, and she asked the first person in a lab coat she met. She was looking for the woman with breast cancer, the one being paid for by the Baptist Mission. The third lab coat guided her to a second-floor surgical ward that held twenty-nine beds. Emma smelled urine and just a hint of fresh milk. The young doctor pointed to a bed against the far wall, and Emma thanked him. She hoped that Misrak would be glad to see her.

The ceiling seemed low, and she passed a nurse at the bedside of a young man in traction, twenty pounds, it looked like. Emma nodded. She passed more beds and rounded the corner to the wall with long, narrow windows near the ceiling. And there she was.

"Oh my God!"

Misrak looked dead. She wore no gown and had no sheet. Her left breast was missing, and in its place was a mess of knotty sutures and a drain that led to a bag filled with red serous fluid. Her eyes were slits and her breathing shallow. Emma pulled the sheet from the floor and covered her with it. Misrak's skin felt cold. Emma looked around to see if the lone nurse could bring a blanket, but she was gone.

Emma took her cold hand. "Misrak." Her voice came out in a whisper. She said her name again, but louder.

Misrak's eyes popped open like a doll. She moaned and tried to lift her heavy arm.

"Oh," said Emma. "Ishi, okay. Misrak?" The bed was ancient, made of iron, painted white, with a flattened mattress.

Misrak's lips trembled. She thanked God that Emma was there and tried to sit up, but fell back. There was no pillow. Just then, the lights dimmed and then went off. The power had shut down.

"Damn," said Emma. Power outages were common in Addis, but at the hospital? Emma held her breath, but had to let it go when the power stayed off. She searched the room but saw no one on a ventilator. The nurse was back in the vast room. Emma waved at her. The sunlight through the high windows made Emma think of a funeral home.

"Ferenj," said Misrak. She squeezed Emma's hand and began to cry, asking about her children.

Emma shook her head. "No problem. It's okay. I'll stay here with you for a while."

Again, Misrak asked about her children.

"You must be cold," said Emma. She waved at the nurse, who saw her. She was giving an injection of penicillin to a man with end-stage syphilis.

Emma just stood there, hunched over, holding Misrak's hand. Her back felt weak, and she squatted halfway. The nurse was coming.

"Yes, what can I do?" asked the nurse.

She was tall and golden, but looked tired in her off-white uniform. Emma noticed that she was wearing black shoes, which made her look like a man from the knees down.

"Cold, she is cold. Is there a blanket?" asked Emma.

"Ai yi," said the nurse. "We have no blankets. I can to bring another sheet."

"Is she getting pain medication?" asked Emma.

The nurse frowned. "Yes, the opium suppository."

"Can you ask her if she is in pain?"

"She will say it if she has pain."

"Can you ask her? She looks to be in a lot of pain." Emma had to let Misrak's hand go because her back was killing her.

The nurse looked around the large, open room and asked Misrak about her pain. Misrak's lips trembled. "I will bring soon," said the nurse, and she walked away.

Emma examined the beds on either side of Misrak, a man with his head wrapped in gauze, and a man sitting cross-legged on his bed reading the Koran. The room hummed with a quiet busyness, but overall, it was dead and now very dim. What could she do? Misrak would need to be in the hospital for many more days, it seemed. But Emma was leaving for Godo in the morning. She would just have to hope for the best.

Emma lingered for another hour, making Misrak as comfortable as possible. The nurse had brought an extra sheet, but not the pain medicine, and had disappeared. Only a tall, thin man pushing a mop was on the unit with Emma. She said her goodbyes to Misrak and set off back to the Mission. As she was leaving, the lights flickered on, and she took that as a good omen.

Back at the Mission, Emma thanked Tesfaw for his patience. He waved her off. It was nothing. She thought about checking in with Teresa, but did not want to deal with Claude climbing all over her. She let the guard open the gate, and she headed left for Guthrie's place. It was maybe two in the afternoon, six in the morning back in Alabama.

A man speaking a mile a minute approached her with his hand out. Emma made eye contact, but did not reciprocate. The man stopped, blocking her, and questioned her in an angry tone. Why would she not shake his hand? Emma looked around. He was furious and would not move, shouting at her. She tried to walk around him without success. The streams of people splitting around them began to circle and form a knot.

"Bucka!" said Emma. Enough.

She lowered her head and butted it against his chest and pushed forward. He pushed back, cursing, calling her an American whore, an American spy. The crowd congealed and created a local heat that Emma could feel to her bones.

"Move, motherfucker!" Emma put her fists into his chest and pushed. The knot of people seemed to turn like an unbalanced tire. Emma wasn't sure if she was headed in the right direction. She breathed deep and shoved the man away from her. He grabbed her shirt and pulled, pressing her to his body. Emma was about to throw up. She thought back to a self-defense class she'd taken after her father had molested her. She grabbed the man's neck with both hands and plunged her thumbs into his thyroid. He fell backward, choking and gasping. The crowd was building a noise. There was laughing, jeering, jostling. Everyone wanted to see.

Emma plowed ahead and pushed through the circle of humanity into a small space of open air. She leaned over and gasped for breath. Whistles and calls. She looked around to gather her bearings and began to walk, and then she broke into a run, a defeated jog to Guthrie's, an image of Reece on the floor of her tiny house.

That evening, Emma sat at the dining room table, telling her story of the awful day. Livvy had made creamed potatoes, fried okra, and a mild goat stew. Emma pushed at the chunks. *Could things get worse?*

"Crowds are mean," said Dr. Guthrie. "But I'm surprised that he attacked you like that. People here like us because we give them food and medicine. That would've never happened if I'd been there. Just shake it off, but let us drive you back in the morning, okay?"

"Heck no. I'm not afraid. I'll walk." She mixed some crispy okra with the fluffy mashed potatoes. "Thank you for dinner." She paused. "And tell me again what Reece said."

Livvy spoke. "Well, he was just asking for you, wanted to talk with you. He sounded just like he did here. I thought maybe he was in the next room, the connection was so good."

"He said he was at his grandparents'?"

"That's right. It was early there. He was trying to catch you during daylight, I suppose."

Guthrie drained his glass of ice water, and Livvy went to refill his glass.

"So, he's still engaged to that other girl over there. He just knows you saved his life. I'd be calling, too. He's worried about you."

That seemed less than ideal to Emma, and she frowned. "I'll call him in a few minutes, after we're finished. He should still be up."

"Sure. You're free to use the phone. Just make sure you write down the time and date and give it to Tesfaw. He'll write you out a bill. Otherwise, we'd go broke paying for international calls."

"Yeah," said Emma. She poured more gravy, a pause of breathiness filling her chest.

An hour later, Emma gave the operator the number to Reece's grandparents' house. He would be up, no doubt, maybe close to the phone, or so she hoped. She checked her watch again, about noon in Alabama. There were the double rings. She exhaled and inhaled, short of breath. She wondered if this was what love was supposed to be like. Was it supposed to be this complicated? Did it have to involve guns, a vulgar man known as the Hyena, and vast distances? The phone kept ringing, perhaps fifteen double rings.

"Hello," said Dora.

"Mrs. Myers? Hey, I'm calling from Ethiopia, for Reece."

Dora frowned. "You are? Well, he's outside."

"Is he...Can he come in for a minute?"

Dora held the phone like a mortar round. "Horace! *Psst!* Horace, go out and get Reece. He's wanted on the phone."

"Do what?" asked Horace.

"Go and get Reece. It's that nurse from Africa." Dora pointed at the receiver, as if it were a baby about to cry.

Horace, a ripe seventy-two, rocked and stood from his recliner. He paused, his vision going black for a moment. "Yeah, where is he?"

"He's outside," said Dora. "Just look around." She had her hand over the receiver and lifted it. "Hold on, Bertha. Horace's gone out to call him in."

Emma laughed. "It's Emma."

"Excuse me, Emma. So, you're a nurse in Africa? That must be exciting and all. You saved Reece's life, and we are sure proud of that."

"That's right, Ethiopia. I just happened to be there when it happened." Emma tried to imagine Alabama, Reece's grandparents, but she could only think of McDonald's. She was in the Guthrie's den, sitting on the couch with her legs crossed, thinking about a double quarter-pounder with cheese. "I can wait, no problem." *French fries.*

Horace lumbered through the kitchen/dining room into the laundry room. He paused at the screen door and pushed outside. He looked around and didn't see Reece in the swing. He walked to the driveway.

"Hey!"

Horace looked around and noticed the ladder leaning against the house between the house and the garage.

"Hey! Up here!" Reece was on the roof, sweeping pine straw from the gutters.

"Jumpin Jehoshaphat," said Horace. "Boy! Get down from there before you kill yourself."

"I'm fine." Reece walked to the crest of the roof and

straddled the pitch.

"You got a phone call, inside."

"From who?" He felt a thrill run through his gut.

"That girl in Africa. You better hurry." Horace wondered that they even had phones in Africa, from what he knew.

Reece got serious, dropped the broom, and mounted the ladder. He was unsteady and descended with care, but missed a rung and fell.

Emma listened as the line went dead. She had no idea why. Sunspots maybe? She held the heavy black receiver and stared at the mouthpiece. Her words had entered and emerged eight thousand miles away. Reece lived there. It seemed to be a matter of chance whether or not she would hear his voice.

"Reece! Holy Toledo, boy." Horace stood over Reece, sitting up on the thick pine straw.

"I'm sort of all right," said Reece. "Hurt my neck, but I'm fine." He tried to stand and fell back on his butt. "Well, damn."

Dora stood at the screen door. "Lord, have mercy."

"What put the idea into you to get on the house?" asked Horace. "Are you special? For goodness' sake, son."

"I'm fine, just slipped."

"And nearly broke your damn neck, boy." Horace held out his hand.

"Gotta keep the gutters clean. You know, causes leaks." Reece pulled and stood. For a second he wondered if he'd shart his britches again.

With the line dead, Emma continued to hold the phone to her ear as if a miracle would take place. After a minute or so, she cradled the phone. She felt dirty, unworthy, and helpless.

"No dice," she said.

Livvy was there, hovering.

"I'm sorry, girl."

"No worries, I suppose. The connection broke." She realized she was sweating and squeegeed her forehead with a palm. "Heck and damnation."

"Was he there?"

"I think so, and the line went dead."

"That happens, just call him back." Livvy moved to the bookshelf, adjusting the books. She saw a copy of *My Utmost for His Highest*. "This is a great book." She removed it and walked over to hand it to Emma.

Emma laughed. "I have it. My preacher gave it to me."

"Oh." She could hear her husband banging in the bathroom, probably brushing his teeth. "Norbert's brushing his teeth." She laughed.

Emma imagined Dr. Guthrie brushing his teeth, wearing a tight tuck-in shirt. She laughed, too. Livvy caught it and laughed some more. Pretty soon, they were both laughing. Emma laughed so hard she wanted to cry, and then it just stopped.

Emma caught her breath. "Well, his teeth are white. That's what matters, right?"

Livvy corralled her laughing. "I guess you're right. Good old Norbert with his white teeth."

The phone rang, and Emma was right there. She stared at the phone. "Want me to answer?" She felt her stomach crawling into her chest.

"Sure, might be Reece." She replaced the book.

Emma reached for the phone. She put the receiver to her ear. There was that sound of a vast distance. "Uh, hello."

"Emma, hey!" Reece pressed the phone to his ear.

"Reece?" asked Emma.

"Yeah, back from the dead. Sorry, I missed your call. I'm calling back."

Emma laughed. "Yeah, well, I figured out that much."

"I fell off the ladder."

"What the heck were you doing on a ladder?"

"I was up on the roof, sweeping off the pine straw."

Emma thought about pine straw, how it was mahogany, kind of like Reece's hair, how it collected in her mother's yard, a soft mattress of pine needles, the woody smell.

"Emma?"

"Yeah, sorry. I'm at the Guthries, headed back to Godo in a bit." She told him about Misrak.

"Oh no." He remembered Misrak cooking over the open fire of coals, topless, her large breasts swinging in the smoke. "God, I hope she'll be okay."

"Me too," said Emma. "Looks bad, though. They took it off, the breast. She looked like hell." Emma played with the long phone cord that had knots in it.

Reece tried to imagine the breast. "She's a tough nut.

She'll do great." What more could he say? "How are you?"

"Doing okay." She wanted to tell him about the helicopter incident. "They're closing the station."

"In Godo?"

"Yeah, cured, done. It's hard to believe." Emma swallowed hard. She just wanted to reach through the phone line and wrap herself around him.

"Holy cow. I suppose it's a good thing, considering. How many at the shelter?"

Emma thought. "Well, about twenty with the kids. That's what I'm most concerned about, although I haven't had much time to think about it." Emma watched Livvy walking around the living room, examining the nooks and crannies as if looking for a prize.

"What about that guy with the rotten leg?" Reece melted into the recliner. He pushed it back, and his feet went up. He was ready to talk for hours, if necessary, and glanced at Dora washing dishes. Horace was still outside. He felt his face and decided that he needed to shave. "The guy I gave my bed to."

Emma took in a deep breath. "I don't know. He might still be in the hospital. I forgot to ask, thinking about Misrak and all."

"Yeah, that's enough."

"Yeah," said Emma, and there was a silence of ten seconds. She so badly wanted to know about Kristin. "How's everything? You're still up and about? No problems with the, uh, the head wound? I thought for sure you were going to die on the floor."

"Yeah, walking okay, still weak, especially in my back.

Weird. Hard to pick up stuff."

"How are the folks, your grandparents?"

"Doing okay. Granny's feeding me, getting me fat." Reece noticed Dora smile at the sink. "Had some fried taters for lunch."

"Fried taters! Dang. Tell her I wish I could be there."

"I will," said Reece.

More silence.

"You coming back soon?" Reece swallowed hard. Was he being too forward?

"I don't know," said Emma. "Not sure if I'll be needed here or not. I've about run my race, though."

"So, you've been there two years, right?"

"Yeah. I miss Alabama."

"Well, you missed a freaking F-5 tornado. I nearly got sucked up to heaven, but Debbie Dee pulled my bed into the hallway. I thought I was a goner." Reece thought about Debbie Dee, the cold sores in the corners of her mouth, how she had kept the TV on MTV. "A good woman."

"Give her my blessings if you see her."

"I will," said Emma. "They came and got you in a special jet. That has to be big bucks."

"No doubt," said Reece. "Maybe Alabama grows enough peaches and pecans to cover my bills."

"Yeah, right, in another universe. Are you thinking about disability at all? You could get a check, take it easy, I suppose."

Reece coughed. "Maybe if I'd lost my arms and legs. I say that within a month, I could be back on the unit working, maybe in CCU or maybe on a floor, something less strenuous, less strain on the brain, if you know what I mean."

"Do you think you've lost something up there? I mean, you sound pretty clear and in control." Emma examined her nails, frazzled to the nubs. "I chipped a tooth, biting my nails."

"That lopsided smile of yours. Has it gone bust?" Her lopsided smile killed him, with or without a chipped tooth, he supposed. "Which tooth?"

"In the front, an incisor, just a square piece, feels rough on my tongue. I guess I'll get it fixed when I get back."

"More reasons to head back," said Reece. He felt the elephant in the room, but what to say?

"When I come back, which could be soon, will you meet me at the airport? I'd rather you meet me than my mom. Maybe we could drive to Hueytown and surprise her at the restaurant, the barbecue place. She'll have a heart attack, but not really."

Reece imagined the logistics with Kristin. She would either freak out and say no or insist that she go with him. "That'd be great, but you know, Kristin and all. She's definitely jealous, and we are engaged. So..."

The couch was feeling hard, and Emma stood, wrapping the cord around her arm. "How is she, Kristin?"

Partially reclined with the TV playing, Reece thought about how best to answer. "I saw her last night. She's fine, I suppose. Working at Carraway...She wants to set up a date for the wedding. But I can't get my head around a wedding just yet. You know?"

"That's pretty final, a wedding." Emma chewed her thumbnail and sat back down, one leg beneath her. "The... the night. The night you were shot. Do you remember?"

"Not really," said Reece. "I can't tell the real from dreams. I was in your house, and then I was on the floor."

"To remind you, you were rubbing my shoulders and..." Emma paused to make sure that she was telling the God honest truth and that Livvy was out of the room. "And you touched me. It felt electric and then *Blam! Blam!* and you should've been dead."

Emma was right. His hands had wandered. *Blam!* After that were blanks, snatches, faces, a jouncing jeep.

"Yeah, I should be dead, no doubt. But here I am, sitting in a recliner talking to you half a world away."

That wasn't quite the answer Emma was looking for. She tightened the cord around her wrist, making her hand turn red. She lowered her voice. "What's strange is that I needed you that night. God provided, and then He took you away."

"God is funny sometimes. You know, I've had a lot of time to think about God, and He just seems to be getting further away, like a plastic bag blowing across a parking lot."

"That's pretty harsh. But I get it. No one invited me here. We were able to work in Godo because of the famine. It seems like we've been riding the famine, trying to get at the underbelly, if you know what I mean. Spread our gospel. Like a hole opened in a fence and here we come crawling through with Bibles and Band-Aids."

"Yeah, bad fences make bad neighbors." Reece felt that he was at the bottom of a well, that Emma was looking down the well, but couldn't see him. Should he tell her that he'd made out with Kristin the night before, that they'd almost had sex to the music of John Denver?

"So, you staying at your grandparents for now?" Emma made eye contact with Livvy and pursed her lips. She wanted to be alone with Reece.

"Yeah, I think that's best. Kristin's parents weird me out. It's just home here, you know. I've got the lake to look at and Horace's garden to help with."

Emma decided to try it again. "Reece?"

"Yes."

"Reece, I think...I love you." Emma felt a flock of doves explode from her chest. She felt her blood surge to her upper body, and her stomach empty.

Reece grinned, but what to say? "I mean, wow." Reece wanted to say the same back to her. "I mean, I'm attracted to you. Who knows what would have happened if I were still there?" He wanted to say thank you, but that would be weird. "What can I say? I miss you, miss working with you. I'm jealous that you're still there and I'm here."

Emma controlled her breathing. She didn't regret saying it. "I just think we're compatible, compadres, you know. It's so hard in the clinic without you. I mean, Afewerki is wonderful, but I don't know. I guess I should just shut up."

Reece leaned even farther back in the recliner and stared at the plain white ceiling. "No, don't think like that." He felt that his life was playing out before him as it should. Would he just tell Kristin that the engagement was off? He tried to imagine such a thing and couldn't.

"So you didn't say it back," said Emma. She took a deep breath. "I guess I'm jumping the gun here. I don't know what to think anymore. Should I just hang up?"

Reece tried to imagine what was best to say, and in a hurry. He couldn't just say it was off between him and

Kristin because Emma said she loved him. "It's so complicated. I'm sorry. Maybe I just need some time to work this out in my head." He felt good about his words. He thought he was making sense and not promising too much. But, *damn,* Emma was always in his thoughts, in a promising manner. With Kristin, he doubted their bond, the engagement, the whole wedding on a stick that he knew would happen. But did that mean he loved Emma?

"Yeah, complicated, inundated, and maybe incarcerated." Emma pondered her left hand while holding the phone to her right ear. A ring would look good there, and Reece would pick something special. She just knew it to be true.

Reece tried to understand the rhyme. "But never fabricated..."

"Can love be a lie?" Emma felt as if poised over the end of a sharp sword.

"Damn, that's hard." He knew the answer was yes, but how would it sound if he agreed? "You're killing me."

"Softly?" asked Emma. "With your song or mine?"

Reece flexed his sockless feet inside his running shoes. He wasn't up to speed on popular music. He'd heard the song, he thought. "If I said you had a beautiful body, would you hold it against me?" It's all he could think of. He frowned.

"Yeah, I would, if you said it and meant it, right? But hell, what are we doing? I'm about to go crazy over here. I need to get back to the States and gather my marbles. We could go to the zoo and watch that poor old, bored orangutan or watch the chimps throw up into their hands."

Reece smiled. "Yeah, and the flamingos and the tigers that smell like piss. Do you like the zoo?" He more or less hated the zoo.

"I guess," said Emma. "But it's kinda sad."

"Sad is the right word," said Reece. "Did I tell you I saw a toucan flying one day while I was driving with Craig? In that huge valley between Lemi and Alem Ketema."

"Ha, Craig. No, you didn't tell me. I'm riding with Craig to Godo tomorrow."

"It had a long brown-and-tan beak, not so colorful as the cereal toucan. It flew alongside the jeep for at least thirty seconds and then veered away."

"Cool," said Emma. "Haven't seen one myself. Have you seen the crocs from the helicopter with Terry?"

"Yeah, he flew down a river canyon one day. They were huge, probably twenty feet long. Up on the riverbanks were tons of gray monkeys."

"That's the place," said Emma. Her mouth was dry, and she needed to pee. How long could they just banter? *Hours?* Had she said she loved him? She had indeed. Livvy was pointing at her watch. The calls were expensive. "Listen, maybe I shouldn't keep you. This is pretty pricey, the phone call."

"Not a problem. I should let you go." He wiggled his toes in his canvas tennis shoes. Everything was okay, or it wasn't.

"Tell your grandparents hey for me." Emma closed her eyes, trying to imagine the house on the lake, what Reece might be wearing, probably some shorts and a t-shirt, maybe a ballcap.

"Yeah, I will," said Reece.

It took them a minute or so to finally say goodbye, and the line went dead. Both, on their respective ends, continued to hold the phone to their ears and stare into space.

Emma felt bad about leaving Addis, about leaving Misrak in the hospital. It seemed she would heal, but had the cancer spread? The hospital did not have the equipment to scan her body for less obvious infiltrations, so hopefully removing the breast would do it.

The morning was slick with rain, the air sparked with what Emma thought of as positive ions. In general, she hated the long, bumpy ride to Godo, but she told herself that she would enjoy the ride today, with hairless Craig, nonetheless. Maybe he was good luck, and she thought she might rub his bald head, except he wore a bad black hairpiece that sat on his head like a flat crow. They had passed through the checkpoint, headed out of the city, and were cruising down a long, empty road that wound its way to a vast valley accessed by a switchbacking road that clung to the cliffs. Occasionally, a car or truck slipped off, sending riders to their instant deaths.

Within two hours, they reached Lemi, the last town before the road dropped to the valley.

"Want to stop for tea and a bun?" Craig wore tan slacks and a short-sleeve dress shirt with brown loafers.

"Yeah, tea would be nice, take a break."

Craig navigated the narrow, dusty street. Single-story square buildings with metal roofs lined the crowded road. A herd of goats slowed them to a crawl, being herded by two small boys in rags, each with a whip they cracked with precision. A few hundred feet more, and a dark green building sat off the road on a slight rise. An Ethiopian flag flew from a pole fashioned to the roof. He parked next to three other vehicles.

"Maybe some ferenji inside?" he said.

"Could be." Emma glanced up at the clouds, feeling their weight in the sky.

Inside was dim, just the light through open squares that shuttered when needed. A golden cloth with long fringes rimmed the crowded room. A bashful young woman approached and pointed to a tiny empty table without chairs. She took a deep breath and asked if they would like tea.

"Ow, shai, dabo?" asked Craig.

The woman bowed and hurried away, her long dress dragging the floor. They stood there beside the table, all eyes lingering their way. They were the only ferenji in the room. Three men eyed them, especially Emma. They looked to be high-ranking soldiers in crisp green uniforms and ballcaps with insignia. One coughed, and Emma noted that he looked puny, perhaps even sick, with a sour look on his face. The fattest of the three stood and brought an extra chair over for Emma, gracing her with a wide smile.

"Amenseganolo," said Emma.

"You are welcome," said the man, speaking English.

Craig said thank you as well.

"Okay if I sit?" asked Emma.

"Yeah, yeah," said Craig. "Beauty before baldness." He laughed and fidgeted, unsure of what to do with his hands.

"Do you feel naked?" She regretted wearing short pants, even though they were baggy with big pockets.

"Ha, no, well not really."

The waitress brought two clear glass cups with thick

handles, an ancient kettle, a sugar dish. She poured, bowed, and backed away. The scalding tea steamed and smelled of cloves and ginger.

"That fat guy looks a little scary." She glanced at the three soldiers, who seemed to be watching her every move.

"Really? He was just being nice." He shuffled his feet.

From a back room, the waitress brought a low stool and indicated it was for Craig. He thanked her and arranged himself, the table hitting his chest. "Better than nothing."

"Those guys seem pretty interested in us." She could see them by just turning left a bit.

"I hope they don't start asking for travel papers." He dipped his finger in the tea. "Yikes. Hot."

Emma took a tiny sip. "Yeah." She tugged at her shorts. "So, will you stay in AK for a night or just head back to Meranya today? I know your wife misses you."

"Probably spend the night. No use driving after dark. Just too dangerous. It could be that I can drive you to Godo tomorrow, if there's no jeep."

"Or maybe Terry will be able to drop me."

"The Mission has halted food drops, I think." He took a swift slurp of tea.

The young woman came with two large, dark brown rolls on clear glass plates.

"Mmm, fresh and warm," said Emma. "Hard to believe they're shutting down. I guess I just thought I'd spend the rest of my life in the clinic."

"The medical side of things is wrapping up. I'm still here, though, doing road and bridge projects. I signed on for two years, have a year left."

"How is your wife, Eve, doing? Is she good for another

year?"

"Yeah, I think so. She doesn't like it when I leave, though. But she's safe with the guards there and Dr. Chuck and his wife. But they'll be leaving soon, so not sure what will happen then."

"I felt much safer when Reece was in Godo. Strength in numbers, you know." She noticed the fat soldier talking to the waitress, pointing their way. It was so unusual to see a fat person, and he wasn't that fat—meaty was the better word.

"Unbelievable, him getting hurt like that." He whistled, and a few heads turned. "Oops. Inside voices, right?"

"He lived and is up and walking the face of God's green earth. It's a miracle, I think."

"You saved his life is the word from Dr. Guthrie."

"I did what I had to." Emma studied Craig's smooth face. He almost looked plastic, somewhat alien, especially with his hairpiece. She wanted to ask him how his disorder had shaped his life. Did he get bullied when he was a kid for being hairless? She tore off some bun. "This is so good." She cut her eyes to check on the soldiers who seemed to be having a merry old time.

It took her and Craig another ten minutes to finish their tea and buns. When Craig motioned the waitress over and asked for the ticket, she blushed, said, "Yellum," and pointed toward the fat soldier. It took a second, but they fathomed that the soldiers had paid their tab.

"That's weird," said Emma.

Craig nodded. "Yeah, sort of." He waved at the men, and they all lifted their eyebrows in approval and nodded back.

"Let's get out of here," said Emma. The room seemed reduced to themselves and the soldiers with their pistols. "I freaking hate those guns."

As soon as they stood, the soldiers stood as well and paused, as if waiting for something to happen. Just then, an old man, who had wandered in, began to play a one-stringed masinqo and sing. Craig fished in his pocket and dropped fifty cents onto a cloth.

Emma jumped in the jeep and watched in dismay as the soldiers followed them and approached. Craig paused with his door open.

The fat soldier motioned for Emma to roll down her window. Emma told Craig to get in and drive, and ignored the soldier.

"Thank you again," said Craig, pausing, perhaps frozen in the moment.

"Craig, let's go. They're up to no good, believe me." She glanced to her right and saw the fat one frowning, while the other two smiled. The fat guy was rapping on the window. "Craig!" She focused on her hands, which were gripping her knees. It could get ugly fast. She felt her heart beating in her throat, but she kept a straight face.

Craig said he was sorry, slid in, and cranked up. He backed out slowly, careful not to run over anyone's feet. The soldiers just held their ground, watching them drive away, but then piled into their civilian Land Rover. They were traveling to Alem Ketema to take possession of cash captured from rebels in the north. It was a kind of holiday for them, something to enjoy, and now the female ferenj had insulted them.

Craig cruised along in third gear, bouncing down the

narrow dirt road, graveled in patches where water flowed during rains. Craig knew it was the work of another civil engineer who worked for Catholic Relief Services.

Emma glanced in her wide side mirror and saw the Land Rover behind them, perhaps a thousand feet back. "Dammit to hell."

Craig watched the Land Rover gain on them and then hold back. "I hope they don't trail us all the way to AK. If they don't pass us, I'll pull over and let them go around."

"Can you out-gun them?" She felt breathless and hot.

"I doubt it. Plus, the roads are so rough and tricky. I think we're fine. Maybe the fat guy has a crush on you, that's all." He laughed but cut it short.

"Yeah, and maybe he has a crush on you. How would that make you feel?"

Craig turned just a bit red. "I was just joking. No need to flare up."

"Have you ever been attacked by men in the middle of nowhere? Are you a woman?"

"No and no." Craig frowned and realized that the jeep was whining at the top of third gear, and he shifted to fourth.

"Well, yes and yes for me." She told him the story about the Hyena and his two minions attacking her during her visit to the old monk building the church into the cliff. Only the shouting of the monk had saved her, the same monk who had traveled to Addis and visited Reece in the hospital. "So, today, you're my monk, got it?"

Craig rolled his eyes. "Yeah, okay." He slowed and navigated a gaping pothole shaped like a pod of star anise. To the right, the cliff edge drew near, lined with huge, jagged boulders. Beyond was the expansive valley. He checked his rearview.

"So, are you and Reece a thing? I mean, I thought he was engaged. May not be any of my business." They rumbled along, approaching the tricky descent to the valley below. "Down we go." A bearded vulture lumbered above them.

Emma thought. "We worked so well together, kind of like magic. And yeah, he was engaged, still is as far as I know."

"Huh." He cleared his throat and moved the jeep inside a tight curve.

For the next half hour, they rode in silence, the transmission whining, resisting the steep decline. The Range Rover behind them often disappeared only to reappear. Steep walls of granite towered above them.

"How did you meet your wife? This is making me woozy."

Craig wrangled another hairpin turn. "I guess I'd rather not say."

Emma noticed his set jaw, smooth as glass. "That's odd."

"Well, love is supposed to be romantic, right?" He held tight to the steering wheel, the distance opening into a hazy vista, a river curling like a bent pin.

"Usually. But you have to tell me, right?" She had to shout over the motor. "Can't keep me hanging like that."

Craig pinched his lips and rolled his eyes. "We're married and that's what's important, right? She loves me, I love her."

"Come on. Am I gonna have to tickle you or what?"

"Tickle me? You'll kill us both." He frowned. "I'll tell

you, but you have to tell me something."

Emma frowned. She felt her face layered in dust and sweat and wished for a hot washcloth. "Okay, you tell me and then I'll tell you. No holds barred. Deal?"

"Deal."

"So…"

"We met at a funeral."

"Jesus, this is like pulling teeth. Whose funeral?"

"Her husband's. He was my best friend."

"I'm sorry." Emma pondered the scenario. "But you had never met her, even though he was your best friend?"

"Yep. He'd moved to Portland and married. I didn't see him for seven years."

"But he was still your best friend."

Craig piled the jeep over a large rock, jouncing them both. He checked the rearview and saw only dust.

Reece had a follow-up appointment at UAB Hospital's ambulatory center. He'd rescheduled twice because he wanted to drive himself, but relented and let Horace and Dora take him. They both wanted to go. His appointment was at one, and they decided to stop at Jack's for a hamburger beforehand. Reece liked the orange-salt fries and the juicy burgers. They took a booth, and right away, Reece looked forward to the entertainment: a black man with a white woman and a baby walked in.

"Would you look at that," said Horace. He held his hamburger halfway between the table and his mouth, like a ping-pong paddle.

"Oh brother," said Dora. "Quit your staring, Horace."

Reece laughed. Horace wasn't racist so much as he was old school. He hailed from Cullman County, still 98 percent white, and had not encountered a black man until he signed up with the Army at the age of 22.

"I bet that's his baby," said Reece.

Horace resumed chewing, his eyes fixed on the spectacle before him. He'd worked for thirty years in the pipe shop side by side with "Negros," but at the end of the day colors didn't mix.

"White trash," he said, his eyes registering disbelief.

"We're in the big city, now," said Reece. "People are people." He couldn't pass up the opportunity, though, to egg on Horace. "I'll bet they're not even married. What do you think?"

"Reece," said Dora. "Behave. You know how he gets.

Better to just leave it alone. Probably a baby with a white man. Looked white to me anyways."

Horace tried to look away, Reece could tell, but he couldn't resist staring. He watched him pick up a French fry and dab it at an empty place on his tray.

"You know I worked with black people in Ethiopia, right?" asked Reece.

Horace wasn't deterred. "She paid for his food. Probably living off her. Oh well, what's done is done." He resumed his fries, finding the ketchup this time, and added extra salt.

"You talk to Kristin today?" asked Dora. Mixed couples made her nervous, but there was no turning back the clock.

"No, not yet. It's hard to get her when she's at work." He savored his food, still wondering at the bounty in the States versus the sparsity in Ethiopia. If he thought too hard, Ethiopia just didn't make sense. It seemed like a dream that he'd even been there. How could someone pay to lose weight in the States while a baby starved to death in Ethiopia? He went back to the night he was shot and tensed. *Was it worth it?* and his thoughts went to Emma.

Kristin washed her hands, breathing in the sweet odor of Hibiclens. It made her fingers itch, especially around her engagement ring. Mrs. Dunlop, the massive coronary with schizophrenia, was still Kristin's patient along with a young woman, a Watkins, who'd been in an auto accident resulting in chest trauma. Both of her breasts were dark purple and blue, and she had a chest tube on her right side.

Kristin adjusted the sheet over Mrs. Dunlop and eyed the bags of fluid pumping into her central line, dopamine and a saline drip. "You good, Mrs. Dunlop?" asked Kristin. "Where are we today?"

Mrs. Dunlop's big brown eyes bugged beneath her ragged bangs. Kristin had washed her hair and combed it out straight. She looked like a little wrinkled boy with a fat face.

"I work at Loveman's," said Mrs. Dunlop. "I have to run the credit card receipts." She frowned, tugging on the loose restraints around her wrists. "I need the scissors."

The intercom buzzed behind the bed. "Hey," said Kristin.

"You got a phone call on hold," said Eudora, the unit clerk. Eudora smoked two packs a day on her off hours.

"Okay, thanks." She stepped out to the long desk, hoping it was Reece. "Hello?"

"Well, hey, working today?"

She recognized his voice. "Brad? Why are you calling me?"

"What, it's not Dr. Phillips today?" He was sitting poolside at his condo on a rare day off.

"No, you're not working, so it's 'Brad.' Disappointed?"

"No, pleasantly surprised. I'm oiled up beside the pool. Jealous?"

"Really? Look, I've got work to do." She wanted to say that she was an inch taller than he was.

"I know, I know. It's a hell of a life. Well, look, you can't blame me for trying."

"I can blame you."

"How about dinner tonight? It's a Friday. I never have

Friday night off." He adjusted his polarized sunglasses, checking out a young mother and her twins in the baby pool.

"No, I can't, and you know why. This is getting to be a little ridiculous, don't you think?"

Brad couldn't stop himself. "But I'm a freaking doctor, for God's sake. What's the problem? I'm grade-A, top-shelf, winner winner—"

"You're making me tired, *Dr. Phillips.* Gotta go," and she hung up. She tried to remember what she was supposed to be doing. "Dang." She glanced at Eudora and shook her head.

"Fox wants in the henhouse." Eudora laughed but cut it short. Behind her, the monitor tech Leslie, who always wore purple scrubs, tried to keep a straight face. Everyone knew about Brad and his fixations.

"Fox can stick his head in a trap." Kristin saw her other patient's chart flagged on Eudora's desk. She grabbed the plastic binder and took a look. "Discontinue lidocaine drip." She handed the chart back to Eudora, who responded with a deep phlegm-rattled cough. Kristin looked at her watch. "Ten-fifteen."

"When will we get to see Reece?" asked Eudora. "We miss him here. I guess he knows that, though."

"I'll get on him about that." Kristin wondered why, too. If he could jump in the lake, he could come for a visit, just to have lunch with her, aside from visiting the unit. "Let me DC this drip on Watkins."

She walked into the room. "Hey, gonna stop your lidocaine drip." She almost called her Watkins, but caught herself.

"Is that a good thing?" Charity Watkins lay in bed with the head up to 30 degrees. She moved with purpose, shifting onto her hip, wincing at the tug of the chest tube.

"Your arrhythmia has quieted down, so that's good. We'll see how you do off the lidocaine. The monitor tech out there is keeping an eye on you, so no worries." She powered off the pump, pinched the line, and pulled the needle from the port into her main IV.

Charity coughed and squeezed a pillow to her chest, wincing. "Shit!" She was young, just nineteen, and had ropy, golden hair. She kind of looked pretty lying there, but out of place among the other patients, mostly older and with heart disease in some form or fashion.

Kristin dropped the needle into the dirty-needle jug and tossed the half-empty bag of IV fluid into the trash. "You look uncomfortable, Charity. What can I do? Lower your head a bit? Get up in the chair?"

"I hate to say it, but I need the bedpan pretty bad. I just can't stand the thought of trying to stand with that damn tube sticking out of me."

"Gotta pee?"

"The other."

"Hey, we'll get you fixed up. Not a problem."

She pulled the curtain and fetched the bedpan, squirted baby powder on the rim. "Okay, lift those hips."

"You wanted to say Big Mama, didn't you?"

Kristin laughed. "No way. Just push the button when you're through, okay. Take your time, though."

"Right," said Charity. And right away she filled the bedpan with a manly fart. "Sorry."

Kristin was out of the room and stopped by the monitors. "Let me know if she starts throwing runs of anything or more than a few PVCs."

Leslie nodded, scanning the monitors.

A group of doctors was back from a code blue on the seventh floor. Just in passing, Kristin gathered that the patient had died and that ribs had cracked during CPR. Only after she was in the break room across the hall did she realize that the deceased was the judge who had been so rude and demanding. She pushed into the bathroom, eager to return to her patients.

As soon as she reentered the unit, the light blinked for Charity's room. She halfway expected to find a hard stool. It seemed that she hadn't had a bowel movement since her admission two days prior. She rushed past Eudora and popped around the curtain. "Done?" The room smelled like a shit house.

"I'm sorry," said Charity. "I just hate this." She slapped her hand on the bed.

"Everybody poops," said Kristin, smiling. "Lift up for me." She almost said, "Wow." A fat coil of feces fit for a giant filled the pan. She decided to empty the pan in the dirty laundry room at the flushing sink. "Roll on your side, and I'll get you cleaned up."

"Hell," said Charity. She turned to her right side and grunted.

With speed, Kristin drew up a pan of warm water, took care of business, and was out of the room in less than two minutes. She'd covered the stool with a towel, pretty sure that Charity had set a personal best.

"Check this out," said Kristin.

Winston, the only male nurse on shift and the only

black nurse in either ICU or CCU, was shoving laundry down the chute. He made a sour face at the big reveal. "Lord, like an elephant shit in that pan."

"A new record, I think, and it's that pretty girl in room seven." She dumped the contents, sprayed the pan clean, and flushed.

"Well, you sure are the nice one to share."

"You're welcome," said Kristin.

"V-tach in seven!" said Leslie.

Winston watched Kristin run across the unit and yank back the curtain.

All the way to the doctor's office, Horace grumbled about the mixed-race couple. Streets were closed due to the tornado, still filled with debris.

"Horace, let it go, for Pete's sake." Dora held her big black purse in her lap. She'd not had her hair done since last Saturday and kept adjusting it.

"I do feel sorry for those little fellas in Africa, hungry and crying," said Horace. "Nobody deserves that."

"I've heard that up to a million died in about three years," said Reece. "Although I was on the tail end, and the worst was over. Emma was in the thick of it, though, at another feeding station before I got there."

"Reece," said Dora. She adjusted her hair and toyed with a turtle brooch on her sweater. "You keep talking about this Emma. You're not calling off the wedding now, are you? Kristin is such a sweet girl. You can't do that to her."

Reece felt he had stumbled. "No, I'm just talking. She was great, though, in the clinic, to work with."

"She did save his life," said Horace. "He owes her something. We owe her something. Could of lost you just like that."

"Yeah, there's that," said Reece. "Kristin did come to see me over there. I don't think I remember it, though. Vague." He asked Dora what time it was. She was the only one wearing a watch. "Been waiting twenty minutes."

They sat there looking around at the dozen others in the room, wondering what "ailed them" as Horace would say.

"Make sure you tell the doctor about having that seizure, boy," said Dora.

"I will." Reece leaned forward, his back beginning to ache. "Her momma lives in Hueytown. I told you that, right? Works at a barbecue place there. I've been thinking about visiting her, just to let her know how Emma was doing."

"There you go again," said Dora. "You got Emma on the brain, boy. You better watch it. You hear?"

"Is she good-looking?" asked Horace. He was twiddling his thumbs.

Reece thought. "She has this lopsided smile, kind of unique. Yeah, she's pretty. That's no secret. But Kristin is too, and thinner than Emma." He wanted to comment on the size of their respective breasts.

"You didn't do anything over there that you'd regret, now did you?" asked Dora. She narrowed her eyes.

Reece laughed. "You are a tricky one, and the answer is no. So there. Enough about Emma. Maybe I should remind them that I'm here."

But a nurse pushed open a door and called his name:

"Rice Myers."

Reece corrected the nurse and followed her to an exam room, where she took his vital signs. She eyed the entry and exit wounds on his head and jotted in the chart. "He'll be right in, hon. Okay?"

"Sure." The paper covering the exam table crinkled beneath him, and he swung his legs back and forth, hitting his sneakers against the metal. He wondered what it would be like to call off the engagement.

The jeep revved down and the first flat stretch of road in an hour unpeeled from the escarpment. Emma realized she'd had her arm in the same position for too long and relaxed her stiff elbow.

"Jesus, that's nerve-racking," she said. "Do you think we lost them?"

Craig's face hardened. "Not sure, but we'll know soon. They can catch us pretty quick if they wanted to for some reason."

"Well, that's comforting, Craig." She wanted to touch his smooth face to make sure he was real.

"That's just the way it is, right? Unless I try to outrun them, which is silly. But, you know, that's something Eve would say."

"That I'm silly?"

"No."

"The way they paid our bill was kind of creepy, like they had a plan." She looked back through the rear glass. "And damn if that's not them."

Craig saw them, too. "Just settle. They may catch up and pass us, but that's no skin off our noses, right?"

"Now I'm worried. You have a gun in here?" She opened the glove box.

Craig accelerated on the straightened road. "I'm speeding up just because I can and not because they're after us, okay?"

"What about a gun?"

Craig huffed. "No gun, not even a knife, but there are

lots of rocks we can throw."

"That's real funny." She kept turning and looking, looking in the side-view mirror.

"So, I told you about how I met Eve," said Craig.

"I nearly forgot. So, what do you want to know?"

Craig pondered how best to ask the question. Had she wanted to kill herself when she jumped from the helicopter? Maybe it had been an accident. But the story was that she'd opened the door in flight, and had it not been for Terry's expertise and quick response, she would have died. He watched the Land Rover gaining on them.

"Just about the helicopter, you jumping." He sped up.

Emma sank into her seat and tugged at her seatbelt. "So, what do you want to know? I was super stressed. It's hard to explain."

"Did you want to, to hurt yourself, maybe even kill yourself? I mean, that's kind of crazy, don't you think, jumping out like that?" He could smell his feet in his shoes, or was it her shoes?

"Oh brother," said Emma. "Those guys are gaining on us, don't you think?"

"No, and you didn't answer the question." The road was open now and running over shallow rises, almost like a roller coaster. The air was much warmer in the valley, and he rolled down his window halfway, felt a tug on his hairpiece, and rolled it up a bit. "You just seem so solid."

"So what you're asking is, am I crazy?"

Craig nodded no and glanced over.

"Well, maybe this place has made me a little crazy. So what? Haven't you ever wanted to die, to just end it all? Maybe on the spur of a moment, just turn the wheel and hit a tree?"

"Honestly, no. It's never crossed my mind."

"Well, lucky you," said Emma. "And maybe that's all I have to say about that."

"Yeah, that's okay. I didn't mean anything by asking. Just curious."

They cruised and bounced along in silence for a few minutes, the Range Rover seeming to hold a distance of a few hundred feet back.

Inside the Rover, the three soldiers were drinking from a bottle of cheap blended whiskey. The fat one, nicknamed Nikita, sat in the front passenger seat, the one who appeared ill in the back, and the driver who was drinking the most. They were not quite roaring drunk yet, but the sky was the limit. Once they had taken possession of the captured cash in Alem Ketema, they could pull out the stops. The driver, with a precise haircut, kept the jeep ahead in view. There was a section of road surrounded by house-sized boulders that he was waiting on. He needed to pee.

Emma squirmed in her seat. Craig's question had given her a headache, and she needed to pee. "I need to pee, but we can't stop."

"Yeah, me too," said Craig. "And there's a good place to stop, maybe in half an hour, a grotto of giant boulders. I've stopped there before. I think I stopped there with Reece when he was riding with me to AK."

"You told me that."

"Yeah, nice guy. Kind of quiet. It's the tea."

"That and the pounding that the road gives your ding-dang kidneys," said Emma. "Seriously, though, don't stop. I can wait."

"It's another two hours, and I can't wait that long. Just relax. Nothing is going to happen. It's a beautiful day, kind of hot, but the sun's out, just a few clouds. We can have a nice dinner at the hotel in AK. The electricity will come on around dusk." He patted his black hairpiece, checking its progress throughout the day.

Emma gazed at the yellow scrub and brown rocks. There were no trees. The escarpment on the other side of the valley rose into the air and seemed as if it was close, but they had miles to go and a river to cross. The jeep hummed with gravel crunching beneath the wheels, like shredded wheat biscuits.

"Was it Reece getting shot, you think?" He still had to drive with two hands to keep the jeep on the road, but could relax a bit on the river plain.

"Yes." She wondered at the speed of her answer. "Or, maybe. That and the misery, the poverty, maybe. But yeah, Reece getting shot was a real shocker. We had a connection in the clinic. It's lonely out here."

"That's why I have Eve. I couldn't do it without her. I could have never come by myself."

Emma thought about that. "Doesn't make it less dangerous. Don't you get nervous leaving Eve up there? I know Dr. Chuck and his wife are there, but still. Anything can happen. The Rover's hanging back. I wonder why they don't pass us."

Craig nodded. "It doesn't bother her, so I feel good when I leave. Or I don't feel bad, I should say. There's a special bond when you're married." The jeep took a breadloaf rock head on and lurched.

Emma grabbed the handle on the dash. "Reece and I

had a special bond. What about that?"

"But I think you forget he's engaged. Right?"

"He told me that he thought getting engaged was a mistake." She tried to remember the specifics.

"Doesn't make it right, though. Marriage is a sacred bond."

Emma rolled her eyes. "Sacred, scared...crades..." rhyming with Hades. "What we had was scared. I mean sacred. Can't I have that, just for me, something to hold onto?"

"If you listen to the Bible...No, you can't." Craig widened his eyes, thinking them suddenly dry.

"Is it in Leviticus, where it says a man can't shave the corners of his beard?" Emma gripped her knees, pulled the tight seatbelt away from her lap.

Craig laughed. "I wish I could grow a beard."

"I guess Eve likes her men smooth." Her jaw was set in stone, and she wasn't laughing.

Craig glanced at her. "You mad about something? It's called alopecia universalis. I'm different."

"Yeah, different, but the same as the rest of these high-minded missionaries." She wanted to spit. She'd given up on her Bible study since Reece had been shot.

Back in the Rover, Nikita sat with his hands on his belly, his shiny Makarov in a holster beneath his left arm. He polished off the last sip of whiskey. "Brother, we'll stop soon. No? The snake is full."

The driver scowled, thinking about the empty bottle between Nikita's feet.

The man in the back spoke up. He wanted to catch the jeep and have his way with the pretty ferenj. He was nauseated from the whiskey, and his mouth dry and frothy in the corners. He wanted to see if he could get it up, which had been a problem lately. Maybe some white pussy would do the trick. The white guy looked like a busheti. She probably needed it hardcore from a black man. "Let's get some pussy," he said. He jounced in his seat, his head in his hands.

The driver laughed. "That would be trouble, right? Unless we killed them."

"No, no," said Nikita. "We will stop to piss and that's it. No pussy until we reach the hotel. You can eat it all night long. No worries." He looked serious in his sharp green fatigues. "Brother, I have to piss, remember."

"Soon," said the driver. He gunned the Rover and crept closer to the jeep. He stayed just far enough back to let the dust blow away before it hit them. He'd heard that the ferenji women shaved down there and wondered if it was true. It would be just like a little girl.

Emma wished she hadn't said it, but she had. She respected Dr. Guthrie and the others, but it seemed too much like a game. Trade some wheat and penicillin for the right to distribute Bibles? Had she even done as much good as she had harm? She had no way of knowing. What about the woman with the broken collarbone? There was nothing she could do for her except give her vitamins and some famine biscuits. *Hell,* the people hadn't invited her to their village. She muttered.

Craig cleared his throat, guiding the jeep along as if in a trance. The giant rocks loomed ahead. "Maybe they'll pass us when we stop."

"I apologize," said Emma.

"I get your frustration. I think we have to articulate our-selves, though. Otherwise, we're just cows in a field."

"Cows in a field are nice," said Emma. "Eating grass, en-joying the sunshine, not bothering anybody."

"The people need us, and here we are." He pulled the jeep over to a soft, sandy embankment. "We can go here. Lots of privacy." He kept his eyes on the side mirror, watch-ing the Rover approach. It seemed to be slowing.

Emma glanced back as well and then to the giant boul-ders surrounding them. They looked like a maze. She had friends back in Alabama who would kill to climb them. They were beautiful to look at, striated and a dozen subtle shades of brown. Emma opened her door but stayed put. "Don't kill the engine until they've passed."

"Well damn," said Nikita, his bladder ready to rupture.

"What to do?" asked the driver. "God has made us all."

"Just pull ahead, fifty meters, and stop. I can't wait."

The driver slowed and as he passed the jeep took a long look, trying to glimpse the young woman, her hair that was called blonde.

The Rover drove past the jeep and stopped.

"What the hey?" asked Craig. "Maybe they have to pee, too?"

"Yeah, right," said Emma. "Let's go. This feels bad." Her heart beat in her neck. "Soldiers creep me out."

Ahead, three doors opened, and the three soldiers piled out, looking back at them, laughing. Off into the boulders they went, apparently to pee or otherwise.

"Just like us. No worries," said Craig. "I've got to go, so let's just do it and be on our way."

"Hell no," said Emma. "I'm not moving, and neither are

you. Stay put until they leave."

"Emma." He realized it was the first time he'd said her name. "I'm going. Be right back, but you need to go ahead and go. It's another hour and a half." He remembered the doors didn't lock.

With Craig out, Emma stepped out. "I'm going with you then. I won't look."

"This is just plain weird. Settle down. We're fine." He tried to stand up straight but had to go badly and hunched over like an old man. "Oh, come on then."

Emma followed him among the boulders and touched one. She imagined the soldiers threading through toward them for a surprise attack. "This sucks, Craig."

"Okay, here, turn around, I'm going."

Emma frowned and stepped around the side of a boulder that was twice her height. Enveloped in shade, she couldn't see the sun. The wind soughed ever so slightly above. She thought about her mother shredding pork back at the barbecue in Hueytown, using her hands to take apart the flesh. She heard Craig's stream hitting the pebbly ground and imagined it soaking into the sandy dirt, bubbles on top. "Hell," and she moved farther away and unbuttoned her shorts. She dropped them to her ankles and squatted. Little gnats floated in the sunbeams, but there were no flies. They were in what was called the kolla, the low place where people contracted malaria. No mosquitoes, though. She heard a horn blow, the Rover. She finished and stood, pulling up her blue underwear. Craig was still peeing. She wondered if his prostate was enlarged and leaned against the boulder.

At the Rover, Nikita was blowing the horn for the others to return. Were they idiots and lost in the rocks? The driver emerged, and then a minute later, the other man, nicknamed Ato, emerged. He looked pale and worn, exhausted.

"You must see the doctor soon, my friend," said Nikita. "You look like food for the hyena."

Ato breathed deep, a look of worry on his face. He looked at the jeep and saw no one there. "Perhaps we should check them for their travel papers?"

The driver liked that idea. "But you are too sick to fuck, my friend. She will fight you and probably win." He laughed.

"Yes, she will tear your balls," said Nikita. He laughed as well. "Do you no longer need your balls?"

"I have this," said Ato. He pulled a long folding knife from his pocket.

"No, no, let's go," said Nikita. "Now I am hungry. We will pay to slaughter the goat. No more delay." He rocked on his heels.

"So, we listen to Nikita, because he wants the goat?" asked the driver. "It's a good idea to check their papers. Maybe they will give us some birr?"

Ato agreed, even though he felt like hell. Someone should pay for his misery. It was too perfect.

Nikita said, "Ishi, but goddamn."

Craig reached the jeep first, and then Emma. They saw the three soldiers looking their way, just a hundred feet ahead.

"Hell, and here they come," said Emma.

Dr. Carpy had worked with the team that cared for Reece before the tornado. "You look mighty good to have been through what you've been through."

Reece nodded. He felt cold without his shirt.

Dr. Carpy examined his vitals on the chart. "Any headaches, auras, or trouble with your vision?" He palpated Reece's neck.

"No, but I did have a seizure. Just went out for a couple of minutes."

"Hmm. I'm going to do a CT scan and see how you've healed inside that noggin of yours." He touched both bullet scars. "Any nausea or vomiting?"

"No. My appetite is good."

Dr. Carpy shined a tiny flashlight in Reece's eyes. He looked into his ears.

"Good. What are these marks on your arms and belly?"

"Leeches. I jumped in the lake."

Dr. Carpy put his hands on his hips. "Kidding me? Stay away from the lake, especially since you've had a seizure. You could drown." He uncoiled his stethoscope and had Reece breathe deep. He laid him back and listened to his stomach. "We'll get some lab work on you, a blood profile, electrolytes, and so on, and schedule that CT scan. Any other complaints?"

"None that I can think of," said Reece.

"Okay, we're done here. Get your shirt and you're ready to go." He scribbled on a piece of paper. "Give this to the lady on your way out."

"Don't I get a sticker or a sucker?"

"Ha, nope," said Dr. Carpy, and he was out the door.

Reece scheduled his CT scan with the secretary. The earliest was a week away, but that was fine. He walked into the waiting room. Horace had the ear of an older gentleman, talking about how they could be related.

"Where's the doctor?" asked Dora. "He not gonna talk to us?"

"I'm done. He didn't find anything. Has me coming back in a week for a CT scan is all."

"I wanted to talk to him. Is he still here?"

"Granny, he's gone. Don't worry about it." He stood there with his hands in his pockets. He felt as normal as corn.

"Did they charge you for the visit?"

"I just had them bill me. Still worried about the hospital bill, though."

Dora batted her eyes. "Your Horace has done taken care of that. Horace, we have to go now. Tell your friend there goodbye."

"Really? How much was it? I have to pay you back."

"Don't you worry, boy. We're just glad you're alive. He cashed out a CD, neat and clean."

"Dang," said Reece. He watched Horace, still embroiled with the stranger, milking him for information.

"My son's wife's people had some Coggins in them," said Horace. Dora was tugging his shirt. "This man here is a Coggins." He looked at Dora as if witnessing to the Supreme Court.

"Well, that's nice," said Dora. "But we have to go. Reece here is finished. I've got supper and laundry."

Horace made a comment about who wore the pants in the family, and the man who was a Coggins laughed. "Y'all take care," he said.

Reece nodded his general appreciation, but was ready to go like Dora. He watched an elderly black woman coughing in the corner. He thought of the word for "What's the matter?" in Amharic. *Mendeno?* He muttered the word. What was Emma doing at that moment? It was probably eight o'clock there. She'd be in her little, tiny house, maybe reading or writing a letter. Most everyone was asleep by nine.

"Reece, son? Reece." Dora touched his shoulder. "Reece, did you tell that doctor about your seizure?"

"Yeah. I think that's why he wants the CT scan of my head." There was something off about the moment as if time had missed a beat. He watched Horace stand, still talking to the Coggins.

Kristin wrapped up her shift, giving report to the evening nurses on Charity and Mrs. Dunlop. Charity's slow V-tach had resolved within a minute, and she had remained conscious the entire time. With the help of the nursing assistant, Kristin had put Mrs. Dunlop in the recliner beside her bed for an hour. It was a chore getting her out of bed. She had flailed her arms, insisting that she was in the swimming pool in Vestavia and that she was about to drown. Kristin kind of felt the same way.

She sped up and merged into the busy I-59/I-20 traffic. She had her blinker on, trying to get over so that she wouldn't be forced to exit onto Twenty-Second Street. Ending a shift felt good, and she had the weekend off.

Brad had done his best to have dinner with her, but that was crazy, or was it? He was a catch, but what was right was right. She imagined that Brad, "Dr. Phillips," she said aloud, drank and was probably into cocaine like the rest of the residents. He drove a red Porsche, a little two-seater, with a Florida license plate that read "DR2BE." She yelled, "Ah!" and squeezed the steering wheel. She didn't even know if Reece would see her over the weekend. Why hadn't he called?

Reece sat in the swing, eying the lake across the road. The late corn in the garden was about ready to pick, and that would be a colossal mess, shucking, washing, and cutting it from the cob. They had a deep freeze in the garage for the corn. Most of the tomatoes and green beans were canned by Dora, but the corn was all on Horace, and he loved it. Reece noted the sun coming down to touch the ridge beyond the lake. He needed to call Kristin and stood.

Inside, Dora was frying potatoes and tending a meatloaf in the oven. "Smells good," said Reece, and he patted Dora on the shoulder. The old black phone clung to the wall by the table, and he sat in a rolling chair to dial Kristin. He hoped she would answer and not her parents.

"Hello?" asked Gert. She'd spent an hour with Kristin, who was inconsolable, crying.

"Hey," said Reece.

"Yeah, let me get her. You need to talk to her, come over even. If you know what I mean."

"What?"

"Kristin needs you to come over." Gert sounded peeved.

"Oh sure. No problem. She okay?"

"No, she's not okay." Gert made wide eyes at Edwin, who was in the recliner watching the news. He made eyes back at her and shook his head.

"Geez. Yeah. I think I'm finally up to drive, so let me eat and I'll be over."

"Can you talk to her now? That might help."

"Sure, sure, no problem." He slumped in his chair. He could tell that she had put the phone down. White melamine plates and paper napkins with a light green design, resembling vegetables, covered the table. Dora was putting the potatoes into a serving bowl, two thin brown stripes around the rim. He waited, hearing the TV in the background, and imagined Edwin in his recliner. He looked back at Horace, who was reading a *National Geographic* with the lamp on. The window AC unit cycled on with a rumble.

"Hello?"

Reece wanted to say, "Hey, Baby," but decided not to. "You, okay? Work go okay?"

"No and yes." She was still in her scrubs. "You coming over? Need a ride over?"

"I'm going to take the truck. Just about to eat, but right after that."

"You can't drive," said Dora.

Reece covered the mouthpiece. "I think I really can. Don't worry."

"You can drive now?" asked Kristin. "You sure?"

"Positive. Chicorilla."

"What? Chigger vanilla?"

Reece laughed. "No, I mean, sure. No problem. I want to come over, and I need to drive. It's now or never, right?"

He watched Dora frown at the fridge, fetching the sweet tea.

"That would be so great. We just need to talk, you know?" She sniffled.

"Sure, no problem." Reece imagined an evening of working out the kinks and then fooling around on the couch. "Talk about what?" He pinched his leg for saying that.

Kristin seemed to be selecting her words. "About us, dumdum. The future. Right now. This doctor at work keeps hitting on me, but we're engaged, right?" She sounded like she was out of breath.

Reece sat up straight. "Is he bothering you? The same guy. I can take care of that."

"You just might have to save the day, rescue me. Right? I love you."

"I love you, too." Reece felt empty.

"That's so good to hear, and you didn't even hesitate. Do you really love me?" She held the receiver to her ear with both hands, sitting at the dining room table.

Reece felt tiny, alone, like he should be somewhere else. "Yes, I do. How could I not? You came to see me in Ethiopia, right?"

"So, what does that have to do with it?"

Reece examined his logic. "I mean, we've been through a lot together, right?"

"Yeah, but either you love me, or you don't. Not just because I flew over there. I was scared to death you would die. And that hospital was so run down. I wanted to fly back with you on the Med-Jet, but there wasn't room. You just keep getting taken away. I'm tired of living like this."

"Look, just believe me, okay?" He watched Dora open the oven door, step back from the yawning heat, and retrieve the meatloaf with a thick layer of ketchup on top.

"Believe what?" asked Kristin.

"That I love you." Reece felt like he was inside a washing machine.

"You better, mister." She laughed a nervous laugh. "What's for dinner? I think we're having spaghetti with meatballs."

"Meatloaf and taters, I think. Smells good right now. I'll eat as fast as I can and then come over. If I'm not there in an hour, it means I drove up a tree."

"Reece, don't say that, please. With your luck, it could happen."

"Nothing to do with luck."

Ato led the way, followed by the driver and Nikita. They looked as if on a Sunday promenade.

"Get in and let's go!" Emma opened her door and stopped.

Craig stood still, watching the soldiers approach. "It's okay. No need to panic. Just be cool."

Even though she had just peed, she felt she had to go again. "Are you nuts? Let's go and now." She watched Craig walk toward them. What the hell was he doing?

Ato closed the distance and put out his hand for Craig. His hand was rough and clammy. He spoke in Amharic.

Nikita translated. "Yes, we meet again, beside the rocks." He gestured toward the boulders around them. He was in the shade, and Craig was looking into the sun.

Emma took her foot out of the jeep, but still with the open door between her and them. The guy who was talking gave her the creeps. His eyes looked yellow and swollen. She could see his jugular veins from ten feet away.

"How can we help you?" asked Craig.

Ato spoke, and Nikita did not translate. He fidgeted and toyed with the pistol beneath his armpit. "Yes, we must to check your travel papers, no? Just to be cautious, to protect us all." Nikita smiled and tried to make eye contact with Emma. "Oh, she is frightened."

At that, Emma came around the door and put her hands on her hips. She was conscious of her shorts and looked down at her maroon long-sleeved t-shirt. She wanted to spit.

"Well," said Craig. "We show our papers at the check-points, but I'll show you if that's necessary. Okay?"

"Yes, that is good," said Nikita. He spoke to Ato in Amharic. Ato laughed. The other guy just stood there sullen and gazing at Emma.

Emma's heart was pounding, but she determined to make a good show. "Maybe we don't need to show you. What gives you the—"

"Emma." Craig held up his hand for her to stop. "No problem, okay?

Emma growled and watched as Craig came to her side and reached into the glove box. "No worries." Before he could hand over the sheaf of purple-stamped documents, the three had maneuvered toward them, now standing beside the jeep.

In the distance was a rumble, and soon a blue mini-bus packed with thirty people lumbered along, slowed, and stopped. The driver yelled through the window. Nikita yelled back. The driver waved and jerked the mini-bus back into drive. Emma saw the faces looking at them, eyes filled with curiosity at the ferenji stopped on the road, standing with the soldiers.

Nikita took the papers and read each page, holding up one to find a watermark. He spoke to the others in Amharic, and they shook their heads. Ato spat.

"Is there a problem?" asked Craig.

"Mmm, there is no letter for this day. Your papers are good for one month ago. Why you do not have the proper papers? This is very dangerous." He sucked on his teeth and then sucked again. "Perhaps you are smuggling something to the north, to Tigray?"

"Get real," said Emma. "Let's go, Craig. Now." She felt the hand on her arm before she saw it, Ato's. "What the!" She jerked away and stumbled backward into the grill of the jeep.

"Hey, what are you doing?" Craig watched Ato press his body against Emma's. The driver was grinning, drooling, and Nikita was standing with his arms folded.

Emma pushed Ato, but he didn't budge. He grabbed her arms and pulled. "You whore," he said in Amharic. "You are a spy and must be punished."

Emma punched him in his chest and stomach. And then Craig was there trying to separate them. Nikita's beefy arm went around his neck and pulled him backward. He flailed but then stopped. Now Ato and the other man had Emma between them, struggling with her.

"Craig! Dammit!" Emma threw elbows and stomped a foot. Ato put her in a chokehold, and she went limp with the pain but rebounded, kicking as hard as she could. They were pushing and dragging her toward a passage between two boulders. Emma looked for Craig. He had his fists raised like a prize fighter, trying to get around Nikita, who had dropped their worthless papers. There was no wind.

Stunned, Craig watched Emma disappear, screaming for him to help her. He stared down the barrel of Nikita's Makarov.

"Emma!" and there was nothing he could do.